Her
LIFELINE

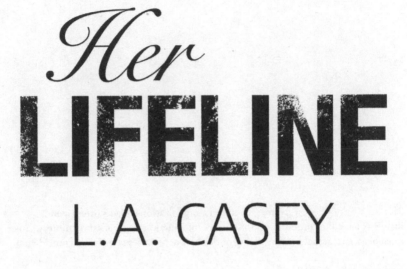

Her LIFELINE

L.A. CASEY

Montlake
Romance

Published by Montlake Romance Publishing, Seattle

www.apub.com

Amazon, the Amazon logo, and Montlake Romance Publishing are trademarks of Amazon.com, Inc., or its affiliates.

ISBN-13: 9781612185774
ISBN-10: 1612185770

Cover design by @blacksheep-uk.com

Cover photography by Wander Aguiar Photography

Printed in the United States of America

AUTHOR'S NOTE

Hi there,

I feel like I should pop this note into *Her Lifeline* just to make everyone aware of the dialect in the book. My characters are from Edinburgh, Scotland, and I did my best to capture a version of the dialect from the city. I went back and forth with friends of mine from Edinburgh so as to use correct phrases and the correct placement of words in sentences as frequently as possible during dialogue between my characters. That being said, I take full responsibility if anything is out of place or just plain wrong. I don't mean to offend anyone from Edinburgh, or Scotland in general, if I've mucked the dialect up at all. I adore Scotland, and I hope my little Scottish tale touches your heart, because it touched mine writing it.

Best,
Lee

Make every second with those you love worthwhile,
because we never truly know how long we have in this life.

PROLOGUE
ERIN

Eleven years ago . . .

"Happy Valentine's Day, Mum!"

Amelia Saunders, my beautiful mum, smiled at me with her dark green eyes gleaming and her arms opened wide. Without having to think about it, I dropped my school bag next to the front door, hustled down the hallway, and tightly wrapped my arms around her midsection as I rested my head against her chest.

"Thank you, my wee love."

She stroked my back as I caught my breath. I had run all the way home from school just like I did most days. I'd never tell anyone other than my brother, but the reason I ran was to avoid the name-calling and laughter of my classmates. Girls who my mum thought were my friends were cruel bullies who made my stomach sick from the moment I entered school until the moment I left.

I tilted my head back and grinned. Mum chuckled and ran her fingertips over my face, tracing them over my skin before she bopped my nose with the tip of her finger, and just like that, the weight of my school day fell off my shoulders. I was safe now.

"You're the picture of your daddy, Erin."

If I had a pound for every time she said that, I'd be a billionaire.

I scrunched my nose. "I dinnae look like a lad."

I normally never minded when people commented on how much I looked like my dad, but lately it was starting to bother me. I was eleven now, rocking double digits, and if I had to look like one of my parents, I wanted to look like my mum. She was the prettiest woman on God's green earth. Dad said so, that's how I knew it was the truth.

"Sorry," Mum smiled.

"What did Dad get you?" I asked, switching the subject back to Valentine's Day.

She looked at our kitchen table. I stared at her face, and almost burst with pride as another beautiful smile stretched across her lips. My mum had to leave for work early every day – she worked in the tower thing at the airport – so after she'd left that morning, my dad had got me up extra-early before school and let me take the lead on how we should set up the gifts he'd got for her.

I'd suggested the dining table because Mum *always* went straight into the kitchen to put the kettle on for a cup of tea when she came home from work. I wanted them to be somewhere that she'd see them straight away, and like I knew I would be, I was *totally* right. I hadn't stopped once during my run from school, just so I could see the expression on her face.

"I dinnae ken," Mum replied, chuckling to herself. "But would you like to help me find out?"

I hesitated. "But they're for *you*."

"Are you sure?" she mused. "I think I spotted someone else's nickname on that wee purple gift bag there."

Nae chance, she's fibbing.

With wild eyes, I searched the pile of gifts until my gaze landed on the bag my mum had described. The bag was *not* there this morning. I'd checked the pile from top to bottom before Dad brought me to school, and I knew he couldn't have snuck it in there because I was the last

2

person to leave the house. He couldn't have come back either, because he had to be at work at nine. He'd have had no time. None.

I checked the name tag, just to be sure it wasn't for my mum.

Doll.

I screeched. "It's from *Ward*!"

Mum burst out laughing, while I jumped up and down with excitement. Ward Buckley was my big brother's best friend, and he was the coolest person, besides my brother, that I had ever met. He had always called me "doll" because he said I looked like a little porcelain doll. He had told me he was going to get me a Valentine's Day present because I was eleven now, a little woman, but I didn't believe him. Until now.

"What does the card say?" Mum asked, still smiling. No matter what was going on, she always had a smile on her face, and I loved that most about her.

"I'm not sure," I said as I carefully opened the envelope, cautious not to rip anything important.

I felt my own smile grow when the front of the card was revealed. It read *You're sweet*, with a big cupcake that had little pink love hearts sprinkled on the frosting. I lost my smile, and tried my best to keep my face as expressionless as I could because I was *very* aware of my mum's knowing eyes on me. Slowly, I opened the card and read what was written inside.

Happy Valentine's Day to my favourite wee lass!
Have a fun-filled day, doll.
Lots of hugs,
Ward :)

My face burned with heat, and the visual made my mum giggle. When I didn't read the card aloud – I physically couldn't, the ability to speak was suddenly lost to me – she moved to my side, peered down and read it slowly to herself. She gave me a little bump of her elbow when she finished, and it only embarrassed me further.

"It looks like I'm not the only one with a Valentine today."

Can she be any more embarrassing?

"Mum!" I scowled up at her.

"What?" she asked, trying her hardest not to laugh. "I'm just tellin' you the truth. Ward sent you a Valentine's Day card; that means he wants to *be* your Valentine."

I willed my face to return to its normal shade of white.

"He's nineteen, like Tommy," I said with a forced roll of my eyes. "And I'm *sure* he has a girlfriend."

I was confident of that fact – he always had different-coloured lipstick marks on his neck *and* on his clothes. He always smelled of different fruity perfume, too.

"So?" Mum said with a perfectly shaped raised eyebrow. "You can have more than one Valentine. I have four: Daddy, Tommy, Ward and you."

I thought on that for a moment, and it brightened my spirit.

"That's true."

"Is there anythin' else in the bag?" she quizzed.

I knew my entire face was doomed to remain the colour of a tomato when I pulled out a light brown teddy bear holding a red heart that said, *I cub you.* I wanted the ground to open up and swallow me whole when Mum said, "Aww!"

"My God," I blurted. "Can you *stop*?"

"Sorry," she giggled. "I take it back, it's not cute at all."

I pushed the cute bear and my cute card back into the cute bag, and folded my arms around it, hugging it to my chest. My mum's eyes glinted with amusement as she turned back to her gift pile and placed her hands on her hips.

"Where does your daddy hide all these?" she wondered out loud. "I do all the cleanin' and I've never come across them."

4

You dinnae clean the attic.

"You'll not get it out of me, woman," I warned her. "I'll take it to my grave!"

Her shoulders shook with silent laughter.

"It was worth a try," she said.

"Go on and open your gifts," I urged. "They'll gather dust just sittin' there."

"Dinnae you think I should wait for your dad to get home? That way we can open our gifts together."

I reared back and stared up at her. "You got Daddy gifts?"

"I sure did," Mum replied, her head tilted to one side. "I wouldn't be a very good wife – or mum – if I only received gifts and never gave them."

I thought about that for a moment.

"I suppose so . . . But what did you get him?"

At that question, Mum snorted.

"Some new socks, underpants, and football tickets to go see Hibernian play next weekend."

I gasped. "He'll *love* that!"

Probably not the socks and underpants so much, but he'd *definitely* love the football tickets. Every single time Hibs were playing a live match on the television, I had to hear my dad announce them as the "magnificent Hibernian Football Club". Every. Single. Time.

"Tommy and Ward can go with him to the match since I got them tickets too, so that's three of my Valentines taken care of with one gift."

I eyed her suspiciously.

"Does that mean you got *me* somethin', since I'm your other Valentine?"

"Me *and* Dad," she clarified.

"Well, where is it?" I asked, hoping I didn't sound too pushy.

Mum grinned devilishly. "You mean to tell me you didnae check under your pillow this mornin'?"

The words were barely out of her mouth before I sprinted down the hallway and took the stairs two at a time until I reached the top. Mum's laughter echoed after me as she warned me to slow down. I heeded it only when I was inside my bedroom, with my hand underneath my pillow. I pulled out a little pink wrapped box that I ripped open. I gasped when I lifted the lid and found a silver heart charm.

I squealed. "I love it, thank you!"

Mum's "You're welcome" was shouted up the stairs. I quickly shrugged off my school blazer and focused on my bracelet as I added my new charm to a link. My mum and dad had gotten it for me when I was five, and each of the trinkets had a special meaning and memory. I brushed them with my fingertips.

The silver shamrock from Ireland had been added to my collection when I went over with my dad a few years ago to visit our cousins in Dublin. It was such a fun trip with just the two of us, and I always thought of it when I looked at that particular jewel. While I adored it, my favourite was the silver rose Tommy had got me for my tenth birthday. I loved it as much as I loved him.

I froze at the sound of the front door opening and closing, but when I heard a familiar cough, I smiled.

"I'm home!" Dad called.

I sprinted down the stairs and ran head first into my dad's open embrace. He laughed as he returned my hug, but quickly pretended to tell me off when Mum angrily shouted for me not to run up and down the stairs.

"How did she react?" he whispered, brushing my white-blonde hair, identical to his, out of my face.

"All wide-eyed and big smiles," I whispered back. "She tried to trick me into givin' up your hidin' spot, but I remained super-strong and refused to crack."

Dad winked. "I'm glad to have you in my unit, soldier."

I saluted him, and though the action made him snicker, what made him smile wide was when my wrist caught his eye. He grabbed hold of my hand and brushed his thumb over my new charm. He flicked his grey eyes to mine and asked, "D'you like it?"

"Try *love* it."

He ruffled my hair. "You're goin' to run out of space soon."

I shrugged. "I can always switch out the charms and wear different ones each day. That way I'll never wear the same bracelet twice."

"How did you get to be so clever?"

I shrugged again. "Mum said I get it from her side of the family."

At that, he barked with laughter. We joked and playfully shoved one another as we walked down the hallway and into the kitchen. The second my dad locked eyes on my mum, I made a puking noise that they both grinned over. He crossed the space between them and caught her lips in a surprise kiss. I pretended to be revolted whenever my parents kissed, but I secretly wasn't. I loved that they weren't afraid to show their love for each other; it'd be weird to me if they acted different.

When Dad suddenly pulled Mum against his chest, placed his arm around her waist and grabbed her free hand, I squealed and happily clapped my hands together before I dug my phone out of my pocket, switched it to record mode and pointed it at my parents. I *loved* when my dad randomly grabbed my mum for a dance. He didn't care where he was or who was around, when he wanted to dance with her, he did just that.

"If you ever," Dad began to sing, "change your mind, about leavin' . . . leavin' me behind. Baby, bring it to me . . . bring your sweet lovin', bring it on home to me."

My mum laughed when I harmonised with Dad on the "yeah" line on "Bring It on Home" by Sam Cooke. I knew the lyrics, and could sing it perfectly in tune without hearing the music. This was a song my dad always sung to my mum, and I'd grown up listening to it.

After they sang and danced they shared one more kiss, prompting me to cheer, which drew their attention. Once they realised I was recording them, they pulled funny faces at me. I saved the video before I tucked my phone back into my pocket.

"I done good this year, huh?" Dad smirked at my mum, nodding towards her presents.

Mum playfully rolled her eyes. "You did all right, I suppose."

He smacked her behind, which prompted her to swat him with a tea towel that she swiped from the countertop. They kissed once more, then had their normal chit-chat about each other's day before they opened their gifts.

My mum was opening some perfume that Dad had bought her when the front door opened and my brother's laughter filled the house. A cold breeze blew in too, prompting Mum to shout, "Thomas, shut the door!"

"I'll do it, Amelia," Ward hollered back.

I froze. "Oh god."

"What?" Dad asked, his brows drawn together in bewilderment. "What's wrong, Erin?"

I looked at my mum and found her smirking into her perfume box, and my heart thudded against my chest.

"Dinnae say a word," I implored her. "Mum, *please*."

She made a motion that her lips were sealed.

Dad looked between us. "Can *one* of you tell me what's goin' on?"

"Nae chance," Mum and I answered in unison.

Dad shook his head, and under his breath he said, "Lasses."

That drew a grin from my mum, but not from me. I was suddenly aware of everything, so I sat perfectly still at the dining table and focused on Mum's gift pile. When Ward and Tommy entered the kitchen, I didn't look their way.

"Bloody hell, Kenny," Ward whistled. "You're settin' the bar a mite high for the rest of us."

Dad laughed, but said nothing. In fact, I felt his eyes on me, and it made me even *more* uneasy.

"Happy Valentine's Day, Erin."

I turned my head and smiled at my brother. "Same to you."

Tommy peered at me. "Why is your face all red?"

Oh my God.

"It isnae red," I said as I quickly turned away.

I hadn't felt the heat on my face before, but I most definitely felt it now.

"I can *see* it and it's re— *Ow!*" Tommy cut himself off, hissing. "What the bloody hell was that for?"

"For being a wee dafty," Ward muttered back.

"But what did I—"

"Haud yer wheesht."

Things were quiet for a second after Ward silenced my brother, and out of the corner of my eye I could have sworn I saw my mum making hand gestures at me, but I was too embarrassed to look and see if I was correct. I sat still, and when a couple of throats were cleared, my brother spoke.

"So," he began. "I need to talk to you, Erin."

I blinked. "What about?"

Tommy moved closer and hunkered down in front of me.

"D'you remember when I was talkin' to you a few months ago about when I go away to uni?"

My shoulders slumped as I nodded.

Tommy smiled affectionately at me. "Well, I got accepted into my first-choice university."

I felt like a weight was suddenly pressed on my chest. Both Tommy and Ward were really into computers, but what they did bored me. They were into programming. I wasn't entirely sure what that meant, but I knew it was what they both wanted to study at university. They want to be computer programmers . . . or something like that anyway.

"Which uni?" I asked, feeling everyone's eyes on me.

I knew I was supposed to say congratulations to Tommy and be happy for him, but I wasn't happy. Him going to university meant he would be leaving me, and it upset me to think about that. Tommy wasn't just my brother, he was my best friend. I was what he called a loner. I wasn't good at making friends, so when I stopped trying, Tommy was there to be the friend he knew I needed. He had always been in reaching distance, and knowing that he would no longer be right next to me made my tummy sick.

Tommy mumbled, "Metropolitan University."

I frowned. "Is that close by?"

Tommy hesitated. "It's a little ways away," he eventually said.

I played with my fingers. "What's a little ways?"

He sighed. "It's in London."

"London?" I flinched. "In *England*? The *country* England?"

At Tommy's nod, my eyes began to fill with tears.

"Nae," he exclaimed, and quickly pulled me into a tight hug. "Please, Erin, dinnae cry. I'll be home every other weekend."

That was the problem.

"Hey now." Dad's voice cut over my sniffles. "Aren't you happy that Tommy and Ward got into their choice university?"

Ward was going too? He was very much another member of our family. I was around him just as much as I was around my brother. There was hardly a night that passed by over the years where Ward didn't ask my parents if he could sleep over, so much so that my parents had bought bunk beds for Tommy's room. He was at every birthday party and family event, and he even came on holidays with us. My parents considered him their son, and while I didn't think of him as a brother, I loved him just as much as I loved my brother. And now I would be losing both of them.

"Nae." I lifted my head and looked over my brother's shoulder. "I'm not."

I wasn't expecting my dad to laugh, but he did, and he said, "At least she's honest."

Mum clicked her tongue. "Come on now, that's enough tears. You dinnae wanna make Tommy sad, d'you?"

"If it will make him stay? Aye."

Everyone laughed, even my brother.

"We'll always talk on the phone, and you'll be with me when I'm back visitin' with Aiden," he said, pulling back from our hug. "I promise."

I was annoyed that he used my three-year-old nephew to try to calm me down. Tommy knew how much I loved Aiden, and for him to bring him up when I was upset was a low blow.

I sniffled, and was mortified to find tears were rushing down my cheeks like a stream. I quickly used my hands to wipe my face free of tears . . . and snot. My mum passed me a tissue as I blew my nose and cleaned my face up as best I could.

"It willnae be the same," I said, hiccupping. "I know it."

Tommy sighed. "But it willnae be awful either, okay?"

I felt like it *would* be awful, the most awful thing ever, but I reminded myself of what my dad had said. I didn't want to make Tommy sad, I wanted him to be happy, and if that meant I had to be happy for him, even if I didn't feel happy, then I would try. I'd be happy for Ward too.

"Okay," I said, forcing a smile. "Congratulations."

Tommy winked at me before he playfully clocked my cheek with his hand. Things were silent for a moment until our dad spoke.

"What's your word of the day, princess?"

I looked at him and shrugged, not wanting to answer.

"You have a word of the day?" Ward asked me, his eyebrows quirked.

I sheepishly nodded. "My teacher asked me to pick one hard word a day to expand my vocabulary, since I know all the easy words everyone else in class is just learnin'. I have to use it five times a day in a sentence and be able to define it on demand. I cannae cheat, because she keeps a list of the words and tests me throughout the year."

Tommy moved back to Ward's side and nudged him. "She's a smart lass, and puts us to shame."

I perked up at the praise. Tommy always gushed about how smart he thought I was.

Ward folded his arms over his chest. "Go on then, wow me."

I laughed. "My word of the day is 'fetid'."

Tommy stared at me blankly; Ward did too. My mum's brow was furrowed as she was lost in thought, but my dad was grinning. He always knew what my words of the day meant.

"Give us a hint," Tommy asked.

"Use it in a sentence then, to help us get the meanin'," Ward suggested at my silence.

"Mum knows the true meanin' of fetid, she's washed the sweaty football clothes that Tommy stuffs under his bed enough times."

Mum started to laugh. "I think I know what it means."

"What *does* it mean?" Tommy huffed.

Mum looked at me and guessed, "Somethin' that smells *really* bad?"

I beamed at her. "Correct."

"Hey!" My brother frowned. "My footy stuff doesn't smell that bad."

We all gave him a deadpan look, and it made my brother throw his head back and laugh.

"Okay," he chuckled, his shoulders shaking, "maybe it *can* be a bit ripe."

"A *bit*?" Mum and I questioned in unison.

This prompted the others to laugh.

"Are all the words you learn hard?" Ward asked me. "Because that was a tough one."

I shrugged, not making eye contact with him. "Sometimes, but I learn them anyway."

"See?" Tommy grinned, nudging his friend with his elbow. "She has brains to burn."

"Well, Miss Smarty Pants . . ." Ward smiled. "I got you somethin'."

Oh my god.

"You already got me so-somethin'," I stammered. At my mum's cough and pointed look, I added, "Thank you, by the way."

Ward winked. "You're welcome, but I got you somethin' else too."

"What did he already get her?" Dad frowned, and to Mum he said, "What is he talkin' about?"

"He got her a card and teddy bear for Valentine's Day," she answered quietly.

My dad's smile was the most embarrassing thing I had ever seen in my entire life. He looked at me knowingly, and I hated it. I felt heat stain my cheeks for the millionth time, and the urge to run away and hide in my room was strong, but I couldn't move. I watched as Ward reached back, as if in slow motion, and pulled out a long-stemmed yellow rose.

Where had he been keeping that thing?

"Are you gonna break my heart on Valentine's Day and not take my rose?" Ward asked, his sky-blue eyes staring down at me, his lips turned up in a pretty smile.

I was mortified.

"Thank you," I whispered, taking the rose in my hand.

Mum laughed when he pulled out another yellow rose from behind his back and handed it to her.

"Are you producin' them?" she asked, cackling.

I paid them no attention. I was too focused on my flower. I was mindful of touching a thorn, but a quick scan of the stem showed all the thorns had been removed. I thought that was thoughtful of Ward, and it only made me love the gift that bit more. I stared at the sun-coloured flower, and with my fingertips I gently brushed the petals, noting how soft they were to the touch. My lips turned up in a tiny smile, but I made sure to keep my head downcast so no one could see.

"You've embarrassed her," Tommy snorted and shoved Ward, who almost instantly shoved him back.

"Lads," Dad said firmly, halting their movements.

"Erin," Mum called, gaining my attention. "D'you wanna put your rose in some water?"

She held the crystal vase that she always filled with her bloomed forget-me-nots, and to appease her, I bobbed my head. I popped my rose in the centre of the flower-piled vase. Later, though, I'd take it out, carefully dry it off, then place it in between the pages of a book to press it and preserve it. My gran had done it for years, and before she died she'd showed me how.

"I'm goin' upstairs to do my homework," I said, and left before anyone could say a word.

I made it up to my room, and closed the door behind me before I exhaled a breath of relief. I looked at my charm bracelet, then to the gift bag on my bed that Ward got me, and squealed a little to myself. I wasn't silly, I knew that Ward was way older and had a girlfriend – I was sure he had one, at least – but I liked that he'd got me gifts for Valentine's Day. It made me feel special.

I took my teddy bear from the bag and sat it on top of my dresser, then quietly slipped back downstairs to grab my school bag. When I returned to my room and spotted the teddy once more, I released another stupid giggle and wondered if I'd react the same way each time I looked at it. I hoped not, because it was embarrassing.

I pushed the thought aside, climbed up on to my bed, opened my bag and got started on my homework.

"Erin," Dad shouted from downstairs not long after. "I'm goin' to get McDonald's, what d'you want?"

"A large Big Mac meal and a Coke with no ice, please," I hollered back as I lowered my pencil. "Give me a sec and I'll come with you."

He paused. "Are you doin' your homework?"

I considered lying, which made me hesitate in replying, and it made my dad laugh.

"You stay and do your homework. I'll be back in twenty minutes."

"Please, Dad, I'm nearly fin—"

"Naw, Erin," he said firmly. "Finish your homework."

"Fine!" I snapped back.

"I willnae be long, love," he called out, but I didn't reply. "I'll get you an ice cream too."

I heard the front door opening and closing, and it only annoyed me further. I wouldn't have been a bother, I'd have just sat in the car like I usually did. With a shake of my head, I refocused on my homework, and before long I finished both my English and Maths work. I glanced at my window and noticed it was already dark outside.

"Mum!" I shouted.

"Aye?" she called back from downstairs.

I imagined her standing at the bottom of the steps with her hands on her hips.

"How long has Dad been gone?"

"About an hour, why?"

I frowned. "He said he'd only be twenty minutes."

"You know your dad, baby. He probably went to get some snacks for later, too."

I relaxed. "Okay, d'you need to use the toilet? I wanna take a shower."

"Naw, but ask your brother and Ward just in case they do."

They were still here?

Ward and Tommy shared a flat about thirty minutes away. When they visited, they never stayed long; Tommy only dawdled when he was on his own. I headed towards Tommy's old bedroom, which now

15

doubled as Aiden's room when he came to stay here. I could hear Tommy and Ward shouting and laughing, and it only amplified the closer to the door I got. I was hesitant for a few moments before I raised my hand and firmly knocked on the door.

"Come in," Tommy hollered.

I lingered in the doorway. Ward and Tommy were sitting on the bed, and they both had Xbox controllers in their hands and headsets on their heads. Neither of them looked in my direction. In fact, they didn't take their eyes off the flat screen on the wall for a second. I wasn't even sure if they blinked.

"What is it?" Tommy asked me, then quickly said into the microphone of his headset, "I'm not talkin' to you, I'm talkin' to my wee sister."

I started at the mention of me.

"How did you know it was me? You didnae even look at me."

Tommy snorted, still focused on the game he and Ward were playing.

"You're the *only* person who knocks on my door. Mum and Dad just walk in."

I frowned. "You told me last month you'd stick my head in the toilet if I didnae start knockin'."

Ward laughed; Tommy grinned.

"That I did – fuck's sake!" Tommy suddenly snapped. "That's *me* you're shootin', dafty."

"Sorry," Ward said, biting down on his lower lip as his fingers moved at rapid speed.

"You cursed!" I stated, pointing my finger accusingly at my brother.

He spared me a glance. "I did?"

"You did!"

"Whoops," he said, chuckling. "I didnae mean to."

He totally *did* mean to. Both he and Ward shouted all kinds of bad words when they played on the Xbox, and more than a few times it had my mum sending them home to their own apartment. I was surprised that she wasn't already shouting up the stairs for Tommy to cut it out, because his door was wide open when he'd shouted.

"Do either of you need to use the toilet? I'm takin' a shower."

"I'm good," Ward said, his eyes not leaving the television once.

"Me too," Tommy added, staring at the screen.

They're like robots.

I rolled my eyes, and without a word, I left the room and closed the door after me. Two seconds had barely passed before their shouting and cursing started back up, and it caused me to shake my head. I put both of the lads out of my mind, and got ready for my shower.

Afterwards, I dressed myself in my favourite flannel pyjamas. I blasted my hair dry and tied it up in a high ponytail. After I put my hair dryer away, I noticed my school stuff was still on my bed. I climbed up, sat back on my heels, and was in the middle of putting my textbooks into my bag when I heard a sound that chilled me right to the bone.

I jumped with fright when the agonising wail came from downstairs. I scrambled as fast as I could to get off my bed, but in my rush I tripped over myself and fell to the floor, banging my head in the process. I sucked in a staggered breath, sat back on my behind and instantly lifted my hands to my head. I checked my hands, and though I was in pain, I was so happy to see there was no blood.

I placed my hand back on my head, forcing myself not to cry even though it hurt so bad. I moved quickly as I left my room, but paused long enough to see that the door to Tommy's room was wide open, and neither Tommy nor Ward were inside. The Xbox controllers and headsets were tossed on the floor.

I rubbed the throbbing spot on my forehead as I descended the stairs. I heard a commotion in the kitchen that slowed my steps.

"Are you *sure* it's him?" Tommy asked, his voice almost pleading.

"Aye, sir, his wallet contained his driver's licence. It was how we were able to find this address to notify next of kin when we plugged his information into our system."

The wailing sound started again, and it distracted me from focusing on the stranger's words.

"I cannae believe this," Tommy replied, his voice sounding not like his own. "Christ."

Believe what? What's going on?

I hustled down the hallway, coming to an abrupt halt at the sight of two policemen in our kitchen. They both had their hats under their arms, holding them tightly to the sides of their bodies with their elbows. I stared at them for a few seconds, before reaching out and gripping the door panel when I saw my mum was clinging on to Tommy, who looked like he was about to be violently sick. Ward was behind the pair of them, his hands placed on either side of his head, and he looked like he had been told something awful.

"Mum!" I shouted when I saw her tear-streaked face. "What's wrong?"

She jerked her gaze in my direction, and I knew for as long as I lived I would never forget the terror, pain and disbelief in her big green eyes. Something was terribly wrong, and the knowledge caused my heart to kick into overdrive. It began to slam into my chest so rapidly I could feel, and hear, each beat. I couldn't sense any pain in my head anymore, only sickness in my gut.

"Mrs Saunders" – the large policeman regained her attention – "we need a member of your immediate family, preferably you or your son here, to come to the morgue and identify your husband."

My heart stopped.

"What does *that* mean?" I stupidly asked. "Why is my dad there?"

The policeman who spoke turned his head and looked down at me. There was great sadness there . . . and pity. I didn't know why he'd pity me though; he didn't even know me.

"I'll go—"

"Naw, Thomas." Mum cut Tommy off. "I'm goin', I need to see him."

"But Mum—"

"Stay here with your sister." She spoke over him again, then to the policemen she said, "I'm ready to go to . . . to that place."

She couldn't even say the word.

"Mum," I said as she walked by.

She didn't answer me, she didn't even look at me. It hurt my feelings, but I hid how I felt when the policemen cast me more pitiful glances as they walked out after her. I looked at my brother when the front door closed.

"What is goin' on?" I demanded. "Why is Mum gone with the polis? Why were they here at all? Is she in trouble? Is Dad in trouble? They spoke about him."

Tommy lifted his hands to his head, and ran both of them through his thick, dark brown hair. He looked a lot like our mum, and in that moment he looked just as terrified as her too.

"Hey, doll," Ward said with a small smile, gaining my attention. "Why dinnae you come and sit down so we can—"

"Naw." I cut him off and refocused on Tommy. "Answer my questions."

"Baby—"

"I'm *not* a baby!" I suddenly shouted. "Tell me what's wrong!"

My brother stared down at me, and I felt like I'd been sucker-punched as sadness radiated from him in waves.

"Come here."

I walked over to him, and stood rooted to the spot in front of him as he kneeled before me and placed his hands on my shoulders.

"Everythin' is goin' to be okay," he said firmly. "I just want you to know that."

My lower lip wobbled. "Tell me."

Tommy inhaled, exhaled, then said, "He's gone, Erin."

"Who's gone?"

"Dad," he whispered. "Dad is gone."

I stood frozen as Tommy wrapped his arms around me and hugged me to his body. He hugged me so tight I felt it all the way down to my bones. My arms remained lifeless at my sides, and with unblinking eyes I stared over his shoulder and up at Ward, who couldn't look me in the eye. The sick feeling I'd got in the pit of my stomach when Mum and Dad told me two years ago that my gran had died reappeared, but this time it felt so much worse.

"What d'you mean he's *gone*?" I asked my brother, turning my head to look at him when he pulled back to meet my gaze. "Where did he go?"

Tommy kept his hold on me, and though his eyes were locked on mine, I saw that he struggled greatly to keep the contact.

"Dad . . . Dad died in a car accident, baby."

I sucked in a sharp breath, and without realising it my legs gave way from underneath me. Tommy stumbled as he stood up, and he held me against him until he was upright and could hike me up his body until my legs were around his waist and my hands on his shoulders. I pushed myself back and stared at my brother. I hadn't properly noticed until then that his green eyes were red and swollen, and his cheeks were blotchy . . . from crying.

"Stop it," I said, my voice breaking. "Stop."

"Erin—"

"Naw!" I slapped him across the face, shocking myself and my brother. "Naw!"

Pain vibrated up my arm, and a sting lingered on my palm.

Tommy didn't move a muscle. "I'm sorry, baby."

Shut up.

"I wanna see Dad," I said, my throat suddenly tight and sore. "Right now. I wanna see Daddy!"

Tommy's eyes glazed over with tears, and I momentarily wondered if it was because I had hit him. There was a nasty dark red handprint forming on his cheek, and I knew it had hurt him, because my palm was throbbing like crazy.

"We cannae right now," Tommy said softly. "We can see him when they bring him home."

Who is "they"?

I placed my hands over my ears as a loud noise sounded. My head began to thump with pain once more, and my chest felt like a weight was on top of it. I didn't notice the high-pitched sound that was hurting my ears was coming from me; it wasn't until my lungs burned with the need for air that I realised I was screaming.

No, not screaming. Wailing.

"Erin!" Tommy pleaded, but I heard it in his voice, he was crying. "Please, stop."

I screamed until my throat was raw, I cried until my vision was blurred with tears, and I fought against Tommy for no other reason than he was trying to hold me.

"Daddy!" I sobbed. "I want Dad! I want him right *now*!"

"I know," Tommy cried as he clung to me. "I know, baby."

I wasn't sure how long I cried, or how long Tommy held me for, but what I did know was that my head was killing me. I wasn't sure if it was because I'd banged it, or because I was crying so much. I pulled back from Tommy's embrace, still sniffling.

"This do-doesnae feel re-real," I wept, stuttering my words. "I want Dad."

Tommy had stopped crying, but his eyes were still red and puffy, and tears still dampened his cheeks. He lowered me to the ground and used both of his hands to brush back the loose strands of hair that had fallen out of my tie. The hairs clung to the wet patches on my skin, but Tommy made sure they were all pushed back before he answered me. It was like the action gave him something to do to keep him from speaking to me.

"I need to make a few calls, baby," Tommy said gently. "I need to call Auntie Jennifer and Auntie Emma, and Dad's friends. Mum . . . she'll need Auntie Jennifer."

Auntie Jennifer was my dad's only sibling, and they were very close to one another.

"Erin," Tommy prompted, kneeling before me once more.

I looked at him. "Aye?"

He looked worried. "Are you okay, baby?"

"I dinnae ken," I answered honestly. "I've a really bad pain in my ch-chest, my stomach feels sick and my head hu-hurts . . . but that's probably just because I ba-banged it—"

"You hit your head?" Tommy frowned, talking over me. He switched his gaze to my forehead and winced. "It's a doozy, but you'll be okay. How'd you hit it?"

"When I heard Mum scream," I answered, my voice barely a whisper. "I tr-tripped and fell."

Without a word, Tommy leaned in and kissed the sore spot on my forehead.

"You'll be okay."

I couldn't bring myself to smile at him, and instead I said, "This hurts way worse than when you said you'd be le-leavin' for uni."

At the very thought of that, I gasped.

"Will you still leave us?" I asked my brother, my eyes widening to the point of pain.

The fear that wrapped around me in that moment almost took my breath away.

"Naw," Tommy said firmly, his hands gripping my shoulders. "I'm not leavin' you or Mum, baby."

"But . . . but you got into your ch-choice uni," I said, my lower lip wobbling. "You're goin' to school in London and wr-writin' the code stuff for the site you're both cr-creatin'."

I had heard them talk about their vision for starting a social-media site, or was it a friend-dating site? I couldn't remember, I never paid it any attention because my dad said I was too young to sign up to any social-media site so they didn't interest me anyway.

"Thomas."

I looked at Ward when he said my brother's name. I had never heard Ward say my brother's given name in my entire life. Not once.

"Stop," Tommy said, his tone clipped. "I know what you're goin' to say and I dinnae wanna hear it."

Upon hearing the tone of Tommy's voice, I remained unmoving.

"Pal," Ward said softly. "We've paid our tuition, we've got a plan."

Tommy tensed, his arms around me tightening.

"My dad is dead, *pal*," he bit out. "My plans have changed."

"Thomas—"

"D'you *really* expect me to up and leave my mum and wee sister when my dad has just *died*?" Tommy snapped at Ward. "D'you fuckin' *hear* yourself, Ward? My dad is dead, and you want me to leave? To leave my family? They *need* me!"

Ward said nothing, he simply stared at my brother's back and looked as lost as I felt. Silence stretched for what felt like eternity until Ward exhaled a deep breath.

"I'm sorry about your dad, pal," he said, and he looked like he meant the words. "I truly am, I love him like my own dad, but plans haven't changed for me. I cannae stay near her . . . y'know that."

He can't stay near who?

I gasped. "Ward!"

He looked at me with his shoulders slumped. "I'm sorry, doll."

"My daddy just *died*!" I said, getting choked up saying those words. "Dinnae talk about this right now."

Tommy humourlessly laughed. "The fact my eleven-year-old sister had to tell you that is shockin'."

"Tom—"

"Leave. Go back home. I'll arrange to have the movers bring my stuff from the flat here instead of our flat in London."

"Tom—"

"Buckley," Tommy growled. "Leave."

Tommy still had his back to Ward, but I had a perfect view of him, and while he looked distraught, he also looked determined about something.

"I'm so sorry, man," he said to my brother. "I'm so fuckin' sorry."

Tommy didn't respond; he hugged me to him instead when I suddenly began to cry. I wasn't sure what I was crying for this time, but I couldn't stop the tears from falling. Through my blurring vision I saw Ward take a few hesitant steps before he walked by me and Tommy, then left the kitchen.

"I need the bathroom," I whispered to my brother.

He let me go, and remained kneeling on the floor as I quickly left the room. I caught up with Ward just as he reached the hall door.

"Ward," I said, almost choking on his name. "Please, dinnae leave us."

I saw his hand on the door handle tense before he turned to face me. I continued to move towards him until I was inches away and looking up at him.

"Dinnae leave us," I repeated. "We need you."

"Doll . . ." He frowned. "I'm so sorry, but I cannae stay. I wish I could, but I cannae. I have to leave."

I instinctively slapped Ward's hand away when he reached out to me.

"Tommy has always been there for you – my mum and dad too," I said, tears welling in my eyes. "We. Need. You. Please, dinnae leave us alone. We're a family, we can't get through this without you. *Please.*"

Ward didn't speak, instead he looked down at me with pain in his eyes, but I saw the same determination in them that I'd seen in the kitchen and I knew that his mind was made up. He was going to London with or without Tommy, and nothing I said, nothing that happened, would change his mind. He was leaving us.

"Offski," I told him, raising my chin. "And dinnae come back. We . . . we dinnae need you."

Ward's lips parted and his eyes widened. "Dinnae say that, Erin. Please."

"I'll take care of my mum and Tommy," I told him defiantly. "I'll be his best friend if you dinnae wanna be anymore."

An emotion I had never seen swam in Ward's eyes, and for a few moments he looked as if he was desperate to explain himself but didn't know how.

"I'm so sorry, doll," he repeated, almost to himself, as he opened the door and backed out of the house.

"Aye," I said, stepping forward and gripping the handle of the door, my lower lip wobbling. "We are, too."

When I closed the door, tears fell from my eyes, and almost instantly I looked down to the floor. Thanks to the light outside from our front porch, I saw the shadow of Ward's feet through the frosted glass in the door. He was still standing outside, and he lingered there for a few minutes, but eventually the shadow moved, and suddenly I couldn't see it anymore. I counted to a hundred before I pushed down on the door handle and opened the door slightly. When I got the courage to open it fully, I was surprised to find the entryway and front garden were empty.

"He's gone," I whispered to no one.

My tears stopped falling in that moment, and began to slowly dry on my cheeks. I wasn't sure how long I stood in the doorway, staring out into the night with the cold wind lapping at my skin, but it was long enough for me realise something. Ward . . . he had really left us. He had really left my brother when he – we – needed him the most. I began to shake, and I wasn't sure if it was because I was cold or if it was because my chest was hurting, but I didn't care.

I forcefully shut the front door of my house, and out loud to Ward I said, "I hope you never come back."

CHAPTER ONE

ERIN

Present day . . .

Vomit.

The revolting stench of it pulled me from my dreamless sleep, and the sound of dry-heaving that soon followed pulled me from my warm bed. I rubbed my tired eyes and dragged my feet across my bedroom floor. I felt for the light switch on my wall, and flipped it. I jumped when a loud thump sounded on my door, but relaxed when I heard the familiar slurs of my mum.

"Erin." She belched. "I've be-been sick."

I counted to ten before I unlocked my door and pulled it open. My mother, who was on the floor outside my room, turned her head and looked up at me when I stepped into the hallway. I took a moment to assess her, and my situation. From her night attire, I guessed she'd vomited in her sleep. I took a few steps down the hallway, glanced into her room then to her bed, and exhaled when my suspicions were confirmed. It marked the third night in a row that she'd thrown up in her sleep.

Like always, I couldn't help but wonder if the next time would be her final time. I'd heard of people choking and dying, but for my mum, it was a regular occurrence and she was still alive and kicking.

I didn't hate my mother, but I disliked her – this version of her – greatly.

"Come on, Mum," I said glumly as I helped her to her unsteady feet. "Let's get you cleaned up."

I resisted the urge to heave as the putrid odour climbed its way up my nostrils. Keeping my stomach contents down became an even more difficult task when my hand pressed against her wet nightgown.

Dinnae think about it.

"You're su-such—" *Hiccup.* "A good—" *Hiccup.* "Girl."

"Thanks, Mum," I said, and steered her in the direction of our bathroom.

I turned my head away and breathed through my mouth in a last attempt not to be sick. Somehow, I forced my focus on to my mum, and not the odour she reeked of. I got her into the shower and began the process of peeling her nightwear from her frail body.

When she was naked as the day she was born, I turned the shower hose away from her body and switched it on. I used this time to blast her clothes with water. After the water heated to a warmer temperature, I turned my attention to my mother and hosed her down. Every so often, when the heat of the water lulled Mum into closing her eyes, I'd drop the temperature to freezing and jolt her into awareness. This step was repeated four times until I finally got her scrubbed and cleaned.

Dressing her wasn't as difficult as it normally was. She was more alert than usual so she did what I told her to do, even if I had to repeat something to her four or five times. Brushing and drying her hair took a couple of minutes. Her new pixie-like haircut made sure of that. When she was dressed in clean underwear and pyjamas, she sat on her bedroom floor with her legs criss-crossed like a child as she watched me strip her bed and remake it with clean linen.

Thank God for mattress protectors.

When I finished, I looked down at her, and I hated that for a single moment she didn't look sick. She looked like her old self, but I knew better than to believe that. Over the years, I had learned the hard way that looks could be deceiving. My mum was clinically depressed, and her medicine of choice was alcohol. She was, by definition, an alcoholic. It didn't matter to her what alcohol she drank; any kind would do. If there was one thing I was certain of in my life it was that she was drinking herself to death, slowly but surely, and I could do nothing but sit by and watch.

With a shake of my head, I got her back into bed and tucked her duvet cover around her body. She closed her eyes almost instantly, and that left me to stare down at her. I wish I could say her behaviour was a once-in-a-blue-moon occurrence, but it wasn't. Drinking till she blacked out and vomited was pretty much all that was on her daily to-do list, and her quota was met every single day without fail. The only thing that changed in her routine were the places around the house that I'd find her when she passed out. It ranged from the sitting-room sofa, to the stairs, in the bathtub, on the kitchen table. You name it, my mum had passed out on top of it, under it or inside of it.

I turned on her bedside lamp in case she woke up. Mum hadn't slept in the dark since the night my father died eleven years ago. I found it ironic that the night she became fearful of the dark was the very night she lost herself to it. When Dad died, a huge part of my mum died with him. His passing devastated her to the point where she lost herself entirely and lost the strength to face her new reality without him, so she found comfort in a bottle. Her addiction happened so fast that none of us could catch it and prevent it. Before we knew it, alcohol wasn't just something my mum wanted to drown out the pain, it became something she desperately needed to function.

I closed my eyes, and thought back to the night my dad died, and saw the first time Mum put a bottle before her children.

I stared up the stairs, and listened as my mum's cries became louder, more desperate. I listened as her heart broke. She hadn't stopped crying since she returned from the morgue. I swallowed the lump in my throat, and slowly I put one foot in front of the other and walked up the stairs. I clenched my hands into fists as I walked to my parents' bedroom. I paused at the open doorway and stared into the dark room. I could make out a body on the bed . . . on my dad's side. I walked over to the bed without a word, and climbed up on to it. I lay down next to my mum, lying on her side of the bed while she wailed into my father's pillow.

"Mummy," I said softly.

She turned to lie on her back a few seconds after I spoke. She blinked as she stared up at the ceiling, but she looked like she was a million miles away. I felt my body begin to shake, and a fear that amplified the pain in my chest that something was seriously wrong with her consumed me. The need to be close to her slammed into me, so I reached over and wrapped my arm around her waist. My face was inches from hers, and I watched as tears slipped from the corners of her eyes, slid down her temples and blended into her hairline.

"I'm here for you, Mummy," I whispered, squeezing her tightly. "I love you so much."

I felt like my world had been ripped away from me for the second time when she removed my arm from her waist, got up from the bed and walked over to the bedroom window. She picked up a pink bag with white love hearts on it – I recognised it as a bag that contained some more gifts my dad had bought her for Valentine's Day – and reached inside. When she pulled out a large, dark bottle, I watched as she struggled to open it, and I was about to offer to help when a sudden loud pop caused me to jump with fright. I sat up and wrapped my arms around my waist, hugging myself as she drank straight from the bottle.

"Mum?" I whispered when she paused for breath.

"He said he would go and pick up the wine I liked after he got the McDonald's because I'm not very fond of this one," she said, staring down at the bottle.

I didn't understand.

"Mum?" I repeated.

"Tommy," she suddenly called, startling me.

Her voice was raspy, but that wasn't what concerned me. What concerned me was I could hear in her words the pain she felt, and it only added to the growing agonising sensation that was slowly spreading outwards from my chest.

"I'm comin'," Tommy shouted, his footsteps pounding against the stairs.

I looked to the doorway when he appeared, slightly breathless. He flipped on the light, and we both frowned when our mum winced as if it hurt her. An expression I couldn't decipher crossed Tommy's face when he saw the dark bottle in our mum's hand. He moved further into the room when she took another big gulp from the bottle. He stood still when she lowered her hand and began to walk out of the room, not giving my brother, or me, a second glance.

"I'm goin' to sit with your aunties so we can make . . . arrangements. Take care of your sister," I heard her say to Tommy as she approached the stairs.

My brother had his back turned to me as he watched Mum walk away from us, and it took him a full minute before he turned back to face me. When he did, his face was harder, and he suddenly looked a lot older than nineteen.

"Are you okay?"

He nodded, and flashed me a smile that didn't reach his eyes – green eyes that were identical to Mum's.

"Aye," he answered. "Of course."

I frowned. "Dinnae lie to me, Tommy."

He lost his smile, and his shoulders sagged as he walked towards the bed, taking up the vacant spot next to me.

"You dinnae miss a thing," he mumbled. "D'you?"

I shook my head. "Naw."

He huffed with small laughter.

"You're too smart for me to trick," he teased.

"Dinnae try to trick me when I ask if you're okay. I cannae help you if you lie."

My brother turned his saddened gaze on me. "You're eleven, baby. You shouldnae have to help me."

"You're my brother," I said firmly. "I will always help you when you need me to."

Tommy put his arm around my shoulders and gave me a squeeze.

"I told Ward we didnae need him," I admitted. "I told him not to come back . . . I think he listened to me."

Tommy was quiet for a long moment.

"It's okay," he said. "I told him the same thing when he phoned me not too long ago."

I looked at him. "You did?"

He nodded, and it made me frown.

"I cannae believe he listened to us."

"Aye," Tommy said, his voice soft. "Me either."

"Why did he listen to us? Ward loves us, and we love him. He's broken about Daddy too, I could see it in his eyes. Why would he want to leave us when we need him most?"

"He has his reasons," Tommy answered gruffly. "I'm too angry with him to let myself think of them right now though."

I heard talking coming from downstairs, but I couldn't tell which voice belonged to who; they all blended together. People had shown up in bunches not long after my mum came home from the morgue. Even as the night dragged on and the hour grew late, Dad's friends and my aunties had stayed to be with us.

"What's wrong with Mum?" I whispered to Tommy, raising my knees up to my chest, leaning my chin on them. "She's actin' really weird."

My brother tugged me closer to his side as he rested his back against the headboard of the bed. His hold on me gave me a great deal of comfort, and it also caused me to burst into tears. Tommy quickly pulled me on to his lap, placed his head on top of mine, and softly sang "You Are My Sunshine".

He always sang that song to me whenever I was sad or when I hurt myself, but for some reason it didn't stop the pain that pulsed in my chest like it usually did.

"Mum," he said softly after he stopped singing. "Mum is really sad about Dad."

I knew she was, but that didn't explain why she wasn't . . . her.

I sniffled. "So am I."

"I know," Tommy said, and kissed the crown of my head. "I'm sad, too."

I knew he was. He loved our dad so much that he didn't even care when Dad told dumb jokes around his friends and embarrassed him. He always smiled, initiated a playful wrestle, then assured my dad that he would get him back. Dad always welcomed the backlash with a teasing grin.

Something he would never be able to do again.

"Mum willnae look at me," I said, my throat hurting. "Why, Tommy?"

He squeezed me.

"She's just—"

"She was lookin' at you and talkin' to you" — I cut him off, my voice sounding husky — "but not me. I've been watchin' her since she came home from the morgue. She made sure not to look at me . . . even when I stood in front of her, she made sure to look the other way." I began to cry again. "What'd I do?"

"Nothin'," Tommy said firmly, pulling back so he could look at me. "You did nothin' wrong, Erin."

"Then why?" I stressed. "Why does it feel like she's changed?"

Tommy tensed, but it was only for a moment, so I wasn't sure if I imagined it or not. I yawned, and my brother suggested I go to sleep, but I didn't want to close my eyes. I didn't want to be left on my own. I ignored my brother's words and repeated my question.

"I think she's afraid," he eventually answered as I snuggled into his chest.

"Afraid of what?" I asked, yawning again despite my not wanting to go to sleep.

Tommy didn't speak for a very long time. I heard commotion, soft cries, talking and even some laughter coming from downstairs. I wondered if everyone was trying to make my mum smile. I wondered if they'd succeeded.

My eyelids began to feel heavy, and when I couldn't keep them open any longer, I let them drift shut. But before I felt myself fall into an abyss of darkness, I heard my brother speak.

"She's afraid to look at you 'cause all she sees is Dad in you. You have his eyes, his hair, his smile," Tommy said, his voice gentle, "and I'm terrified that when she does eventually look at you . . . he's all she'll be able to see."

I opened my eyes, staring at my mum in the present, and my chest hurt as much as it did the night Dad died. That night changed – and ruined – everything.

"Night, Mum."

"Di-Dinnae tell To-Tommy about this, Erin."

I looked over my shoulder and saw she was already halfway into her self-medicated slumber.

"I willnae say a word," I lied, though I knew she couldn't hear me.

I left her bedroom door open in case she needed me, and brought all the dirty linen downstairs, where I put it in the washing machine. I walked back upstairs to my room, still dragging my feet. I locked my door behind me out of habit. I'd rather wake up to my mum banging on my door than her falling on to my bed covered in vomit.

With a sigh, I unplugged my phone from its charger, and climbed back into my now-lukewarm, but cosy, haven. It was just after 2 a.m., and knowing my brother was working the graveyard shift at his security job, I texted him a play-by-play of what I'd just had to deal with, even though I'd told my mum I wouldn't. He knew what she was like . . . but only to a certain extent. He knew she drank herself into a near-coma daily, but he didn't know about the verbal venom she sometimes spat my way, and I'd never tell him about it.

Tommy worried about me and my mum too much as it was, so keeping these things from him was a blessing. If he knew how she treated me when she was drunk, he'd try and fix it, and it wasn't something he could easily resolve so I didn't bother him with it. Neither of us had much going for us in our lives, Aiden was our only saving grace. If Tommy and I didn't have him, we would both work long hours and have nothing other than our mum to take care of. Neither of us had the time to date, and even if we had I wasn't sure either of us would be very good at it. Tommy had always been my protector, and now that I was old enough, I wanted to be that for him, too. If I could keep my brother from experiencing hurt, even if only a tiny bit, I'd move mountains to make it happen.

I was startled when my phone began to vibrate in my hands. Tommy was calling in response to my text, and I momentarily wished I hadn't told him the situation with Mum.

"Hi, Tom," I said softly when I answered the call.

"Hey," came my brother's response. "Is she sleepin'?"

"Aye," I sighed. "I just hope she stays down for the night. I've to get up for work soon."

My first job, at the local Tesco, started at 8 a.m. and finished at 2 p.m. My second job, a waitress at the local TGI Friday's, started at 4 p.m. and ended at 10 p.m. I didn't always work both jobs in the one day, but when I did, I prayed when I got home from work that Mum would already be asleep so I didn't have to deal with her. I didn't need both jobs, but they kept me out of the house, so I worked as many shifts as I was offered.

My mum didn't work, but she did have money that she received from welfare. She claimed disability through an injury she'd sustained in her hip a few years ago when she fell during one of her many drunken hazes. She owned the house we lived in, so after paying the bills, insurances and putting food on the table – I split each bill with her – she had money to spend as she chose. She always chose alcohol.

I had put every penny I didn't need into a savings account. Over the years, I'd managed to save just over eleven thousand pounds. I'd started saving the money the first time I realised that the environment I was living in wasn't healthy, that it was toxic, and it scared me to think that my mum's habits could rub off on me. I was only sixteen when I came to this realisation, and I'd had every intention of getting out of her home – out of her life – but six years later, I was still living with her.

There were days where I would spend hours listing reasons why I should leave my mum and never look back, but the one thing that always kept me rooted to her was Dad. He'd always taught me to never give up on the people you love, even if they make you want to. He lived and breathed for his family, and there was nothing he wouldn't do to keep us together. I knew that he would advise me that this situation was different, that I shouldn't stay with a mother who only cared about the next drink she could get her hands on, but giving up on my mum made me feel like I was giving up on my dad too, and I wasn't ready to do that so I'd planned a future that included her.

The years got tougher as my mum's addiction became stronger, but I pushed through it and put myself through college while working two part-time jobs, and it had paid off as I'd recently graduated with a teaching degree. I had just been hired to teach at a primary school thirty minutes away, when the new term started back after the summer holidays.

Everything I had worked towards my entire life was finally happening for me . . . but I didn't feel excited about it in the slightest, and that baffled me. Becoming a teacher had been my dream since I was little. The idea of helping children to learn and grow filled me with such yearning to bring out the potential in them. Growing up, many of my teachers in school had pushed me aside because I'd learned quicker than the other students – they'd classed me as a know-it-all and I never felt like I was given the chance to be the best I could be, because of how little guidance I was shown.

I wanted to be a better person, a better teacher, because of that.

But my mum, and my relationship with her, made it difficult to be excited for that new chapter in my life. She was at rock bottom, and it almost felt like she was a permanent bookmark in a sour chapter in my life that I couldn't escape. I loved my mum, I loved her even though she was a shell of her former self, and for that reason I took things one day at a time. I never thought about tomorrow, I always stayed in the now. For my sanity's sake, I had to.

"How was your day?" my brother asked me, pulling me from my thoughts.

I snorted. "Same as every day. Long and hard."

"I hear you," Tommy grumbled before yawning.

I tilted my head. "Did you see Aiden today?"

He sighed deeply. "No, his mum thought it was best for him to focus on studyin' for his summer school exams."

"You always spend Fridays with him after school." I scowled. "She cannae do that, Tommy."

"She can," he replied, sounding crestfallen. "She has full custody of him, she can do whatever she wants."

I felt both rage and devastation on my brother's behalf. When I thought that my life was tough, I just had to think about Tommy's and it put things into perspective. When he was fifteen, he'd got his then seventeen-year-old girlfriend pregnant and he became a father at sixteen. Lucy Hayes had always been controlling and manipulative, and those traits only intensified when she and Tommy broke up not long after they became parents. I was only eight when my nephew was born, but for as long as I could remember my only memories of Lucy and Tommy were of them fighting and her taking Aiden away from him for no other reason than she could.

From the moment my nephew was born, he was used as a weapon against my brother. For years the arrangement was simple – Tommy and Lucy worked out a schedule between themselves – but after my dad died and my mum's drinking became a real problem, Lucy didn't trust that

Aiden was safe with us anymore . . . and she was right. When Aiden was only a child he found an open bottle of vodka that belonged to my mum and drank from it. I found him vomiting as he lay unconscious on the floor, and Tommy and I rushed him to the hospital. That day changed my brother's life.

Lucy took Tommy to court and won full custody of Aiden on the grounds that our home was an unsafe environment. He didn't even fight her on it, because my brother was an incredible father and he wanted what was best for his son even if that meant having nothing to do with him. He just couldn't help that he had an alcoholic mum with whom he shared a house.

For Aiden's safety, Lucy only allowed my brother to have him for six hours a day every Friday. She considered it a great gift, because she didn't have to let Tommy see Aiden at all, and as Tommy's hands were tied, he jumped through every hoop she presented him with.

Aiden, who was now fourteen, had told me the moment he turned sixteen he wanted to permanently live with Tommy, who had recently moved into a beautiful two-bedroom apartment not far from Aiden's house. Lucy's years of spitefulness and withholding him from his father had backfired on her, and Aiden could finally see just how awful she had been to my brother.

"Things are goin' to change, Tommy," I said, hoping he believed me. "You'll see."

My brother chuckled. "I sure hope so, kid."

I rolled my eyes. "I'm twenty-two, a grown woman, *not* a kid."

"Sure you are . . . kid."

I growled and Tommy laughed.

"It could be worse," he mused. "I could still call you baby."

I paused. "Aye, you win."

He laughed again, and the sound brought a genuine smile to my face. It was a sound I didn't hear often from him, so when I did hear it,

I made sure to memorise it for the days when silence was overwhelmingly loud.

"I'm goin' to get some sleep. I'll talk to you tomorrow, okay?"

"Okay," he said, still chuckling. "Night, Erin."

"Night, Tom," I yawned. "I love you."

"I love you too, kid."

When we hung up, I put my phone back on charge and lay on my bed, staring up at my ceiling. I flinched when I heard a bang come from somewhere in the house. I remained still for a couple of moments, then I heard groaning.

"Erin," Mum called, then yelped after another bang was heard.

I closed my eyes and counted to ten.

"I'm comin', Mum."

I pulled myself from my bed and went to see what she needed me for this time, and all the while a voice in the back of my head told me that this pattern wouldn't last forever. She was going to drink herself to death eventually. It was only a matter of time, and since Tommy no longer lived here, I'd be the one who would find her when her body finally decided to give out.

Sometimes I thought about what things would be like if she died. Not out of anger or hatred, but more so out of relief for her. She was in awful pain, and had felt that way every single day since my dad died. A part of me selfishly knew that if she died, it would make my life easier and give me a lot less hassle, and I hated thinking that. I hated thinking that she was a burden, because no matter what, she was still my mum, the same woman whose smile once made my heart happy. The same woman whose arms had made me feel so safe and warm.

She was lost in darkness, but things that were lost could be found and brought to light once again. I had to hold on to the hope that one day she would return to us, because I had already buried one parent and it had nearly killed me.

I couldn't do it again.

CHAPTER TWO
WARD

"Ward?"

Fuck.

I looked over my shoulder, locked eyes with the red-headed bombshell from the night before, and gave her my best, or what I hoped was my best, innocent smile.

What the hell is her name?

"Sweetheart," I chirped, sounding a hell of a lot merrier than I should have for six in the morning.

I was still smiling, and I still had my death grip on the door handle. Escape was mere inches away, so close that I could almost taste it. I had to be smart about this departure, otherwise things could get messy, and I didn't like messy once it was outside of the bedroom.

"What are you doin'?" Red asked, folding her arms over her ample, and very bare, chest.

Jennifer. Her name is Jennifer. I mentally paused. *Or is it Jessica?*

My focus was quickly diverted from mindless questions to the woman before me. The action of folding her arms across her chest had pushed her tits up, and made them appear even bigger, rounder . . . tastier.

Don't go there, mate. I shook my head clear, and concentrated on the woman's eyes to get myself out of dangerous territory. The eyes were always a safe bet. I could see what a woman wanted from me through her eyes, and this time I wasn't disappointed to see the lust and greed that dwelled within the brown orbs staring back at me.

"I have to get to work, sweetheart."

Johanna, it's Johanna . . . or did she say Jessie?

Red pouted. "But it's Saturday."

"There's no rest for the wicked." I winked.

She smiled at me devilishly, and I knew just how wicked she thought I was.

"Can I see you later?" she asked sweetly.

Her request was a demand that was dressed up as an innocent question.

"Sure," I lied with another smile. "Your number is in my phone, right?"

I always made sure the women I slept with put their number in my phone and the date on which I bedded them when they wanted to see me again. Most women would normally refuse to do so – if her heart was in the right place where I was concerned – but a woman who wanted status, and money, would do just about anything asked of her.

The women I met with were usually professionals and wouldn't dream of insisting they contact me outside of work, but there were a few women, like this one, who chanced their arm. I only ever took numbers; I never gave mine out, if I could help it. My number was easy to get, and the last thing I needed was to answer a phone call from a woman and not know that I'd already bedded her. Numbers were my thing, dates even more so. I could remember a day, or the woman of that day, once I knew the date. Once I remembered the date, I'd decide whether the woman was worth calling when the mood struck.

Did that make me an inconsiderate prick? Most likely.

"Yep." She bobbed her head. "I saved it under Jacey and yesterday's date like you told me to."

Jacey!

"I *knew* it began with a J," I said quietly to myself.

"What was that?" Jacey asked, straining to hear me.

"I said" – I grinned at her – "I'm looking forward to your call."

She lifted a hand to the end of her shoulder-length but beautifully wild hair, and twirled her fingertips around the strands. This exposed one of her breasts, and the rosy pink nipple called to me like a bloody dinner bell. I tightened my hold on the door handle, and reluctantly dragged my gaze away from Jacey's breast. I pulled the door open, stepped out into the shockingly cold hallway, then turned and winked at Jacey before I closed the door behind me.

I exhaled deeply, but instead of lingering around and waiting for her to open the door and watch me leave, like I knew she would, I buttoned up my coat, hurried down the hall and entered the stairway. I lifted my phone to my ear when it rang.

"Buckley," I answered.

"Good morning, sir," Hope, my assistant, said in her too-chirpy tone for 6 a.m.

"Good mornin', Hope," I replied as I descended the stairs of the hotel. "What's my schedule like today?"

"Four meetings, and your first one is at eleven," she replied. "I had it changed from nine since it's a Saturday."

I pushed open the entrance door to the lobby, and at the reception desk I gave my room number and waited for the valet to retrieve my car. I sat down on one of the large sofas to wait.

"Speakin' of it being a Saturday," I said to Hope, "why're you up and callin' me so early when you dinnae start till ten?"

"These meetings are important – I wouldn't have them scheduled on a Saturday otherwise – but our first meeting is a *board* meeting,"

Hope said, as if I was stupid for asking. "I've been prepping for it the last five days."

"It's a board of advisers' meetin'," I chuckled. "I'm founder, owner and chief shareholder. They're representatives and that's it. You *know* I'd never relinquish any real power to them. This meetin' is just a recap of the first six months of the year for the company, nothin' more."

"I'm just covering all of your bases, kiddo."

"And *that* is why you're my number-one girl."

Hope snickered. "I'm sixty-one, happily married for the last thirty years with five children and six grandchildren, and *I'm* your number-one girl?"

"And you always will be," I said with a genuine smile.

Hope was someone I'd trust with just about anything. She had my – and my company's – best interests at heart.

I raised my head as a man signalled to me from the hotel entrance. He was wearing a valet uniform, so I got up and headed towards him. We exited the hotel and I found my new Bentley parked out front. I thanked the man, tipped him fifty pounds and slid into the driver's side.

"We need to get you a nice girlfriend, son."

That drew a laugh from me as I settled into my car, buckled my seatbelt and started the engine, switching my handheld conversation over to Bluetooth.

"I *have* a fiancée, Hope."

I could practically feel her scowl. "That woman is venom."

Hope's blatant honesty was another reason to adore her. She was my employee, but she didn't treat me like her boss. She treated me like her son, and I loved it too much to ever put a stop to it.

"You dinnae have to tell me," I sighed as I pulled away from the kerb.

"Where are you right now?" Hope asked, an underlying meaning to her question. "Not with her, I assume?"

It was my turn to scowl. "Never you mind."

She gleefully laughed. "Did you get a signature from the girl?"

The signature she was referring to was one on a confidentiality agreement. When I wanted the pleasure of a woman's company, I used a high-end escort service that promised complete and total privacy. Still, I required any woman I slept with to sign a confidentiality agreement to ensure she wouldn't try to extort me with threats of going to the press. It was public knowledge that I was engaged, and the shitstorm that would take place in the press if it was exposed that I was unfaithful would be damaging to my brand.

"The woman pre-signed the agreement. She's from the agency and they know the drill."

Jacey was a new escort and had just recently joined her agency – she'd told me as much during our time together – and I already knew I wouldn't be requesting her again when the time came to make another appointment. Her forwardness during sex had been warmly welcomed, but her playful antics of wanting more from me this morning didn't interest me.

"You're sure you weren't recorded or snapped in a picture with her?" Hope asked, a hint of worry in her tone.

I relaxed as I merged into the early-morning London traffic.

"I'm sure," I assured her. "We met in a hotel room like always."

Hope hummed. "Send me her name so I can pull her information from the agency's files. I'll have a tab placed on her so I can be sure."

I shook my head. "Okay, double-o-seven."

Hope laughed, and it brought another smile to my face.

"I'm headin' home to shower and dress. I'll meet you in my office at ten, no earlier, to go over your notes for the board meetin'—"

"Wait," Hope suddenly shouted. "While I have you, and my planner open, when are you taking a holiday?"

I sighed. "I dinnae need—"

"Yes, you do," Hope cut me off. "You haven't had one all year, and you agreed to take one. I have it in writing if you'd like a recap. You promised that you'd take twenty-eight days to be *out* of the office. I don't care if they're all together or separated, but, Ward, you *will* take these holiday days if it's the last thing I do, or so help me God I will make your life miserable."

The urge to bang my head into the steering wheel was a tempting one. My work was my life, and if I didn't work, it would give me time to think, and when I thought too hard, ugly monsters from my past reared their heads.

"I'm not dropping this, Ward," Hope continued. "You haven't had any holiday time in . . . forever."

I smirked. "Are you tryin' to get rid of me?"

"Always," she replied instantly. "I get more work done when you're out of the office."

I snorted. "I'll get back to you on it . . . Okay?"

"Fine," she sighed. "I'll see you at ten."

When the phone went silent, it only remained that way for five seconds before it rang again.

"Buckley," I answered.

"Good morning, sir."

I relaxed. "Mornin', Keller."

John Keller was the head of my security team, and apart from Hope he was the closest thing I had to a friend.

"Do you need me to clear the woman you spent the night with?" he asked. "I only have the hotel's address from your Bentley's satnav, but I'll have the rest of her information in three minutes. Two if the downloading speed increases."

My lips twitched. "Naw, but you can forward that information to Hope. She wants to keep a tab on her."

He huffed with laughter. "Very good, sir."

"Anythin' else?"

"No. I'll meet with you after your board meeting to discuss your team for tonight's event."

At the reminder of my charity event, I brooded. Not because of the event itself – I loved anything that would bring awareness and attention to my charity – it just annoyed me that *she* would be my date.

When the call ended, I turned on the radio and listened to the early-morning broadcast. The drive to my townhouse was quick and uneventful. I pulled into my underground car park, then headed into my house. It was deathly silent when I stepped foot in the hallway, and it caused me to breathe a sigh of relief.

She isn't here.

I headed into the kitchen to get a cup of coffee and some food before I went to shower. I was in the middle of pouring the coffee when I heard a noise from behind me. Before I turned around to see what had caused it, a voice spoke and it caused my muscles to tighten.

"How was your night, my dearest *husband*-to-be?" she asked, and even without looking at her I knew she was smirking. I could practically feel it.

I ground my teeth together. Escaping women came naturally to me, I did it so often it had become second nature, but there was nothing on God's green earth that could enable me to escape from Tara Welder – my fiancée. Heaven knows I'd tried.

I scowled as I poured milk into my cup and stirred in a spoonful of sugar.

"Why're you here?" I asked, trying to conceal my annoyance. "We agreed we wouldn't be in the other's company unless absolutely necessary."

Not having to see Tara every minute of the day gave me some peace of mind considering the fucked-up situation I was stuck in with her.

"This *is* absolutely necessary," Tara pressed. "I wanted to check in and see if I had to go to the charity fundraiser tonight with you."

"Of course you do," I stated with an incredulous shake of my head. "If you don't show up with me, the press will have a field day."

I turned to face her when she didn't reply, and when I saw her in very revealing lingerie, I deadpanned. Almost every part of her chocolate-brown skin was on display.

"You slept in *that*?"

"Slept? Sure," she mused. "If you could call it that."

I eyed the dark hickey on Tara's neck after she spoke, and rolled my eyes, knowing damn well that I didn't give it to her. We hadn't been intimate in over a year. Hell, we hadn't so much as held hands since she threatened to drop the bombshell that would ruin my carefully built image if it was made public.

"Who was the poor soul unlucky enough to find his cock buried inside of you?" I asked with a shake of my head. "Your yoga instructor or personal trainer? Or both?"

Tara tittered, not offended in the slightest.

"Neither," she replied as I lifted my cup to my lips. "I decided to spread my wings and take a dip in the waters of *your* team."

I froze. "My *security* team?"

"Maybe." Tara grinned.

I forced myself to take a sip of my coffee, and fixed her with a glare. "Who am I givin' the sack?" I asked, nonchalantly. "C'mon, tell me."

She merrily laughed. "It's not fun if you don't guess."

That fact that she thought my guessing who she'd cheated on me with was a game pissed me off. Not the cheating part – I was just as guilty of that – but the fact that she thought our engagement was a game, instead of an arrangement, really ground my gears.

"I dinnae have time for you, or your bullshit games, today," I informed her, my tone clipped. "I've a meetin' with the board this mornin', and three other meetings throughout the day before we've to attend the fundraiser at seven."

Tara rolled her contact-lens-blue eyes. "Fine, it was Calum Jefferson."

I mentally flicked through the names of my team in my head, and a light went on when a twenty-three-year-old with golden-blond hair and a mole on his left cheek popped into my mind.

I snickered. "You couldnae let the kid get to six months on the job before he lost it?"

"He was too easy." She shrugged.

Considering her attire, I highly doubted that.

"*He* was easy?" I belly-laughed. "I think you'll find that *you* are the easy one, sweetheart."

Tara scowled. "Says the man whore."

I smiled brightly, knowing I was starting to strike a nerve.

"I fuck women, they don't fuck me. When I use the escort service, the women argue with one another just to be the one to spend the night with me. You're the one who chases men, and cannae keep their interest long enough to give a fuck about somethin' other than what's between your thighs. You're trappin' me with a marriage . . . Surely you know you arenae a catch by now. You're a gold-digger, a waste of space. Take your pick, *sweetheart*."

I ducked when Tara grabbed a coaster from the table and hurled it at me before stomping out of the kitchen, cursing up a storm as she went. My laughter followed her, and it only aggravated her further.

"I may be a gold-digger," she venomously shouted, "but *I'm* not the one pretending I started Friendzone by myself. You *co*-created it, and you've left that man, your so-called *best friend*, high and dry back in your hometown while you live the high life. You're a fucking *coward*. Keep fucking with me, Ward. I *dare* you!"

My laughter dried up and my smile was indefinitely wiped from my face.

"Fuckin' bitch," I growled as she continued to stomp away until she was out of view.

I was on a good streak of not thinking about my hometown – and who I'd left there – going on a week now, but that was well and truly ruined. I tossed the remainder of my coffee into the kitchen sink before angrily setting my cup aside. I placed my hands on the counter edge and gripped it tightly, lowering my head as the familiar feelings of guilt and sickness spread outward from my lower abdomen.

Tommy Saunders.

If there were ever a person on the face of God's green earth who wasn't Hope or Keller that I'd trust with my life, it'd be Tommy. From the time we started preschool we were the best of buds, and it lasted right up until I hightailed it out of our hometown with my mind focused on growing what we'd both created, not long after his father was killed in a car accident when we were nineteen.

With my shoulders slumped I left the kitchen and headed down the hallway and into my den, where I sat down and stared around the room. The den alone was bigger than the entire two-bedroom apartment I'd grown up in back in Edinburgh. By anyone's standards, I had made it and then some. I had become a billionaire three days after my twenty-fourth birthday, and now, a month after my thirtieth, I had earned my twenty-second billon.

Friendzone started as a drunken idea, then developed into lines of code for a website and from there it grew into an empire that I was truly proud of. It was something the world had never seen before, and it became *the* social-media platform that all future platforms would be compared to. It was revolutionary.

From an outsider's perspective, I had it all, but really I was drowning in a success that I knew deep down wasn't just mine to claim. I did claim it, though – I had written an autobiography about my early life and how I started Friendzone, and not once did I mention Tommy. I'd done hundreds of interviews where I could have mentioned him, where I could have told the truth, but I didn't. My anger, hurt and bitterness towards him for cutting me out of his life, and for wanting me to drop my dream all those years ago, had started a lie that had grown over the years and now couldn't be recanted, as my image would be ruined.

Despite my possessions, I wasn't a vain or materialistic person . . . but before Friendzone became a worldwide success, self-image was all I'd had. I had spent years painting a picture-perfect life, just so no one knew what my childhood was actually like, and now that I was an adult, something inside of me couldn't allow any cracks to form in that facade. If my success suddenly stopped and my life were to change, that created image of the person the world perceived me to be would remain my most prized possession, so I'd go to *great* lengths to protect it.

It was the only thing that was really mine . . . even if it was all a lie. I couldn't imagine what would happen if the world knew the truth about Friendzone, about Tommy, about . . . my upbringing.

Dinnae think about it.

I was living a rags-to-riches fairy tale, and if word broke that I wasn't single-handedly responsible for creating Friendzone, the resulting media frenzy would consume my name and my brand. I couldn't *begin* to fathom how differently I would be viewed, be treated, if my childhood was made public. My image was everything, and fear wouldn't allow for me to be less than perfect, so that image *had* to be upheld, no matter what the cost. Whether it was lies, deceit or even a fake marriage, I'd do what I had to do to ensure it remained intact.

That didn't mean that I didn't feel like a piece of shit whenever I thought of Tommy, because I did. For years, I tried to compensate him to make sure he and his small family were living a great life, but every cheque I wrote and sent to him was sent back to me not cashed. I lost count of how many times I picked up the phone to call him, or how many emails I began and letters I wrote only for them to be abandoned, erased or ripped up.

Tommy didn't just want nothing to do with Friendzone, he wanted nothing to do with me. And I'd begrudgingly accepted that when I shouldn't have. I never fought for our friendship, for the family who took me in and made me one of their own. I threw it, and them, away.

"Tara's right," I grumbled to no one. "I'm a fuckin' coward."

CHAPTER THREE

ERIN

"Auntie Erin?"

I looked up from my book of choice for the day at the sound of the familiar voice.

Reading was my one and only escape into different worlds where I didn't have to think about my mum, my dad or anything that was real to me. I could pretend I was a damsel in distress, a heroine with the weight of the world on her shoulders, the badass CEO of a billion-pound company or even a vampire who had a soft spot for humans. It was a time where I was carefree and happy, and I loved it.

"Aiden!" I beamed when my nephew entered the break room at Tesco. "I didnae know you were stoppin' by today."

I really shouldn't have been surprised; he dropped by during my break as often as he could, since it was the only way we could spend any time together thanks to the schedule his mum set years ago.

He crossed the room and gave me a hug. He rested his chin on my head, and like always, I was struck by how grown he was. He was only fourteen, but at five-foot-nine he towered over my five-foot-two frame. His height was just one of the many things Aiden had inherited from his father.

"You make me feel like a kid when you stand next to me," I said, pinching his sides.

He jumped away from me, grinning. "It's not *my* fault that you're as tall as a wee lass."

I pointed my finger at him. "Those are fightin' words, laddie."

He raised his hands and shook them from side to side.

"I'm *so* scared," he teased.

I eyed him. "Keep it up, and I'll cut you down to size real quick."

Aiden laughed merrily, and it made my heart happy. He put his school bag on the table, then took a seat next to me. He unpacked his lunch, and began eating it as I tucked my book into my bag and resumed chowing down on my sandwich.

"How's school so far?" I asked after I took a sip of Diet Coke.

"Borin'," Aiden said, rolling his eyes. "Sixth to eighth period is going to be the *worst*. I have back-to-back maths class. Double periods are rubbish."

I winced, knowing how much he struggled with maths.

"Anythin' I can help you prep for?" I quizzed.

He shook his head, his shoulders slumped. "It willnae help. I'm not as smart as you, Auntie Erin."

"Hey!" I frowned. "You're plenty smart."

Aiden remained unconvinced. "I'm not . . . Maths goes in one ear and out the other. I dinnae care what *x* or *y* is . . . what I should *really* be learnin' about is taxes, mortgages, interest rates, life's expenses. I should be learnin' about stuff I'm *actually* going to encounter in life, not about the cuntin' square root of pi."

I gasped at his casual use of such a vulgar word, and part of my food lodged in my throat for a moment.

"Aiden Saunders!" I chastised him when I caught my breath.

Aiden avoided my gaze. "Sorry, I shouldnae have said that around you."

"Or *at all*." I scowled.

He shrugged in response but still didn't look at me.

"Oi," I said, and waited for him to meet my eyes. "I was in your shoes before, bud. I know how tryin' school can be."

"But you *understood* what you were being taught," Aiden argued with a huff. "You're the smartest person I know, Auntie Erin."

The fact he believed that touched me.

I laughed lightly. "I may have excelled at schoolwork, but I never seemed to fit in. The kids teased me, and teachers pushed me aside because I sometimes corrected them when they were wrong. That made school hard for me. I lost count of how many times I pretended to be sick just so I wouldnae have to walk through those gates. I didnae have chums like you do."

Aiden, who was watching me with his large green eyes that were carbon copies of his father's, frowned. "Dad said you used to be bullied. I was kind of hopin' he lied about that."

I wish.

"It wasnae a lie. I was bullied." I nodded solemnly. "But I didnae let it get the best of me, even though it was very hard. I buckled down and got through school, and you will, too. Maths and English are your only downfall, but I still believe when push comes to shove you'll pass any exam put in front of you. I know it."

He gave me a pleased smile. "Thanks, Auntie Erin."

I winked. "I'm always gonna be your biggest cheerleader."

Aiden stared at me, a twinge of horror in his gleaming eyes. "Not in front of my mates though. Right?"

I tipped my head back and laughed. "And risk public humiliation for you? Never."

He leaned over the table, raised his hand in the air, and grinned when I lifted mine and clapped my palm against his.

"What's your word of the day?" I prompted when I relaxed back in my seat.

From the time he was ten and I found out how much he struggled at school, I had been doing words of the day with him. He had no mental disadvantages and he was a smart lad, he just found school a bit overwhelming at times.

His lips twitched. "Temerarious."

The *perfect* word to describe Tommy before Aiden came into our lives.

"In a sentence," I said, gesturing for him to speak with my hand.

"Skippin' sixth to eighth period would be temerarious and unwise of me."

I laughed. "Aye, it would."

"Doesnae mean I dinnae wanna skip though."

I raised an eyebrow. "Did you come here *hopin'* I'd let you skip?"

"Maybe?" he said, laughter laced through his words.

I clicked my tongue. "Your dad would redden *both* our arses if I allowed that."

Aiden lips twitched. "Aye, I figured as much."

"If you learn new formulas, or an old one is being revised, I'll help you with them," I assured him. "You like how I explain maths better than your teacher."

"Because you explain everythin' in straightforward terms," Aiden said, his shoulders slumping. "Teachers at my school use big words, like from word of the day, when explainin' somethin', and it just makes me feel stupid when I dinnae get it."

"You arenae stupid, Aiden. I'll help you with whatever you're stuck on. I've got you, bud."

Aiden reached back into his school bag and pulled out more food. He unwrapped another sandwich and began to eat it as we chatted. I kept an eye on the time so I wouldn't overrun my break, but also so Aiden would have enough time to get back to school. Some of my male co-workers, who were used to Aiden dropping by during my shift, bumped fists with him in greeting. Jensen, the shop's manager, jabbed his thumb over his shoulder when he entered the break room.

"You've another visitor, Erin." He smiled, the lines around his eyes deepening.

Jensen was nearly sixty years of age, and I rarely saw him without a smile on his face.

"Thanks, Jen."

I didn't get up to see who my visitor was. I only ever had three visitors, since Mum didn't know which Tesco I worked in. One was in front of me, Jesse Buckley worked day shifts at his construction company but sometimes visited me on his own lunch breaks, and the other had just walked through the door.

Aiden jumped up when Tommy walked into the room, and he instantly made a beeline for him, wrapping his arms around his dad. Tommy laughed, put his arms around his son and planted a kiss on the crown of his head. I grabbed my phone and quickly snapped a picture of their embrace before either of them could protest.

"Dad!" Aiden scowled as he pulled away, his cheeks tinged with a hint of redness. "I *told* you about kissin' me."

Tommy apologised with a grin and I snorted.

"What?" I teased. "You're too cool to receive a kiss from your dad?"

"Obviously," my nephew countered, shooting a grin – identical to his father's – my way.

I playfully rolled my eyes. "I'm never stoppin' my kisses, they're somethin' you'll just have to live with."

Aiden sighed dramatically. "I know."

I smiled, Tommy laughed and Jensen shook his head, still smiling as he left the room with a coffee cup in his hand. My brother joined us at the table and exhaled a deep breath.

"Long night?" I asked.

He nodded. "I got overtime, which is great, but my arse is killin' me from sittin' down for so long. I must have patrolled about one hundred times last night, just so I could move around. I jogged back and forth a lot too, just to keep active."

Tommy was the night guard at the National Museum of Scotland, and he had assured Aiden a hundred times that nothing came to life at night time that made his job exciting.

Aiden looked at his father. "Dinnae you have work tonight?"

Tommy nodded. "Only four hours though while I cover some of a friend's shift for him, thank God."

"We're still on for footy in the park tomorrow, after I'm done studying?"

Since Aiden was studying for his summer exams over the weekends, it meant he got to spend almost no time with his dad. It hurt him just as much as it hurt Tommy when they were forced to stay apart.

"Like you even have to ask." Tommy grinned. "I live for my days with you, you know that."

As far as Lucy knew, Tommy only saw Aiden on Fridays, but he was around at Tommy's as much as possible. When he told his mum that he was going out to play with his friends or going football training, he snuck around to Tommy's and spent a while with us. At first, Tommy was against it out of fear Lucy would find out and take away his Fridays with Aiden, but Aiden swore he'd never tell, and that was good enough for Tommy – and me.

"I dinnae understand your obsession with football," I said after I took a sip of my drink. "It's so bor—"

"Lemme stop you right there, Auntie Erin," Aiden said, giving me a pointed look. "Football is God's sport and Hibs is his chosen team, and we shouldnae talk bad about all things holy, isn't that right?"

Tommy muffled his laughter with his hand, but I could still hear his amusement at my being scolded by a fourteen-year-old.

"I suppose so," I said with a ghost of a smile.

"Glad we settled that," Aiden said with a nod.

"Aye," I mused. "Me too."

I gave Tommy my second sandwich, insisting I was full up from my first, and while the lads ate, we talked – and, as usual, we had a ball of a time together. It was simple moments like this that made up for all the hardship with Mum. Time with Tommy and Aiden was never time wasted . . . but sometimes it could be annoying as hell when sports were constant topics of conversation.

After we kissed and hugged Aiden goodbye, and sent him on his way back to school, I sat back down at the break table. Out of the corner of my eye, I saw Tommy tap on the screen of his phone. I leaned to the side to see what he was doing, and when I saw what app he had open, I gasped and snatched the phone from his hand.

"You *dinnae* have this piece-of-shite app downloaded!"

Tommy scratched his head. "It's not a piece of shite, it's the number-one social-media platform worldwide."

I gripped his phone tighter and scowled. "You know bloody well why I think it's a piece of shite."

Tommy silently held out his hand for his phone and waited. With my lip curled up in disgust, I dropped it into his open palm before folding my arms over my chest in annoyance.

"I understand your distaste for it – I do, Erin . . . but I helped create it—"

"Even more reason for you to avoid usin' it, since the *other* co-creator has never given you so much as a speck of credit. He's a billionaire now, livin' in London with a model fiancée, and hasnae looked back to Edinburgh since he left here without a backward glance eleven years ago."

"Ward . . . he isnae—"

"I dinnae wanna hear it." I cut my brother off. "I cannae stand the thought of him, and hearin' his name only makes me sick."

My brother exhaled a deep breath, but complied with my request by keeping his lips sealed. I was in a foul mood from that point on, and Tommy knew it. He told me he'd see me later, and gave me a hug and a kiss goodbye. I had ten minutes left of my break, but I went back to work anyway just so I could keep busy. Usually work helped keep my mind preoccupied, but not when Ward Buckley was mentioned.

I despised him.

At one point in time he was my brother's best friend – another member of our family, and someone I secretly had a crush on. He was so cool, always nice, and made me feel included when he joked around. I'd loved him when I was little, and that's why it hurt so much when he left us when we needed him most. Over the years, that hurt had turned to loathing. When he first garnered success with Friendzone, I fully expected him to credit Tommy, because they'd thought of it together, coded it together and designed it together.

But that didn't happen.

The first interview I saw that featured Ward was when he was twenty-one. I was thirteen at the time, so stupidly I'd believed the Ward I'd known and cared for was still somewhere inside the perfectly presented Ward who was wearing a suit and tie and being interviewed on *This Morning*. I watched that interview from start to finish seven times before I gave up on Ward altogether and began to hate him. His voice was different – he spoke more slowly, clearly – and not only did he fail to mention Tommy, but he said Friendzone was something that had been on his mind for years and that he'd taken a risk when he started developing it after moving to London to attend university. He said, "It was a lot of hard work, building it from the ground up by myself, but it's been worth it."

My bitterness towards Ward, and Friendzone, grew the more successful he and the company became, because I knew how different my brother's life would have been if he'd been part of it. Ward never gave Tommy the recognition he deserved, because he was a spineless coward who only cared about himself. When I encouraged Tommy to go public about it, he shut me down and told me never to bring it up again.

I knew part of my anger towards Ward came from Tommy and I being stuck in our lives while he went on to achieve great things. I couldn't speak for my brother, but I was horribly jealous that Ward had everything he and my brother had once talked about, while we were trapped in a never-ending cycle of darkness with our mum.

I finished my shift at Tesco in a sour mood, and lingered around town for a while until my shift at TGI's started. My night didn't improve between annoying consumers, staff drama, and the foul weather that fell from the sky. By the time I served my last customer, bussed my last table and clocked out, I was more than ready to fall into bed. The thought of my mum and her antics didn't even faze me, I just needed to get home and put the day behind me.

I left the restaurant, only to come to an abrupt halt outside under the shelter of the restaurant's awning.

"Shite," I groaned when I saw how hard it was still raining.

Rain was a common thing in Scotland, but the current downpour had the makings of a bad storm. I took out my phone and checked my bus's timetable, and groaned when I saw my bus route had been flagged red because of traffic. I remembered Tommy had said earlier in the day that he didn't have full shift at work that night and would be finished around this time, so I dialled his number.

"Hey," Tommy answered on the third ring.

"Hey," I said. "Is there any chance you could come and pick me up from TGI's? It's pourin' out."

"Aye, of course. I just finished up my shift," he replied. "I'll be there in twenty minutes – probably thirty with the traffic."

"Thanks, Tom," I said. "I owe you for this."

My brother snorted. "I'll add it to the list."

But after forty-five minutes of waiting, my legs were starting to hurt from standing in the one spot. I got fed up and sent Tommy a text that the rain had eased off enough for me to walk, because he was taking too long. I pocketed my phone, buttoned up my coat, pulled up my hood and adjusted the strap of my bag around my shoulder, then left the shelter of the awning. I kept my head down as I walked, to deflect the gales from slapping against my face. It proved futile, because the wind came from every direction.

"Hawaii," I said aloud as I walked. "One day you'll be able to sit on a beach in Hawaii and you *willnae* be cold."

It was a holiday I knew would most likely never come to pass, but thinking of hot sand, warm waters and the scorching sun helped keep my mind off the rain that sunk through my clothes and began to seep into my bones. I pulled my hood as low as it would go, trying to shield my face from it.

I shuffled from foot to foot when I reached the first pedestrian crossing on my journey, and waited for the green signal so I could cross the road. I glanced up, scanning multiple cars in the hope of seeing my brother's, but I didn't. However, I did notice that traffic was a lot heavier than normal. It wasn't rush hour, nowhere near it, but cars were backed up as if everyone had just been let out of work.

I crossed the road, ignored the multiple beeping horns and continued making my way home. I thought of Hawaii some more, and every desert I had ever learned about in school. I tried to focus on how high temperatures can aid in speeding up dehydration. Random facts ran through my mind, and so did multiple words of the day. I was distracted when flashing blue lights on the road up ahead came into view.

"Oh God."

There had been an accident, and from what I could see of the two cars, it had been a nasty one. There was a fire engine, as well as two ambulances and lots of police. I intended to continue my walk home, but something told me to stop and observe like the other pedestrians. The rain didn't bother me so much when I looked and saw the first wreckage. Whoever had been involved in the crash would be lucky to survive, because it looked bad.

"How did a crash this bad happen with all of the traffic?" I asked an older man who had stopped next to me, observing the scene with interest.

"There wasnae much traffic when it happened," he answered without looking my way.

I gasped. "You *saw* it?"

"Sure did." He nodded. "The driver of that red car broke the pedestrian crossin' light. I had barely made it across the road when he came speedin' through the junction. The driver of that black car was in his path, and the red car was goin' too fast to avoid a collision."

My heart leaped at the mention of a black car, but I told myself I was being silly – thousands of people had black cars, not just Tommy.

I turned my gaze to the black car that the man had pointed out, and scanned it, scrutinising every inch to try to spot some familiarity, but I couldn't. Not only was it dark out, but the car was badly damaged. I found myself wondering how the emergency services had got the person out of the car . . . until I saw parts of the vehicle had been cut away.

I jumped when I heard loud groaning that was quickly followed by a shrill scream. I instinctively reached out and gripped on to the forearm of the man next to me, and he didn't seem to mind; in fact, he used his hand to cover mine. He even gave it a reassuring pat. More people had stopped to watch the scene, and together we collectively winced when the driver of the red car was pulled free. His screaming caused the hairs on the nape of my neck to stand to attention.

"I bet that son of a bitch will walk away from this," the man next to me said. "Careless drivers like him do the damage and walk away. That other man hasnae made a sound since they got him free."

Now that the reckless driver from the red car was out of it, the paramedics moved him straight to a stretcher, and it cleared a path for me to see another group of paramedics and firefighters who were gathered around the other man involved in the crash. There were a lot of bodies doing important things, it was dark out and the rain was pouring down, so I shouldn't have been able to see much . . . but when I spotted bright orange running shoes on the feet of the injured man from the black car, my heart stopped.

Tommy had ugly shoes like that. Aiden had bought them for him for Father's Day, and Tommy loved them, not caring that they were neon. Someone's headlights shone on the scene, and when I saw thick black scribbled writing on the heel of the right shoe, I felt like I was going to scream. Aiden had written a silly quote for runners on the sole of his dad's right shoe.

The man who was in the destroyed car . . . It was my brother.

"Tommy?" I whispered.

"I'm sorry, love?" The man next to me nudged my side. "Did you say somethin'?"

"I know him," I said, staring at my brother's unmoving legs. *He's so still.*

"Oh God," the man said, and gripped my arm tightly. "Who is he?"

"My brother," I answered. "He's my brother."

"Christ!"

Without another word, I pulled free of his hold, dropped my bag to the ground and shot forward. The policeman saw me coming, and he straightened up to his full height and glared at me when he realised I had no intention of slowing down.

"Oi, you cannae—"

"That's my *brother*!" I screeched, forcefully pushing my way past the officer, not caring that I'd shoved him aside, and rushing towards the team of people that surrounded my brother as they performed CPR on his battered body.

"Thomas!" I screamed. "Oh God. *Thomas!*"

Arms came around me from behind, and I was lifted into the air for a moment.

"Miss," the officer's voice said firmly. "Let them work. Let them save him."

I fought his hold, but quickly stopped and put my entire focus on my brother.

"Dinnae let him die," I begged the people who worked on him. "He's all I have. *Please.*"

No one answered me, no one looked at me, and apart from the policeman restraining me, no one touched me. I saw lips moving and cars in motion, but I could hear nothing except the rain as it fell from the sky and pounded against the battered remains of my brother's car. Each droplet sounded like a resounding bang inside of my head. I gripped the arms that were still tightly wrapped around me, then I stared unblinkingly at my brother's feet, as they were now all I could see. I willed them, with every ounce of energy that I had, to move, to twitch . . . to *something*.

But they didn't.

CHAPTER FOUR
WARD

I'm the biggest fraud that I know.

This thought resonated with me as I shook the hands of another person who'd contributed greatly to my charity. I had to be polite and welcoming, because every person that came to one of my fundraisers helped my charity grow, and I'd deal with anything thrown my way to show my thanks. I'd lost count of how many people I'd greeted, smiled at and laughed with when they told a horrible joke since I'd entered the gala. And that was perplexing, because numbers were my thing, numbers helped me concentrate – but not tonight. Not with *her* on my arm.

"You're glaring awfully hard at our guests, my love."

I resisted the urge to squeeze the fingers that were intertwined with mine, and swallowed down a bitter taste in my mouth. "I'm just thinkin'."

"About what?"

Like you give a fuck.

"About how much perfume you have on," I said with a discreet sneer, as I turned my head and glanced down at my fiancée. "I could smell you from across the room."

I could tell Tara was clenching her teeth; the muscles in her jaw rolled back and forth as she tensed.

"Arsehole," she mumbled.

My lips twitched as I lifted my head and scanned the room. I held back a sigh that I was desperate to release. I hated that she had to come to these events with me. If these fundraisers didn't benefit my charity – Preventing Secrets – or another charity I cared about, I wouldn't go.

Had I been alone, I could happily smile, laugh and talk to people whose only purpose was to kiss my arse so they could achieve whatever was on their agenda. Everyone wanted something from me in one way or another, and if I could get something out of them that benefitted Preventing Secrets in return, then I'd do it with a smile on my face.

"Stop scowling," Tara mumbled, her hold on my hand becoming increasingly tight. "Someone will snap a picture, and the last thing we need is another headline saying our relationship is in trouble."

"It's in a hell of a lot more than trouble, sweetheart," I said, smiling widely for good measure as I spoke.

Tara snorted and leaned her body into mine. "The world doesn't need to know that, though."

I held back a glare and kept my eyes on the crowd.

"Aye," I begrudgingly agreed.

Tara removed her hand from mine and slipped her arm around my waist. Like clockwork, I switched the hand that held my glass of champagne and put my free arm around her, tugging her as close to me as I could get her. Part of me wanted to throttle her out of existence, while another part of me was appreciative that she didn't make these events harder than they needed to be. Tara knew her role in our arrangement, and she played the besotted fiancée very well. For a single moment I believed her act, but then I remembered how she had trapped me, and all civil thoughts vanished.

I was so wrapped up in my own head that I didn't realise Tara was speaking until I forced myself to focus on her.

"What do you think?"

I blinked down at her, causing her lips to thin into a line.

"You didn't listen to a word I said, did you?" she asked, narrowing her eyes accusingly.

I grinned. "Sorry."

I wasn't sorry.

Tara scoffed. "I said, we've been engaged longer than a year. Our wedding is in two months, and I want to be pregnant before we walk down the aisle."

Here we go again.

"You're the only woman I know who would *want* to be pregnant on her weddin' day."

Tara beamed up at me. "The sooner we have a baby, the sooner our agreement will be fulfilled, and the sooner we can get our divorce."

It can't come quick enough.

Not only did Tara want spousal support and a huge chunk of my money after we divorced, she wanted monthly child support, too. She knew I had the best team of solicitors that money could buy, and when we eventually divorced they would help retain as many of my assets as possible, so she wanted a baby to trap me for life. I'd never turn my back on a child, and the vindictive bitch knew it. I had agreed to her demands; it was the only way she'd sign a confidentiality contract. She would get money, houses and support for life once she agreed legally to never reveal the secret I had been harbouring for years.

One of the secrets – of those she knew about – anyway.

"I'll look into IVF—"

"We're *not* having IVF treatments when we can just have sex," Tara hissed under her breath, while managing to keep a smile on her face. "We've had sex plenty of times."

To anyone who cared enough to watch us, it would seem like we were gazing into each other's eyes and smiling as we spoke. We appeared to be the perfect couple, but it was a lie, a sham. Something entirely fictitious.

"That was *before* I was repulsed by you, sweetheart."

Tara's nails dug into my waist. "We're conceiving this child the *natural* way. I'm not being prodded with needles when your cock works perfectly fine."

I laughed humourlessly. "And how, pray tell, do you expect me to get it up?"

"I have my ways, you know that."

I looked away from her, disgusted with both her and myself. I despised Tara, and she truly did repulse me, but I also knew that if she wanted to have sex with me, she'd take my cock in her hands and make it happen. I knew it, and so did she. Sex was an outlet for me, and had been since I was a teenager.

"I hate you. Y'ken that, right?

Tara smiled up at me lovingly. "I hate you too, darling."

She loved my money, though.

I continued to smile down at her as she spoke to me, very aware that flashing cameras, and video cameras, were being pointed in our direction, waiting for something incriminating they could record and attach a headline to. I stroked my thumb over the material wrapped around Tara's waist, and I pressed a kiss to her temple, then to her cheek, which she quietly rebuffed because she didn't want me to ruin her highlighter. Whatever the fuck *that* was.

When the dinner started, I was grateful because I knew that meant the night was drawing to a close. Of course, things would continue at the after-party, but it was common knowledge that I never attended those. I always made sure that my event planners spared no expense, so my guests never missed my presence. Each time I held one of these events, they cost me a pretty penny, but the return in donations to my charity, and the exposure they brought, made them worth their while.

Preventing Secrets was something that I held very close to my blackened heart. It was a helpline for children who suffered neglect or physical, emotional, verbal, sexual – and, not least, mental – abuse. I wanted my charity to do more than help the victims of child abuse who came forward. I wanted to help the ones who suffered in silence . . . the ones who had to keep the harrowing secret and continued to endure the pain. And I wanted to prevent that secret from ever forming in the first place, if I could.

I worked with the government in order to have highly trained social workers on my payroll, so they could act as agents on behalf of the charity. They attended schools and other functions, meeting with children under the facade of working as school counsellors to the children, but of course the school board and its staff knew of their true purpose. While they were there, they used their training to watch for signals that a child was suffering from abuse.

In the current calendar year, Preventing Secrets had so far aided 407 children in the UK being freed from their abuse – whether it be at home, from a family friend, a family member, a teacher at school and so forth. And the aftercare for survivors didn't stop after the children's abuse was made known; it continued long after their court cases were closed and they returned to their new lives. It helped them work through what they experienced, until they reached a point where they were stronger than their fear of their abuser and could see light at the end of the dark tunnel.

Preventing Secrets was everything I'd needed as a child, and it was my duty as a human being to help children in need . . . so that was exactly what I was doing.

I felt a hand on my shoulder. I looked to my left, then down, and smiled when I found Hope's bright hazel, ever-loving eyes. But my smile slowly faded from my face when I took in her worried expression.

"Hope" – I frowned – "what's wrong?"

"Your brother," she said quietly. "He could only get your voice-mail, so he called me to reach you . . . Something has happened, Ward. Something bad."

Christ.

I tensed. "Go on."

"Your childhood friend you once told me about . . . Tommy Saunders . . ." Hope said, her face crestfallen. "He's been involved in a very serious car accident. The reports I could gather from your brother – through his hysterics – was that things don't look good for him."

My ears began to ring, and I could hear every beat of my heart as it punched against my chest.

I focused on Hope. "Get my jet prepped and ready to go to Edinburgh."

She nodded, raising her phone to her ear. "For when?"

"Right now."

Hope spun as she tapped on the screen of another phone, while holding the first to her ear with her shoulder.

I turned to Keller, who was, as usual, behind me on my right side.

"Change of plans," I told him. "Bring the car around."

He nodded once, pressed his fingers to his earpiece, and into his wrist he spoke a low command to the team.

"What's going on?" Tara asked, leaning into me so the guests around the table couldn't hear.

I flicked my eyes over them, and found they were too immersed in eating their dinner, talking to one another or draining their wine glasses to pay any attention to what was happening on my side of the table.

"I have to go," I replied. "My friend . . . he was involved in an accident, and I need to go to Scotland and see what I can do to help."

"You can't just *leave*," Tara hissed, her hand finding its way to my thigh, her fake nails digging in. "What will everyone think?"

"For once, Tara," I said as I brushed her hand from my leg and stood up. "I dinnae give a fuck what people think."

As my security team hustled together and guided me out the rear of the building, my brisk walked turn into a jog, then a full-on sprint as I spotted my town car. I wasted no time in jumping into the back seat, with Keller sliding in next to me. He handed me my phone, which he always kept when I attended an event. It rang the second the device touched my palm. I quickly pressed Answer when I saw my younger brother's smiling face filling the screen.

"Jesse," I said after placing the phone to my ear. "Is he okay?"

"Naw." Jesse choked on the word, his voice thick with emotion. "He's in surgery right now. Both of his legs are badly broken, and he has severe trauma to his head, too. They havenae said what the next step is with that; their focus right now is stabilisin' him. His heart stopped in the ambulance for thirty or so seconds, but the paramedics got him back."

"Christ . . ." I breathed, pain filling my chest. "Christ."

"I dinnae ken what's wrong with Erin, either," my brother continued. "When I got to the hospital she was screamin', Ward. Fucking *screamin'*, but now I cannae get her to talk to me. She's just starin' at the wall and tears are runnin' down her face. Her mum is the same. They're like statues. I'm beyond worried, man."

"They're in shock," I told Jesse. "Keep an eye on them until I get there. I'm on my way."

"Okay," he said, inhaling and exhaling deep breaths. "I'll text you the hospital's information. Just . . . just hurry, Ward."

"I'm comin', Jesse," I said through gritted teeth, before I hung up and looked at the eyes staring at me in the car's rear-view mirror.

"Where to, sir?" the driver asked, an eyebrow raised.

"The airport," I barked. "I'm goin' home."

CHAPTER FIVE

ERIN

Surgery.

My big brother was in *life-saving* surgery.

Three hours ago, I'd discovered it was Tommy who was lying in the middle of the road with a team of people surrounding him, trying to keep him breathing. I didn't listen to the details when Jesse Buckley explained it to me, but the driver of the red car that had slammed into my brother, the man who *caused* the crash after he ran a red light, had died on an operating table.

My mind and emotions were all over the place, but the one thing I was certain of was that I didn't care about the other driver. I didn't care that he had died. My focus was entirely on Tommy, and the only thing I could feel for the other man was an abundance of hatred because this was all his fault. He'd hurt my brother, and killed himself in the process.

Good riddance.

That thought process scared me. I had never wanted another person to die before, but this man . . . His actions had put Tommy's life at risk, and there was nothing I wouldn't do for my brother to protect him. Absolutely nothing.

I shifted in the plastic chair I had been sitting on for the past two and a half hours. My legs were tingling from sitting still for so long, and my behind was numb, too. I knew I wasn't the only one who was uncomfortable; everyone was shifting in their seats. Mum, Auntie Jennifer and Jesse kept me company while we waited in a family room at Edinburgh Royal Infirmary.

Jesse Buckley was Ward's younger brother, but unlike his older sibling, I adored Jesse. He had always been a great friend to Tommy and me in the years after Ward left, and he was always there when we needed him. The same couldn't be said for Ward.

I glanced around for what seemed like the hundredth time in the space of thirty seconds. We were in the trauma ward, and had been told to wait in the family room until the doctor came in to tell us whether my brother had made it through his surgery. The wait was agonising.

When Tommy was rushed to the emergency department, they'd stabilised him after his heart stopped beating, then sent him for X-rays and an MRI scan. Based on those results, they were going to repair a puncture in his lung first, and then something to do with his legs, but after that I was clueless as to what they would do to my brother.

Pain wrapped itself around my chest as I considered Tommy possibly dying. When I thought of death, I remembered my father and how I'd felt when I lost him all those years ago. It cut me like a blade. I didn't want to feel that way about Tommy. I wouldn't be able to survive it.

I felt a hand on my shoulder and I heard talking, but it sounded far away.

I turned my head when the hand on my shoulder gave me a shake, and when my eyes landed on Jesse, I simply stared at him. His sky-blue eyes, identical to his older brother's, gazed at me with concern. I didn't know how Jesse had found out about Tommy; in fact, I had no idea how my mum or auntie had found out either, because I hadn't called anyone. I didn't do much other than scream and cry as the police brought me to the hospital after Tommy was packed up into the back of the ambulance.

"Huh?"

Jesse frowned. "I've been speakin' to you . . . Did you not hear me?"

I shook my head. "My mind was elsewhere."

He bobbed his knee. "Are you okay?"

Fear pinched my heart.

"Ask me that again when Tommy comes out of surgery, and I might have an answer for you."

Jesse's gaze was full of pity, and helplessness. I related to the latter, because I desperately wanted to do something – anything – to help my brother, but there was nothing I could do. I could only wait for strangers to do their best to save him.

"Erin," Jesse said.

I blinked, then focused on him. "What?"

"Babe, I'm talkin' to you," he said, his forehead creasing as his frown deepened.

I lifted my hand, and gestured with a wave that I was fine. "Pay me no mind, Jesse. I cannae think straight. My thoughts . . . they just keep goin' to what the doctors are gonna say when they come to speak to us."

His hand on my shoulder gave me a comforting squeeze. "He'll be okay."

I didn't move.

"He has to be, Jesse," I said, more to myself than to my friend. "He has to be."

"When Ward gets here, he'll get the best team of doctors and—"

"What?" I cut Jesse off, turning my body to face him, the action causing his hand to fall from my shoulder. "When *who* gets here?"

Jesse opened his mouth to speak, but when he picked up on my tone and saw my facial expression, he swallowed.

"I . . . I had to call him."

Nae.

If there were two people in this world that were the opposites of one another, it was Ward and Jesse Buckley. The only similarities between them were their looks – that was it. Jesse was everything Ward wasn't.

He was loyal, reliable, down to earth, and, above all, he was a real friend to Tommy. Something Ward *definitely* wasn't.

"Jesse," I said slowly. "I *know* you aren't sayin' what I think you're sayin'."

Jesse cleared his throat. "I'm sorry, Erin."

"You phoned Ward?" I asked, baffled. "*Why?*"

"Because Tommy is like a brother to him, and he'd want to be here for him."

I choked on a humourless laugh. "He'd want to be here for him when he's possibly on his deathbed, but not the last *eleven years* while he's been livin' it up in London?"

"I cannae answer that." Jesse frowned. "I know you dinnae like him—"

"I hate him," I corrected.

"Fine." Jesse straightened. "You hate him, but Tommy doesn't, and this is about Tommy. Not you."

"How the hell do *you* know Tommy doesn't hate your piece-of-shite brother?"

Jesse shrugged. "He told me so."

Words of denial were clogged in my throat.

"I'm not lyin', before you even suggest that I am," he continued. "The only reason Tommy never spoke about Ward to you was because you lashed out every single time his name was mentioned. We've chatted about him from time to time. He never indicated he wanted to be buddies again with Ward, but he told me he had no hard feelings against him."

No hard feelings against him?

"That . . . that man took away what could have been a whole other life for my brother."

"Erin, if Tommy wanted that life, he could have had it even with your dad dying. He chose to stay here with you and your mum. Ward took nothin' away when you think about it, he just put himself first and pursued his dream."

My jaw dropped. "He claimed to start Friendzone on his *own*."

"I know, and that's rubbish of him – trust me, I've told him so – but Tommy is the one who never challenged that. He, again, chose not to. Have you ever asked your brother *why* he never followed Ward to London or had any involvement with Friendzone?"

I swallowed, and didn't answer because I knew the answer. I never allowed anyone to talk about Ward or Friendzone because whenever I thought about him, about him leaving us, the pain and anger still felt as fresh as they had on that life-changing day.

"I'm not talkin' about this, Jesse."

He sunk into his chair, casting his gaze downwards.

"Fine," he said when he eventually looked back at me. "If Tommy wakes up, you can talk to him about it."

"*When* he wakes up," I corrected.

"When." Jesse swallowed. "I meant when."

"*When* my brother wakes up, I'll talk to him about everythin', but until then you can go ahead and phone Ward." I spat his name. "Tell him not to come."

"Erin—"

"Naw, I dinnae care. You get him on the phone, and you tell him that he isn't welcome, Jesse. I mean it."

Jesse stared at me, and I stared right back at him. After a few moments, he sighed deeply as he picked himself up off the chair, dug his phone out from his pocket and walked out of the room without a word or a backwards glance. My eyes locked on the door that Jesse had shut behind him when he left the room, but my attention was pulled back to my thoughts as what-ifs plagued my already-troubled mind.

I squeezed my eyes shut and tried my hardest to force out the negativity, but it was hard because while I knew Tommy was stable, he'd only been barely so before they took him to surgery. He'd lost a lot of blood at the scene of the accident, and would no doubt need a transfusion. The odds were stacked against my brother, but then again, they'd always been stacked against him, and he always came out on top.

He'll be okay.

I opened my eyes, and stared at my mum, who had her head leaned against Auntie Jennifer's shoulder. She was crying softly, tears silently rolling down her cheeks, and I wondered if she was shaking because she was worried for Tommy or because she hadn't had a drink in a few hours. I snorted to myself when, for a single moment, I considered leaving the hospital to grab her something to calm her nerves.

"What's funny?"

I flicked my gaze to my auntie when she spoke.

"Nothin'," I mumbled. "I just thought of somethin' stupid."

I dropped my gaze down to my fingers, and began to pick at the chipped purple varnish that coated each nail.

"Erin . . ." Auntie Jennifer spoke softly, then when I didn't answer she said, "Honey . . ."

I didn't look up, because I didn't want to see pity in her eyes – or worse, worry for Tommy.

"I'm fine," I answered, my voice low. "I'm just antsy."

That was the understatement of the century, because I was terrified.

"He's a tough nugget, that brother of yours," she said. "He's too bloody stubborn to not come out of this A-okay."

I laughed a little, then without warning, my laughter turned into soul-splitting sobs. I covered my face with both of my hands as I rocked myself back and forth, willing my tears to dry up and go away. I hated crying, it solved and changed nothing, but I couldn't deny that it was a relief to force out some of the built-up agony that was perched upon my chest.

"I'm fine," I repeated as I sniffled and wiped away my tears. "I'm fine."

I wasn't fine, but it felt right to say that I was.

When I looked back at my mum and auntie, neither of them had moved an inch. They were both staring at me with pain in their eyes. I always saw pain in Mum's eyes, but it was the first time in a long time that I'd seen the agonising emotion in my auntie's eyes. Auntie Jennifer was always the one person you could rely on to bring happiness to any situation, but looking at her before me now, I knew not even she could make what we were going through any easier . . . not that she was even trying.

Normally, I stared at my auntie every chance I got, because she reminded me so much of my father. Not physically, but personality-wise – she was carefree and outgoing just like my dad was. I was the only member of our family who'd got Dad's white-blonde hair, lustrous grey eyes, button nose and full pink lips.

Here in the waiting room, I couldn't even try to hold my auntie's gaze – there was too much uncertainty there, and I needed reassurance that Tommy was going to be okay. I couldn't think of him not being anything other than perfectly healthy.

"Where's Auntie Emma?" I asked, my focus returning to my nails.

Emma was Auntie Jennifer's wife, and where there was one, usually there was the other.

"She's on a plane back from Manchester," my aunt answered me. "She'll be arrivin' shortly."

I forgot that she'd been away on business. Auntie Emma had just completed culinary school a year ago, and in the time since she became fully qualified to run her own kitchen, she had been going to masterclasses, workshops and conferences up and down the UK, learning all she could about everything a chef needs to do *besides* cook food. Presentation and staff management weren't her forte, but Auntie Emma said the workshops and classes taught by experienced chefs had given her invaluable knowledge.

"Does she know . . . does she know how bad his accident was?"

Auntie Jennifer hummed. "I didnae wanna tell her over the phone, but she said she couldn't sit in the airport, then on the plane for hours, without knowin'."

My shoulders slumped. "Did she have to leave her conference early?"

"Naw," Auntie Jennifer answered. "The classes she attended finished this evenin', but she planned to stay one more night just to avoid travellin' after a long day, but an army couldn't stop her from comin' home once I told her our Tommy was . . . injured. She booked a ticket on the first flight out."

I swallowed the lump that had formed in my throat.

"I hope it didnae cost her too much money to get a ticket at the last minute."

Auntie Jennifer chuckled softly. "Nae cost is too much when it comes to family."

I continued to pick at my chipped nail varnish, but when the door to the room suddenly opened, I jerked my head up, gripped the arms of the chair and held my breath. An unfamiliar woman popped her head into the room, and after a quick glance around she said, "Sorry, wrong room."

I exhaled when the door closed once more, and a glance at my auntie and mum showed that they were now sitting back in their seats, having shot upright when the door opened.

"I dinnae think we've ever been so on edge," I commented.

"We have," Mum muttered. "You were probably just too young to remember it."

I couldn't believe my ears. I looked at my mum, hard. She'd completely caught me off guard. She *never* brought up that night.

"If you're talkin' about Dad, and the night he died," I said, not caring that the mention of him made her wince, "then know that I remember *everythin'* about that night. Every. Single. Thing. I can describe it to you in detail if you'd like?"

I'd dreamed about it nearly every night since . . . It wasn't likely that I would ever forget the night that both of my parents died: one physically, the other emotionally.

"Hey now," Auntie Jennifer said softly. "Let's not talk of the night your sweet dad passed away. Let's focus on what we need to do to take care of Tommy once he comes out of surgery."

"Definitely," I agreed. "Once we know the plan, I'll go and get whatever he needs from his apartment."

My auntie looked at my mum when she said something to her under her breath, and she shook her head in response.

"It's almost two in the mornin', love. Lucy and Aiden will be asleep, and callin' them now will only cause worry."

"But they should know," Mum argued. "Tommy is his dad."

"We shouldnae tell them until we know there *is* somethin' to worry over. Mornin' will come soon enough for us to discuss how to break the news to Aiden, okay?"

Mum exhaled, and bobbed her head.

Auntie Jennifer had always been the peacemaker in the family, always the one to find a solution when things seemed bleak, so I wasn't surprised that she was trying to force into our subconscious that Tommy was going to be okay, even though I could tell she was just as unsure as the rest of us. I appreciated her and I truly loved her to pieces, but I wanted to show her it was okay if she wanted to be sad. Tommy was her nephew, and she didn't have to remain strong just for our sakes. It didn't seem fair that she felt the need to help raise everyone else's spirits when her own were in disarray.

I just didn't know how to begin to comfort her.

"I'll go by Aiden's house in the mornin'," I offered. "Once we know where we stand with Tommy, of course."

"Tomorrow is Sunday," Mum said to no one. "Aiden was supposed to go and play football in the park with Tommy tomorrow."

I swallowed. "Aiden will come here once he knows about Tommy, so he'll still have him tomorrow."

My mum nodded, but I knew her mind was elsewhere. Trying to connect to her when she was spaced out was futile, so I returned my attention to the waiting-room door. I spent minutes willing a doctor, nurse – *someone* – to walk through it and update us on my brother, but no one came, and I began to get extremely anxious.

I stood up, causing my auntie to raise her eyebrows in a question.

"I'm goin' up and down the corridor to stretch my legs," I said with a forced smile. "I'll break out into squats otherwise."

My auntie snorted. "I wouldnae mind seein' that, since you *never* do them correctly."

"Whatever," I joked as I headed out of the room.

When I closed the door behind me, a glance to my left and right showed an empty corridor. I leaned my head back against the wooden door and stared straight ahead. After a moment, I pushed away from the door, and headed towards a small nurses' station. Facing it was the entrance to a large area of cubicles, which were empty of patients. Three nurses were behind the counter of the station, and each was too busy filling out documents to notice my approach.

"Excuse me," I said softly.

All three looked up, but the oldest of the trio, who had greying hair and lots of smile lines, was the one who beamed up at me and dropped her pen, giving me her full attention.

"Hello, love," she said, revealing an English accent. "What can I do for you?"

"Um . . ." I swallowed, but relaxed when the other two nurses went back to filling out their paperwork and paid me no attention. "I just wanted to see if there was any update on my brother, Thomas Saunders? He's been in surgery for a little while now."

Two hours and twenty-five minutes, give or take a few seconds.

The nurse kept her smile in place as she tapped on the keyboard in front of her, looked at the computer screen, then back to me.

"I'm afraid there have been no updates from the OR yet," she said, putting one small hand on top of the other. "But as soon as there is, I'll come and give it to you right away. Your family is in family room two, correct?"

"Aye," I said, my shoulders slumping. "Thank you for your help, I appreciate it."

I turned away from the smiling nurse, and began to walk in the direction that led to the ward's exit. I wasn't planning on leaving, I just wanted to stretch my legs. I glanced around as I walked, noting the place was very quiet for a ward that dealt with the most severe trauma patients. I decided that silence meant nobody was in a dire enough state to cause chaos among the staff. Silence on a hospital trauma ward was surely like music to the nurses' ears.

That silence was disrupted when I heard a phone ring back down the corridor, at the nurses' station. They were no longer sitting calmly behind the counter, they were quickly moving around while the nurse who'd spoke to me had the telephone to her ear, frantically writing on a clipboard.

The other two nurses rushed towards the empty cubicles and disappeared out of sight. I put two and two together and realised they must have received a call about an incoming patient and were prepping for the situation. Two men, clearly doctors from their attire, hustled on to the ward and jogged past me. Talk among the doctors and nurses faded into the background as I walked further down the corridor.

I came to a stop when a vending machine caught my eye. I was about to purchase a bottle of water but then I spotted the self-service tea and coffee machine next to it. My feet practically glided across the floor. The adrenaline from the past few hours was fading, and the late hour was starting to register with my body. Tea with plenty of sugar was exactly what I needed.

I popped some loose coins from my pocket into the vending machine, and when my teabag packet fell to the bottom of the machine, I retrieved it and got to work on making the delicious cup of excellence. I grimaced at the styrofoam cups, but quickly got over it. I wasn't in any position to hold a real mug, so I'd take what I could get.

Being annoyed over something so trivial felt stupid.

I wasn't sure how long I stood at the machine making my drink, but when there was a sudden loud commotion to my left, I almost spilled my tea. A group of people were pushing a bed trolley with a patient through the double doors and into the ward. They zoomed past me, shouting different orders at one another. A person was sitting on top of the person on the trolley, performing chest compressions.

"This is bad," I whispered to myself.

Three grown men, one elderly woman and a woman closer to my mum's age made up the group that came barrelling through the doors next. I tensed at the tears streaking all their faces.

All five of them looked how I felt – terrified.

"Sorry," the man closest to me said. "D'you know where—"

"Lisa!" the oldest-looking man of the group suddenly shouted.

I didn't know who Lisa was, but when he took off running down the corridor, the others quickly followed behind him. I stared at them as they all came to a stop outside the cubicle area, holding on to one another, crying. I guessed the person that was brought in on the trolley was their loved one – Lisa.

For a long while, there were no sounds other than crying, machines beeping, and the hospital staff calling out vital signs and requesting the family to move away. The family didn't move an inch, and I didn't blame them.

"Call it," I heard a male voice say.

There was a moment of silence, then another voice announced the girl's time of death. I froze, and though I desperately wanted to move, to run in the opposite direction, I couldn't move a muscle.

"*Naw!*" the middle-aged woman screamed as she fell to the floor. "Naw! Lisa! My baby!"

The pain-filled wails from the entire group were too much for me. I dropped my tea into the bin next to the vending machine, and ran back towards the family room. I opened the door and stepped inside in a hurry, slamming it shut behind me.

"Where'd you get off to?" Auntie Jennifer asked as I entered the room.

It was only then that I realised my eyes were closed. I slowly lifted my lids but kept my gaze on the floor.

"I was makin' tea."

"Is somethin' happenin' out there?" Mum asked. "We thought we heard shoutin'."

I swallowed. "A family got really bad news about their loved one."

Silence.

I exhaled, and was just about to raise my head and walk back over to my seat when a voice stopped me.

"Hello, Erin."

I remained unmoving for a few seconds before I could force my body to shift so I could face the piece of shite who'd addressed me. I'd know his voice anywhere. I'd listened to it many times over the years through the interviews on different podcasts he appeared on. I used to hope that if I listened to them enough, Ward would change his answer and he'd credit Tommy with helping to create Friendzone, but he never did.

Though I knew it was his voice, I held out some hope that my mind was mistaken, but when my eyes landed on all six-foot-something inches of him, I knew he was here.

"Ward," I said, my voice sounding strange to myself.

Even though I'd actively avoided any news pieces about him or Friendzone, I had seen pictures of him, and it made me sick to think they didn't do him justice. He was so incredibly handsome that it almost hurt to look at him.

His hair was as dark as night and presented in a clean-cut, taper hairstyle. He had dark facial hair, not thick or long enough to make a full beard, but it suited him. His skin was fair and looked soft to the touch. He was perfect. The image was lost on me though, as the only thing I saw when I looked past his beauty was his lies. I curled my lip in a sneer and glared at him, hoping I projected how much he disgusted me.

"What the *fuck* are you doin' here?"

CHAPTER SIX
WARD

Well, shite.

I'd known that I wouldn't exactly be welcomed with open arms by the Saunders family, but *shite*. Erin was *not* happy to see me, and while I'd expected glares, cursing, and maybe even a slap or two being thrown my way – slaps that would be rightly deserved – what I was not prepared for was the raw hatred in her eyes.

"Jesse," I said, shoving my hands into my trouser pockets. "He phoned me, then I phoned your mum, who told me to come."

A mixture of emotions played out on Erin's expressive face. An expressive, *beautiful* face. I felt my surprise at that particular observation, but I pushed it aside and focused on her. She was shaking, her cheeks had dried streaks of tears on them, her clothes were wrinkled beyond belief . . . and she looked completely, utterly terrified.

"Leave," she said, her voice sounding rough. "I dinnae want you here."

I shouldn't have felt a pang of hurt at her declaration, but I did.

"I'm here for Tommy, Erin," I said as gently as I could.

"*He* doesnae want you here either," she snapped. "He doesnae want anythin' to do with you. None of us do."

"Erin," her auntie chided softly. "This is not the time and place for this."

I had never agreed with a statement more in my life.

"He shouldnae be here," Erin said to Jennifer, her voice cracking. "He should be in London, far away from here."

"Erin," Jesse said with a frown. "This is his home, too."

I wanted to argue with that. Scotland hadn't been my home in a very long time, but as Jesse and Jennifer were currently the voices of reason here, I kept my mouth shut.

"He walked away from *home* without a care for us a long time ago, Jesse," Erin said with a sneer.

Jesse didn't reply, but I saw his shoulders slump in defeat. He couldn't argue with Erin's jab and he knew it. I had walked away from my home and my family a long time ago, but what Erin, Jesse, and everyone else *didn't* know was that I'd had my reasons for walking away – and *staying* away. But if I had any say in it, they'd never find out those reasons.

There was one person on the planet who knew my suffering, and he was currently in life-saving surgery.

"We can argue till we're blue in the face later about me being here," I stated. "Right now, we need to focus on Tommy. What's his status?"

"Like I told you," Jesse answered, "he's in surgery. They never gave us a timeframe, everything happened so fast. He was here one minute, then whisked away the next. We dinnae even know if broken bones are the worst of his injuries."

I rubbed my face, not liking my brother's reply. I wasn't what one would call a patient man. When I wanted results, I usually got them fast, but this situation was out of my control, the one thing I usually had a handle on . . . in my adult life, anyway.

"The three of you sit down," Jennifer said with a sad smile. "You're makin' me nervous, facing off with each other."

But the only person facing off was Erin with me, and everyone knew it.

Jesse and I took a seat next to one another without hesitation, while Erin sat on the far side of the room, away from everyone. She was watching the door, and I was watching her. She *definitely* wasn't a kid anymore. She didn't have any social-media profiles, so the only visual updates I'd got on her over the years was when she was with Jesse and he snapped a picture of them and put it on his Friendzone profile. I told myself that was the reason why I was so taken aback by her appearance.

It was foolish to assume she'd have remained that cute kid who used to giggle whenever I was in her presence. She wasn't a young girl with shoulder-length white-blonde hair and the most adorable smile I'd ever seen. She was a twenty-two-year-old woman with a face so beautiful it was hard not to stare. Her thick, white-as-snow wavy hair hung to her waist, and she was couple of inches taller than five foot, if that. Though her crumpled clothing covered her well, it did nothing to hide the swell of her breasts, the dip of her small waist and the delicious flare of her curved hips.

Erin had grown up, and I found myself taking notice of it.

Dafty.

I shook my head, scowling at myself for thinking such things when Tommy was in a critical condition on an operating table. Not to mention, the woman clearly fucking *hated* me and I didn't have a clue how to go about dealing with it. The last time a person had looked at me with that much hate, I was hurt. Physically. Over and over again. I'd run away from that situation, but I couldn't run away from Erin.

I'd already done that to her before, and I refused to do it again.

I turned my gaze from Erin to Amelia Saunders, and found she was looking right at me. Her appearance shocked me to the core. She looked as if she'd aged thirty years since I last saw her. She was only fifty-one, but she looked so much older. She looked like she might even be sick, and I made a mental note to bring it up to Erin at a later time. A time when she wasn't so hostile towards me.

I hoped to God there would be such a time.

I cleared my throat. "I wish I were here under better circumstances, Amelia."

Amelia didn't blink. "Me too, son."

My heart thudded against my chest. Did she mean to call me son, or was that just a slip-up? She'd once told me I was just as much her son as Tommy was, but then I'd left her. I'd loved her, and I still loved her, I just didn't know how to make things right between us. Between all of us.

I felt eyes on me, so I turned and looked back at Erin. Her plump pink lips were thinned to a line, and her grey eyes were narrowed to slits.

"Have all the conversations you'd like, but dinnae make yourself at home," she warned. "You arenae stayin'."

"Erin," Amelia whispered. "*Please.*"

Erin looked at her mum and I could see that she wanted to argue with her, but she didn't. She relented with a nod, and turned her attention back to the door of the room. I focused on making sure I was allowed to stay at the hospital.

I looked at my brother, who got up and walked out of the room, giving me a nod to follow him, so I did.

"She hates me," I said to my little brother after I gently closed the door to the waiting room. "If looks could kill, I'd be dead and buried."

Jesse raised an eyebrow. "Were you expectin' hugs and kisses?"

"Naw," I admitted. "Nothin' like that. I expected anger, just not hate. She really hates me, Jesse."

"Erin doesnae know the meanin' of the word," Jesse said, patting my shoulders. "She's a good lass . . . She's just conflicted because she hates what you've done."

I lifted my hand to the bridge of my nose and pinched it as pain started to pulse there, before dropping my hand with a sigh.

"I'll have to do things in baby steps," I said. "I have to show her I have no ulterior motive, and that I'm just here to be by Tommy's side."

"*Is* that all you're here for?"

I frowned. "Why else would I come back?"

"I'm not goin' to dignify that with an answer."

"Jess," I sighed. "I fly you down to see me so I don't *have* to come back here."

My brother shrugged. "It'd be nice for you to stop by and say hello to Dad—"

"It's not goin' to happen, Jesse," I interrupted, my voice firm. "We've been over this."

"Yeah, we have," my brother agreed. "And I still think it's a bullshit excuse for either of you to not talk to one another."

"How is me not wantin' to be anywhere near your mum a bullshit excuse?" I questioned. "Dad is standin' by his wife, and I'm standin' by my decision not to have her in my life."

"It's so stupid though, Ward," Jesse said, exasperated. "You never got on with my mum, I get that – but Jesus, man. Seeing her a few times a year just to keep a relationship with Dad is surely doable?"

Nothing was doable if I had to be anywhere near that woman.

"I'm not talkin' about this again, Jesse," I said with a glare. "Focus on the problem at hand: Tommy."

The muscles in Jesse's jaw rolled back and forth as he tensed it, but he gave me a curt nod that drew a relieved breath from me before I scrubbed my face with both of my hands.

"This is fucked up."

Jesse nodded grimly. "Aye."

"I have to speak to his doctor," I said. "If it's serious, if there's anythin' wrong with his brain and he needs special care or treatment, I want him transferred to London. I'll arrange for him to be under the best care."

Jesse stared at me blankly.

"What?"

He shrugged. "You're here five minutes and already makin' decisions that arenae yours to make."

I scowled. "I'm thinkin' logically. If he cannae get better here, he needs to go where he *will* get better, and *that* is in London."

"Why London?"

I threw my hands up in the air. "Because that's where the National Hospital for Neurology and Neurosurgery is! An employee of mine had his mum treated there when she was in a skiin' accident, and they worked miracles on her after she sustained a brain injury. They're the best."

"What if his brain is okay?" Jesse questioned. "What if he needs to stay here?"

"Then he'll stay here *if* this place provides the best treatment for whatever might be wrong with him!" I countered. "Why are you arguin' with me on this?"

"Because it's not your decision to make . . . It's Erin and Amelia's if Tommy can't speak for himself."

I shook my head and began to pace back and forth.

"Arguin' over this is futile," I told Jesse. "Everyone will want Tommy to get better. *Everyone.* The location of where it happens doesn't matter once it happens."

"Agreed. But you have to let others come to that conclusion on their own. Dinnae force it on them like you just did with me."

I stared at my younger brother, wanting to wring his neck.

"You're a pain in the arse, y'ken that?"

Jesse grinned. "Aye, I do."

And, just like that, my annoyance with him washed away and I chuckled. Jesse was only five years younger than me, but he knew good and well how to push my buttons.

"Come here," I said, opening my arms. "It's good to see you, Jess. I missed you, little brother."

Jesse walked forward and gave me a tight hug and a firm pat on the back, which I returned.

"Missed you too, man," he said, stepping out of our embrace. "It's been awhile."

It was four months to the day since I'd last seen him in person.

"It has," I said, and frowned. "I'm sorry I've been so busy. It seems every day I launch more apps. Ever since I expanded the company to other projects, things have been crazy. That means more business, and while more business means more money, it means more work."

Jesse patted my shoulder. "Naw need to explain, I know how run off your feet you are."

"If you accepted my job offer you could see me more often," I hinted.

"Me? In London? Surrounded by suits day in and day out?" Jesse snorted. "Naw, bro. Thank you again for the offer, but I'm happy here with my tools. My business is doin' well."

"Aye?" I said, already knowing what he was going to tell me. "Any new contracts?"

Jesse's eyes gleamed.

"Aye," he practically squealed. "I was gonna call you next week with the details once it had all been finalised, but a new hotel is openin' on George Street in the city. A really big luxurious Hilton, and I placed a bid, not really thinkin' I'd even be considered for a call back . . . My bid was on the pricey side since I havenae got enough jobs under my belt to be in good with buildin' providers yet . . . but they fuckin' *accepted* my offer, Ward!"

I had practised my response to this repeatedly the past few weeks, to make sure I got it genuine, but I didn't even have to try. Seeing the joy on my brother's face was all I needed.

"Jesus!" I stated. "Jesse, congratulations! Fuck, I'm so proud of you. I *told* you your break would happen!"

We hugged again.

"Thanks, man," he beamed. "It means a lot, comin' from you."

"From me?"

"Aye, from *you*." Jesse snorted. "Self-made billionaire with one of the most successful businesses on the planet? Praise from you means a lot, man. I aspire to be successful like you."

"Jesse," I said, clearing my throat. "Thank you, I dinnae ken what to say."

"Nothin' to say," my brother replied.

I smiled. His happiness about his business let me know that what I'd done was the right thing. I'd never tell Jesse, because he'd feel like I was spoon-feeding him, but I'd been keeping an eye on contracts that popped up in Scotland, too. When I found out that Jesse had bid for the Hilton job, I'd made a few calls and recommended that my brother's bid be accepted. But I didn't have to twist arms, or pay any money to make it happen. Jesse's previous work spoke for itself.

When he left school he'd followed in our father's footsteps and dived into construction. He'd always loved it, and would even accompany our dad on jobs and help out when he was a kid. I never knew what to get him at Christmas or on birthdays because he wasn't a materialistic person, but when he announced he was starting his own company – Buckley's Construction – I finally knew of gifts that he would accept. He'd saved up enough money to purchase a small plot of land outside of Edinburgh, and after two years he'd levelled it all out and built a warehouse and small office building by himself, as he hadn't had the money to hire a crew to help him. When Christmas rolled around, I gifted him with ten of every tool, machine and vehicle a construction company needed. I made sure he had the best that money could buy.

That was the second time I had ever seen my brother cry, the first being when I told him I was moving to London when he was just fourteen.

"How'd Dad react?"

"He cried." Jesse laughed. "He's just happy for me. Y'ken how he always wanted his own company but couldn't afford it and had to work for others – well, he's kind of livin' that dream through me now. He offered to help me, without pay if needed."

I smiled. "Good ol' Dad."

"Aye." Jesse nodded. "Good ol' Dad."

"How many men are you goin' to hire?"

"It's a big job," Jesse said, sighing. "I've got my ten lads who I've had since I got the company up and running, but I think about twenty-five more and I'll be comfortable meetin' the deadline."

I nodded. "When does construction start?"

"It could change, but right now, work starts in two months. The deal closes on Friday next, and on the Monday followin' that I meet the architect to go through the plans and give my input. They wanted it done in six months, but I stretched them to ten. The amount of detail they want is honestly outstandin'. They want the structure to appear like old Scotland – to keep in theme with Edinburgh Castle, which the guests can see from their hotel rooms – but the interiors will be a mixture of old and new Scotland. I made some design suggestions, and the architect was impressed by them and is workin' them into the final design. I'm so excited I could honestly piss myself."

I laughed but quickly quietened down, not wanting Erin or her family to think I was having braw banter with my brother while they were nervous wrecks waiting for news.

"I'm chuffed for you, man," I told Jesse. "You deserve it."

"Thanks," he replied. "I told Tommy about it yesterday. He just about lost his mind."

I lost my smile and sense of joy altogether at the mention of him.

"He needs to be okay," I said, my voice tight. "I need to make things right with him, I need to fix what I've broken."

Jesse placed his hand on my shoulder and gave it a firm squeeze.

"You will," he said, sounding sure. "He's goin' to be okay, and you can have your chance with him to make everythin' right."

I nodded, choosing to think positively for my sanity's sake.

"I dinnae think Tommy will be the problem though," Jesse said, cringing. "There's someone else who you'll need to make amends with."

Erin.

"Aye," I agreed. "Too bad she isn't painfully shy anymore. That'd make things easier."

"Shy?" Jesse asked, wide-eyed. "*Erin?*"

"She was always shy around me, like a little kitten . . . but now? She a full-grown hellcat."

"One with a mean bite when it comes to Tommy," Jesse said with a grin. "Good luck, man . . ."

We both knew the end of that sentence.

Because I'll need it.

CHAPTER SEVEN
ERIN

Ward. Fucking. Buckley.

Only the fact I knew I'd either be thrown out of the hospital or arrested for murder kept me from wringing his bloody neck. He had some nerve, showing his face around my family, but to show up at the hospital where my brother was in surgery after a horrific car accident? He had a death wish, one I *more* than wanted to grant.

For the hundredth time since he showed up three hours ago, I scowled to myself, hating that he was consuming my thoughts. I had got extremely good at forcing all memories and fleeting thoughts of Ward from my mind. I usually was only ever plagued by him when I saw his face in a magazine, or if I overheard someone mention Friendzone. I could deal with that, but being in the same room as him, just a couple of metres away? That was too much.

I didn't want him to be here, but it appeared that everyone else in the room did.

I refused to look at him, but it didn't stop my mind from conceiving thought after thought about him. His presence here was shocking, but what confused me more was that he was wearing a fucking three-piece tailored navy suit that looked like it cost more than my mum's house. His shoes were black, and so shiny that I knew if I was close enough I'd see my reflection in them. I'd bet my life savings that they were made from the best leather, too.

Ward's attire boasted money, and his face and body accompanied that perfectly tailored suit. His look screamed model, and it bugged the shite out of me because I noticed it. I noticed *him*. I found myself wondering why he couldn't be short, bald and ugly like multibillionaires were *supposed* to be? It wasn't enough that he was filthy rich – and famous – he just had to be drop-dead gorgeous to boot, too.

"Bloody typical," I muttered to myself, just as the door to the room opened and in stepped a doctor.

A very tired-looking doctor.

I jumped to my feet, and in my peripheral vision I noticed everyone else shot to theirs, too.

"Hello, everyone. I'm Dr Liddle, one of the surgeons who headed Mr Saunders's surgery tonight," he said, his voice rough – probably from tiredness given the late, or rather early, hour. "I'll get right to the point, as I can see the apprehension and worry on your faces. Mr Saunders isnae out of the woods just yet, but he made it through the surgery."

I cried out with relief and stumbled back. My knees buckled, and I thought I was going to drop to the ground, but arms suddenly enveloped me and held me up against a firm body. Every fibre of my being told me it wasn't Jesse's body I was against, but I was too relieved about Tommy to care.

"Thank God," Auntie Jennifer cried as she hugged my now-sobbing mum.

"I need to be clear," the doctor continued, "that while he is stable, Mr Saunders is still in critical condition and has been admitted to the ICU for round-the-clock observation."

My breath hitched.

"Why?" I asked, tears sliding down my cheeks. "Why is he in intensive care?"

"After his accident, and the injuries he sustained, ICU admittance would be textbook protocol for any patient for monitorin', but in Mr Saunders's case it is highly required as he has other injuries. More complex injuries, to be frank."

"Complex?" Ward spoke for the first time since the doctor entered the room. "Please explain."

"That's the thing," Dr Liddle said with a shake of his head. "I'm not entirely sure *what* I'm explainin' yet. It could be somethin' or nothin' at all, brain injuries are tricky."

"Brain injuries?" I repeated with a sob. "Tommy is *brain*-damaged?"

"Naw, nothin' has been determined yet," the doctor said quickly, trying to calm the rising cries from my auntie and mum. "The only thing we've detected through scans is swellin' on the parietal lobe of his brain. No bleeds, abrasions or cuts of any kind. Just swellin', but that in itself can be dangerous, dependin' on the type of swellin'."

"Type of swellin'?" Jesse asked. "There are types of brain swellin'? What type does *Tommy* have?"

I lifted my hands to Ward's arms, which were still wrapped around me, and I gripped them tightly as we awaited the doctor's response.

"We willnae know until he wakes up," the surgeon answered. "The problem with brain injuries is, the majority of the time, we need to monitor the patient while they're conscious to determine how much function, if any, was lost due to the swellin' sustained from the injury. As Mr Saunders is a patient with a TBI – traumatic brain injury – after we stabilised him we decided to perform a procedure called a decompressive craniectomy."

I held on to Ward for dear life as the doctor spoke.

"We removed a moderate-sized piece of Mr Saunders's skull, which will allow the brain to be relieved of some intracranial pressure that the swellin' has caused."

My heart slammed into my chest and my stomach rolled. All I heard were words that, for once, I did not understand. All I could comprehend was that Tommy had had brain surgery, and a piece of his skull had been removed.

"What now?" I managed to rasp.

"Now we wait," the doctor replied. "We've done what we can, and as scripted as it sounds, the rest is up to Tommy. We'll monitor him round the clock, and when the swellin' has gone down, we can perform surgery to replace the piece of skull we removed. That can take days, or weeks. No one knows. I know this will be difficult, but we need to restrict all contact. His room will have a window for viewin', but entry to the room from non-staff, right now, isnae possible. After such surgeries, infection is our greatest worry."

My mind became a puzzle of words. Of their own accord, over and over, words from words of the day floated through my mind one after the other, with no stop in sight. My ears were ringing, and I felt like I was floating. I thought I heard screaming and shouting, but I couldn't be sure. I tried to look to see who was making such noise, but it was only then that I realised that my eyes were closed.

"Erin?" a familiar voice called. "You're scarin' me, doll. Wake up."

I blinked my lids open, and stared at the face inches from mine. I had never seen eyes as blue or eyelashes as thick and long before in my life, and for a moment I was envious of them. I was envious of a pair of ocean-blue eyes, and bloody eyelashes. I was losing my mind, I knew I was, especially since I knew who those eyes belonged to.

"Get your face out of mine before I bite your nose off, Ward Buckley."

He exhaled. "You're okay. Thank God."

"Of course I'm okay – why the hell am I on the floor?"

"You fainted," Jesse's voice answered. "It wasn't anythin' like the films, either. It wasn't gracious or ladylike at all, you just dropped like a sack of potatoes and took Ward down with you."

"I *told* you it was unexpected and caught me off guard." Ward scowled at his brother without looking at me.

"This is not a time for jokin'!" Mum bellowed.

"Amelia," Auntie Jennifer chided. "Tommy's surgery went well and he's in recovery. If we focus all our energy on a negative outcome, we'll be even more miserable. We need normalcy. We need the dynamic happenin' in front of us right now. It willnae hurt us, or Tommy, to not be sick with worry constantly."

At the mention of Tommy I tried to sit up, but I halted my movements when I realised I was about to butt heads with Ward. He was still holding on to me, and he still had his face next to mine.

"You can get off me now."

He raised an eyebrow. "I'm not *on* you, I'm beside you."

"A thousand metres is too close to me when it comes to you, Ward."

Hurt flashed in his blue eyes for a moment, then a blank look took over as Ward robotically got to his feet, and without caring whether I wanted him to or not, he helped me stand and didn't release his hold until he was certain I had my bearings. I gritted my teeth to keep from apologising to him. I shouldn't have felt bad for hurting his feelings, but I did, and that infuriated me because the arsehole deserved hurt feelings.

"I cannae believe I fainted," I muttered, embarrassed.

"Why?" Ward asked. "You just received terrifyin' news that your brother had brain surgery. I think your faintin' is warranted."

The mention of the news had me looking around the room.

"Where's the doctor?"

"He got a call," Auntie Jennifer answered. "Another trauma patient needed emergency surgery. He was literally just leavin' when he saw you comin' around, he said he was sendin' someone—"

She was cut off when the door to the room opened and a nurse entered.

"Someone fainted?" she said, looking around.

I felt my cheeks flush. "I'm fine."

"Are you sure?" she asked.

"Aye."

She didn't look like she believed me.

"Did you hit your head?"

"Naw" – Ward answered for me – "I broke her fall."

The nurse nodded, her eyes still on me.

"When was the last time you ate somethin'?"

I couldn't remember.

"I dinnae ken," I answered honestly.

The nurse's lips thinned to a line. "I'll go get you some orange juice and a few slices of toast."

Not giving me a chance to object, she turned and left the room as quickly as she'd entered.

"If you tell her naw when she comes back," Jesse commented from the other side of the room, "she might force it down your throat."

"Aye, I second that." Auntie Jennifer smiled tiredly. "She seems to be a woman who doesn't take nonsense from patients."

I blinked. "I'm not a patient."

"Because Ward caught you," Jesse said. "You'd have hit your head if it werenae for him."

"Enough, Jesse," Ward grumbled.

I gritted my teeth, not liking being in debt to him.

"Thanks," I muttered.

He was silent for a moment, then said, "You're welcome."

"How long was I out?" I asked hurriedly, moving away from Ward and returning to my earlier seat.

"Thirty seconds, if even," Jesse answered as Ward returned to his own seat.

"I cannae believe this about Tommy," I said, my voice tight. "He's had *brain surgery*."

Everyone was silent.

"He's in ICU right now," Ward said. "The doctor said we'll have to wait until a reasonable hour to go and see him. Through the window of his room, that is."

I turned around, looking up at the clock on the wall. My heart dropped when I saw it was only 5:14 a.m. I faced forward, then leaned back against the chair, sighing. It felt like a lifetime had passed by, instead of only a night.

"I'll bring Mum and Auntie Jennifer home for a few hours' rest before we go and speak to Aiden," I said, dread in my tone.

"Naw need for that," Ward replied. "The gettin' home part, I mean. I'll have a car brought around to take you three home."

I looked at him. "You'll have a car 'brought around'?"

He nodded, and I don't know why, but I snorted.

"That's such a rich-person thing to say."

"Erin!" Mum scowled at me like I was a child.

I snorted again and got to my feet. "Come on, let's get home for a few hours."

Everyone stood, and for a moment it was awkward until Auntie Jennifer said, "We appreciate the offer to take us home, Ward. We're ready whenever you are."

And *that* was such an Auntie Jennifer thing to say. No matter what, she was always the peacemaker.

We all left the family room that had housed us for the night, but the nurse who had checked on me after I fainted wouldn't let me leave the ward until I'd consumed a whole slice of toast, half a glass of orange juice and promised to go see my doctor if I felt out of sorts in any way.

Every step it took for us to leave the hospital felt like running a marathon with weights on my back. I didn't want to leave, and more importantly I didn't want to leave my brother there; but I had to remind myself that I couldn't see him yet, and when I did see him, I would be no use to him, or anyone, if I was running on fumes.

I was exhausted, there was no denying that, but I didn't want to admit it around Ward. I didn't want to appear weak in his presence. The last time I was vulnerable around him, he'd broken my heart, and I refused to give him – or anyone else for that matter – the power to ever do it again.

When we exited the hospital, it wasn't raining any longer and things were eerily silent. My mum was shaking so badly that Ward thought she was cold, and he shrugged off his suit jacket and draped it around her shoulders. I kept my mouth shut. No one, apart from Tommy, Jesse, Auntie Jennifer and Auntie Emma, knew that Mum had a drinking problem. But even they didn't realise how bad it was, because Tommy and I tried to shield them from it as best we could, and then I tried to shield Tommy from the worst of it.

And I planned on keeping it that way.

When a very expensive-looking, large black car pulled up in front of us, I looked from the car to Ward and found he was already looking at me. I flinched, and I hated that I did that. I didn't want Ward to think he made me nervous, because as much as I hated to admit it to myself, he *did* make me nervous. I only had memories of a nineteen-year-old Ward, and that was not the Ward before me. This was a man, a thirty-year-old mountain of a *man*. He was ridiculously handsome and in what looked to be great shape, with hands so big I found myself staring at them. He was, without doubt, a very attractive man, and the tailored navy suit that he was wearing was sure to raise the temperature of any room he stepped into.

I hated that I noticed all that, and I utterly despised that I physically responded to his looks. I detested Ward, and I had better remember that fact when his pretty face tickled my interest.

I turned my eyes away from his intense stare, and focused on the car that my aunt had already climbed inside. I helped my mum in, then slid in next to her. There was another row of seats behind us that Ward and Jesse sat on. We remained silent after Auntie Jennifer gave the driver our house address. I leaned my head back against the headrest, and absent-mindedly reached for my bag only to realise I didn't have it.

"Naw," I whispered.

"What?" Auntie Jennifer asked, her tone worried. "What is it?"

"My bag," I replied, dumbfounded. "I left it at the car crash site. When I realised it was Tommy, I screamed and just dropped everythin'. I haven't given it a second thought. My phone, my keys, my purse . . . everything is inside it. It's gone."

I banged my head twice against the headrest.

"Fuck!" I growled to myself.

My auntie reached over and patted my hand. "It can all be replaced, honey."

I could get a new phone and sync it with my cloud, so all my photos and whatnot would be restored, but in order to do that I needed my purse. I'd only recently got paid from both of my jobs, and I had yet to settle the house bills out of that money. I'd withdrawn the cash from an ATM and placed it safely inside my purse, with plans to go to the post office and pay everything tomorrow. We wouldn't be cut off just for being a few days late on our bills, but it was a headache I didn't want to deal with.

"Aye," I replied, my shoulders slumped.

Before I knew it, we were home and I was helping my mum and auntie out of the car. Auntie Jennifer used her key to let us inside, and she guided Mum into the house before she returned to the car. She would be going on to her own home, to be there when Auntie Emma got back – which would be very soon – and then she would stay with us until we knew what we were dealing with where my brother was concerned.

Jesse got out of the car and stopped in front of me, enveloping me in a bone-crushing hug. I held on to him for a long time, and when we separated, a small smile touched my lips when he leaned down and kissed my forehead.

"I'll see you in a few hours," he said, brushing loose strands of hair from my face. "Okay?"

I nodded. "I'll call you from the house phone when I wake up."

He kissed my forehead once more before he walked back towards the car. I stayed standing in the doorway of my house, and when I noticed Ward was leaning against the car, one leg crossed over the other and his hands in his pockets, staring directly at me, my pulse leaped. When he pushed away from the car and started coming towards me, passing Jesse without a glance, I knew I should shut the door before he reached me, but I couldn't move.

I was transfixed by him.

"Get some rest," he said when he stopped a metre or so away from me. "We've a long day ahead of us tomorrow."

"*We?*"

"We."

I didn't reply, so he turned and began to walk away.

"Ward," I called.

He turned to face me. "Aye?"

"Please . . ." I began.

He stepped forward. "What is it?"

I remained silent, staring at him intently.

"Erin," he said, my name sounding foreign on his tongue. "Tell me."

"Please . . . go home," I said finally. "The last time you stood here in front of me, you walked away from us, and do y'ken what?"

Ward looked at me with tortured eyes and said, "Tell me."

"I prayed that you'd never come back."

I closed the door in his face, just like I did eleven years ago – and just like then, I pressed my head against the door and waited until I could no longer see his shadow through the glass. I waited another few minutes before I opened the door, and found the porch empty and the car gone.

"Go away," I said to Ward, hoping his subconscious would hear me. "And stay away."

I shut the door once more, and locked it before I went in search of Mum. I found her in the kitchen with a bottle of Jack in her hands. Half of the contents were already drained.

"Mum . . ." I frowned. "Come on, put that down and let's get you to bed—"

"Dinnae you dare," she interrupted. "Not right now. Dinnae lecture me. I need it."

I stood, unmoving.

"Fine," I said after a moment. "I've naw energy to argue with you. Drink. Dinnae drink. I honestly dinnae care."

I left the room, and headed up the stairs and into my bedroom, locking the door behind me. I removed my still-damp jacket, dropping it on the floor without a care, then walked over to my bed. I stripped out of my remaining cold, damp clothing, and changed into dry pyjamas. I then sat on the edge of my bed for close to thirty minutes, the last fifteen of which was in utter silence. I pushed myself to stand upright, and quietly walked out of my room to go in search of my mum. I'd already decided to leave her wherever she'd passed out, but I had to check on her. There was some part of me, today at least, that needed her to be okay.

Her room was empty, as was Aiden's room, and she wasn't downstairs either, so in a rushed panic I ran up the stairs. I found her in the bathroom, inside the bathtub, the now nearly empty bottle of Jack clutched tightly in her hands. Her eyes were closed and her head was leaning against the tub's frame, hiding most of her features from me. My eyes found their way to her chest and I stared at it, relaxing when I saw it rise and fall steadily.

She's breathing.

I wasn't sure how long I stared down at my mum, but it was long enough for me to understand her for a change. I hated her narcotic of choice to deal with her darkness, but right now I understood it. She was trying to block it out – Tommy, my dad . . . me. And, for once, I hoped it worked for her.

"Erin," she suddenly slurred.

I was hesitant, not knowing whether to reply or not, but I had no choice when she opened her eyes and focused her dilated pupils on me.

"Aye, Mum?"

She stared at me, long and hard. "You did this."

Out of all the things I'd expected her to say, that was not it.

"What?" I said, frozen to the spot.

"Everythin'," she whimpered, then hiccupped, "is all your fault."

I swallowed, pain constricting my already broken heart.

"Dinnae say that, Mum."

I reached out to steady her when she struggled to push herself up on to her feet, but she slapped my hand away with a cry. Then, with a pained-filled scream, she hurled herself out of the bathtub and flung herself at me. I cried out when her fist connected with my face, but luckily I quickly gained my bearings and grabbed her flailing arms, pinning them to her sides. I stumbled back, my body slamming into the bathroom wall, the towel rack prodding into my flesh. The stinging pain was a reminder that I was still alive and breathing.

"Mum!" I shouted. "Stop!"

It took her all of five seconds to slump against me. I held on to her so she wouldn't fall to the floor, which proved difficult because, just like she gave up on living, she gave up trying to hurt me. Her body was heavy as she leaned against me.

"I'm sorry, baby," she cried, her face pressed against my chest. "I'm so so-sorry."

I was in shock. She'd hit me. She had never hit me before.

I struggled to hold her up. "Come on, Mum."

I hooked an arm around her waist, slung one of her arms over my shoulders, and together we walked slowly into her bedroom. I used my foot to flip back the cover enough that I could sit her on the bed. When my hands were free, I pushed the cover back further, and help Mum lie back. I took off her shoes and trousers, but left her underwear and T-shirt on.

"If Tommy dies," she hiccupped. "Bury me with him."

I didn't reply, but I understood where that declaration came from. If Tommy did . . . die, then I wanted to be buried with him, too. Without him, I would be broken, and it seemed our mum felt the same way.

"He'll be okay, Mum."

"Naw, he willnae," she replied, her eyes closing. "I love him, so he wi-will die. Everyone I lo-love leaves me."

I felt sick.

"I'm still here with you, Mum."

With that one sentence, I realised that as much as I hated the person my mum had become, I'd still do anything possible to help ease her pain.

"I know, ba-baby," she replied. "You're my re-reminder."

I swallowed. "Of what?"

"That he's dead."

Dad.

I knew what she meant. It took me until I was fourteen to fully realise that she rarely looked at me because I was too much of a reminder of my dad.

"This is a nightmare," Mum said to herself. "I know it is."

I didn't correct her, because I agreed with her. We were trapped inside a whirlwind night terror that neither of us would wake up from. It was our reality, and we couldn't do anything but face it head on. Or, in my mum's case, drink herself into oblivion to escape it.

"Night, Mum," I whispered as I tucked her blanket around her.

Robotically, I went into the bathroom and began to clean up the broken glass from the shattered Jack Daniel's bottle. I tried not to think about Tommy or my mum, and especially not about Ward, so I focused on my throbbing cheek instead. I was surprised it had taken me this long to acknowledge it, because it *hurt*, but I was glad it hurt – it relieved me of some of the pain in my chest.

Once I'd brought the broken glass downstairs and binned it, I checked once more that the house was secure before I dragged my feet up the stairs. I paused outside my mum's room, making sure I'd left the light on even though it was light enough outside already. I headed into my room, locked my door behind me and walked over to my bed. I climbed on to my mattress and pulled my blanket over my body, hugging it tightly to my chest.

Then, like most nights since my dad died eleven years ago, I cried myself to sleep.

CHAPTER EIGHT
WARD

I groaned into my pillow when there was a knock on the door, disturbing me from my dreamless slumber.

"What is it?" I called out groggily.

I felt exhausted, and that was odd for me. I normally never needed much sleep, but at the current moment, it felt like I'd never get enough.

"Erin just called," Jesse said, opening the door. "They're headin' over to speak to Aiden, and she asked if I'd be there because she thinks my presence will help Aiden deal with the news."

I opened my eyes, and shot upright when I realised I wasn't in my house in London. I was in the spare bedroom at my brother's apartment in Edinburgh. Tommy was in intensive care, and his little sister hated me and the very ground I walked on.

"Fuck," I said, rubbing my eyes.

"Did last night's events just hit you?" Jesse asked.

I dropped my hand, nodded and looked at him. I grinned when I saw he was leaning against the doorframe and had an extra cup of what I assumed to be tea in his hand for me. I pushed away the blanket that covered me and stood up from the bed. I took five steps and stopped in front of him, taking the cup from his extended hand.

"Thanks," I said and raised the cup to my mouth, gently blowing on the contents and taking a sip, followed by a bigger gulp that made my brother laugh.

"Pace yourself, buddy," he teased.

My lips twitched. "You always did make a good cuppa."

Jesse gestured to himself. "I'm a man of many talents."

I shook my head, amused.

"Has Keller stopped by to—"

"He's been here the past hour," Jesse said. "He's currently readin' the paper at the kitchen table and drinkin' coffee."

"Sounds like Keller."

"He's very . . . intense," Jesse whispered, glancing over his shoulder as if Keller would suddenly appear like the Ghost of Christmas Past.

I resisted the urge to laugh. "What did he do?"

Jesse returned his attention to me. "He checked the apartment from top to bottom, just like he did before he let you enter this mornin'. I dinnae ken why, though. The most dangerous things he'd find around here are my dirty socks."

At that, I did laugh.

"He's my head of security – this is his job, and he takes it very seriously."

Jesse nodded. "I get that, I just don't get *why* you need protection."

I blinked. "I get fifteen hundred death threats a year, little brother."

Jesse's jaw dropped. "What fuckin' for?"

"All different reasons." I shrugged. "A recent one was because I didn't stop to give some man business advice when I was leavin' a restaurant with Tara last month."

Whenever I left a high-profile restaurant, the paparazzi were always tipped with the location by my team of publicists. Getting my name – and face – all over the papers and media sites was free publicity, especially when I had a new app launching. This man who approached me for help would have been drowned out by the paps shouting my name.

I didn't purposely ignore him but he'd felt as if I did, and he threatened to mutilate me over it. He was very descriptive in his letter about how he was going to kill me.

"That's ridiculous!" Jesse exclaimed, his eyes wide with disbelief. "And have any attempts on your life been *made*? Dinnae lie to me either, I'm pissed you've never spoken of this before."

I hadn't told him about it because I knew it would make him worry, like he was worried right now.

"Just the one," I admitted. "Five years ago, before I hired Keller."

Jesse's eyes nearly popped out of their sockets. "Ward, what the fuck?"

"I dinnae panic people unless there's a need to," I replied. "That's why I've never told you, or Hope for that matter. She'd have up and died on me."

I saw the moment Jesse considered tossing the contents of his cup over me, and it amused me greatly.

"Dinnae you dare," I warned him. "Keller would be on you faster than you could blink."

Jesse looked over his shoulder again, and he relaxed when he saw Keller wasn't there. It made me laugh, again.

"Tell me," Jesse said, looking at me. "What happened?"

"I was in the toilets at an event, when a man approached me with a gun – that later turned out to be fake – and demanded one hundred and three thousand pounds."

"Ward!" Jesse said, shocked.

"I know, it was intense."

Terrifying, more like.

"What'd you do?" Jesse asked.

I shrugged. "Called Hope and had her transfer him the money."

Jesse looked like he was about to drop to the ground. "You just *gave* him the money?"

"He had a *gun* pointed at my head, Jesse. Of course I gave it to him, but only after he told me why he wanted it."

"And why did he want it?" Jesse asked, mockingly.

"To pay for life-savin' cancer treatment for his six-year-old daughter. It was only available as part of a special trial and his insurance didn't cover the total bill."

Jesse opened his mouth to speak, but when nothing came out of it, he pressed his lips back together.

"He was desperate to save his daughter's life, and I had the money to help him," I said with a shrug. "He was very clear that he was deeply sorry for the situation he put me in, but he had no other choice, and he hoped I'd understand someday. He was honest and regretful, but he stood by what he needed to do, and I liked that. He came aboard my charity a few weeks later and he works for me now. He's a great man who did what he needed to do to save his child. I respect the hell out of him for it."

I respected *any* parent who would go to any lengths necessary to protect their child.

"Wow," Jesse said after a few moments. "Is his daughter okay?"

"Yes." I smiled. "She's in complete remission, and just celebrated her eleventh birthday."

Jesse shook his head. "You're wicked, man. Heart of gold."

I turned the conversation back to the problem at hand.

"How far away does Lucy live?" I asked, wondering how quickly we could get to Tommy's ex.

"Five minutes from me, twenty-five from Erin," he answered. "They havenae left yet, she said she'd ring me when she got her mum ready."

"When she gets her mum ready?" I repeated with a frown. "What is she? Five?"

Jesse avoided eye contact with me, and I knew what that meant. He couldn't look anyone in the eye when he was lying to them, and the fact he was doing that worried me. I was the liar in our family, not Jesse.

"Jesse," I said firmly. "What's with your change of demeanour?"

He groaned. "She'll kill me if I tell you."

Erin.

I glared at my younger brother.

"I'll kill you if you *dinnae* tell me."

"Bloody hell," he grumbled before he looked at me. "Dinnae tell Erin that y'ken, okay? Not even a slight indication. Promise me."

"Know *what*?"

"Promise first," Jesse pressed.

I gritted my teeth. "I promise."

"Amelia . . . she's an alcoholic."

"The fuck she is," was all I could say.

Jesse shrugged. "She has been for years . . . since Kenneth died."

The mention of Kenneth Saunders was like a jab to the ribs but I kept my composure, or at least what I could of it. That man was as much of a father to me as my own dad was. I'd loved him, and I was still sick with myself that I'd left my family when they needed me after he died. I knew I couldn't stay, but just leaving the way I did . . . it wrecked everything.

"Tommy does what he can to help, but Erin is the one who looks after her since she still lives with her. She willnae let Tommy know how bad Amelia is. I think she tries to shield him from it, y'ken? She thinks I dinnae notice, but I do. She's a good lass, and she's had it tough-going since her dad died."

Since I'd left she'd had it tough . . . when she was fucking *eleven*.

"I had naw idea," I murmured, more to myself than to Jesse.

"How could you?" he asked. "Erin made me swear not to tell you any of her family's business, and you didnae live here so you couldnae see the change in Amelia."

That didn't excuse it.

"I should have known," I protested.

Jesse didn't reply, he just watched as I processed the information I'd threatened out of him.

Amelia was an alcoholic.

"Fuck," I said quietly.

"Aye," Jesse replied glumly. "Fuck."

"Rehab," I then said. "Have they not tried rehab?"

Jesse nodded. "Twice. It failed both times when she signed herself out."

"Fuck," I repeated.

"She cannae get over his death," Jesse continued. "Erin said she doesnae think she'll ever be able to accept that Kenneth is dead."

I knew how that felt. I thought about my mum, and the last image I had of her: in a hospital bed, all pale, weak and drained from the cancer that eventually killed her. I was four when she died, and that memory was only one of two that I had of my mum. The other was of her laughter and the expression on her face when she smiled at me.

She'd been beautiful, and though I'd been alive a hell of a lot longer than I'd known her, I missed her every single day. She was one in a billion, so on some level I understood Amelia. Not her methods of coping, but I understood the "why" behind it. She wanted to forget reality, and being spaced out was better than living every day with the knowledge that someone you loved was gone and never coming back.

Covering up that crushing pain was better than facing it.

"I'll do somethin' to help," I said, scratching my chin.

Jesse folded his arms over his chest. "What can you try that we already haven't?"

"A rehab where she cannae sign herself out," I suggested. "Somewhere that she'll be a patient, and willnae be released until she's sober and has her life back on track."

"Let me guess," Jesse said. "In London?"

I rolled my eyes. "They have facilities like that here in Scotland, dickhead. They just aren't advertised on billboards because they're exclusive and cost a pretty penny."

"Erin will refuse you," Jesse countered. "She willnae wanna be in your debt."

I shrugged my shoulders. "If she wants her mum to get better, she willnae refuse."

Jesse remained silent for just a moment, then his eyes dropped to my near-naked form. "You wanna borrow some clothes, or wear your suit again?"

"Has Keller had it dry-cleaned?" I questioned, looking down at my body.

I only had my boxer briefs on.

Jesse snorted. "Yeah, and dinnae ask me how, because nowhere is open this early on a Sunday."

"What time is it?"

"Twenty past eight."

"Fuck," I repeated for the umpteenth time. "Naw wonder I feel like shite. We're runnin' on a couple hours of sleep, if even."

"I think I got forty minutes," Jesse said, drinking his tea. "I could-nae switch my mind off."

I couldn't either.

"I'll grab a quick shower and wear some of your clothes, thanks. Keller will go out and buy me a few things while we're at the hospital."

Jesse blinked. "He's your personal shopper, too?"

"Naw." I grinned. "But he'll get me jeans, shirts and the basics for both of us, since this trip was unexpected."

Jesse left the room with a nod. I drained the contents of my cup, left it on the dresser and headed down to the bathroom. Jesse had shouted which room it was, so I found it easy enough. I showered quickly, and dried myself just as fast before securing a towel around my waist and heading back to the spare room.

Jesse had laid out blue jeans and a black long-sleeved T-shirt. Black socks and black boxer briefs were next to the clothing, still in their packets. I dressed quickly, pleased to find that my brother and I were close to the same size. The jeans were a perfect fit; the T-shirt, however, was a little short at my wrists, so I rolled the sleeves up to my elbows. My dress shoes worked well with the outfit so I put them on, pushed my damp hair out of my face and left the room with my phone in my hand.

"Morning, sir," Keller said when I entered the small kitchen/sitting-room combo.

"Mornin'," I said to him. "Has Hope been in touch?"

"Only fourteen times," he replied, his lips twitching.

I smiled and shook my head. "Any less and I'd have been worried."

"She's cleared your schedule until further notice, and ensured me she has everything under control so you are not to call her with business talk. She threatened to put her foot somewhere unpleasant if you do."

I laughed, and Keller grinned.

"Can you grab me some clothes and other essentials for a few days? Get yourself everythin' you need too, on my card. I'm not sure how long we'll be here."

Keller nodded. "I'll head out after I bring you to the hospital."

I nodded and ate some toast that Jesse had put on a plate, as well as drinking another cup of tea. When Jesse entered the kitchen, he had his jacket on, his keys and phone in hand.

"Good to go?" he asked. "Erin just rang, they're ready to head out."

I hesitated. "She asked *you* to be there, not me."

"True," Jesse said, bobbing his head, "but Aiden is obsessed with Friendzone, and, to be honest, you."

"*Me?*" I asked incredulously.

"Aye, you," Jesse chuckled. "He knows you were his dad's best friend for a long time, and he thinks Friendzone is the coolest thing since sliced bread. You might help calm him."

I exhaled. "And Erin?"

"She'll just have to deal with it." Jesse shrugged. "Today is about Aiden and Tommy, no one else."

He was saying that now, but wait until Erin spotted me.

Together, along with Keller, we left Jesse's apartment and made our way to Erin's house. The journey was silent, but I noticed that my leg started bobbing frantically when we pulled up outside. I was nervous, and that surprised me because I rarely got nervous, if ever. Erin got to me though, and I didn't know how to handle the knowledge of that, let alone how to handle *her*.

Jesse and I got out of the car, and the first thing I heard was, "You're *still* fuckin' here?"

I turned my head to face Erin, and was surprised by what I saw. Last night she'd had on a damp coat and a creased-beyond-belief work uniform. Her white-blonde hair had been a mess of tangles and stray curls, and she'd looked like she was drained of life.

While she still looked like she could use a full night of sleep, she didn't look a mess. Not even close. Her hair was plaited into two sections, keeping the strands tight to her head while the ends hung over her shoulders. She had on grey skintight jeans, black ankle boots and a hip-length leather biker jacket. I knew it wasn't real leather, but it looked good on her. Fitted. Tight.

Dinnae go there, man.

I cleared my throat as she marched towards me. "Good mornin', Erin."

"Save it," she snapped, stopping in front of me, craning her neck to glare up at me. "*Why* are you still here?"

"Erin—" She held up her hand to cut Jesse off.

I didn't spare my brother a glance; instead, I was entirely focused on Erin's face. Her bruised face. Her right cheek was swollen, and her eye was black and blue. The eye looked a little bloodshot, too.

"What happened to your face?" I asked a little forcefully.

The tips of Erin's ears flushed scarlet.

"I walked into a door," she answered sternly. "My mind is all over the place, in case you havenae noticed."

I frowned down at her, because I sensed she was telling a lie, though she didn't give any visual indication that she was. But I had a feeling, and I always trusted my gut.

"You sure about that?" I grilled her. "That's an awful big bruise to get from a door."

She rolled her eyes. "You want to go inside and beat up the door for bruisin' me up? Be my guest, London-boy."

London-boy?

My lips twitched as I looked at my brother, who had his head tilted back and was staring up at the sky, as if silently asking for guidance. Then I looked back down at Erin and found her still glaring up at me.

"I'm not leavin' anytime soon," I informed her. "I'm not goin' to be in the way, or causin' any bother. I just want to be here."

"We dinnae always get what we want," she countered. "Do we."

"Naw," I agreed, thinking of Tara and how she'd trapped me. "We *dinnae.*"

With a shake of her head, Erin said, "Just stay out of my way, okay?"

"Okay. Whatever you want."

She grunted, then turned and waited for her mum, auntie and her other auntie. Emma Saunders smiled widely when she saw me, and gave me a bone-crushing hug. She was Jennifer's opposite. Where Jennifer was tall and slim with dark hair, Emma was short, curvy and had a mop of bright red hair.

"Long time no see, stranger!"

I smiled as she released me. "How are you, Em?"

She sighed. "I'll be a lot better once that nephew of mine is home and on the mend."

"When he's home, everythin' will get better."

"You bet!" Emma chirped.

Erin opted to sit in the front of the car with Keller, just so she didn't have to sit in between me and Jesse in the back. I didn't blame her. She wanted to keep her distance from me and I respected that, but I made a pact with myself that, before I returned to London, I would be on good terms with her. I'd have to move mountains to make it possible, but I was willing to do whatever it took just so she didn't hate me anymore.

I needed her not to hate me.

We drove to Lucy Hayes's house, and before any of us had a chance to close the car doors, the front door opened and Lucy stepped out. She was still in her pyjamas, which was fitting considering it was early on a Sunday morning. Apart from her attire, she looked exactly liked she had the last time I saw her. She was still attractive, still had a body made for wet dreams, and seemingly still very youthful. That sucked, because Lucy . . . she was a horrible person whose looks should have reflected just how ugly she truly was. Or, at least, how she had been when I knew her all those years ago.

"Erin?" she called, and I could see the frown forming on her face. "What's goin' on?"

Erin started up the pathway to the house. "It's Tommy . . . he's been in a car accident."

"Oh my god!" Lucy gasped, and flung her hand to her mouth. "Is he okay?"

"He's really hurt, but he's hangin' in there," Erin replied, and she sounded calmer than I knew she felt. "We've come to talk to Aiden about it."

"Of course, come in," Lucy said, then quickly headed back into the house, most likely to wake up Aiden.

We all entered the house, and it instantly brought flashbacks of drunken parties and sex from when I was a teenager. My childhood, and the things I'd gone through, hadn't exactly encouraged me to trust in women. I'd never wanted a steady girlfriend, and I was happy flicking through girls like the pages of a book. I thought of all the times I'd cheated on Tara, and realised I was still in that same mindset as when I was a teenager. I grimaced to myself.

Back when we were teenagers, Lucy's parents had owned the house and they'd gone on "social visits" every weekend. According to Jesse, shortly after Lucy's dad died a few years ago, her mum remarried and moved into her new husband's home, and she signed the house over to Lucy and Aiden.

The decor had all changed, which I was pleased about, because I wasn't too keen on sitting on the same furniture I had drunkenly fucked different girls on. Worse, I didn't want to see *Erin* sitting on the furniture I had drunkenly fucked different girls on. Those memories were dirty, and to me, Erin was pure. I gritted my teeth at the idiotic thought, reminding myself that Erin was Tommy's little sister *and* that she hated me.

I remained standing in the kitchen, as did everyone else, and this unnerved Aiden when he walked into the room, shirtless in pyjamas trousers. He was rubbing his eyes, but dropped his hands when he saw our group. He scanned each face, and when his green eyes, identical to his father's, landed on me, he looked bemused.

"*Mr Buckley?*" he said.

"Hey, Aiden." I smiled. "You've grown up since I last saw you."

And he had. He was a teenager now, taller than Erin by a good six or seven inches. There was nothing baby about him anymore, and I felt saddened that I'd missed him growing up. I was his godfather, and the kid didn't even know me.

"What's goin' on?" Aiden said, looking from Erin to his mum. "Where's Dad?"

"That's why we're here," Erin said. "Listen to me and dinnae panic."

Aiden *instantly* panicked.

"Is he dead?" he choked, his eyes darting around the room.

"Naw," Erin quickly reassured him. "He isn't, baby."

"Dinnae lie!" Aiden screamed. "Is he dead?"

"Naw!" Erin said firmly. "I swear to you. He's *really* hurt, but he isn't dead."

Aiden's eyes filled with tears that streamed down his face seconds later.

"What happened?" he demanded, his chest now rising and falling rapidly.

"A car accident," Erin, who was now crying herself, replied. "In town, last night."

"I read about that on Friendzone, a few of my friends saw it happen and posted about it," Aiden gasped. "They said it was bad."

Erin held Aiden to her. "It was bad, but he is going to be okay."

"Where is he?" Aiden asked, squeezing his auntie tightly.

"The hospital," Jennifer answered. "Run upstairs and get dressed, honey. We're goin' back up to see him now."

Aiden was out of the room not a second later, his feet pounding up the stairs.

"How bad is it, Erin?" Lucy asked.

She looked genuinely worried. Erin swallowed and wiped her face with the back of her hand, wincing when she pressed too hard on her bruised and swollen eye. I fisted my hands to stop myself from stepping forward and putting an arm around her. The protective urge to do that shocked the hell out of me.

"Bad."

"Jesus," Lucy whispered.

"You're free to come with us," Jennifer said, her voice small. "If you'd like."

"I've work at ten, and it's a double shift," she answered. "I'll try to get off as early as I can, though."

Erin said, "Dinnae stress yourself. We'll look after Aiden until you can get there."

Lucy, who was now chewing on her nails, nodded. "Text me to keep me up to date with him, okay?"

Erin replied, "Aye, I'll use Jesse's phone. I lost mine."

I watched Erin and Lucy's interaction. Lucy was comfortable around Erin, but Erin was tense and looking anywhere except directly at Lucy. Erin either didn't like her or didn't feel comfortable around her, or maybe both. I didn't pass comment on it; in fact, no one did. We all remained quiet until Aiden came hammering down the stairs dressed in a grey tracksuit, pulling on his white Nike trainers.

"I'm ready," he panted. "Let's go."

Amelia moved to his side and Aiden put his arm around her shoulder, and the two of them walked out of the kitchen, huddled close. Erin spoke to Lucy quietly, and when Lucy nodded, she followed her nephew and her mum. Then the rest of us left, too.

"Lucy," I nodded, passing her by.

"Ward Buckley," she said, and her tone sounded catty. "I thought you'd turned your back on Tommy, and Scotland for that matter, a long time ago."

I gritted my teeth but kept walking. "Things change."

"Aye." She snorted. "I can see that . . . See you in another eleven years when someone else is in the hospital."

Bitch.

That panicked fear that had gripped her minutes ago had suddenly disappeared, and she was replaced by the Lucy I knew well. The piece of shite who used her son as a weapon against his father from the get-go. I'd done lousy things in my life, but Lucy Hayes was the biggest piece of shite I'd ever met, except for *one* other woman.

I left the house, glad to be back in the fresh air. Everyone else was already in the car, and I slid in beside Emma, who was next to Jesse. Aiden sat in between Jennifer and Amelia. Erin remained in the front of the car with Keller, and her body was still while she stared out the window. I found myself willing to pay a lot of money just to know what was going through her mind.

The journey to the hospital was uneventful, and when we entered the building, we were directed to the ICU. Right away we hit a bump in the road when we were told only four people could visit at a time, and all had to be family. Before Erin could have me and Jesse kicked out, Jennifer stepped up and said we were all family and would take turns. Erin, Aiden, Amelia and Jennifer went in first, of course, while Jesse, Emma and I sat on the plastic seats outside the ICU ward. Only Keller remained standing.

"I'll go and get the items you need," he told me, pocketing his phone, which reminded me that Erin was without a phone.

Before Keller left, I said, "When you're out today, buy a new iPhone – whatever is the latest model. Prepay, and load it up with a couple hundred pounds on credit."

Keller nodded, then he was gone. I looked to my right when I felt eyes on me.

"What?" I asked Jesse and Emma.

Emma only grinned, while Jesse shook his head.

"I hope y'ken what you're doin'," he said.

I was lost.

"It's not a big deal," I said. "She needs a phone."

"Aye, she does," Jesse agreed. "But I'll say it again, I hope y'ken what you're doin' with her."

"Sure I do. I've got everything under control."

I had never told a bigger lie in my entire life, because when it came to Erin Saunders, the only thing I *was* sure of was my uncertainty when it came to her. Becoming her friend would require a lot of work, but I knew she was worth it. She needed a friend, and I needed her to be in my life again.

"There is always good that comes out of a bad situation," Emma suddenly said. "You just have to recognise what parts are good."

I looked from Emma to Jesse and then to the ground, lifting my fingers to my temples and rubbing in circular motions. There were two things I'd realised since returning to Scotland: I hadn't ever had a bigger headache, and people here still spoke in riddles.

Home sweet fucking home.

CHAPTER NINE
ERIN

"I'm scared, Auntie Erin."

I threaded my fingers through my nephew's and squeezed his hand reassuringly. I didn't speak, fearing that nothing would come out – because, just like Aiden, I was scared. And that was putting it lightly. When we entered the ICU, we were greeted by a nurse named Carl. He informed us that we could not enter Tommy's room under any circumstances, but we could look in through the window as much as we wanted to. There was room next door to Tommy with a television and large cushioned chairs that I *knew* would be an upgrade from the chairs we'd sat in all night in the waiting room on the trauma ward.

"Before I open the curtain," Carl began as we filed into the side room. "Be aware that Mr Saunders is hooked up to many machines, so there are lots of wires and tubes surroundin' him. It looks very scary, but they're only there to monitor him and allow us to give him medicine directly through IV lines."

"Okay," we all said in unison, our voices wary.

"As you can imagine, he's also a little banged up from his accident. He's quite swollen and bruised around his face, but that's also because of the surgery."

These warnings were freaking me out. I knew that Carl's aim was to relax us and keep us calm, but the more he spoke, the more apprehensive I became. I squeezed Aiden's hand as a reflex, and he squeezed back. The gesture comforted me. As Carl reached for the curtain, I closed my eyes just to give myself an extra moment to prepare myself for what I was about to see. But I wasn't granted that moment because my eyes popped open when I heard Aiden gasp and my auntie and mum whimpering.

I couldn't contain the cry that climbed up my throat when my gaze locked on the figure through the window. I pulled my hand from Aiden's as I stepped forward and pressed my hands against the glass and stared at my limp brother.

"Tommy!" I rasped.

Helplessness. Worry. Fear. Pain.

I felt each of the emotions so deep within my soul that for a moment I wondered if I'd ever know what happiness felt like again. I placed a hand over my mouth as my stomach churned. I focused on taking deep breaths in and out, but it was no use. I knew I was going to be sick. I fled the room and rushed down the hallway, and once inside the ladies' bathroom I vomited.

"Erin!"

After my name was called, heavy footsteps pounded against the floor, and the door to the stall I was in was pushed open. I vomited once more just as hands touched my back before they moved up to my head and bunched my two plaits into a tight grip, pulling them away from my face.

"It's okay," Ward said. "You're okay."

I couldn't even tell him to go away, because when I opened my mouth I vomited again. I groaned loudly, and clutched my aching stomach with my hands. I wondered how I could be vomiting so much when I had no food in my system. I hadn't been able to stomach any breakfast, and with the sight of Tommy all battered and bruised, eating was not on my to-do list for the day.

"Good lass," Ward said as he placed a hand on the centre of my back and rubbed it in circles. "Get it all out."

I groaned in response. He still held my hair tightly in his hand, and with the other he continued to rub my back. I knew everyone rubbed someone's back when they were being sick, and I never thought it did much good, but I found it helped relax me and I didn't know how to feel about that because it was *Ward* who was relaxing me.

"I'm fine," I rasped.

Ward didn't back up. "You arenae fine, so dinnae feed me that bullshit."

I stood upright, wiped my mouth with the back of my hand and tilted my head back so I could stare up at Ward. He was almost glaring at me, as if daring me to challenge what he was saying.

"Whatever," was all I managed to say.

I moved around his body, and when I reached the sink I gargled some water to clean out my mouth, as well as splashing some of the water on my burning face to cool it. I heard Ward leave, but I didn't turn to look at him. I didn't know if I was heating up because of Ward, or because I'd just vomited in front of him. For my sanity's sake, I chose to believe the latter.

When I left the bathroom, I came to an abrupt halt when I found Ward leaning against the wall outside, waiting for me. With his shoulder pressed against the wall and his arms folded around his chest, he looked the picture of seriousness, but I couldn't take him seriously in his brother's clothes.

"I once spilled ketchup all over that shirt," I commented.

Ward glanced down at his body, then looked at me with amused eyes. "On purpose?"

I think we were both surprised when I laughed.

"Naw," I said. "It was an accident. I tried to squeeze out the sauce at a restaurant and it wouldnae come out. Jesse reached for it as he sat down to help me and – boom! – ketchup covered him."

Ward's lips twitched. "You hang out with Jesse a lot?"

"Whenever we're not workin'."

"Are you both just friends?"

I raised an eyebrow. "Not that it's any of your business, but aye, Jesse is just my friend. Why?"

"Just curious."

Why would he be curious about that?

I began to feel uncomfortable, so I changed the topic.

"You arenae gonna leave no matter how many times I tell you," I said with a sigh. "Are you?"

"Naw," Ward replied. "I'm not."

"With your track record, you understand why I'm sceptical, right?"

Ward's shoulders slumped ever so slightly, his lips turned down and his eyes just . . . looked right through me.

"Nothin' I say will make you believe me," he said. "My actions will just have to speak louder than my words."

I rubbed a hand over my face.

"Why now?" I asked, dropping my arm back to my side. "Why does Tommy have to be gravely injured for you to be here?"

Ward was silent for so long, I thought he might not respond.

"I'm a coward," he eventually replied, shocking the life out of me. "Everyone here knows it."

I couldn't begin to form words so I remained silent.

"You think when I walked away from your family that I forgot about you? I didnae," Ward continued, his jaw tensing. "I've thought about you, *all* of you, every single day for the past eleven years. I hate what I did. Hate. It. I cannae take it back – if I could, I would. I'd change everythin' about that night just so you wouldnae look at me the way you are right now. So Tommy would still be a brother to me, so your mum would still be my mum. Believe me, Erin. I have no ulterior motive for being here. I just want to be with my friend, my brother, and help him in any way I can. Please . . . please, let me."

I stared at Ward. I just couldn't believe him, he wasn't someone I knew anymore. He was a stranger to me, to my family . . . but . . . He was once our family, once someone I loved, and I tried to tell myself that people could change. I wished it for my mum every day, so why couldn't I wish for it with Ward, too? Bitterness and hurt made it very difficult, though.

"I dinnae trust you," I said firmly. "But I also dinnae think you would want to hurt Tommy . . . no more than you already have."

"I dinnae want to hurt anyone," Ward said hurriedly.

I lifted my chin. "Time will tell."

"Erin." Ward frowned. "I'm not a monster."

"Funny that," I said, balling my hands into fists. "You've been a monster hauntin' me for a very long time, only now I'm not a helpless eleven-year-old girl. If you hurt my family, you *will* be sorry."

I turned away from him and walked back towards the room next to Tommy's. I was surprised to find everyone in there, Jesse and Auntie Emma included.

"We're here ten minutes and you lot are already breakin' the rules?" I said with a tilt of my head. "That nurse will kick us all out."

Auntie Jennifer smiled. "Ward spoke to a doctor in passin' outside, and they allowed us all to come stay in the room as long as we were no trouble."

"They're daft," I replied. "We're nothin' but trouble."

Everyone chuckled. When Ward entered the room, I turned to him and said, "What'd you say to the doctor for us to be allowed in here at the same time?"

Ward's lips thinned to a line. "Nothin' important."

"Uh-huh," I said, not breaking eye contact with him.

Ward held my stare, but only for a few moments.

"I made a donation to the ICU," he said quietly, jamming his hands into the pockets of his jeans. "Hospitals are always in need of fundin'."

I blinked. "You bribed a doctor?"

"Maybe."

My lips twitched, and I was appalled to find that I wanted to *laugh*.

"Well," I said, clearing my throat roughly. "Thanks."

"Dinnae mention it," he said, turning his gaze to the window to my right.

I watched as he saw my brother in person for the first time in eleven years. He sucked in a strangled breath, took a step forward and placed a lone hand on the glass. He stared into Tommy's room with wide eyes for a long moment before he whispered, "Tommy."

A lump formed in my throat.

"He's gonna be okay," I said, my voice cracking. "You'll see."

Ward bobbed his head without looking away from my brother, so I turned and stared at Tommy, too. For a long time, after all I had been through I didn't think anything else could break me, but staring at my brother caused nothing but fear to dwell within my body. It was raw terror, and it hurt so badly it felt like physical pain. It felt like my heart was shattering.

Tommy was laid on a single bed, with tubes coming from what seemed to be every part of his body. His head was wrapped in a large bandage and his face was swollen and bruised beyond belief. He didn't look like the brother I knew, and that scared the life out of me.

"Why him?" I thought aloud.

"What?" Ward asked softly.

"Why is this happenin' to my brother?" I asked, hoping he could answer me. "He doesnae deserve any of this. He's the best person I know, and this shouldnae be happenin' to him."

"I cannae answer your question, Erin," Ward replied. "No one can."

I knew that, and I hated it.

"None of this feels real," I murmured.

For the next two hours, we remained in the viewing room, simply gazing at Tommy. I couldn't speak for anyone else, but I prayed and prayed that he would suddenly wake up and say it was all just a big joke. I knew that wouldn't happen, just like I knew he wouldn't wake up and be perfectly okay. I had a sickening feeling this was only the beginning of a hard journey for my brother and our family.

"Auntie Erin."

I blinked and looked to my right, directly at my nephew, who was sitting next to me. I smiled at him as he hooked an arm around my shoulders and tugged me closer to him.

"Everythin' will be okay," I murmured. "It will."

Aiden didn't respond, he only gave me a squeeze.

"Uncle Jesse said he'd be asleep for a while," he mumbled eventually, staring through the glass at his father. "How long is a while?"

I swallowed. "No one knows, sweetheart. Your dad was hurt badly and had serious surgery. Rest is somethin' his body desperately needs to get better. D'you understand?"

"Yes and no," Aiden said sorrowfully. "I hate that no one can say whether everythin' will be okay."

"But it will be—"

"You dinnae ken that for definite, and that's what I mean," Aiden said, his voice cracking. "No one knows for certain."

I didn't know what to say, so I held my nephew to me and comforted him as best I could.

"Maybe Uncle Ward will know," Aiden muttered after a few moments. "Dad said he's the smartest man he's ever known, so he might know."

I felt my breath leave my body as I turned my head and stared at Ward, who was looking at my nephew, his mouth agape. He'd heard every word Aiden had just spoken. I knew Ward wasn't shocked over Tommy and Aiden thinking he was smart, because everyone knew how smart he was. It was the reference to him being Aiden's uncle that threw him, and if I was being honest it had thrown me, too.

In no way imaginable did Ward deserve the title of uncle, because he hadn't earned it like Jesse had over the years of *being* an uncle to Aiden. I wanted to correct my nephew and set him straight that Ward was *not* part of our family, but I couldn't. I couldn't tell someone else how to feel about Ward, no matter how much of a problem I had with him. That was my issue to deal with, not Aiden's – or anyone else's.

I had to accept that, no matter how difficult it was for me to do so.

For the next ten minutes, Aiden spoke to me about Ward. From him possibly knowing if his dad would be okay to his social-media business ventures. I listened, and I knew Ward listened, as Aiden all but gushed over him. With Aiden, everything was suddenly "Ward Ward Ward", and it frightened the life out of me.

"Ward," I suddenly snapped.

He jerked his gaze to mine. "Aye?"

"Outside," I demanded as I stood up. "Now!"

I felt everyone's eyes on us, but no one said a word as we left the room. When we were both in the hall, Ward closed the door to the viewing room and turned to face me.

"You cannae let him down," I said firmly.

"Erin—"

"Naw. You *cannae* let Aiden down. You heard him talkin' about you, he knows everythin' about your business, your accomplishments and even silly stories from your childhood that his dad obviously shared with him. He's never spoken like that about you before, and that's most likely because I could never stand the mention of your name so I had no idea he looked up to you so much."

"I had no clue either."

"You're weasellin' your way back into this family and I cannae help it," I all but snarled. "I know you're here for Tommy, but getting chummy with the rest of my family is *not* happenin'. You're not makin' yourself someone they think they can rely on."

"Why not?"

"Because you're *not* reliable!" I stated. "You say you're here for Tommy, and that you just want to be helpful, but I – *we* – dinnae ken you anymore. You could be genuinely sorry for everythin', but you cannae just expect me to believe that. You're a stranger to us. Something else could go wrong and my family could need you, but you willnae be here to help them and I'll have to clean up the mess when you leave. I'm not havin' it, Ward. I refuse."

I was surprised when his face hardened.

"Listen to me, wee lass, and listen carefully," he chided. "I. Am. Not. Goin'. Anywhere. D'you understand that? Even when I eventually go back to London, I *willnae* be out of your lives. I *refuse* to be out of your lives."

"You listen to me, *wee lad*," I replied. "I cannae make you leave, and I cannae choose whether other people will want you around or not, but what I can do is shove my foot up your arse if you hurt my family again, are we fuckin' clear on *that*?"

"Fine. If I go back on my word, I'll bend over and make things easier for you."

I scowled at him. "You're a real piece of work, y'ken that?"

"And you think you're a ray of sunshine to deal with?" Ward taunted. "I think not, princess. I've been nothin' but nice to you, and you've cut me deep at every turn. Accept that I'm here or dinnae, I dinnae care. I'm not here for you, I'm here for Tommy."

"I dinnae give a flyin' fuck who you're here for," I snapped. "You're nothin'!"

Ward glared down at me, his chest rising and falling as if he'd just been running.

"Like you said," he said through gritted teeth. "You dinnae get to decide whether the others will want me around or not, it's not your choice."

"Lucky for you it isnae, because you'd never see anyone I care about ever again if I had my way."

"I dinnae doubt it."

I began to pace back and forth in front of him.

"He called you uncle," I stated. "Aiden called you his *uncle*. I hate it, you have no idea how much, but he doesnae call just anyone uncle. He cares for you, and that means he'll be sad if he never sees or hears from you again when you leave. You *have* to live up to being the uncle he thinks you are, d'you understand? He cannae have people takin' off on him, especially now—"

"Erin!"

I jumped when Ward said my name and placed his hands on my upper arms, bringing me to a halt before him. He kept his firm but gentle hold on me and stared down into my eyes, his brow furrowed and his eyes unblinking.

"I heard him," he said clearly. "I heard his words, and I heard his emotion when he spoke them. I felt it. He likes me, and he thinks of me as his uncle . . . D'you understand how incredibly happy I am?"

"Happy?"

"Aye," Ward said. "Happy. That kid is my godson, and he doesnae know me from Adam, but he thinks of me as his uncle and he thinks that on his own. No one has forced him to perceive me that way."

"You're right about that, because I have definitely never had a good word to say about you."

I hadn't meant to say that out loud, but I didn't regret saying it, either. I couldn't help how I felt towards Ward. I had eleven years of hurt, anger, bitterness and confusion built up, and being an adult didn't suddenly mean I had to put all that to one side and accept him. The real world didn't work like that. *I* didn't work like that.

Ward's lips twitched. "I'm goin' to earn it, just like you said. I'm goin' to be his uncle in every way. I promise."

I set my jaw. "You swear on everythin' you love that you will be in his life and be good to him?"

"I swear," Ward said firmly.

I nodded. "Then I'll never speak an ill word of you to Aiden, or within earshot of him, ever again. *I* swear."

"You'll speak ill of me when he's out of earshot though?" he asked, a smirk playing on his lips.

I rolled my eyes. "Most definitely."

Ward's chuckle was low as I brushed by him and re-entered the viewing room, taking up the vacant seat next to Jesse so Ward could sit next to Aiden. Everyone watched us, silently trying to figure out if there was any tension, but when I smiled, each person in the room relaxed. Especially Jesse.

"I thought you were goin' to kill him."

"I considered it," I muttered. "I had half a mind to give him a Glasgow kiss."

Jesse laughed, and it made Aiden, who glanced at us, smile. I guessed that seeing us smile and laugh relaxed him, and maybe, in a way, even comforted him. No one smiled or laughed when they thought someone was going to die.

That's what I told myself, anyway.

"What do we do now?" Aiden asked Ward.

Ward glanced around the room before focusing on my nephew and replying, "The only thing we *can* do, bud."

"Which is what?"

"Wait."

CHAPTER TEN
WARD

"If you keep starin' at her, she'll most likely try and fight you."

I just about leaped into the air with fright.

"Christ, Jesse." I scowled, looking to my right where my brother now stood. "You scared the shite out of me."

Jesse chuckled as he nudged me aside and started the process of making himself a cup of tea. I had yet to finish making mine, but I said nothing because Jesse could make a hell of a cup of tea – even with shitty hospital tea, which was quite a feat in my opinion. I leaned against the wall, folded my arms across my chest and fought off another yawn.

It marked thirteen hours since we'd come to the hospital, and any minute now we were going to be told visiting hours had already ended. I'd happily sat in the hospital all day, and I knew I'd continue the routine for the next few days, but I'd be lying if I said I wasn't looking forward to returning to Jesse's apartment and getting some sleep.

"Are you gonna pretend you didnae hear what I said?" Jesse asked, not looking away from the task at hand.

I rolled my eyes. "I wasnae starin' at anyone."

"Aye, you were," Jesse replied casually but firmly. "I can tell you how many times you looked at our lovely Erin in a sixty-second period. D'you wanna know the number?"

"You're daft, d'you know that?"

"Twenty," Jesse continued as if I'd never spoken. "Seven of those moments you stared at her without blinkin' for at least five seconds."

"Numbers are my thing, not yours."

"Not tonight, big brother."

I shook my head. "Dinnae you have anythin' better to do?"

"Nope," Jesse replied as he stretched his arms above his head. "There's not a lot to do in the viewin' room, so I had to improvise."

At that, I snorted.

"And starin' at me was the best you came up with?"

"Aye, because you're nervous around Erin and you're nervous around *no one*, so I find it rather interestin', if I'm being honest."

I sighed. "Leave it alone, Jesse."

"Leave *what* alone?" my pain-in-the-arse brother pressed. "What exactly is goin' on with you and Erin?"

"Nothin'," I snapped. "Absolutely nothin'. The woman cannae stand me or the ground I walk on."

"So?"

"So?" I repeated. "What the hell do you mean *so?*"

"I mean exactly that – so?" Jesse chuckled. "Since when has being hated stopped you from getting what you wanted?"

I froze. "I dinnae want Erin, Jesse."

"Ha!" the arse chortled. "Dinnae think me stupid, because I'm not."

I glared at him as he continued to make our tea.

"She's attractive," I admitted after a few tense moments of silence. "Really, *really* attractive. I wasnae expectin' to be attracted to her. It's caught me off guard, okay?"

Jesse only smirked. "You dinnae ken what to do about it, huh?"

"Not a bloody clue."

My brother laughed. "Try gettin' to know her . . . She's not the same lass you once knew."

I exhaled a breath, taking the cup when it was offered to me.

"That's puttin' it lightly."

I blew on my tea before taking a sip and humming with appreciation. I glanced at the still-closed door of the viewing room, and instantly Erin popped into my mind. Her beautiful scowling face, her petite body, her long white hair that I was sure smelled like the aftermath of a rainstorm, which I found oddly appealing. She wasn't a little girl anymore, that much I knew already, but being attracted – *very* attracted – to someone who despised me seemed like I was setting myself up for disaster.

"I dinnae have a chance for friendship, let alone anythin' else," I confessed. "Our history will not allow for anythin' to happen."

"Is that the only thing stoppin' you from tryin'?"

I raised an eyebrow. "Aye, why?"

"Because you're not exactly single?" Jesse reminded me.

I gritted my teeth before taking another sip of my tea.

"Tara is not important," I said, my tone clipped. "No doubt she's probably fuckin' another man in my bed right now."

Jesse stared at me, not blinking.

I shrugged. "What?"

"Why are you with her?" he quizzed. "You dinnae love her. Hell, I dinnae even think you *like* her. You would have introduced her to me and Dad if you did."

You've got that right.

"It's complicated."

"Is she pregnant?" Jesse asked.

I shook my head. "Not that I know of."

And if she is, the kid isn't mine.

"So break up with her." Jesse shrugged like it was the obvious choice.

"I cannae do that," I grumbled. "I'm stuck with her."

"Why though?"

I sighed. "It's—"

"Complicated," Jesse finished. "Yeah, you've said that already."

"And I meant it."

Things were silent for a few moments, and my brother knew me well enough to realise that the conversation wasn't going to go anywhere, so he dropped it, which I was thankful for.

"How long are you goin' to be here for?"

I had been waiting for that question from him since the moment I'd arrived in Scotland.

"Not sure yet," I answered honestly. "Hope has been badgerin' me to take a few days off to use up my holiday time, so I'm gonna do just that. That gives me twenty-eight days out of the office, and I see no reason why I cannae spend them here."

"Tommy could be asleep . . . in his coma . . . for that long," Jesse said. "I've been googlin' the procedure he had done and the recovery time is normally just a few days, but Tommy could be in a coma for a long while until the docs take him off the meds keepin' him asleep. And then it could take even longer for him to wake up by himself, and when that eventually happens, it can take him years to get back to being *half* of his usual self."

I felt the dull ache of a headache forming at the base of my skull.

"Dinnae do that to yourself," I said. "Dinnae play the 'what if' game. We'll take it day by day, hour by hour if need be."

Jesse's shoulders slumped. "I cannae help thinkin' the worst, ye'ken? Thinkin' is all I can fuckin' do and I hate it."

"I know," I agreed. "The helplessness is a sickenin' feelin', but if being here is all we can do right now, then at least we're doin' that much."

Jesse nodded. "We're gonna have to leave soon before they kick us out. We dinnae want to overstep our boundaries with the staff, we need to stay on their good side so we can all visit together."

I rubbed my eyes. "I'm not objectin' to leavin', because I'm done in, but we won't be kicked out."

"How d'you know?"

"Because I'm donatin' to the ward to fund them with new equipment and so forth, and they won't risk that by kickin' us out. But that being said, I dinnae want to overstep when other families aren't gettin' leeway like us."

"Agreed," Jesse replied. "We'll just pretend we have to get gone."

"*You* can be the one to say that to Erin," I said. "She'll be nice to you, especially since she trusts you when it comes to Tommy's well-being."

Jesse snorted. "You really dinnae have much experience with her when it comes to Tommy."

"I thought we covered that I don't have experience with her at all."

"And isn't that a bitch, considerin' you're *really* attracted to her?"

I glared at my brother as I took a gulp of tea.

"Keep it up," I dared him. "Go ahead, and see where my foot ends up."

Jesse just laughed, but quietened down when the door to the viewing room opened, and one by one the Saunders family members exited the room. Erin was the last to leave, and even then I saw that she was leaving unwillingly. She hugged Aiden before he left the ward with his mum, who had shown up not long ago to be with him. I didn't speak or look at Lucy, and luckily she didn't seem to acknowledge me either, which suited me just fine.

"We're past visitin' time," Jennifer said, displaying a tired but pretty smile. "We dinnae wanna to step on the staff's toes so we're gonna head home before they kick us out."

Smart woman.

"I was just sayin' that to Ward," Jesse said as he finished the remainder of his tea.

I didn't bother finishing mine, I binned it instead and hung back so I could give Keller a call. It took two seconds for him to answer, four seconds for me to tell him I needed the car brought around, and a further two seconds for him to acknowledge my request and hang up. That was what I liked most about Keller: he didn't like bullshit, and always preferred getting straight to the point so he could act.

"I cannae believe it's only five past ten," I said to myself as I glanced at a clock on the hallway wall.

"I know," Erin answered as she walked by me, dragging her feet tiredly. "It feels a hell of a lot later."

"Tell me about it."

Erin glanced up at me. "You sound . . . wrong."

I looked down at her in confusion.

"I beg your pardon?"

"How you speak," she clarified. "Sometimes, it doesnae sound like you."

I don't sound like myself?

"I had to enunciate my words better down in London so I could be understood durin' meetings and at events," I explained. "I also had to speak slower, and use the 'correct terms' for things instead of our slang. I never realised how heavy our accent was until I was in London surrounded by people who'd strain to understand me when I spoke."

Erin frowned. "But we all speak English."

"We put our own twist on it, doll." I grinned.

She scowled at me. "*Stop* callin' me doll."

I watched her go with a grin on my lips. She'd had a slip-up. For those twenty seconds, she'd forgotten that she hated me and had spoken to me like a regular person. But when I used my old nickname for her, it had seemed to remind her that I was the bad guy and she shouldn't be talking to me. It was most likely a stupid thing for me to think, but that little moment of normalcy gave me hope that things wouldn't always be so hostile between us.

After we left the hospital, we repeated the same routine as the day before. Keller brought the women home, then he took Jesse and me back to the apartment. I had no need of him then, so he was free to spend the rest of his night the way he wished. Both Jesse and I showered, but instead of going straight to bed, we sat in his sitting room with a beer in hand and relaxed as best we could.

"This is fucked up, isn't it?" Jesse said. "Us sittin' here with beers while Tommy is in the hospital."

I leaned my head back against the sofa cushion.

"The only thing that's fucked up is the fact that Tommy is in the hospital."

"Aye," Jesse mumbled. "You're right."

I took a swig of my beer, and closed my eyes in satisfaction as the cool liquid flowed down my throat and quenched my thirst.

"I have somethin' I need to tell you."

I opened my eyes and sat upright, placing my bottle on the coffee table.

"Okay."

Jesse, who was picking the sticker off his beer bottle, was tense. I could see his right knee bobbing up and down at a fast pace. Whatever he wanted to talk to me about, it was serious enough to cause him distress.

"I dinnae want you to get mad at me over it, either," he added. "It's not a conversation I wanted to have over the phone with you."

I pressed my hands together and rested my elbows on my knees.

"You're worryin' me, Jess."

He sighed. "They're not together anymore."

I frowned. "What?"

"They're not together anymore," Jesse repeated, flicking his eyes up to mine. "My mum and our dad."

My mouth dropped open ever so slightly.

I sat back and stared at my brother. "What exactly are you sayin'?"

"They're separated, and are gettin' a divorce."

I couldn't remember the last time words failed me, but in that moment I couldn't begin to form a coherent sentence.

"They separated about three months ago," Jesse continued, taking my silence as a nudge to speak on. "I noticed they'd been fightin' a lot more, and growin' apart, but I didnae think it'd go this far."

I ran my fingers over my mouth.

"Who filed?"

"Dad."

I almost choked.

"*Dad* is leavin' *her*?"

Jesse nodded. "I didnae find out until after they began sleepin' in separate rooms."

I rubbed my jaw. "I cannae believe this. I never imagined he'd be the one to leave her, not in a million years."

"Me either," Jesse said glumly.

I looked at my brother, and frowned when I saw he was crestfallen. To me, it was my father divorcing a wicked stepmum who I had long despised, but to Jesse it was his parents splitting up, his family breaking apart, and I felt for him because I was sure, even if he didn't say it aloud, that it was hurting him.

"Sorry, man," I said, hoping he heard the sincerity in my voice. "I know I've been at odds with your mum for a long time, but I'm sorry to hear she and Dad are divorcin'."

That was a partial lie. I *was* sorry for my brother, but *not* sorry about the overall divorce. I'd prayed every night for years when I was a child that my dad would divorce her and she'd be out of our lives forever.

"It's for the best." Jesse sighed as I dropped my arm back to my side. "Dad said they'd been fightin' a lot, and then when she . . ."

I leaned forward at his pause.

"When she what?"

Jesse closed his eyes. "She hit him."

My body froze, and a knot formed in my stomach.

"What?" I asked, my voice a rasp.

"She punched him in the nose and busted it open after a stupid disagreement about the kitchen," Jesse said with a shake of his head. "After she hit him, he fell, and she kicked him in the stomach twice before she stomped on his head and stormed upstairs. That's what Dad told me when I showed up after he phoned me, and she didnae deny it when I confronted her about it. She just looked furious with Dad, like she hated that he'd spoken about it."

My head felt a little light, and my stomach churned as a sensation of dread consumed me.

"When I got Dad to the hospital and he got some medicine for the pain, he admitted she's hit him multiple times over the years, but this one was the furthest she ever went. I haven't spoken to her since Dad kicked her out that night when we got home from the hospital, and I dinnae plan to either." My brother looked at me, agony weighing heavy in his eyes as he said, "She's been abusin' him, Ward."

CHAPTER ELEVEN
ERIN

I couldn't sleep.

I had been tossing and turning all night, and finally gave up on any semblance of sleep just after 5 a.m. I got showered, dressed, and after I checked on Mum to make sure she was okay, I left a note on the back of the front door to let her know where I was going. I had no purse or phone to bring with me, since I had lost them all on the night of Tommy's accident, but I did grab an old tablet that Aiden had given me after his dad got him a better one for his birthday a few months ago and put it into another bag I had. I probably wouldn't have any use for it in the hospital, but there were some gaming apps on it that I could play if my mind became bored of staring at my brother through a window.

Of course, I had to be allowed into the hospital in the first place in order to become bored.

I walked the thirty-five minutes to the hospital, thanking God for small favours when the rain held off. By the time I got up to the ICU, it was ten past six. We had been given a code yesterday to enter the ward, but I wasn't sure whether the code only worked during visiting hours. I held my breath as I punched in the numbers, and exhaled when a green light shone and a click sounded as the door to the ICU unlocked.

I pushed the door open, and hurried so I could reach Tommy's room and slip inside the viewing room connected to it before anyone could stop me. My heart thumped and my palms became sticky with sweat. I was convinced that someone was going to spot me and call me out for being on the ward before visiting hours had started, but I got lucky. The two nurses that walked past looked so exhausted that I wasn't sure if they even saw me.

When I entered the viewing room and my eyes landed on Tommy, I stared right through the glass without moving, and my heart hurt when I saw he was still in the exact same position as yesterday. His bruises looked worse, and his swelling did too, but I told myself that was normal, and if it wasn't then he was in the right place for it to be fixed. I sat on the chair closest to the window, and for a long time I just watched his chest rising and falling.

I comforted myself with the realisation that he wasn't on a machine to aid his breathing, he was doing that all by himself, so I knew that was something to be pleased about. As I gazed at his bandaged head, I wondered if the swelling in his brain had increased or decreased since his surgery. I hoped it had decreased; any sort of increase would be bad. I didn't need a medical degree to know that. I hooked one of my legs under the other and got comfortable in my chair. It was a chair with a lot of padding, but no matter which way I sat, it just didn't feel right.

I turned the chair completely so the back of the chair was facing the door, and I propped my feet up on an empty end table against the wall. That helped. I was semi-comfortable, and I could still see my brother. That was enough to make me feel more relaxed.

I held my breath when a nurse came to take my brother's blood pressure. She went about her business, got what she needed, then left without sparing a glance my way.

I practically deflated with relief.

Not long later, I took out the tablet from my bag and switched it on. I flicked through my camera roll, smiling at different pictures of my brother, nephew, myself, and even some of my mum when she had a good day. When I stopped scrolling and a video file appeared on the screen, I hit Play without putting much thought into it.

I sucked in a sharp breath the second my parents appeared on the screen, laughing and smiling widely as they danced in our kitchen. The quality of the video wasn't the best since I'd filmed it on my phone camera when I was eleven, but it was the last piece of footage I had of my dad and I cherished it. I'd always kept that phone just so I could watch it, and when Apple released iPhones, iPads and iCloud, I transferred the video file to my account so I'd always have it. As my dad sang to my mum, his love for her, and hers for him, was clear as day. It shone in their eyes, their smiles, and showed in their touch, too. They'd loved each other so much.

"Your dad was a helluva singer."

I jumped with fright, having not heard anyone enter the room. I shot to my feet and all but fell over when Ward came to my side. I placed my free hand to my pounding chest and tried to calm myself.

"You scared the crap outta me."

"I'm sorry." He winced. "I thought you heard me come in."

I dropped my hand.

Ward looked down at my tablet. I focused my gaze back on the screen where my parents continued to dance, oblivious to the fact that our entire lives would change later that very day.

"I recorded this the day he died," I said, my finger brushing over his face on the screen, which caused the video to pause. "It's the last video I have of him before he was taken from us."

Ward was quiet the entire time I spoke – so much so, in fact, that I looked up to see if he was still next to me. He was.

"I know you won't believe me," he began, "but I'm so sorry that he died. He was a gentleman, and I was lucky to know him. He meant a lot to me."

I looked into Ward's eyes. "Just not enough to stay as we buried him."

Ward lips parted. "I was there when he was buried."

"Naw, you wer—"

"Erin," he spoke firmly. "I *was* at your dad's funeral. Not front and centre like I wanted to be, but I was there. In the church for the service, and at the graveyard for his burial. Naw matter what you think of me, I wouldnae have missed sayin' goodbye to that man, not for the world. I loved him."

I blinked, uncertain of what to say.

"Why are you here?"

He shrugged. "Same reason as you, I assume."

"You couldnae sleep?"

"Not a wink." He sighed. "I'm exhausted, but my mind keeps goin' back to Tommy, and before I knew it, I was on my way into the hospital."

I glanced behind him at the closed door. "Where's your shadow?"

Ward's lips twitched. "He's gone back to his hotel."

"Why didnae you just come here without him?"

"Because he'd have a heart attack if he didnae know my every movement." Ward snorted. "He takes his job very seriously."

"I think I feel sorry for him."

"I'm sure you do."

I glanced around the empty room. "I suppose you want to sit here with me?"

"D'you think you can manage that?"

I rolled my eyes at him, earning me another snort, before we both took a seat. I fixed the chair I was previously sitting on back in its original position, and I placed my tablet on the empty chair next to me. For an unknown amount of time, Ward and I sat in silence as we watched over Tommy, and I was ruffled to find it wasn't uncomfortable.

"Jesse says you're startin' a teachin' job come autumn?"

I didn't look at Ward as I nodded.

"Teachin' year four," I answered. "I'm not sure you'd know the school, it's fairly new. It wasnae around when you lived here."

"Congratulations," Ward said, and my skin prickled hearing the genuine praise in his voice. His smile was wide and his eyes lit up as he spoke to me, and I found myself taking in-depth notice of it. "You must be delighted."

"Sure."

"Nervous about it?"

"Like you wouldnae be," I answered, surprising myself with my honesty.

"Surely an erudite aspirin' teacher such as yourself won't have trouble succeedin' at the job."

I snorted in spite of myself. "Having a wide vocabulary doesn't mean I'll be good at the job, Ward. I learned how to leave a lot of big words out of conversation over the years. What if I forget, though, and use them in front of wee ones? I dinnae want to confuse them because my brain picks words to explain things that most people dinnae ken."

"If anyone has a problem with you knowin' and understandin' words beyond their ability to comprehend, that's *their* issue. Not yours. Besides, Aiden told me he comes to you for help with schoolwork because you explain it in terms he can understand. That doesnae sound like someone who will talk above her students' heads, Erin."

I looked at my brother through the glass and smiled. "He said somethin' along the same lines."

"Of course he did," Ward said. "He's not daft."

Silence.

"Erin?"

I looked at him.

"Are you okay?"

I nodded.

"Erin," he said, giving me a pointed look, like I should know better than to tell white lies.

"Ward," I said firmly. "Whether I'm okay or not okay is none of your concern. Please dinnae fash yersel with me."

"And what if I *want* to bother myself with you?"

My throat became dry.

"Why would you want to?"

"Because I care about you, maybe?"

I shifted in my seat as my heart rate picked up.

"Good one."

I felt Ward's glare, but paid him no obvious attention. My lack of response annoyed him, it was as if I could sense it.

"Truculent as ever," I said when I glanced at him.

Ward narrowed his eyes at me. "Is that your word of the day?"

I stared at him in shock. "You . . . you remember my words of the day?"

He looked away from me and back to my brother.

"I created an app for it because of you."

I gasped. "*What* app?"

"Word of the Day," he replied with a snort.

Without thinking, I blurted out, "*You* created my favourite app?"

A huge smile spread across Ward's face as he returned his gaze to mine.

"It's your favourite app?"

Annoyance gripped me.

"Of course. I always thought it was made for someone like me because I was interested in uncommon words. Aiden told me about it, and I fell in love with it from day one."

"You inspired it."

I didn't know what to say so I remained silent.

"I never thought you'd use it," he admitted. "I never thought anyone would bother, to be honest, but it's had fifty-six million downloads since its launch, and is used by twenty million people daily. That number will rise as we're now addin' other languages to the next update. You arenae the only one who's interested in expandin' their vocabulary, it seems."

I folded my arms across my chest. "Well, you're welcome for the idea."

When he laughed, my own lips twitched, and I had to bite down on the inside of my cheek to keep from smiling. Sitting with him and talking felt too comfortable to me, way too comfortable considering he was someone I was supposed to be at odds with.

"Thank you," he chuckled. "I'm glad you like it, though."

I loved the bloody thing.

"I'm glad we're talkin', Erin," he said then. "I know nothin' has changed, but I appreciate your conversation."

"I still think you're a pig," I informed him. "But as much as I hate to admit it, arguin' with you changes nothin'. What's happened in the past is done. Just because I'm speakin' to you, though, doesnae mean I've forgotten . . . I just have bigger fish to fry than you right now."

"Understood," Ward said. "I still appreciate it."

I relaxed into my chair as best I could. I wasn't sure why, but now that Ward and I had conversed about mundane things, I wanted to ask him some questions.

"Can I ask you somethin'?"

He sat upright. "Aye."

"It's about your job."

"Okay," he said tentatively.

"What are your duties?" I asked. "I mean, what does a CEO *actually* do?"

He looked thoughtful for a moment, then said, "My job is everythin' that isn't explicitly someone else's job."

I stared at him, unblinking, and this drew a chuckle.

"I have overall leadership of the organisation, I'm the final decision-making authority and I have overall responsibility to shareholders."

"You dinnae fully own Friendzone though, right?"

"Stock-wise, no. I own eighty-six per cent of it, and the remaining fourteen per cent is divided among six shareholders. I needed money to get it off the ground, and that's where my shareholders came into play. They invested, gave me the money I needed, and in return I sold them shares of the company. I'm the legal owner, majority shareholder, and I decide everythin'. They just get a share of the profits."

"So they get money for doing . . . nothin'?"

Ward laughed. "Pretty much."

"That doesnae seem fair."

"They took a huge gamble on me – and Friendzone – by investin' money in a new company not knowin' what the future of it was. That's how it works. They take a chance to see if it'll pay off."

"Considerin' you're filthy rich, I imagine they are too, so it paid off more than nicely."

Ward's lips quirked. "You could say that."

"I checked your net worth a few months ago," I admitted after a pregnant pause.

"And were you happy with what you found?" Ward asked, an eyebrow raised.

"Naw," I quipped, "because half of that money should belong to my brother."

Ward kept eye contact with me, and for a minute I thought he would remain mute, but he surprised me when he said, "I know."

"What d'you mean ye'ken?" I asked incredulously.

"I mean exactly that, I know half of my fortune is Tommy's." Ward flicked his eyes to Tommy's form. "He willnae take it though."

I froze. "What the hell does *that* mean?"

Ward sighed, and tilted his head back so he could look up at the ceiling.

"Dinnae do that," I warned him. "Dinnae contemplate whether to answer my question or not."

Ward straightened up in the chair and focused on me, an emotion in his eyes that I couldn't decipher.

"There's a reason Tommy hasnae told you this, Erin."

"Aye," I angrily agreed. "Because he tries to protect me from everythin', but trust me when I say he *cannae*."

"What does *that* mean?" Ward asked, an edge to his voice. "What cannae he protect you from?"

Life.

"Dinnae change the subject." I glared at him accusingly. "Answer my question, Ward."

He kept his eyes on mine, and when he realised I wasn't going to back down, he laughed to himself and shook his head. He looked at me like I was something foreign, and like he didn't know where to begin to try to understand me. I wanted to wish him luck with that endeavour, because I knew myself better than anyone and even I still struggled to understand who I was, so I knew no one else would ever come close.

"Can we take this conversation somewhere—"

"Naw. I need to know this, Ward. I need to."

Ward's only response was a curt nod.

"So," I continued. "Start talkin'."

Amusement flashed in Ward's blue eyes, before those eyes flicked to my brother and sobered. Then he focused on me again.

"Every year since the company turned a profit" – he hesitated, but only for a moment – "I've sent your brother exactly half of my earnings, after tax. Every year I do the same thing, just addin' it on top of the amount from the year before."

I opened my mouth to speak, but nothing came out.

"Erin." Ward frowned. "Are you okay?"

Naw!

"You're tellin' me you tried to give Tommy *billions* of pounds . . . and he wouldn't take it?"

Ward nodded, and my focus switched to my brother.

"You're ly-lyin'," I stammered when I looked back at Ward. "Tommy wouldn't have . . . he just . . . he just wouldn't have sent it back when we've been strugglin' so much over the years with our finances."

Compassion that I didn't want filled Ward's eyes.

"I cannae explain why he never accepted the money, but a part of me always thought it was a 'stick your money up your arse' gesture whenever I received the uncashed cheque back from him."

"If what you're sayin' is true," I said, scowling, "I'm sure that *was* part of the reason."

Ward nodded. "We can ask him when he wakes up."

When he wakes up, not if.

"I've a hell of a lot of questions to ask him when he wakes up," I grumbled.

"I just want to talk to him," Ward said, staring at my brother. "God, I really just want to kick back and talk absolute rubbish with him. I've missed him like you wouldnae believe."

"Why'd you never come back to see him then?"

"A reason I dinnae care to discuss," he replied. "I know you think I left Scotland to better myself and live a life of luxury, but I didn't. I left to pursue a dream, but also to escape . . . somethin'."

"That is so vague."

"I know, and I'm sorry," he said. "It's just somethin' I cannae talk about."

"When Tommy wakes up, maybe you can talk to him about it."

"He already knows," Ward replied. "And he's the only person I can discuss it with."

I had turned back to look at Tommy when Ward said, "Oh, I got you somethin'."

Out of instinct, I took the box that was being handed to me. When I studied it, my eyes widened to the point of pain. I tried to thrust it back at Ward, but he wouldn't have it.

"I cannae accept this."

"Sure you can," he said. "I got it for you because you didnae have a phone anymore. Dinnae overthink it, Erin. You willnae be in debt to me for acceptin' it. You'll be doin' everyone a favour."

"How so?"

"We can contact you directly now instead of callin' your house phone or aunties to reach you."

I looked back down at the box, and when butterflies exploded in my stomach, I told myself I was just hungry.

"Thank you," I said as I placed the box on the end table next to me.

"You're welcome."

Both Ward and I started when the door to the room opened and a lady in a skirt suit stepped inside.

"Sorry to intrude," she said with a smile. "My name is Mary McCarty. I'm the insurance manager here at the hospital. I was on my way to my office and a nurse notified me that you were in here. I'm terribly sorry to bring up such a matter while your relative is in such a serious condition, but I hoped I might snag a moment of your time?"

I looked from Ward's suddenly hardened expression to the woman and nodded. "Aye, come in."

Mary smiled, closed the door and took a seat across from Ward and me.

"You're Erin Saunders, correct?"

"Aye," I said, leaning over and shaking her hand.

She looked to Ward. "And you, sir?"

"Ward Buckley," he answered, shaking her hand also. "Friend of the family."

Mary hesitated a moment, then looked at me. "Is it okay to discuss this matter in Mr Buckley's presence?"

I scratched my neck. "What matter?"

"I was hoping I could discuss your brother's insurance situation with you."

There is a situation?

"Sure, you can talk about it."

Mary smiled and got some documents from the folder she'd been carrying. "I was hoping you'd have information on your brother's health insurance that I seem to be missing."

"What information are you missin' exactly?"

"Well . . ." She swallowed. "An insurance policy."

For a moment, time stood still and a numbing sensation attacked my legs. The feeling fled as quickly as it arrived, but the confusion of what I was being told didn't subside.

"Hold on a minute," I said, bewildered. "His care is to be covered by the NHS, so why would you be lookin' for an insurance policy?"

"I dinnae think this is really an issue—"

I looked at Ward, and he stopped talking the second he caught my glare.

"Miss Saunders," Mary said, regaining my attention. "Standard care is covered by the NHS, *not* private care."

I stared at her. "Neither myself nor my mother opted for Tommy to be under private care, though."

The woman furrowed her brow, then looked down at her documents for long seconds, before she looked back up at me. There was confusion in her hazel eyes.

"He has been placed under private care on request of the family, miss."

I straightened in my seat, and felt my eyes widen. "There has to be some sort of mistake, Mary. There *has* to be."

She flicked her eyes to Ward for a moment, then moved them back to me. "I have a signature to prove it, miss."

Fuck.

A train of thoughts flooded my mind, wondering just what the hell was going on, then my mum popped into my head. Did she sign the document Mary held in her hands? I felt sick at the thought of her possibly signing something when she was most likely under the influence of alcohol. I racked my brain trying to think of a time when a member of staff had approached my mum, or she had approached them, and I drew a blank. A lot of the time I'd been staring at my brother, willing him to wake up, so it was entirely possible that I'd missed my mother requesting Tommy to be placed under private care.

I tried to remain calm, but I felt as if the walls of the room were suddenly closing in on me. My breathing was becoming laboured and my chest began to ache terribly. I jumped when I felt hands on my shoulders. I jerked my gaze forward and stared at Ward, who was now hunkered in front of me, concern written all over his face.

"This isnae a problem," he said firmly. "Dinnae fash yersel with the bill, *I'm* paying for it."

I pushed his hands from my shoulders, forcing myself to take deep breaths.

"He didnae want your money when he was healthy," I stated. "Why would he want it now?"

"Because" – his jaw tensed – "now he needs it."

I placed my hands on either side of my head. "I cannae think."

"Can we have a few minutes alone, Ms McCarty?"

I didn't hear the woman's response to Ward, but I heard the door opening and closing.

"I cannae believe my mum did this."

"It wasn't your mum, Erin."

I froze.

"Listen to me," Ward said, pushing my hands away from my head and replacing them with his. "And *please* dinnae get angry with me."

I slowly looked into his lustrous blue eyes.

"Why would I be angry with *you*?"

He inhaled and exhaled a deep breath. "I've done somethin' that I didn't ask permission for. I am sorry about it, I just . . . I just wanted to help."

I shook my head. "What are you *talkin'* about?"

"It's *my* signature on Mary's documents," he explained tentatively. "The night of his accident, I arranged for Tommy's care to be private, with *me* footing the bill. There's a reason he's in a room like this, and receiving so much staff attention, Erin. NHS patients don't get this kind of room for their family; when a person is paying, even the family gets benefits in these situations."

Words clogged in my throat, disabling a reply.

"There must have been a mix-up with administration about me paying the bill and not Tommy, because that woman shouldn't have come here at all."

I felt my body begin to tremble, and I had no idea why. All I could focus on was Ward barrelling back into my brother's life and making a decision on his behalf that was never his to make.

"I cannae believe you've done this," I said, my voice gruff. "What you've done is *illegal.*"

"Yes," Ward agreed. "Very much so, so I'd appreciate it if you wouldnae cause a scene. Normally, I would have never been able to do this, but when you have money that a hospital ward could avail of, things change."

I was seething. "Who the *fuck* do you think you are to make this decision?"

"I'm sorry," Ward pressed. "I swear I didn't do it to upset you, or take charge, I just wanted to make sure Tommy had the best care possible."

"And you thought *lyin'* about it was okay?"

"I was goin' to tell you." He swallowed. "I promise I was, but I wanted everyone's focus to be on Tommy and not on money."

I tried to push him away, but he didn't budge.

"I'm goin' to take care of everything. The NHS is great, but things get done faster . . . more efficient when it's paid directly by the patient, or the patient's family. There's a reason private patients never complain about the care they receive, Erin. Let me make Tommy's care like that, please."

"Naw," I almost growled. "I cannae allow that."

"Put your stubbornness and anger towards me aside, and think of Tommy."

"I *am* thinkin' of Tommy!" I snapped. "He's my priority."

"Then why are you fightin' me on this?"

"Because!"

"Because?"

"Because when you walked away from my family I swore to myself that we would never need you for anythin'."

Ward was silent for a long time as he remained crouched down in front of me with his hands on either side of my head and his gaze locked on mine.

"You were eleven when you made that promise," he said. "You were angry, hurt and confused. You still are, and I get it, but you cannae hold yourself to what you said when you couldnae foresee somethin' like this happenin', Erin."

He was right, and realising that was tremendously hard on me.

"Tommy *needs* to get better," Ward continued. "I have the money to make the treatment he needs happen. I'm *so* sorry I went behind your back, behind everyone's, but he needs the best care."

My eyes welled with tears.

"Erin," Ward prompted. "You know I'm right. We *need* Tommy to get better. End of story."

Once Tommy got better, who paid the bill at the end of it all wouldn't matter. I would lick my wounds and protect my bruised pride over accepting Ward's help another time. Right now, everything *had* to be about my brother.

Ward was right.

When I nodded my head in acknowledgement, tears fell from my eyes and splashed against my cheeks. Ward moved his hands and used his thumbs to wipe them away, careful of my bruised eye. Then he did something that surprised me: he pulled me forward into an embrace, and held me while I cried. What surprised me more was that I didn't push him away. I had despised Ward for almost as long as I could remember, but right now, at this moment in time, my family needed him. Needed his money. And for my brother's sake, I'd swallow my pride, suck it up and accept the help willingly.

I just hoped I wouldn't live to regret it.

CHAPTER TWELVE
WARD

Something old, and something new.

That thought ran through my mind as my eyes roamed around Erin's bedroom and spotted something from when she was a wee lass, then something I had never seen before. The balance was perfect: the Erin I once knew filled the small space, but so did the Erin I was getting to know.

The open door of her bedroom had caught my eye just as I was about to descend the stairs after leaving the bathroom. I wasn't sure why it made me pause, and I was confused further when my feet moved and I found myself inside her room. I wasn't a nosy person – I cherished my privacy, and the privacy of others – but Erin was an enigma to me.

I had been around her for a week, and even though we spoke more and more every day, I wasn't close to scratching the surface of who she was as a person. I had never been so completely immersed and interested in someone as I was with Erin, and if I was being honest with myself, it terrified me.

My only experience with women was bedding them and then walking away. I never made promises or let silly notions take root in a woman's heart. I never searched for romance because it never interested me. It had never presented itself to me in my thirty years on this earth, and I found it laughable that the feelings I had been experiencing since I returned to Scotland were textbook romantic ones. Because I was physically attracted to and emotionally interested in a woman who had to train herself to tolerate my presence.

It was a joke, and *I* was the punchline.

I shook my head, placed my hands on my hips and wondered how I had gone from zero to one hundred where Erin was concerned. Since my return, I'd looked past her physical beauty and seen how pure her heart was, and how mean her bite could be when she was protecting the people she loved most. She was a good lass, someone who deserved the world and then some, but she wasn't someone who *needed* the world. She just needed her family, her friends . . . people she could count on.

I was desperately trying to be someone she could put into that category.

"What are you doin' in my room, Ward Buckley?"

I jumped about a foot in the air, spun around and lifted my hand to my chest where my heart was beating like a drum.

"You nearly gave me a heart attack, Erin!"

Her lips twitched as she folded her arms under her ample breasts, and she waited for an answer to her question.

I gathered my bearings and straightened. "I'm sorry, this is horribly rude of me."

"It is," she agreed.

"I didnae mean to barge in here . . . I just . . . I just wanted to see."

"See what?"

"Part of you."

I spoke the words before I realised what I was saying, and Erin froze. She looked shocked, confused and, dare I say, interested. I didn't know what she was interested in, but I could see the curiosity in her pretty grey eyes.

I cleared my throat. "I remember so much about you from when you were a wee one, I just wanted to see somethin' new since you're still pretty guarded with me."

Erin loosened up as she shifted from foot to foot. "And what did you find?"

I glanced at the mountain of paperback books on the floor in the corner of the room. There were two bookshelves that were full to the brim, and dozens more books littered the floor around them. It made me grin.

"You hate readin'. Clearly."

Erin laughed, but quickly covered her mouth with her hand.

"You're a romance junkie," I noted with a teasing smile.

Her cheeks flushed a pretty pink.

"Lorelei James, Yessi Smith, J. R. Ward, T. Gephart, Tillie Cole, L.A. Casey . . ." I read each author name, and my lips twitched when I noticed something similar about each book based on the covers. "Are some of those *erotic* stories? The covers sure have a lot of half-naked men on them."

"Some of them are," Erin answered with her chin in the air. "Some are more graphic than others. Romance is the baseline of each book, though," she added. "Sex is part of romance, but there's so much more to it . . . at least, in the books there is."

"D'you not think there's more to romance than sex in real life?"

Erin shrugged. "I've never been in love, so I have no idea."

Me either.

I glanced at her wrist and smiled. "I've always loved that charm bracelet."

Erin lifted her hand and brushed her fingers over the charms.

"Me too. It's somethin' I have that's still the same as it was when I was wee, but it's always different because I switch out the charms."

"That's clever."

She smiled. "My dad thought so, too."

I swallowed at the mention of him.

"He'd be proud of you, y'ken? How hardworkin' and lovin' you are."

Erin locked her eyes on mine, and for a moment I thought she wasn't going to say anything, then she softly said, "Thank you."

"You're welcome."

Erin glanced at her book pile then back to me.

"D'you want to see somethin'?"

"Aye."

She walked over to her books and plucked one off the shelf. She opened it, and in the centre was a perfectly pressed yellow rose. The pigment of the petals was faded, but its beauty was not lessened.

"You gave me this on Valentine's Day . . . the day my dad died."

I looked at Erin's face, and blinked.

"I remember." I cleared my throat. "Why have you kept it?"

I tried my hardest to remain cool and collected, but my heart was beating a mile a minute. She'd kept my rose. All I could think of was that she couldn't truly hate me if she'd kept something from such a long time ago. Especially from a day that had brought her so much heartache. Hope surged through me.

"I've been askin' myself that for years . . ."

"And what did you come up with?"

"It was the last thing you ever gave me before you left and everythin' changed. I guess . . . I guess I wanted to keep somethin' from when you were still mine."

My breath caught at the mention of the word.

"Yours?"

The tips of Erin's ears flushed pink.

"Y'ken what I mean," she said, as she carefully closed the book and placed it back on the shelf. "From when you were just our Ward, and not a famous billionaire."

I nodded. "I know what you mean, doll."

Erin playfully rolled her eyes. "I'm not a wee doll anymore, Buckley."

"Naw," I agreed. "You arenae."

"You'll have to come up with a new nickname for me, since I cannae get rid of you."

Her tone was teasing, and it made me snort.

"Maybe I will, short stuff."

A ghost of a smile graced her lips.

"Come on," she said. "Tommy's skull surgery is gonna start in a few hours, and I want us to be there early to talk in depth with his doctor and the team."

I gestured towards the door.

"Lead the way, I'm right behind you."

She gave me a quizzical look, but walked ahead of me. She glanced over her shoulder, and when she saw I was following her, her shoulders relaxed. She knew I couldn't stay in her room, so I knew she wasn't surprised that I had followed her, but I think just looking over her shoulder and knowing I was right there if she needed me meant something to her. The small action meant the world to me. A week ago, my presence had hurt Erin, and now I could see that she was slowly coming to rely on me just as she did Jesse, and I'd have been lying if I said it didn't make me one of the happiest men in the world.

CHAPTER THIRTEEN
WARD

Over the past two weeks since I returned to Scotland, I'd fallen into a routine. Every morning, I'd wake up, get showered, have breakfast, get updates from Hope, Jesse and Keller, then head to the hospital to see Tommy. His family and I would spend all day there, talking to one another and staring at Tommy, willing him to wake up.

He never did.

Seven days after his accident, the swelling on his brain had decreased enough for the doctors to reattach the piece of skull they'd removed to let his brain breathe. The surgery was a success, but Tommy was still being kept in a medically induced coma to aid his brain's recovery. Though his state was unchanging, there *was* change among our group. A small change to most, but a huge change to me.

Erin could now tolerate me.

I'd tell myself "tolerate" just to stop myself from thinking it could be more, but deep down I knew that she was beginning to warm to me. Just like she did when she saw Jesse, she'd smile at me now. Not a strained smile, a genuine one. Most days it was just a small curve of her lip, or a slight twitch here and there, but it was something other than a scowl. She rarely got angry with me anymore, she never targeted a glare in my direction, and she talked to me. We didn't talk about anything important, not really, but it was a step in the right direction.

With each passing day, I found myself wanting to be closer to her.

It was a dangerous line I was walking, I knew that, but it didn't deter me from my chosen path. I liked Erin. I liked her a hell of a lot, and the more I was around her, the more I found my attraction to her growing. She was an incredible woman. She worked her arse off at two jobs, helped her mum run the house, took care of said mum, and was always there for Tommy and Aiden. She didn't have much of a social life unless Jesse dragged her out somewhere, and I liked that about her. She was a homebody.

Another thing that I found incredibly attractive about her was that she didn't give a damn about my business, or the fact that I had money coming out of my ears. Since I'd become successful, I had never been in the presence of another woman, except Hope, who treated me like a normal person and not a meal ticket. It was refreshing not to feel like she had an ulterior motive to talk to me.

I learned early on that she didn't like talking about her mum, and from what I'd seen over the past couple of weeks, the pair's relationship had drastically changed. It was like their roles had reversed and Erin was the one catering to her mum, making sure she had everything that she needed. That saddened me, because I could remember a time when Erin was a mummy's girl, a time when life had no hardship for the Saunders family.

Nothing stayed the same forever, though.

"Earth to Uncle Wardddd?"

I looked to my right, and blinked when I saw Aiden.

"Sorry, kid." I cleared my throat. "I was miles away."

"Nae bother," he said, tucking one of his legs under his thigh. "I wanted to give you some feedback on Friendzone . . . if you'll hear me out, that is?"

I leaned back in my chair, and gestured for him to continue speaking.

"It's about the messagin' option," Aiden continued as he dropped his eyes to his hands. "Can you *please* have someone add a bulk option when deletin' old messages? Deletin' them one by one *kills* me."

When I laughed, Aiden looked up at me, his shoulders losing some of the tension that had built in them, and a smile stretched across his face. It told me he'd been worried I might take his feedback the wrong way. With a grin on my face, I took out my phone and sent a note about adding the bulk delete option to Hope. She'd have the programmers add it to the next update.

"Done," I said, placing my phone back into my pocket.

Aiden blinked. "Just like that?"

"Just like that."

Aiden grinned. "My pals are going to *love* hearin' that I suggested that."

"If you have any other feedback," I said, "let me know. It's quicker when I make a decision instead of it goin' through our customer service. There's a big chain from customer service up to me."

Aiden bobbed his head. "If I think of anythin' else, I'll *definitely* let you know."

I winked. "Good man."

We chatted for the next hour about sports, mainly football, and throughout my entire conversation with my godson, I felt eyes on me. It didn't take a genius to figure out whose gaze was drilling holes into the back of my skull. Erin and I were on good terms, but I knew she didn't trust me when it came to her nephew. She was terrified I'd do something to hurt him, and because of my lingering past I could do nothing to assure her I wouldn't. I had to let time be a factor. Eventually, she would see I wasn't going to turn and run away again.

I *hoped* she would see that, anyway.

"I'm hungry," Aiden announced.

As if on cue, my stomach rumbled, making Aiden snicker.

"You're hungry, too?"

I nodded. "Starvin'."

Aiden placed his hands on his stomach. "I'm sick of takeout."

"I can cook you somethin' back at the house," Erin offered. "What d'you want? I'll make it for you."

I looked at Erin as she came to Aiden's side, and I grinned. "Does that offer include cookin' for me, too?"

She flicked her eyes to me, and a ghost of a smile graced her lips.

"Naw," she answered. "Just this growin' lad here. You can starve."

I clicked my tongue. "Am I not a growin' lad?"

"A growin' man-child . . . maybe."

Aiden laughed at my and Erin's teasing, and she grinned down at him while I flat-out smiled at her. I liked this. The harmless back-and-forth bickering that we'd had going on the past few days had really begun to cement the foundation of a possible friendship between us. The pair of us were getting there, slowly but surely.

"What if I get hands on and help with the cookin', then can I get some grub?"

Erin's lips parted with surprise. "*You* know how to cook?"

"I think I'm insulted by your obvious shock."

She looked at Aiden, then back to me. "Can you *really* cook?"

"Of course I can cook," I said. "Why would you think otherwise?"

"Because at one point in your life you'd manage to mess up boiling water."

Laughter filled the small room, and for the first time in the weeks we had been its occupants, the atmosphere that surrounded us didn't hold an ounce of tension. I didn't want to read too much into her remembering something like that about me, but I couldn't help but feel happy that she did. I told myself it was a good thing that she knew I had once been an awful cook; it meant she had possibly thought about it once or twice, since it had spilled from her mouth so easily.

"I've learned a thing or two over the last decade," I assured Erin with a wink. "I even know how to switch an oven on."

She smirked at me. "Watch out, Gordon Ramsey."

My shoulders shook with laughter as she turned to her nephew then glanced around the room.

"Does anyone want to come help us?"

A chorus of "No" answered Erin's question a little too fast for it to go unnoticed. I looked around the room, and so did Erin. She missed the wink my brother shot my way, though. I frowned at him, wondering what the action was for.

"I want to stay with Dad a little longer." Aiden cleared his throat, nudging Erin towards me. "Call me when dinner's nearly ready, and we'll all come back to Nana's."

Erin looked at her nephew with a puzzled expression that I think I mirrored. When she locked eyes me with and raised an eyebrow in question, I shrugged my shoulders in response. I was as clueless as her.

"Well, okay," Erin said tentatively.

Aiden looked between us, and the kid had a shit-eating grin on his face. It was at that moment that I knew exactly what he – and I think everyone else – was doing. For some reason, they were putting me and Erin in a situation where we would be alone together. I wasn't about to call anyone on it because alone time with the temperamental lass would only aid in her getting used to me. Either that or it would cement her hate in me.

It was a toss-up, really.

"Do we need to stop by Tesco?" I asked Erin as we left the viewing room and walked down the hallway side by side.

She looked at me, blinked, then said, "Aye, we seem to be cookin' for plenty of mouths."

"Then let's go cook somethin' good to feed these hungry bellies." I rubbed my hands together. "I'm with Aiden – if I have to eat takeout one more time, I'm goin' to need a new arsehole from curry damage."

Erin did something that surprised me then: she erupted with laughter. The sound was light, carefree and something I realised I wouldn't mind hearing more of in the future.

CHAPTER FOURTEEN
ERIN

"Let me help you with those, Miss Saunders."

I looked up at Keller, Ward's driver, and smiled at him as he took the two heavy carrier bags full of food off my hands.

"Thank you, Mr Keller."

"Please," he said, his London accent wrapping around me like a warm blanket. "Just Keller."

I clicked my tongue. "I'll call you Keller if you call me Erin."

"It's not proper, Miss Saunders."

"I promise not to tell Ward."

His lips twitched. "I sense that I won't win this battle, and that I should concede before any arguments can occur."

I smiled brightly. "I'm glad we understand one another, Keller."

"Me too, Erin," he chuckled.

"I hope this doesnae sound out of turn, but you're nicer than I thought you were."

Keller blinked. "Have I done something to make you feel like I might not be nice?"

"Naw," I said. "You're just very . . . serious around Ward. Today is the first time I've seen you smile."

Keller nodded. "Ward is my boss but he's also my friend, and his well-being is my priority. Even if he wasn't payin' me, I think it would still be my priority. He's a good man, and I can't say that about a lot of the men in his industry."

I glanced at the house, then back at Keller.

"What kind of man *is* he?"

"He's hard-working, and a *lot* more serious than me, but he's also . . . pure. He worries about strangers and helps people in need when he can. He's terrified that Hope, his assistant, will overwork herself, so he offloads her work pile to a team of interns but pays them well to deal with it. He knows my custody agreement with my ex-wife, and every single time that I have my son, he puts it in the calendar as my time off."

I didn't speak.

"I know you can't trust me from Adam, Erin, but believe me when I say that Ward isn't the man you've decided he is. He isn't here to hurt anyone, he just wants to make everything better."

I digested his words, and was glad when a noise from my right snagged my and Keller's attention. We both looked towards the door-way of the house and saw Ward jogging out. He'd brought in a few shopping bags ahead of us, and was coming out to get more. He glanced at the bags in Keller's hands and slowed his pace.

"D'you need a hand?" he asked.

Keller shook his head. "No, sir."

He passed Ward by and carried the shopping into the house. I looked into the boot of the car, and when I saw it was now empty of carrier bags, I jumped up to close the door. But I wasn't tall enough to touch the door, let alone grasp it and close it.

"I've got it, Bilbo."

I rolled my eyes at Ward's teasing as he came to my side, lifted his arms and pulled the boot door closed.

"There's a reason short people don't buy big cars like this," I said as I walked around Ward and headed towards my front door.

"Ah, but short people can buy big cars. They put buttons on car keys that open and close boot doors automatically nowadays."

I snorted. "I wouldnae know, Tommy's car was older than Aiden. We were lucky the radio still worked."

Ward didn't reply, he only followed me into my house. Once inside, I invited Keller to join us for dinner three times before I accepted his polite refusal. I watched the man as he left my home, and Ward's gaze moved in sync with mine.

"He's very private," he said. "He prefers his own company to that of others."

I frowned. "Why? He seems lovely."

"He is," Ward agreed. "But he's an introvert. He won't linger in crowds unless he has to."

"But doesnae he have to be in crowds when he goes places with you?" I quizzed. "Or does he just mainly drive you places?"

Ward raised an eyebrow. "Keller isn't my chauffeur, Erin."

That surprised me.

"What is he if he's not your chauffeur?"

"He's my bodyguard."

I almost choked. "*Bodyguard?*"

I had suspected he might have to have security when he was at a fancy restaurant in London, somewhere the paparazzi would swarm him, but no one seemed to pay him any mind here in Scotland. I'd seen a few people take pictures of him, or ask for pictures with him, pictures he gladly took, but for the most part people didn't seem to know who he was. He wasn't that type of celebrity. Or, at least, I thought he wasn't, until I reminded myself that his looks had caused him to grace the covers of many magazines. He wasn't a regular CEO, I wasn't dumb enough to think that. He was uber-successful, and gorgeous to boot – and I was sure a lot of other people thought that of him, too.

Maybe he did need a bodyguard, after all.

Ward laughed at my reaction. "Aye, he's my bodyguard."

"But why?" I asked. "Why do you need someone to protect you?"

He shrugged. "He's just there in case anythin' ever goes sideways."

"I dinnae understand what that means."

"You dinnae have to," he said. "It's nothin' to worry about."

I huffed. "I'm not worried about you, Ward. And Keller isn't as quiet as you think. I had a whole conversation with him out in the garden. He even smiled at me. Twice."

I thought I saw his lips twitch, but I wasn't sure so I didn't comment on it. We worked silently to remove all the food from the carrier bags and began opening the packaging. While we were in Tesco – one close to my house, not the one I worked in – we'd decided to make a large chicken stir-fry. It was easy and quick to make. I was too tired to spend hours cooking something else.

When my phone rang, I answered it without looking at the screen. "Hello?"

"Erin," a familiar voice said. "It's Jensen."

"Hi, Jensen," I said after a pause.

"Hi, love. How are you?" he asked. "How's your brother?"

"Still the same," was all I could say.

"Sorry to hear that." Jensen cleared his throat. Twice. "Look, I hate to call you and add to your stress . . . but your two weeks of sick days are almost up. I'm short on staff as it is, so I need to know if you'll be returnin' to work? I can give you the weekend off, still with pay, but that's the best I can do for you. D'you understand, love?"

"Aye," I sighed. "I understand. I'll see you on Monday."

"I'm so sorry, Erin."

"Don't be, Jen," I said. "None of this is your fault."

"See you on Monday."

"See you then."

When I pocketed my phone, I turned in Ward's direction and found him looking at me.

"Is everythin' okay?"

"My manager at Tesco said if I dinnae come back to work, he'll have to let me go. Well, he didn't say that, but it was implied. I've nearly used up the two weeks of sick days that I've saved up at both of my jobs, but they're runnin' out. I'll no doubt get a voicemail off my manager at TGI's sometime soon, tellin' me the same thing."

Ward processed this.

"Maybe you should quit—"

"I cannae quit," I said sharply. "I'll have no income if I do that, and I spilt everythin' down the middle with Mum, so I need to be able to pay my bills."

"What about reduced hours?" he suggested. "You'll still work, earn a wage, but have more time to be at the hospital."

I considered this.

"It's the best form of action I can think of," I admitted. "I'll speak to both my managers about it."

"I'm sure they'll work with you on this."

"And why are you so sure?"

"From what Jesse tells me, you're incredibly hard workin'. They willnae want to lose someone who's as efficient as you seem to be."

I turned my face away as heat crawled up my neck.

"Right," Ward said, as he clapped his hands and rubbed them together. "Put me to work, doll."

My lips twitched. "Okay. If you want to make yourself useful, chop up the peppers over there on the bunker while I dice these onions and the chicken breast."

"On it."

Ward couldn't see that I was smiling, and I was glad of that, because if he had asked me why I was smiling, I wouldn't have been able to give him an answer. I wasn't sure myself why I was smiling, or why I had seemed to be doing so much of it lately, especially in Ward's presence. Granted, it mostly came in the form of a lip twitch here and there, but it was still something.

I forced that thought from my mind and focused on preparing dinner. I moved to Ward's side of the counter, and in silence we cut up the food on the chopping boards.

"When you were wee, you'd wear this hot-pink apron and chef's hat when you helped your mum in here."

My mouth dropped open. "I cannae *believe* you remember that!"

Ward barked a laugh. "You'd be concentratin' so hard, especially when you were helpin' cook a meal that I would be eatin'."

I refused to look at him. "Shut up."

Another hearty laugh.

"I knew, ye'ken?"

I glanced to the side. "You knew what?"

Ward's dimples creased as he grinned.

"That you fancied me when you were a kid."

I widened my eyes to the point of pain as I looked up at him.

"I did *not*," I said firmly, but I couldn't help the blush that stained my cheeks. "I just thought you were a nice person."

Ward's laughter was loud, joyous, and one hundred per cent genuine.

"Give over," he teased, playfully jabbing me in the side with his elbow. "You were head over heels in love with me."

I scowled at him, but couldn't help the grin that tugged at the corners of my mouth.

"You're very sure of yourself," I said, my nose in the air. "You must think you're a real catch, huh?"

Ward's smile was wide, and his eyes seemed to glisten with amusement as he bobbed his head.

"I'd make a fine husband," he claimed.

My smile slowly fell from my face. "I'm sure your fiancée agrees."

It was like the flip of a switch. One moment, Ward was carefree and happy, and the next he was tense, reserved and looked like he'd swallowed something sour.

"Aye." Ward nodded solemnly. "I'm sure she does."

I didn't understand why the mention of his soon-to-be wife would make him look and sound so miserable.

"Are you okay?" I asked, shocked that I was concerned about him. "You look sad."

Ward shot me a grin, and though I had only been in his presence a couple of weeks, I could tell it was forced.

"I'm as well as can be, doll."

He wasn't giving up on that nickname.

"I used to love when you called me that," I said with a shake of my head. "It made me feel all special."

"That's only because you fancied me so much."

I looked at him, noting that some of the tension that had gripped his body at the mention of his fiancée began to slowly melt away. I decided then not to mention his partner, their relationship or impending nuptials ever again. Two weeks ago, I didn't want to be near Ward at all, but now I didn't want to be near a sad Ward; I wanted to be in the presence of the man whose laughter made me smile, whose self-confidence made me ambitious, whose teasing made my stomach erupt with butterflies . . . whose interest in my life made me feel worth something.

I didn't know when that change had occurred, but I didn't hate Ward anymore. I wasn't sure I'd even hated him in the first place. Disliked him? Of course . . . but not real hate. I'd convinced myself it was hate, and I didn't think I'd ever fully accept what he'd done to my family back when he was a teenager, but if they could forgive and move on from it, then so could I.

"Y'ken that rose I gave you? The one you pressed?"

I nodded.

"Did you ever press any of the others I sent you over the years?"

I paused, and blinked in confusion.

"What do you mean? You've only ever given me one rose."

Ward looked at me. "I've sent you a bouquet of mixed-coloured roses every year on your birthday, and I have done since you were twelve."

My mouth dropped open.

"You *have*?"

Ward looked baffled. "Are you tellin' me you've never received *any* of them?"

"Not a single one," I answered. "Apart from that yellow one on Valentine's Day when I was eleven, but you know that already."

Ward lowered his hands to the bunker and simply stared at me. I could see he was trying to figure out how I hadn't received the roses he said he'd sent me, but in the back of my mind I knew who I'd have to ask. I'd just have to wait until she was sober, so she could hold a conversation and answer my questions.

"Why?" I asked after a few moments of silence.

Ward blinked. "Why what?"

"Why would you send me roses every year on my birthday?"

Ward held my gaze for a moment before he tipped his head back until he was looking up at the ceiling, and a sigh escaped him.

"I want to say because I know roses are your favourite flower, but if I'm being honest" – he sighed again, returning his gaze to mine – "I felt guilty."

"Guilty?" I asked, bemused.

Ward nodded. "Yeah, guilty."

"For what?"

"*For what?*" He guffawed. "For everything, Erin. You don't know how many times I've relived my last conversation with you," he said, rubbing a hand over his face. "You were so wee, and you looked at me like I could save you, like I could make everything better after your dad died, and I let you down. I didnae only walk away from Tommy, I walked away from you, your mum *and* your dad, when all any of you ever did was be a family to me. I will never forgive myself for that, Erin, not even if you all do."

My heart thrummed inside my chest.

I didn't know what to think, let alone how to form coherent words and reply to Ward. He'd been carrying around the guilt of what he did? When I thought he never gave any of us a second thought? This dramatically changed how I perceived Ward.

"I won't lie and say you didnae hurt us – hurt *me* – because you did," I said, biting my lower lip. "As dumb as this is goin' to sound, you were like a knight in shinin' armour to me. You were always there to help Mum and Dad whenever they needed you, and you were the best friend to Tommy, and so sweet to me. I thought there was no one better than you, and when you left . . . it changed somethin' in me. I've never opened up to trust anyone like that ever again, because in my mind, if you could walk away when I needed you most, any stranger could too."

"I'm so sorry, Erin," Ward exclaimed as he leaned forward and took both of my hands in his. "For the rest of my life, I will be sorry."

"I believe you," I said, shocking both of us.

"You do?" Ward asked, his mouth agape.

"I do." I answered. "Part of the reason why I held so much anger towards you was because you moved on with your life without us. You've lived wild and free, while we've been here with nothin' changin' except the house decor. I envied you . . . I still do."

"Erin—"

"Let me finish," I cut in, then, at his nod, I continued. "When I think back to my dad dyin', and you leavin', I dinnae see it through the eyes of an eleven-year-old anymore. I'm seeing it through my eyes now, and you were right to go to London and better yourself and your life. Maybe if me and Tommy weren't so hurt and angry with you, then we could have all stayed in touch."

Ward swallowed.

"Everythin' happened for a reason, so I'm not goin' to play the 'what if' game. I just want you to know that I dinnae hate you, and I don't blame you for anythin'. It wasn't your fault that my dad died."

He exhaled a deep breath. "I cannae even begin to tell you how happy that makes me feel. I told myself that before I went back to London I would be on good terms with you. I knew I'd never be able to leave if we were anything other than friends."

I was shocked to find that the thought of him leaving upset me, and then I was completely astonished to find that being just friends with Ward disappointed me.

"Are you okay?"

I looked up, smiled and nodded.

Ward frowned. "Dinnae do that."

"Do what?"

"Lie."

I swallowed. "I'm not lyin'."

Ward scowled at me, and I grunted.

"How can you tell I'm lyin'?"

"Because I know you."

"Naw, you dinnae."

"I do," he countered. "Not as well as I'd like, but I've been with you nearly twelve hours every single day since the accident. I'm gettin' to know you, doll, whether you like it or not."

I considered this. "I guess we aren't strangers anymore."

Ward smiled. "I never wanted to be a stranger to you."

"If I say me either, would you believe me?"

"I would if you said it was the truth."

"It is. If you'd have told me two weeks ago that I would even consider wanting to be anythin' other than a stranger to you, I'd have called you crazy."

"And now?"

"And now . . . now I think it's time we walk over that bridge we've built over the last two weeks, and leave our past where it belongs. Behind us. You're sorry for what you did, and I'm sorry for my part in keepin' this feud goin' for so long. I'm sorry for not considerin' your life and what you wanted to do with it. We can move on from it; we deserve to. What d'you say?"

I had barely finished speaking before Ward dropped the knife in his hand on to the bunker, rushed at me, gathered me up in his warm embrace and hugged my body to his.

"Aye," he said into my hair. "I want to *run* across the fuckin' bridge with you."

I laughed as I slid my arms around his waist and hugged him back. "You're daft."

I felt Ward plant a kiss on my head. "I've been called worse."

"By me, no doubt."

Ward chortled before we separated and continued preparing the dinner. We had just finished dicing and slicing everything when his phone rang. He dug it out of his pocket, checked who was calling, then placed the device against his ear.

"Hello," he answered.

He patiently listened to whoever was on the phone, then sighed and said, "Have the jet prepared to depart tonight at nine. I'll be on it, and I'll see you in the office in the mornin'."

Two things happened in that moment.

The first was that I realised Ward was leaving us, and the second was that I knew I undoubtedly didn't want him to. My desperation for him to walk out of our lives and never come back had changed to an urgent need to have him close – not only for my brother, but for me, too. Somehow, Ward did what I'd never thought possible.

He'd worked his way back into my life . . . and I wanted him to stay in it.

CHAPTER FIFTEEN
WARD

"You're leavin'."

"Aye," I sighed as I pocketed my phone. "I have to handle a few things back at the office, but it willnae take very long. I should be back tomorrow evenin' at the latest."

There was a pregnant pause before Erin whispered, "You're comin' back?"

I looked down at her, noting the look of disbelief on her face.

"Aye, of course."

Her face flushed red, and for a split second I thought she was going to cry.

"Erin . . ." I frowned. "Did you think I was leavin' . . . for good?"

She looked away from me.

"D'you think everyone will be happy with a chicken stir-fry?" she asked, busying herself around the room, clearly trying to change the topic. "I'm not too sure they will."

I stared at her back, and I knew she could feel my gaze on her.

She'd thought I was leaving and not coming back. I'd heard it in her voice, and I'd seen it in her eyes. There was a touch of fear in her tone, and a hint of uncertainty in her demeanour. If I didn't know any better, I would think that she didn't *want* me to leave.

I stepped closer to her and placed my hand on her waist, bringing her movements to an abrupt halt.

"Look at me."

She was stiff as a board, but she slowly turned to face me and drew in a shallow breath when her breasts brushed against my body. I didn't step back, nor did I remove my hand from her small waist. I stared down at her, and when she didn't raise her head to meet my eyes, I put my hand under her chin and tipped her face upwards.

When her gaze locked on to mine, her lower lip wobbled ever so slightly.

"I'm never leavin' you."

As soon as the words left my mouth, I knew them to be true. Erin, Tommy, their entire family . . . I wasn't going to leave them.

When we separated, Erin kept her eyes on me and I lifted my hand to brush a few strands of hair from her face. What happened next caused my heart to drop to my stomach. Erin flinched at my hand, as if she were afraid I was going to strike her.

"I'm sorry."

I blinked a bunch of times before I opened my mouth to speak, only to close it without saying anything. I repeated this action twice more before I shook my head as if to erase what had just happened.

"Did you . . . did you think I was goin' to *hit* you?" I asked, astonished.

She stared up at me.

"Answer me," I said, my voice firm. "Did you think I was goin' to *hit* you?"

Erin shook her head.

"No," she said firmly. "You just startled me."

"No one just reacts like that when someone reaches for them, Erin."

"I'm just jumpy, that's all. Dinnae fash yersel."

"Dinnae tell me not to worry about you."

I knew my gaze was making her uncomfortable when she couldn't keep eye contact with me anymore. She turned back to the counter and checked on the food that was still cooking in the pan. She busied herself with tidying up our workstation, and all the while I didn't move a muscle.

"Erin," I said, my voice calm and collected.

"Huh?"

"You can talk to me without judgement of any kind," I said softly as I stepped back into her space. "I promise."

In that moment, I was willing to pay any amount of money just to know what she was thinking.

"It's complicated," she eventually managed to say.

"Well," I said, staying put. "It's a good thing I've got nothin' but time."

"You once said in an interview that time is not a luxury you can afford."

"Time with – and for – you is somethin' I'm making a priority."

Erin's lips parted ever so slightly.

"Why?" she whispered, her cheeks tinged with pink. "Why do you care about what happens to me?"

"Do I need a reason?"

She snorted. "Considerin' two weeks ago we were at each other's throats, I'm goin' to say *aye*."

My lips twitched. "I dinnae think I have a good enough reason for you. There's a part of me that's desperate to help Tommy, and being his wee sister—"

"You want to help me too." She nodded, her shoulders slumping. "Because of Tommy."

"Naw," I said, shaking my head. "Despite him."

She blinked. "Really?"

"When I think of you now, Erin, your brother doesn't come to mind." I stared into her eyes. "Not at all."

She licked her lips, her tongue slowly sliding back and forth. The action sent blood rushing to my cock. I tensed my muscles to have some control over my body, but it was futile. I was so attracted to Erin that I couldn't think straight. In that moment, I was desperate to touch her, kiss her . . . to have her.

"I dinnae . . . I'm not sure I understand—"

"Aye, you do," I almost growled. "You know *exactly* what I'm sayin'."

"Ward."

The way my name slipped from her parted lips in a throaty rasp was all I could take. I leaned down and covered her mouth with mine. For a moment, my lips just lingered on hers, and I was almost certain that at any second she was either going to ram her knee into my bollocks or whack me upside the head while spewing curses at me. I couldn't have been more surprised when neither scenario happened. I groaned as I absorbed the sensation of her soft, plump lips. God answered my silent prayers when Erin slowly parted those lips and tentatively flicked her tongue against mine.

My entire body burned with need.

I knew where this was going to end. Us both naked, sweating and completely wrapped up in each other . . . and I wanted that. Fuck, I *desperately* wanted that. I slid my hands up from Erin's waist to her cheeks, where I cupped them and deepened the kiss. I felt her shiver, and when she moaned ever so slightly into my mouth, I had to force myself not to strip her bare then and there.

I had to go slow with her, I *wanted* to go slow with her. I wanted to savour every kiss, touch and moment of being with her, because I knew that after this was over, she'd probably never look in my direction again. I had to make it last, I had to have my fill of her. I had never wanted that with another woman before; usually I wanted sex and *just* sex, but that's not what I wanted with Erin, and it scared the crap out of me . . . but it wasn't enough to stop me, even though I knew nothing would come of us being intimate together.

I kissed her slowly, deeply, and every little moan and groan that escaped her sent blood to my already-hard cock.

"Make me forget," she whispered against my lips. "Make me forget everythin' but the two of us."

There were a lot of things I couldn't do, but fulfilling that request wasn't one of them.

CHAPTER SIXTEEN
ERIN

I was kissing Ward Buckley.

Or he was kissing me . . . I wasn't too sure who was in control of the kiss, but one thing I was certain of was that it was happening – and that I *wanted* it to happen. When Ward had invaded my space and said he wasn't leaving me, my heart warmed. I knew he wasn't leaving my family, but he said he wasn't leaving *me* specifically, and it wasn't until then, when I saw how he was looking at me, that I realised the attraction I had to him might be returned.

The second his lips touched mine, there was no doubt.

I wanted him. I wanted, just for a little while, to forget about how scared I was for my brother, to forget how lost my mum was, to forget that my dad was dead. I wanted sensation, peace and Ward. I wanted him so bad. When I asked him to make me forget everything, he didn't acknowledge my request with words; instead he backed me up against the bunker and deepened our kiss. I felt his hardened length press against my stomach as it strained against the material of his jeans.

I shifted against him, and the movement caused him to groan into my mouth. The rush that shot through me sent a heatwave to my body, causing my skin to flush. I lifted my hands to Ward's neck, and pulled him as close as I could get him. When he made a sound dangerously close to a growl, pleasure pulsed between my thighs. I ached, and there was only one person who I wanted to rub it better.

"Ward," I rasped against his lips.

He snagged my lower lip between his teeth the second his name left my mouth, and he sucked on it. When I moaned and my fingers dug into the flesh of his neck, he pressed his entire body flush against mine and made a gruff sound in the back of his throat. It was *so* sexy, so primal. My hands slid down his torso and went to the hem of his jumper, where I gave it a firm tug. Without a word, Ward pulled back ever so slightly, putting a few inches of space between us, and reached up to the back of his neck to pull his jumper, and the T-shirt underneath, up over his head in one swift motion. He tossed them somewhere behind him, but my eyes were too focused on his bare torso to see where the items of clothing had landed.

"Holy shite," I breathed. "You're so toned."

"You dinnae need to sweet-talk me, babe." He gave a low chuckle. "I'm a sure thing."

I ignored his teasing as I lifted my hands and lay them flat against his stomach. He had abs – nothing that showed he was a gym junkie, but I could feel, and see, the ridges as I slid my hands over them. I swallowed when my fingers traced over the dips at his hips, the drool-worthy lines making my stomach clench. My fingers brushed over the hair of his treasure trail, and when I heard his sharp intake of breath, I knew he was enjoying my hands exploring him as much as I was.

"You're beautiful," I said, and I tipped my head back to look up at him.

His blue eyes were already on mine, and they looked overcome with desire.

"Naw," he almost growled. "That'd be you, love."

I watched his face as I slid my hands lower and rubbed over his erection. I felt it throb against my hand, and when I tried to squeeze it, Ward's eyes fluttered shut. With my eyes still on him, I felt my way to the button of his jeans and popped it open. I tugged his zipper down, and eventually moved my fingers to the waistband where I pushed the material down to his mid-thigh. Ward's eyes shot open when I lowered myself and came face to face with his cock.

It was long, thick, and appeared to be as hard as a diamond.

I clasped my hand around the length, giving it a gentle squeeze, and Ward's legs seemed to buckle at the contact. I heard him fumble as he gripped on to the bunker, and when he stilled I could hear his laboured breathing. I looked up at him the moment I opened my mouth and placed my tongue against the head of his cock, then gently licked. His eyes almost instantly rolled back, and his lids shut.

"Christ," he rasped, a hand blindly finding its way to my hair, fingers grasping the strands tightly. "Are you sure about this, Erin? You dinnae have to do this if you dinnae want to."

Something told me he'd probably cry if I backed away.

My response was to close my mouth around the head fully and suck. Not hard, just a soft bit of suction to get his full attention. Ward moaned out loud, and his reaction gave me courage. I had only ever given a blow job once before, and that was back when I'd first had sex, in my first year of college. I'd seemed to do an okay job that one time, but it was different now, and I found myself wanting to please Ward immensely.

I removed my lips from the head and kissed the base, then licked it from root to tip. When Ward hissed, I took the head of his cock back into my mouth and sucked again. He whimpered. I tentatively began to bob my head, learning how much of him I could take in my mouth. I relaxed, telling myself I would *not* be sick. Not a chance in hell. I wrapped my hand around Ward's wet cock, and worked it as I moved my mouth up and down.

He began to talk to God out loud, and thanked Him an awful lot.

Things got messy then. The sounds my mouth made while I sucked and licked seemed to add fuel to the fire in turning Ward on. He opened his eyes a few times to look down at me, but when he found my eyes were on his and realised I liked watching him while I gave him head, his eyes rolled back again and he bit down on his lip as if he were in pain.

I *loved* that.

I loved that I made him feel so good that he reacted in such a way. I had never seen Ward be anything other than in complete control, but right now, as I kneeled before him, he was at my mercy. When I reached up with my free hand and cupped his balls, his entire body twitched. I kept my touch light, and if his vocals were anything to go by, it hit the mark.

I hummed around him, letting him know just how much I was enjoying myself, and the vibrations from my throat were too much for him to handle.

"Stop," he suddenly choked.

I frowned when he pulled his hips back and his cock slid from my mouth with a pop.

"Did I do somethin' wrong?"

"The fucking *opposite*," Ward hissed. "I was afraid I'd come before I was inside you."

My clit throbbed at his words.

I got to my feet and reached for him, but he slid his hands around to my behind, and in one swift motion he lifted me into the air. I sucked in a sharp breath as my arms and legs instinctively wrapped around him. Ward turned and walked us over to the kitchen table, trailing kisses along my jaw and neck. When he sat me down, he gently pushed my shoulders until I was lying flat on my back. After he removed my boots, I began to tremble as he gripped my leggings and my underwear and pulled them down south.

"You're perfect," Ward murmured as he slid the clothes off my body and, like he'd done with his own garments, tossed them over his shoulder.

"I've ne-never," I stammered before clearing my throat. "No one has ever gone down . . . on me . . . before. I mean, I dinnae ken if I'll—"

Ward hushed me, his hands flat on my stomach.

"You'll like this, baby," he said. "Trust me."

I did trust him, and that knowledge surprised the life out of me.

I closed my eyes when his hands drifted over my skin, squeezing my flesh here and there. I moaned softly when he trailed kisses, along with a few nips of his teeth, up the insides of my thighs. My body bucked of its own accord when I felt his wet tongue slide over my sensitive folds. He licked up and down but didn't directly touch my throbbing clit, which ached so much I ground my teeth together. My eyes crossed when he tongued around the hood, teasing me. Then he moved to my labia, and sucked on my lips before dipping his tongue inside me.

"Ward!"

He moved upwards, and *finally* I felt hot air on my clit, followed by his warm tongue lapping at it.

"My . . . *God!*"

Ward hummed as he hooked his arms around my thighs and pressed his hands at the base of my stomach. He inhaled a deep breath, then curled his tongue around my clit *slowly*. It felt so good that it almost hurt. I pulsed with need, and the urge to reach down and fist my hands into his hair became difficult to ignore.

Breathe, I told myself. *In. Out. In. Out.*

My body was like a live wire as I twitched and bucked with every swipe of Ward's tongue. My flesh was flushed with desire, and my skin burned with need. The passion I felt was as intense as it was intoxicating. This brief escape from reality was just what I deserved. Ward . . . *he* was just what I needed.

"Ward," I whimpered. "Dinnae st-stop."

His hands flexed against my stomach in response.

Jolts of pleasure became more constant then, and with an abundance of attention focused on my clit, an orgasm began to build. My breathing suddenly became irregular, and I couldn't focus on any one thing. I began to lose myself to Ward's touch. My body felt like it was on fire, and my thighs were quivering. I lost my fight against the urge to bury my hands in his hair, and the second I did that, he sucked my clit into his mouth and my body began to convulse.

I screamed, before I drew in a sharp breath and held it.

For a moment, I felt a sharp sensation like pain, followed by a split second of numbness before an inexplicable wave of bliss started at my clit, and with each pulse pushed the sensation outward. My eyes rolled back, my spine arched and my lips parted in a silent scream. My lungs burned for air, so I exhaled the breath I had been holding before greedily gulping more down. My body spasmed, but Ward still sucked and lapped at my now oversensitive clit. I bucked against his face and turned my body, forcing him away as I continued to twitch. I felt his hands all over me, I felt his lips kissing my hips, my behind and any section of skin he could reach, and I heard his murmured sweet words.

"Erin?"

My eyes were closed, and I wasn't sure how much time had passed.

"I cannae move."

Ward's chuckle was low as he gently rolled me on to my back once more and hooked his arms around my thighs, pulling me to the edge of the table. My muscles were lax and depleted of energy. I felt heavenly. Ward stepped between my parted thighs, and when I felt his hand sneak its way up my T-shirt to cup my breast through my bra, I chuckled and lifted one eyelid.

"You just *had* to grab my boob, huh?"

"Had to, sorry."

I opened my eyes fully and smiled up at him, feeling almost sleepy.

"I dinnae have condoms," he said, and I heard the strain in his voice.

"I'm on birth control," I said, "and I havenae had sex with anyone in three years. I'm clean."

"I am too," Ward replied eagerly. "I get tested often."

I pulled a face and he shrugged. "Better safe than sorry."

I couldn't argue with him there.

"Then we're good."

He hesitated.

"What is it?"

"I've never fucked raw before."

I raised an eyebrow. "If you dinnae want too, I under—"

"Naw, I want to. You have no idea how much. I'm just . . . *fuck*, I'm excited as hell."

I hummed. "What are you waitin' for then?"

Ward moved and leaned over my chest, and before I could blink he reached for my T-shirt and pushed it up. The material bunched above my breasts, but they were still covered. I quickly unclasped the latch at the front of the bra, and when the fabric fell away, Ward groaned.

"I *love* practical bras."

I laughed, but my laugh quickly turned to a moan as Ward lowered his head and latched his hot, wet mouth around my right nipple. I licked my lips and lifted my hands to his head, where I slid my fingers through his soft, thick hair.

"Oh, that feels *good*."

My body tingled in a frenzy of static as Ward moved from my right breast to my left and showered it with attention from his wicked tongue. I arched my back ever so slightly when another ache began to build between my thighs, and my heart pounded with excitement.

"Ward," I pleaded. "Please."

He released my nipple with a pop, then he grinned knowingly as he stood upright. He looked down to my parted thighs and hissed a breath.

"You're so wet," he growled. "I can *see* your clit throb."

His words caused my muscles to clench, and he growled.

"Your pussy wants to be filled," he hummed. "Should I keep it waitin'?"

"Naw!" I almost whimpered. "Please, Ward, fuck me."

Something changed in his eyes. Before, he'd watched me with a lust-filled gaze, but now? Now he looked like a predator who was about to consume his prey, and God help anyone who got in his way. I looked down at the same time he wrapped his hand around his cock and pumped his wrist once, twice. He groaned. With his left hand on my thigh, he pushed my legs open wide, and with his hand still on his cock he stepped forward and used the head to rub up and down over my aching clit.

"Omigod!"

Ward continued to rub my clit with his cock until my legs quivered and my breathing was erratic. He lifted his hooded gaze to mine, then his rolled his hips forward, and inch by inch he slid inside, stretching me wide and filling me completely. I cried out in pleasure, and Ward hissed. He began to thrust in and out of me slowly, his eyes never leaving mine. When he lifted my leg and placed it over his shoulder, my breath caught. When he repeated the action with the other leg and thrust forward, my eyes rolled back as his pelvis slapped against me.

"Fuck. Yes."

I agreed with those sentiments exactly, but I couldn't voice that. I could do nothing but blindly reach out and grip the sides of the table as Ward fucked me. His slow pace became merciless, and before I knew it I was screaming and begging him to fuck me harder, faster.

"Dinnae stop," I pleaded. "Dinnae st-stop!"

Ward pounded into me in response, and then time was forgotten. His pelvis rubbed against my thighs as he thrust in and out. *He* was completely in control of the sex, of my pleasure, of me. I surrendered completely, becoming a slave to the rhythm of his hips. I hadn't realised how much I'd missed having sex, how good it could be, until that moment. I reached up for Ward, craving him, wanting his tongue to dance with mine. We were both caught up in the moment, our hands were erratic, touching as much skin as possible. Our kisses became starved, like we would die if we didn't taste every part of the other.

Then, Ward switched it up. He reached for my breasts, his hands roughly palming them. He stepped back, the action causing his cock to slip out of my body, and I whined in protest. He pulled me to my feet, wordlessly turned my body and applied pressure to my back to push me forward. Before I knew it, I was lying flat on my stomach on the table, my arms stretched above me. Ward slid into me from behind and his hands latched on to my hips, his fingers biting into my flesh. I sensed everything, this immense magnetic field between us. Electricity. Fire. But did he feel it? Was this as good for him as it was for me?

God, I hope so.

With no warning, sensation became me and a startled screech slipped past my lips. My body convulsed, and my back arched as bliss flowed through my veins and touched my every nerve ending. I felt a stinging bite of pain in my hips, but it only heightened my pleasure and drew a whimpering cry from me. I bucked back against Ward, riding out the ecstasy that had a hold of me, then as quickly as it had slammed into me, it began to recede.

I collapsed forwards, my cheek pressed against the cold wood, and closed my eyes.

"Jesus," Ward panted, still inside of me. "Christ."

I grunted, not able to respond vocally as I was too focused on breathing. For an unknown amount of time, I lay on the table and Ward leaned against me. When he eventually slipped from my body and tapped my bum twice, I managed a snort. I was about to push myself up when I heard water suddenly running from the tap. I sluggishly placed my palms on the table and prepared to draw what energy I had left to get me upright, but then I yelped when a warm, wet cloth was suddenly pressed against my behind.

When I realised Ward was cleaning me up, I smiled.

"There you go," he murmured, a chaste kiss placed against my labia making me flinch and him chuckle. "All pretty again."

I glanced over my shoulder as Ward stood upright. He shot me a wink as he cleaned himself up, then he tucked himself into his boxers and pulled his jeans up, zipping and buttoning them closed. He picked up his T-shirt next and shrugged it on, and when he realised I was still watching him, he laughed.

"D'you want me to dress you, too?"

"You'll have to," I said, yawning. "I may fall asleep otherwise, and it'll be a shock to see me like this when everyone comes home for dinner."

With a shit-eating grin, Ward gathered up my clothing and helped me get dressed. He boasted about the sex rendering me useless, and I couldn't disagree because he was right. I felt like a marshmallow, and I didn't care – not even a little bit. So I let Ward's ego swell, telling myself that I'd cut him back down to size later. When I was clothed, he placed his hands on my waist and lifted me back on to the table. He parted my thighs, stepped forward and then leaned down, capturing my lips in a breathtaking kiss.

I ran my hands up his arms until they clasped together behind his neck, and I hummed with contentment as I kissed him. His hands stilled at the base of my spine, and he jolted me forward until my parted thighs were pressed against him. I broke our kiss and looked down when I felt something hard poking uncomfortably into my thigh, and when I saw the bulge in his jeans, I looked up at him, my eyes wide.

"I cannae do it again." I blanched. "I'll die."

Ward tipped his head back and laughed. When he looked at me again, he was still smiling and his hands went to my face. His fingers brushed loose strands of hair out of my eyes. My breath caught when I realised how small the action was but how giddy it made me feel. I felt like I was sixteen, and had finally been noticed by a boy I fancied, but that wasn't the case with Ward – he was a fully grown man, and the butterflies he gave me were real.

I didn't know what to think.

I liked Ward touching me, kissing me and being close to me. That was a huge change in my behaviour towards him from two weeks ago. Getting to know him, slowly but surely, and learning how much guilt and regret he carried because of his leaving eleven years ago had changed everything. The sex we'd just shared, and the moments before and after it? That changed everything, too.

My heart noticed Ward now, and that frightened the life out of me.

"What's that look for?"

I blinked, then swallowed.

"What look?"

Ward rubbed his thumb over my lower lip.

"The look where you just realised we had sex and you dinnae ken what to do about it."

I exhaled a breath. "*Do* we do anythin' about it?"

"Do you *want* to?"

It freaked me out that my instant thought was "yes".

"If I say I dinnae ken, will you be weird around me?"

"Naw." He smiled. "But if you say that, then would you be okay if I kissed and touched you a little?"

"What's a little?"

"A little bit of a lot."

I wanted to smile. "I wouldnae mind that."

"Thank God, because I want you so much it hurts, Erin."

My breath caught. "Ward."

"I like you," he said, a ghost of a smile on his lips. "You're like no other woman."

Ward *liked* me.

"I cannae process that right now."

Ward pressed his forehead to mine. "You dinnae have to, I just wanted to be honest. I dinnae like playin' games, so lettin' you know up front is easier for me."

"You like me?" I repeated.

"Mmm." He nuzzled his nose against mine. "You remind me of fine whisky . . . I think I'll call you that from now on."

"What, whisky?"

"Aye." He nodded. "I called you doll when you were a child, when I viewed you as a wee darlin' who was always under everyone's feet. The woman before me isn't cute like a dolly, she's delicious and as rare as they come. *Just* like fine whisky."

That was . . . hot.

"I dinnae have a nickname for you," I said, dumbly. "I cannae think properly . . . I think you've gone and bloody broke me."

Ward laughed again, and I noted that I liked the sound of it. When I realised that I wouldn't mind hearing it often, my stomach dropped. I knew then that Ward wasn't the only one who'd caught feelings, because I liked him, too. I closed my eyes, my mind going into overdrive and my heart slamming into my chest. When I opened my eyes and looked up at Ward, I swallowed.

The wave of lust that had previously consumed me slowly lifted, and reality was waiting with a sickening twist.

"Wa-Ward," I stammered, my hand lifting to my mouth as a devastating realisation hit me. "You're *engaged!*"

CHAPTER SEVENTEEN
WARD

"*Ward.*"

I jerked in response to a hand clamping down on my shoulder, and when I found the owner to be Keller, I relaxed.

"What?"

I had heard him speak, but it was lost on me what he had said. From the moment I'd left Erin's home, travelled to London and arrived at my hotel – there was no way I was going to my townhouse – my thoughts were filled with her, of our lovemaking and then of our fight. It was all pushed to the side the second Hope phoned me to tell me there was a rescued child my team had taken into their care that very morning. My meeting with Hope was rescheduled, and my charity and this child became my focus.

"I said," Keller frowned at me, "that you don't have to go in there, one of the agents can handle the introduction."

"Naw," I said, my voice wrapped in emotion. "I need to talk to her myself."

I stared through the narrow window of the hospital room door, and observed the little girl who was sitting not on the bed but in the corner of the room, with her knees drawn up to her chest and her long red hair covering her face completely. This wasn't the first time I had been called to a rescue. I was in attendance for every single child my charity had rescued, but this was the first time a child's abuse had made me hesitate.

"Tell me everythin' about her case again."

Keller retrieved a mini-tablet from his coat pocket and tapped on the screen.

"Her name is Hannah Burke. She called the hotline at 9:06 a.m. and reported that her stepfather had just sexually abused her and she needed help. The suspect was intoxicated and barely coherent when he was arrested. The mum's whereabouts are currently unknown, and from what I've gathered from the system, she has a rap sheet of arrests for drug offences."

"A junkie," I commented.

"Yes. Heroin is her drug of choice – it's what she has constantly tested positive for during her arrests." Keller looked back down at the tablet in his hand. "The girl has been assessed, and apart from bruising, she is physically okay . . . or as okay as she can be after what she endured. They confirmed she was sexually abused, and the examination showed that this wasn't the first time."

I felt like I was going to pass out.

"How old is she?"

"Eleven."

My heart stopped.

"Christ." I reached out and placed my hand on the wall for balance. "Jesus Christ."

Keller pocketed his tablet.

"She hasn't spoken much to our female agents, and she wouldn't utter a word to the police."

"She's terrified," I said, understanding. "She's waitin' for the rug to be pulled from under her feet."

"I know," Keller answered. "They all think that at the start."

My heart hurt for her.

"I'll make my introduction," I said, clearing my throat. "You know the drill . . . Go observe."

Keller nodded and entered the connecting room, which had monitors and speakers for the cameras and microphones that were in the room Hannah was in. Two of my agents followed Keller, as standard protocol. I looked back at the door of the room and stared through the window at the little ball huddled in the corner. Any doubt and apprehension I had about the introduction faded away the longer I looked at her. I knew I could talk to her, just like I did to all the other kids we rescued.

I knew how to relate to this child because she *was* me.

Hannah didn't move an inch – she didn't even flinch – when I entered the room, though I knew she'd heard me. I closed the door behind me and sat down on the floor, just like she was. I kept a space between us, so as not to scare her further.

"Hello, Hannah," I said. "I'm Ward."

She hugged her knees tighter to her chest, and remained silent with her gaze downcast.

"I'm the man who founded Preventing Secrets," I continued. "And I want you to know that even though you're really scared, and you dinnae know what's goin' to happen, I want to be really clear when I tell you that you will *never* be returnin' to the people whose presence you grew up in. Never. You have my word."

Her head moved slightly, causing her hair to part enough for me to see a pale blue eye staring right at me, unblinking. The girl was eleven years old, but I saw endless days and nights of pain in that little glimpse. My chest tightened. It felt like looking into a mirror, and the realisation that someone felt as I once had – as I still did – caught my breath.

"I think you're very strong and brave for phonin' us when you did," I said, clearing my throat. "I know how hard that was for you, how scared you must have been, but I want you to know that I'm *very* proud of you for it."

The fingers that were clasped around her knees, holding them to her chest, loosened slightly.

"If you have any questions, or want to talk to me – or anyone – all you have to do is say the word. If you want me to leave and not return, that's perfectly okay as well. You are in control of everythin'. What you say goes, no questions asked."

Silence.

"You also dinnae have to speak to me if you dinnae want to," I said softly. "But the police will need to hear you say a few words, if that's okay? They'll ask very important questions, and it will help put him in prison for a very long time."

I remained sitting on the floor for a minute longer, and when it became crystal clear that Hannah didn't want to talk, or talk to me at least, I decided to leave. I didn't want to scare her any further than she was already, so I made a move to get up.

This got a reaction from her.

"Where are you from? You talk different."

I halted my movements, and slowly eased back down into my sitting position.

"Edinburgh," I answered. "It's in Scotland."

Slowly, she nodded her head. "I'm learning about that in geography."

I couldn't yet see her face, it was still covered by her hair, but I looked at her as if I could, just so she could relax a little bit more.

"D'you like what you're learnin'?"

"Sure." She shrugged. "I don't get the whole . . . skirts thing for men, though."

I chuckled. "Kilts are just part of our culture is all."

Hannah slowly nodded.

"You seem nice," she then said.

I smiled. "Thank you."

"I wasn't sure if you were," she continued, "but I don't have a bad feeling so I think you're nice."

It ripped me apart inside just wondering how many bad feelings she'd got from the man who'd hurt her and who she couldn't escape. Until today.

"Can I ask you a question?"

I nodded. "Of course."

"Why?"

"Why what?"

"Why did you make Preventing Secrets?" Hannah asked, her voice so soft I had to strain to hear her. "I've seen the different posters all over school for it, and in the community centre. I saw the advert on the telly, too. I memorised the number because I saw it so much."

Gratitude filled me, but I pushed it aside and focused on the question I was being asked.

"I started the charity, because when I was your age, I needed somethin' like Preventing Secrets."

Hannah drew in a sharp breath, and the silence stretched.

"Can *I* tell *you* a secret?" I asked her, part of me hoping she'd say no.

She nodded slowly, and apprehension swirled in my gut.

"Someone . . . someone hurt me for a long time when I was a wee lad, and they continued to hurt me until I was older than you are now, but I wasn't as brave as you. D'you want to know why?"

Hannah lifted her head and her hair fell away from her face. Not all the way, but enough for me to see the little girl who hid behind it. Fair skin, a bruised eye, a swollen lip, and eyes so blue it was like all the myriad shades of the colour swirled together, creating a colossal ocean of strength.

"Because you kept the secret?"

For a moment after Hannah spoke, I stared at her, my heart thumping as she said the words I had protected for years from becoming public knowledge.

"Aye," I said, my voice strained, "I kept the secret."

Hannah blinked. "You don't have to keep the secret anymore."

I closed my eyes as she said one of the taglines that was printed in bold on the posters that decorated her school – and thousands of others nationwide. I'd made it clear that the word "the" would be underlined, and I'd made sure it wasn't the word "your", because an abused child's abuse wasn't their secret, it was their abuser's, and it was forced on to them to keep.

I kept my eyes closed as a range of emotions swam through me. Doubt took centre stage the second I remembered that the interaction with Hannah was being recorded, and Keller and two of my agents were observing every word that was spoken.

I wanted to kick myself, to scream, and run away until I was as far away from my demons as I could get. I hadn't meant to tell the secret I harboured, it had come out before I could put an ounce of thought into it. I swallowed and forced myself to breathe, to relax, to calm down, but it was futile. I thought of everyone knowing, and it felt like the walls of the room were closing in on me.

Jesse. Dad. Aiden. Tommy. Keller. Hope. And, Christ . . . Erin.

Fear slammed into me, and the thought of everyone I cared about looking at me and seeing only my past scared me half to death. I drew my own knees up against my chest and wrapped my arms around them, and rocked myself back and forth, just as I had done so many times before. I knew it wouldn't work, it never did, but I tried to rock the pain, the memories, the reality of my life away. I wasn't sure how long I rocked, but a small hand touched my shoulder, and when I lifted my head and stared into blue eyes, I still saw pain, but I saw something else that outweighed the pain. Something I could only pray for for myself.

Courage.

"You don't have to keep the secret anymore, Ward."

I stared at Hannah, and when my eyes filled with tears, shock tore through me. I hadn't cried in years. When a tear spilled over the brim of my left eye, Hannah reached out and swiped it away before it had a chance to roll down my cheek.

"You're a remarkable wee lass, Hannah. I hope you know that."

When Hannah smiled at me, I knew it was the first genuine one that had graced her small face in a very long time.

"I'm still scared," she said, swallowing. "But I was scareder to keep the secret."

"You're brave," I said, lifting a hand to rub my eyes. "And I am in awe of you."

The child had *just* been rescued from her hell, and she was sitting in front of me, comforting me and encouraging me not to keep the secret that tormented me. I wanted to pull her against me and hug her tightly, but I didn't. She was one of the bravest little women I had ever had the honour of meeting, and I knew that for as long as I lived, I would hold her in my heart.

"You're brave too, Ward," Hannah said, brushing a large chunk of her hair behind her ear. "We all are."

We, I mentally repeated. *We. Us. Survivors.*

CHAPTER EIGHTEEN
WARD

"Ward."

"Hope."

"Boy, if you don't cut the attitude I'll slap the sense you're lacking back into you."

Hope wasn't just my assistant, she was my dear friend and practically my adopted mum. When she frowned at me, I knew she knew that something was wrong with me. I watched as she put her phone down on the desk, closed the file in front of her and clapped her hands together.

She was giving me her undivided attention.

"Ward," she said, sternly. "Tell me what's wrong, and *don't* lie to me. I'll know if you do."

My lips quirked. "You're a human lie detector now?"

She winked. "Always have been."

"I'm fine, honestly."

"No, you're not." She frowned. "Is it about that little girl? Because she's safe now, honey."

"I'm not worried about her safety," I said. "Just about a conversation I had with her."

"What conversation?"

I exhaled a deep breath. "I told her something that I've only ever told one other soul about."

"May I ask why?"

"I've been askin' myself that since I told her," I answered. "The only conclusion that I've come to is that I saw myself in her sufferin', and I just sort of . . . broke for a few minutes."

"You saw yourself in an abused child's suffering?"

I cast my gaze downward and nodded once.

"Ward," Hope said softly. "I know."

I jerked my head up. "What?"

"I know."

"You know what?" I asked, my heart pounding.

"I know that you suffered something at the hands of another when you were younger."

It felt like the floor gave way beneath my feet, and I gripped on to the arms of my chair to keep upright.

"How?" I choked.

Hope smiled sadly. "After the first one hundred rescues, you mumbled, 'I wish someone would have helped me.' I've never forgotten it. I put two and two together and realised that you suffered just like the kids you rescue. It's why you're so dedicated to helping children in need."

I could hear my heart beating in my ears.

"Why didn't you say somethin'?"

"I never pushed you to talk because I figured you'd do so at your own pace."

I swallowed down the lump that formed in my throat. "I . . . I was abused."

I flicked my gaze up to Hope's, and when I saw no judgement of any kind in her eyes, a muffled sob escaped me. She quickly rounded the desk and wrapped me in her embrace. I pulled her against me, not caring that she was practically on my lap. Hugging her, and knowing she knew what had happened to me and still hugged me, made me regret ever feeling dirty because of what I had gone through.

"I'm sorry," I croaked. "I never cry."

Hope leaned back, tears on her cheeks, too. "It's good to cry every now and then; it's like a cleanse. Everyone needs to get rid of what's bothering them eventually, and tears are usually the best way to achieve that."

I rubbed my eyes with the back of my hands.

"I guess I do feel a little better."

Hope kissed my cheek, chuckled, then returned to her seat in front of my desk.

"Good," she said. "Now, tell me what else is bothering you."

I looked at her, into her wise eyes, taking in her knowing face, and sighed. She wasn't going to let up unless I told her the truth. Hope didn't care that I was her boss; I knew she loved me like a son, and she'd risk losing her job by poking me with uncomfortable questions to make sure I was okay. It was just one of the many reasons I loved her.

"I dinnae want to be here," I said, not looking directly at her.

Hope was silent, but only for a moment.

"In the office?"

"Naw. In London."

"You don't want to be here for the day?"

"Naw," I answered, revealing something I'd realised on the flight back to London. "I dinnae want to be here long-term."

Hope was silent, but only for a moment. "And may I ask why?"

"Multiple reasons."

"Lay them out for me."

I locked eyes with her, and began to list off the reasons why I wanted to stay in Scotland.

"I miss my brother. I've spent more time with him this past while than I have in years."

"Good reason. What's the next one?"

205

My lips twitched. "I miss Scotland. I didnae realise how much until I went back."

"I can tell, your accent has thickened back up since you've been gone. It sounds just as it did when I first met you."

I grinned. "It's nice not having to talk slowly, or in perfect English just so people can understand me easier."

Hope snorted. "What's the next reason?"

I tapped my finger against my desk.

"I miss Tommy, and I want to be around for his road to recovery . . . once he wakes up, that is."

"Uh-huh, and the next?"

"I want to be there for Aiden," I answered, thinking of the kid who looked at me like I was his idol. "He's my godson, and he's a great kid. He calls me his uncle. I want to live up to that, and earn the title. I want to *be* an uncle to him, and not from afar."

"Glad to hear that. Is there *another* reason?"

I tipped my head back and looked up at the ceiling.

"Aye," I said. "I miss Erin. Not the kid I once knew, but the woman I've gotten to know."

"Tommy's little sister?"

I grunted. "She's not so wee anymore."

"Oh," was all Hope said.

When I glanced at her and found her smiling, I raised my eyebrows.

"What's that look for?"

"You've found yourself a woman."

I nodded without thinking, and it caused an even bigger smile to stretch across her face.

"Relax," I told her. "We arenae thinkin' of anythin' other than her brother right now. Erin made that perfectly clear."

Hope's smile didn't falter. "You care for her?"

"More than I should," I admitted. "I . . ."

"You what?"

206

"I cannae *believe* I'm tellin' you this," I said, shaking my head. "I was intimate with her."

"Oh . . . *oh.*"

I nodded. "Yeah. Oh."

"Oh" didn't cover it. There wasn't a known word, not even in Word of the Day, that could accurately describe how incredible the sex was. Erin . . . she'd ruined me for any other woman, and she didn't even realise it. I had never been so content in my life as I was when we shared our bodies with one another. I wanted to rewind and play the entire act on a never-ending loop, just to feel her, taste her, fill her.

Christ.

Unfortunately, like most situations in life, something could be perfect one minute and a complete disaster the next. Three words uttered by Erin had started that, but the words I spoke in return are what sealed the deal. I closed my eyes, and for the thousandth time in the hours since the conversation took place, I thought back to that moment with Erin, mentally kicking myself for saying what I did.

"Wa-Ward," she stammered, her hand over her mouth, her grey eyes widening with shock. "You're engaged!"

I froze, my stomach sinking at the reminder, but the knots that formed and twisted were because of the horror that had overtaken Erin's face. I quickly moved towards her and grabbed her shoulders, hoping my touch would calm her. It didn't; it only made her more agitated.

"Dinnae touch me," she demanded, pushing me a few inches back. "What have we done?"

Like the snap of my fingers, she had gone from blissfully satisfied to an emotional wreck, tears welling in her eyes.

"Dinnae cry," I pleaded, my hands dropping helplessly to my sides. "It's okay."

"It isnae okay!" Tears splashed on to her cheeks. "Oh God, Ward . . . we're horrible people."

"Erin, just relax."

"How can I relax?" she demanded. "I feel so dirty, so disgustin'. How could I have done this to another woman?"

I hated that she was hurting on Tara's behalf, when she was unaware that Tara cheated on me just as much as I did on her. I couldn't tell her that though, because then I'd have to tell her why Tara had me cornered, and I couldn't do that. I couldn't because she'd hate me.

"That woman," Erin griped. "I helped you betray her . . . I helped!"

"Listen to me!" I pleaded. "It'll all be okay, she won't find out—"

"What?" Erin interjected, her voice raised. "You'd keep such a dirty secret from her? How could you even think of doin' that to her! D'you have no shame?"

She slapped her closed fists against my chest in anger.

"I cannae believe I've done this," she continued, pressing her hands to her face. "I feel sick!"

The situation was unravelling around me and I was at a loss as to how to contain it.

"Erin," I said, my voice calm. "This isnae as bad as you think it is."

"You just fucked me, and you're engaged to another woman!" she bellowed. "How is that not as bad as I think it is?"

When she said it like that, it was bad, but it was only bad because she thought Tara was an innocent party. But she wasn't.

"I cannae answer that."

Erin stared me, and I watched as any affection she'd felt for me minutes ago faded away.

"You're . . . you're horrible. Are you always so quick to toss someone's feelings, and respect, to the side?"

"Nae," I answered instantly. "But this situation is different."

"How?" Erin demanded. "Tell me how."

"I cannae," I said through gritted teeth. "I want to, but I cannae. You have to believe me."

Erin shook her head and looked away from me.

"I'm not playin' this game," she said. "You clearly have a secret and dinnae want me to know about it, and you know what? I dinnae want to *know. If you wanna keep what happened from your partner, that's on you, but I'm allowed to feel shame for my part in hurtin' her, even though she may never know about it. She's a person, and what we've done to her is lower than low . . . It will not be repeated, not with me, anyway."*

My gut twisted.

"Nae," I almost pleaded. "Please, we started somethin' here, Erin. You know we did . . . You feel the same pull to me as I do to you. I know you do, Whisky. I saw it in your eyes when you looked at me. You're terrified to even consider somethin' happenin' between us long-term."

"Long-term." She blanched. "You. Are. Engaged. To. Be. Married. You dinnae get more long-term than that with a person."

I couldn't disagree with her, so I didn't even try.

"You should leave."

My heart stopped. She was sending me away again?

"But . . . the dinner, and Tommy . . . "

"I'll finish the dinner and invite everyone round for food. I'll tell everyone that you got a call and had to go back to London, but you'll be back tomorrow."

"You want me to leave the house? Not altogether?"

"You care for my brother, and my nephew. I have accepted that you're goin' to be in their lives, and for that I am happy and grateful, but I cannae have you in mine in any other capacity than a friend."

"Erin—"

"Please," she said, turning her back on me. "Please, just leave. I'm beggin' you."

Hearing the pain in her voice cut me like a blade, and instead of arguing with her, I did what she asked and turned to leave.

"And Ward?"

I paused, but didn't look over my shoulder. "Aye?"

"Dinnae call me Whisky ever again."

When I opened my eyes and came back to reality, my stomach was twisted in knots. I hadn't waited around after Erin dismissed me, instead I'd rung Jesse and told him I had to go back to London for the night to sort out some business, and that I'd be back the following day. He suspected nothing, which relieved me.

"You were thinking pretty hard."

I didn't look at Hope. "Just relivin' an argument that I had with Erin over Tara after we were intimate. She's devastated that she broke another woman's trust, and she's fiercely upset with herself – and me – for doin' what we did, because of my relationship."

"I'd be hurt too if I had sex with a taken man. I'd feel pretty evil doing that to another person."

"I know," I grumbled. "I understand that, but if anyone should feel like shite, it's me. I'm the one who's engaged to Tara, no one else."

"But you don't feel bad?"

"It probably makes me a real prick, but naw, I dinnae feel anythin' close to regret."

"Did you tell Erin that?"

"Aye." I grunted. "She got furious then . . . She thought I was cruel for disregardin' Tara like she was nothin'."

"Did you tell Erin *why* you don't feel sorry for cheating?"

I hesitated, and Hope groaned.

"You're so smart, Ward, but God, you can be so stupid at times."

My fingers flexed. "I know."

"Why didn't you tell her?"

"Because," I said, "if I told Erin that Tara was blackmailin' me and why, she'd . . . she'd never look at me the same ever again, Hope. She already hates that I never credited her brother. Can you imagine what she'd feel if she knew I was willin' to marry someone I don't care for just to keep that a secret?"

"She'll never look at you the same if you keep this from her," Hope stated. "The truth always comes out in the end, and you want her to hear about this mess from you, not by reading it in a newspaper."

"She wouldnae accept me."

"I think you're not giving the girl enough credit," Hope said with a shrug. "Who are you to know how she'd react or how she'd perceive you? You don't know what goes through her mind. It's your own fear that's making you hold back on being honest, and you know it is."

I hung my head. "Why do you always have to make sense?"

"Because I am a woman, son," she said, reaching over and patting my hand. "If we didn't make sense of things, the world would be a worse place."

"You think I should take a chance?"

"What's it they say in Scotland?" Hope quizzed. "What's fur ye'll not go by ye?"

I laughed. "Where did you hear that?"

"You've said it plenty of times."

I shook my head, smiling.

"Well, it's true," she continued. "If you come clean with Erin, it'll go one of two ways, but at least you'll know where you stand. I know I'd rather take a chance instead of being plagued with what-ifs for the rest of my life. Some secrets aren't meant to be kept, son."

As always, Hope was right.

"I'll talk to her when I go back to Scotland this evenin'."

"Good. And now that we've got a plan for your love life, take a look at the items listed for the next update on Friendzone, and then sign off once you're happy."

I took the tablet from Hope's outstretched hand, and as I was scrolling through the list, a light bulb went off in my head.

I looked up at Hope. "I've one addition to make to this list of updates."

"You do?" Hope said, tilting her head to the side.

"Aye." I smiled. "And I need *your* help to do it."

CHAPTER NINETEEN
ERIN

"What's wrong with you?"

I looked at Jesse when he spoke. "Nothin', why?"

"Dinnae bullshit me. You've been acting like a zombie since last night. Did something happen between you and Ward that's gotten you all wound up?"

I tensed at the mention of Ward, and Jesse noticed it.

"Aye," he said, "something *definitely* happened between you and Ward."

"We just argued," I said, shrugging it off. "That's nothin' new."

"It is, actually," Jesse commented. "You've both been gettin' on like a house on fire the last while."

"Yeah, well, we were bound to clash eventually."

Jesse was quiet, and that silence screamed for my attention. I turned to face my best friend, leaned my hip against the bunker in my kitchen and said, "Say whatever it is you wanna say, Jess, I'm in naw mood to try and guess."

He snorted. "What makes you think I've got somethin' to say?"

"Because I've never known you to keep that big mouth of yours shut, that's why."

Jesse smirked. "You've got me."

"Aye, I do. Now, talk."

"Ward likes you."

Out of all the things I'd expected him to say, that was *not* it.

My lips parted, but I quickly masked my features and said, "We get on well enough."

"Y'ken what I mean." Jesse scowled. "Dinnae act stupid."

"This conversation is givin' me the fantods."

Jesse blinked. "The what?"

"It's makin' me uneasy."

He pinched the bridge of his nose before dropping his hand to his side. "My point exactly – you use words like that in a sentence and understand them. You arenae stupid."

I rolled my eyes. "I'm plenty stupid, trust me."

"I'll be the judge of that," he quipped. "Name *one* stupid thing you've ever done."

Your big brother.

"Jesse," I sighed. "I like your brother well enough to be civil with him. I'm not sure what you want me to say, I've no interest in anythin' other than Tommy. I dinnae want my focus on anythin' – or anyone – else."

I needed my focus to be on my brother. What happened with Ward was supposed to have been a quick getaway from reality, but now it was a big mess and we were no better off than we were before we had sex. He'd cheated on his fiancée with me, and even if he never told the woman about it, I would always know my part in it. I would always feel dirty, and that hurt, because that intimacy with Ward had made me realise more than a few things.

The first was that I had feelings for him, feelings that he returned, but feelings that could not be pursued. What was worse is that even though I was mad at him and at myself for what we had done, I still couldn't get him off my mind. His ocean-blue eyes, his lips, his smile, the way he touched and looked at me so intently that my knees knocked

together. One thought of him sent my heart racing, and I didn't understand it. I didn't think it was possible to catch feelings for someone so
rapidly, but I had caught them with Ward and I didn't know what to
do about it.

What should have been simple had turned into one colossal fuck-
up of a situation, and I had only my bloody self to blame for it.

Jesse jerked his head in a nod. "Okay."

I frowned. "What's wrong with you?"

"Nothin'."

"Jess."

He grunted. "I love havin' Ward live with me. I'm sorry that Tommy
gettin' hurt is what brought him here, and kept him here, but it's just
been great, y'ken? He's my big brother, and I miss him. It's gonna sting
when he leaves. I guess I was hopin' if you both . . . y'ken, got together,
that he'd stay."

My bruised heart hurt for my friend.

I smiled sadly. "Ward said he wasn't leavin' – and, Jesse, you're a
big part of the reason why. I've watched you both together, you're so
similar and so different, it's captivatin'. He loves you just as much as
you love him."

"When did he say he wasnae leavin'?"

Shite.

"Last night when we were makin' dinner." I cleared my throat. "I
think he's gonna put down roots here."

Jesse's eyebrows flew up. "You're serious?"

"As a heart attack."

"My dad is goin' to up and lose his mind." My friend beamed.
"He's been bidin' his time since I told him Ward was stayin' with me.
He wants to see him so bad, but he's worried Ward will rebuff any sort
of reconciliation."

I frowned. "But I thought Ward just butted heads with your mum,
not your dad?"

"When they butt heads, Dad had to interfere, or at least he used to." Jesse shrugged. "He's set on divorcin' her, so he's free to see Ward whenever he wants now."

I'd known about Jesse's parents' plan to divorce for a few months, but realising it was going ahead was surreal to me. I'd always thought Jesse's parents had the perfect marriage, but it only went to show that not everything was what it appeared to be.

"Meanin' that he couldn't before?"

"Not without receivin' hell from my mum."

I winced. "Sorry, Jesse, I had no idea things were that bad."

"You never liked talkin' about my brother." He shrugged. "So I kept anything involvin' him to myself."

I wanted to punch myself for making him feel like he couldn't talk to me just because I couldn't stand hearing the mention of Ward's name. I wrapped my arms around my midsection, feeling sick with myself for being such a horrible friend.

"I'm sorry, Jesse," I said, lowering my head. "I'm so sorry for makin' you feel like you couldnae talk to me about Ward. I've been the worst friend to you when you've only ever been the best to me."

"Hey," he said, and didn't speak until I looked up at him. "Dinnae beat yourself up about it. I can talk to you about him now, right?"

"Right."

"And just so you know," he continued. "You *are* my best friend. You have been since we were kids. I love you."

"I love you, too."

He grinned. "You're a good lass, d'you know that?"

I dropped my arms to my sides, trying to make myself look tough. "I'm not a lass, I'm a grown woman."

"Y'ken what I mean," he chortled. "You've a good heart."

I felt my cheeks warm.

"Thanks, Jess."

"D'you want to hear somethin' interestin'?"

I perked up. "Always."

Jesse's lips twitched. "When you and Ward left the hospital last night, the staff changed like they normally do and I noticed the nurse who came in to check Tommy was new. Or new to me, at least. I introduced myself to her, and we talked here and there, and guess who asked her out for a drink?"

"Bud!" I beamed. "It's about bloody time you dated someone."

"Steady on." He winked. "It's only a drink."

"She agreed, then?"

"Aye," he grinned. "Her name is Louise Chambers, and she's twenty-nine."

"Ohhhh, shackin' up with an older woman. Your brother will be proud."

Jesse playfully shoved me away, though he was clearly amused with my teasing.

"She seems great, and to be honest, now that I have an upcomin' project at work, havin' someone to distract me so I'm not obsessin' over it 24/7 would be nice."

"What upcomin' project?"

Jesse's lips parted. "*Please* tell me I've told you about the score I landed?"

"Um, no?"

"I thought I had . . . Oh, naw, wait. I was goin' to, then Tommy got hurt and I didnae want to bring it up."

I balked. "Well, don't keep me in suspense. Tell me now!"

Jesse launched into an in-depth explanation of the construction job he'd landed in the city for the Hilton hotel empire, and by the time he'd finished speaking, I had my arms wrapped around him and I was screaming and jumping for joy. Jesse's laughter rang in my ear as he hugged my body to his and gave me a tight squeeze.

"I knew you'd be made up."

"I am," I gushed. "I'm *so* proud of you. No one deserves it more."

"Thanks, sis."

Sis. The perfect word for him to describe me. Jesse wasn't just my best friend; we were as close as brother and sister, though a lot of the time, I knew I didn't deserve him in my life. I had been very bitter where Ward was concerned, and I knew that was hard on Jesse. I decided then and there that I was always going to be open with Jesse, and would harbour no more secrets from him.

"Does Ward know?"

"Yeah, I told him the night of Tommy's accident," Jesse said. "He's so pumped for me. We went over my design plans back at my place, and he was impressed. Not because he's my brother either, I could see it in his eyes that he was genuinely impressed, and I'd be lyin' if I said that didn't make me as happy as a pig in shite."

I laughed. "I've been tellin' you for *years* that your designs are great, but what really puts me in awe is how you follow through. I know you need skill to draw up a detailed design with all the specs and whatnot, but followin' through and buildin' it with your bare hands? That's some masterclass talent right there, Jess."

When a tinge of pink stained Jesse's cheeks, I pinched them.

"You're adorable when you blush."

"That's enough of *that*," he said sternly, but he had a grin in place as he spoke.

"I'm goin' to go back to my apartment and grab a quick shower," he said. "I'll meet up with you at the hospital later, okay?"

"Jess," I said, placing my hand on his arm. "You dinnae have to spend so much time in the hospital, y'ken that, right? Tommy wouldn't expect your life to go on pause just because he's hurt."

"I'm goin' to pretend you didnae just say that." Jesse frowned. "I dinnae want to be anywhere else than by you and your family's side during this, Erin. If I wasnae there in that room with you all, I'd lose my mind. I love Tommy. He's my family, too."

I squeezed his arm. "I love you, Jess."

"I love you, too."

We hugged, and when we separated, the front of door of my house opened and closed.

"Erin?" Auntie Jennifer called.

"Kitchen!" I shouted, making Jesse wince at the volume.

I snorted.

When Aunt Jennifer, Aunt Emma and my mum walked into the kitchen, all yawning, I smiled at them.

"We came home for some food. The nurses are cleanin' Tommy's room, changin' his bed sheets and so on. We figured we'd pop home then go back later."

"He's okay?"

"As can be," Auntie Emma answered, stretching her arms above her head.

I frowned at her. "Why dinnae you and Auntie Jennifer go home to your place, and we can meet up at the hospital later?"

My aunties shared a look before looking back at me.

"Are you sure?" Auntie Jennifer asked.

"Of course."

They hesitated, but only for a second before they said, "Okay, what time are you goin' back up to the hospital?"

I glanced at the clock on the wall.

"It's just after three now, so how does seven sound? That way we can all get some rest and food before we head back."

When everyone agreed, Jesse moved towards my aunties and said, "I'm passin' by your place on my way home; let me escort you lovely lasses."

Both my aunts snorted, but neither of them declined Jesse's offer, just like I knew they wouldn't. Everyone loved Jesse; it was no hardship being in his company. They said their goodbyes, and just like that, the house was coated in a veil of silence. When the front door clicked shut, I kept my eyes on Mum. She was sober, that much was obvious – since she'd just been with my aunties – but just to be cautious, I waited for her to say or do something first. When she looked at me, and stared at me, I swallowed.

"Any change with Tommy?"

She shook her head. "He's not any worse, so I'm countin' it as good news."

"Me too," I said.

Things were quiet then, and I realised how awkward I felt in her presence when she wasn't under the influence of alcohol. When she was drunk, I took care of her. That was my role, and had been for as long as I could remember. I hardly ever saw my mum sober, and I'd never realised how much of a toll that had taken on me. But still, while it made my daily life a struggle, trying to think of something to say in that moment while knowing that she was sober was a bigger struggle to me than picking her up off the floor unconscious.

"Havenae seen Ward today," Mum commented. "Did you succeed in runnin' him off?"

I ignored the jab, because I deserved it for how mean to him I'd been when he first arrived.

"He had to go back to London for work last night, he'll be back this evenin'."

"I forgot," Mum replied. "Jen said he was payin' for Tommy's hospital bill since he's goin' private to get the best care now."

"Yeah," I said, folding my arms across my chest. "He offered."

I didn't tell her that Ward went over our heads to make my brother's private care happen. It didn't matter now. The only thing that mattered was that Tommy had the best care available to him, thanks to Ward.

"Did you try and turn him down?"

"Of course," I answered instantly. "But he insisted, and since we don't have the funds for private care, I couldnae let my pride be the only thing stoppin' me from acceptin' the help that was offered. I don't know the charges, but I know it'll be expensive. We'd have gone into debt payin' back the bill if we went private ourselves."

"I know," Mum answered. "I was preparin' for that, but I didnae think you'd let Ward help. I know you hate him."

"I dinnae hate him." I cleared my throat. "When he never credited Tommy . . . it hurt me. I hurt for Tommy, but that was a long time ago, and if you can all forgive and forget, then so can I."

"I forgave Ward," Mum said. "I love him, but I'll never forget what he did. He knows he was wrong not givin' Tommy credit, and he has to live with that."

I exhaled. "It is what it is. None of us can change what happened, and if we stay stuck in the past, nothin' good will come of it."

"The only happy times I have are in the past," she said, her eyes looking through me. "If I want to dwell there, then I will."

I gritted my teeth. "Then that's your choice."

Mum grunted, but said nothing further. She turned and messed with the dying flowers in the vase on the kitchen window. Some people from the neighbourhood had left flowers and well wishes for Tommy. New ones appeared on our doorstep every few days from a different neighbour.

I stared at Mum, then the flowers she was fiddling with, and something Ward had said resurfaced in my mind.

"Mum?"

"Hmm?"

"Ward said somethin' to me yesterday that confused me."

Mum glanced at me. "What'd he say?"

"He said that he's sent me roses every year on my birthday, but I've never received any such flowers . . . Would you know anythin' about that?"

She looked away from me, but not before I saw the guilt in her eyes.

"Mum?" I pressed. "D'you know why I didn't receive those flowers?"

Her shoulders slumped.

"I was so hurt by that boy. My anger at him lasted a long time."

"What do you mean?" My mouth dropped open in shock at her admission. "You loved Ward as if he were your own son!"

"I did," she acknowledged. "I still do, but then he abandoned Tommy when he needed him and started their business, and reaped all the credit and rewards. The first few years, I binned the flowers out of spite. I wanted him to think you were ignorin' him by not sendin' a thank-you card, or somethin' silly like that. It was small-minded and petty, but it made me feel better." She swallowed. "Then . . . then you started to hate him, for the same reason, all on your own. You got upset if someone mentioned his name, so I binned the flowers every single year just so they wouldn't upset you."

I stared at her when she finished speaking, and my emotions were torn. Her intentions had started out as vengeful and childish, but ended with, in her mind, what she thought was best for me. I didn't know how to feel about that, because my mum . . . she wasn't my protector anymore. That part of her died the night my dad did.

"Why didnae you ever tell me?"

She looked at me, her eyes red with tiredness.

"Because I didnae need to give you another reason to hate me."

My breath caught.

"Mum . . ." I frowned. "I dinnae hate you."

I hated that she drank, I hated that she was killing herself slowly, I hated that she wasn't the woman I once knew, but I didn't hate *her*. She was my mum, and she'd fallen apart and lost herself the day my dad died, and just hadn't found her way back again.

"Aye, you do, baby."

A lump formed in my throat. "Look at me."

She did.

"I said I *dinnae* hate you, and I mean it," I said firmly. "You arenae my favourite person, not by a long shot, but I dinnae hate you."

Mum's eyes welled with tears, and she looked away from me so I couldn't see them fall.

"I miss your daddy so much it hurts."

I almost choked at her mention of him. She hadn't referred to him as my daddy since the day he died.

"I do too," I answered. "Every minute of every day."

"I'm tired, Erin," she said, and swallowed. "I'm so tired of feelin' pain."

"I know, Mum."

"I hate drinkin'," she almost whispered. "But it's the only way I can get away from the hurt, at least for a little while."

I knew that, too.

"Please, Mum," I pleaded. "Would you not consider the rehabilitation programme I found to help you? It's in the city, and the success rate is incredible."

She was silent for a long minute, then she asked, "D'you think it would help me?"

"Aye," I answered instantly. "It won't erase the pain you feel, but you'll learn new ways to cope, Mum. I promise I'll be right there with you, every step of the way. You'll never be alone on the road to recovery, I'll always be there."

"You cannae promise that," Mum said, her eyes darkening. "You dinnae ken whether you'll leave me."

I had never been able to leave her, but now I realised that was always out of fear of *me* being truly alone, not her. This time was different. This time, being by her side might just bring back the mum I'd loved and adored.

"I'm not goin' anywhere," I said. "I *promise*."

When tears fell from Mum's eyes, I found myself right in front of her, wrapping my arms around her tiny frame.

"I love you," I choked.

"I love you so much. I'm so sorry for being a horrible mum. You're my whole world."

I didn't argue with her or assure her she wasn't a bad mum, because as much as I hated to admit it, she was. But she was not her addiction, she was not the person she became when she consumed alcohol, and I would do everything I could to help her find herself again.

"I love you too, Mum," I said, squeezing her tightly. "I love you."

As I hugged her tightly, I was distinctly aware of a voice in the back of my mind saying this wouldn't last and that she'd be drunk again. I fought back with the reassurance that if that did happen, I would be there to put an end to it. Things were going to change for me and my mum. I could feel it, and I knew she could, too. We were tired of living in darkness.

It was time to walk into the light.

CHAPTER TWENTY
ERIN

I felt him approach me before I saw or heard him coming.

I tensed, and turned around to see if I was going crazy, but just like I suspected, Ward Buckley was walking up the hallway, his eyes locked on mine. I took a moment to assess him. He was wearing dark blue jeans, black boots and a navy long-sleeved T-shirt that had the sleeves pushed up to his elbows.

God, he was gorgeous.

His focus was all on me, until a passing nurse stopped him and asked for a picture. He obliged, and leaned down and smiled as she positioned her phone to take a selfie of them. I gritted my teeth, and spun back around to the tea and coffee machine. I couldn't focus on making a cup anymore, so I abandoned it, tossing the teabag into the rubbish bin next to the stand. I turned, and kept my gaze on the floor as I walked back to the viewing room. But I came to a stop mere feet away from the door, because he was standing in front of it.

I looked up, and locked eyes with Ward.

He crooked his finger at me, and though I wanted to run in the opposite direction, I lifted my chin in the air and walked towards him. Each step matching the rhythm of my heartbeat.

"Whisky," he said, when I stopped in front of him with my arms folded across my chest. "We need to talk."

I felt like the wind had been knocked out of me.

"So help me God, Ward, if you call me that again, you'll need the aid of a wheelchair to leave this hospital."

Ward didn't smile, but his eyes lit up with amusement, and that was just as bad.

"We have nothin' to say to one another," I continued.

"I think we have a wee somethin' we need to discuss, dinnae you think?"

"Naw!" I growled. "I dinnae think anythin'. You and me . . . we never happened. It was a . . . it was a . . ."

"Mistake?" Ward finished, his lips twitching. "Is that the word you cannae bring yourself to say?"

"Shut your stupid face," I hissed. "It *was* a mistake, nothin' good came from it."

"Nothin' good *came* from it?" he repeated, tilting his head. "Really?"

The adolescent in Ward couldn't let the word "came" slip by unnoticed when we were discussing sex, and it made me roll my eyes.

"God save me from daft men."

"And save *me* from lyin' lasses."

I choked on air. "I have lied about *nothin*!"

"You just lied when you said what happened between us was a mistake!" he bit back, his voice low. "It's *wasnae* a mistake, it was the best decision I've ever made, and I *know* the only reason you're feelin' regret, guilt and embarrassment is because of Tara!"

I flinched at the mention of her name.

"So what?" I hissed, glancing around to make sure I'd attracted no attention before refocusing back on him. "I'm sick with myself. Fuckin' sick! You're goin' to marry this woman, and I—"

"We," Ward interrupted. "*Me. I* was the one who was engaged to her, not you. I was the one who was in a relationship, so this shame is mine to carry, not yours."

"But you arenae ashamed!"

"Naw," he agreed. "I'm not."

"You're fuckin' heartless! She's a *person*!"

"Oi." Jesse's voice suddenly got our attention as he left the viewing room, firmly closing the door behind him. "Either lower your voices or leave the bloody hallway. I could hear every word you both just said. The others are on their phones, or listenin' to earphones, so your secret is safe with me, but please, take this shite somewhere *private*."

"We're done speakin', Jesse." I said to him, but I was looking at Ward, my eyes narrowed to slits.

"Will you listen to me for once in your bloody life?" Ward demanded, reaching out and grabbing hold of my arm when I tried to walk away from him. "I'm not ashamed because I dinnae love her, and she doesnae love me! The entire relationship was a fuckin' sham."

My mouth dropped open, and for once, no words left my parted lips. Jesse stilled, and his gaze was on Ward, but his brother paid him no mind, he kept his focus entirely on me.

I began to tremble. "That woman—"

"Is vile. She's vile, and our entire relationship was a complete lie."

I felt like the floor had vanished from beneath me.

"What are you sayin'?" I demanded.

Ward ran a hand through his hair. "It's complicated."

"Well, it's a good thing I've got nothin' but time."

He blinked slowly, then his lips twitched, though I had no idea what he found so amusing.

"It was a lie," he continued. "It wasnae real."

"Why do you keep referrin' to everythin' in the past tense?"

"Because it *is* in the past," he answered. "I ended it."

I stumbled back, but his hold on my arm wouldn't let me go far. "Because of me? Because of what we did?"

"Naw," Ward answered. "Because the only reason I was with her was because she was blackmailin' me to marry her for a lot of money."

My mouth dropped open once more, and I was so happy when Jesse spoke, because I was speechless.

"What the fuck?" Jesse snapped. "What did she have on you?"

Ward shared a look with his brother, then glanced at me, but before he could say anything Jesse said, "Dinnae you even *think* of pushin' me to the side. I want to know, you can tell me and Erin together."

Ward jerked his head in a nod, but before he could speak, a voice behind us said, "Just the people I wanted to see."

The three of us turned to face the head doctor on Tommy's team. I tugged my arm free of Ward's hold and gripped his hand instead. We had to talk, to really talk, but right now I needed Ward, because the doctor looked like he had something to say about my brother, and it scared me half to death.

"Is everythin' okay with my brother?"

The doctor looked at me and smiled. "Everythin' is goin' well."

I almost sagged with relief.

"We're reducin' the drug that's keepin' him in his induced coma," he explained. "Since we reattached his skull fragment last week, there's been no increase of swellin'. In fact, there's been a two per cent decrease, which is good news. I've seen people conscious with the level of swellin' Mr Saunders has. Swellin' on the brain is always dangerous, but he isn't critical anymore, so that should enable everyone to take a deep breath."

Ward wrapped his arm around my waist, hugging me to his side, while Jesse's hand went to my shoulder and gave it a squeeze. I had to fist my hands to stop me from stepping closer and snuggling into Ward's embrace. It scared me that he was the person who I automatically sought for comfort; I didn't know what to do with that, not with what had happened between us and what he'd just revealed. I couldn't be close to him, not with the guilt of what we'd done hanging over my head.

"When can we go into his room?" I asked the doctor, forcing my attention back to my brother. "Is he still at risk of infection?"

"No to the latter," he answered. "His wound from surgery is healin' nicely, but it's always advised that you wash your hands and use the disinfectant gel provided before you enter a patient's room, just to be safe."

"We can go in and see him?" I asked, hopeful. "Can I hold his hand?"

The doctor smiled. "Aye, love."

Tears welled in my eyes, and my lower lip wobbled.

"Thank you," I gushed. "Thank you so much."

"For your brother's sake, keep talkin' at a low volume in his presence," the doctor said, his tone stern. "It could take days, weeks or months for him to wake up naturally now that we're reducin' the drugs that were keepin' him asleep, but we dinnae want to startle him. He's been in a silent room for fifteen days now, and sudden noise could hurt him. His brain is still healin', so let's not make it work any harder than it already is, okay?"

"Okay," the three of us said in unison.

"Could it really take months for him to wake up?" I asked then, my voice just louder than a whisper.

The doctor frowned. "Aye, it could."

I nodded in understanding, but I didn't miss the worry that played out on his face for all to see. I practically heard what he was thinking. It could take months for Tommy to wake up . . . but who was to say he would wake up at all?

CHAPTER TWENTY-ONE
WARD

I hung back outside of Tommy's room with my brother, as Erin, his mum and both of his aunties went in the room to see him up close for the first time in more than two weeks. I phoned Aiden and told him the good news about him being able to enter his dad's hospital room, and I had no doubt he would come barrelling up the hallway soon enough just to see Tommy.

I smiled at the thought.

"What the hell are you smilin' about?"

I schooled my features, then looked to my brother. My extremely pissed-off brother.

"I'm sorry I didnae tell you."

"Bullshit," Jesse hissed. "You've been engaged to that woman for more than a year, and *now* you're sorry you didnae tell me? You're just sorry you had to tell Erin, and that I happened to be standing right next to her when you did."

I gritted my teeth, but didn't deny the accusation.

"I'm sorry," I repeated. "Whether you believe me or not, I *am* sorry."

Jesse huffed and shook his head. "Is this why you didnae want me to meet her?"

"Aye. I knew you'd see through her, and I didnae want you to judge me for being with someone like her."

"How in the hell did you let yourself be roped into this situation?" Jesse asked. "What does she have on you? Naked pictures, a sex tape?"

I snorted. "Naw, nothin' like that."

"Then what?"

I rubbed my jaw with my hand, before letting my arm fall to my side. "Tommy."

Jesse frowned. "Tommy what?"

"Tara had Tommy on me."

My brother stared at me, and I watched as realisation dawned on him. "She knew Tommy co-created Friendzone?"

"Bingo," I said. "I told her about Tommy one night when I was drunk off my arse."

"What does the bitch want?"

"What do all gold-diggers want?"

"Money," Jesse spat.

"Aye, but Tara is clever. She wanted a lifetime of money, not one lump cash sum."

"Meanin'?"

"Meanin' a divorce settlement wouldn't have been good enough for her. She wanted a baby with me to secure monthly payments."

Jesse blanched. "That . . . that *tramp!*"

I snorted. "That's a nice way of puttin' it."

My brother scowled. "I'm fuckin' furious on your behalf."

"Thanks, man."

"What now?" he continued. "You said to Erin that you ended things with her. Arenae you worried she's goin' to expose you?"

"If you'd asked me that two weeks ago, my answer would have been a resoundin' *definitely.*"

"And now?"

"And now I'm not afraid anymore," I said with a smile.

"What's changed to make you feel that?"

I shrugged. "You, Erin, Tommy, Aiden . . . and a wee lass called Hannah."

"Hannah?"

"I'll tell you about her sometime."

Jesse eyed me, but nodded before turning his gaze back to Tommy's room.

"Women like Tara don't bow down easily, Ward."

"I know," I answered, "but I have Hope on my side, and she may as well be God."

Jesse snorted. "What are you goin' to do?"

"What I should have done a long time ago."

"Which is what?"

"Publicly credit Tommy Saunders as co-founder of Friendzone," I said with my head held high. "I'm done keepin' it a secret."

I was done keeping secrets altogether.

"And Jesse?"

"Aye?"

"When we're back at your place later," I said, ignoring my pounding heart. "I want to tell you somethin' that I should have told you years ago."

Jesse stared at me for a long moment, then nodded in response. Neither of us spoke for a few minutes, then out of the blue, Jesse turned my way and said, "Dad wants to see you."

I blinked. "He does?"

"Of course he bloody does." My brother scowled. "You're his son."

"Dinnae take my shock as an insult," I soothed. "I'm just surprised. He's never expressed an interest in seein' me before."

"You've never expressed an interest in seein' him either."

"Aye." I nodded. "You have me there."

"Since he and Mum arenae together anymore, I guess he has no reason not to see you."

I was surprised at how much I wanted to see my dad. I had buried my feelings for him deep down over the years, just to avoid the hurt of missing him, but I didn't have to do that anymore.

"I *definitely* want to see him."

A bright smile stretched across Jesse's face. "I can have him come by my flat tomorrow, if you want?"

"Aye," I nodded. "That sounds good to me, man."

Jesse clapped his hand against my shoulder, and I put my arm around *his* shoulders and said, "I'm not goin' back to London."

Jesse was silent for a minute, then without a word he put his arms around me, hugging me tightly. I wanted to laugh, to tease him for showing such emotion, but I couldn't. I knew if I spoke a word, it would sound choked. I returned his hug, and after a lot of manly back-slapping we separated, then we both laughed.

"I'm glad, man," he said, clearing his throat. "I've missed you."

"I've missed you too, little brother."

Jesse smiled, and it was only then that I noticed I had never seen him so happy before. It looked good on him.

"D'you think we should leave?" I asked as my eyes went to the viewing-room door. "This is a very private moment."

"Ward," Jesse said, rolling his eyes, "we're *family*."

I paused. "Am *I* though?"

"Aye. You are, and Erin knows that."

"Who says I was talkin' about Erin?"

Jesse snorted in response. We both went into the viewing room and watched as the others interacted with Tommy. Erin and her mum sobbed the entire time, and it was gut-wrenching. I knew they were happy tears because they could finally touch him, but it hurt me all the same to see her cry. I hated it, and I wanted to make it so she'd never cry again. A foolish wish, I knew, but it didn't stop me from wanting it all the same.

Time passed quickly, and hours later a pretty nurse popped her head into the room. She shot a brilliant smile Jesse's way, and when he sat upright upon seeing her, I raised an eyebrow, but he pointedly ignored me. His focus was entirely on the nurse.

"Hey, Jesse," she said shyly. "It's really late, and I have to be movin' your family on home now."

Jesse stood. "I'll tell them."

The nurse relaxed. "Thanks. I hate being the one to tell the family. I'd let everyone stay all the time if it were up to me."

She seemed to notice me then, and flushed crimson.

"Hi, Mr Buckley," she said. "I'm Louise Chambers."

She knew who I was outside of this hospital room; her behaviour told me so.

"Pleasure, Miss Chambers."

"Ward is my brother," Jesse said. "He's—"

"I know who he is, Jesse," Louise interrupted in a hushed whisper.

I grinned at Jesse's confusion and then instant annoyance.

"How'd you know him?"

"Because he's famous," Louise replied, her cheeks getting redder by the second.

"Oh." Jesse relaxed. "I forgot."

"You forgot that your brother was famous?"

"Aye." He shrugged. "You'd be surprised how often, too."

Louise giggled and my brother smiled. I looked between them, and stupidly found myself smiling, too.

"Do *you* two know each other?" I asked.

"Aye," Jesse answered, his eyes still on Louise. "We're goin' on a date on Friday."

"I have to get back to work," she said in a rush. "I'll see you tomorrow?"

"I'll be here."

Louise disappeared, and Jesse had a shit-eating grin on his face that made me snort.

"She seems nice."

"Nice?" Jesse chuckled. "She seems downright perfect to me."

"And you're goin' on a date?"

"Aye, and I'm shittin' myself. I've never been on a date somewhere fancy. McDonald's has always been my go-to place."

I laughed. "How old is she?"

"Twenty-nine . . . A grown woman who I suspect isn't interested in playin' games, so I have to be on the ball."

That surprised me.

"You're only twenty-five, you shouldn't want to settle down."

"Says who?" Jesse asked. "If Louise is the right woman, I'd be crazy not to. I'm not interested in a string of women and meaningless sex. I had enough of that in my teens and early twenties."

"You've a solid head on your shoulders then," I praised. "I couldn't decide if I liked redheads or brunettes when I was twenty-five."

Jesse glanced at me. "You arenae into either."

"And how do you know?"

"Because Erin has white hair."

Normally, my instinct would be to lie and say Jesse was wrong, but I shrugged my shoulders instead, knowing good and well that he was right. I didn't like black, brown or red hair. I only liked blonde hair, white-blonde hair to be exact, and only on one woman. Erin.

"I'm goin' to make a play for her."

"I figured you would," my brother said. "Just be smart about it. Dinnae try to take control of the situation, just explain yourself and then let Erin make her move."

I exhaled.

"I'll take your advice, little brother" – I glanced at Erin through the window pane – "because God knows, when she finally talks to me I'm goin' to need it."

CHAPTER TWENTY-TWO
WARD

I hadn't been able to sleep a wink.

After Jesse and I told Erin and the others that we had to leave the hospital, I knew she was in no place to talk to me. She was so exhausted from crying and fussing over Tommy that I wanted nothing more than for her to get a good night's sleep. Jesse was wiped too, and while I intended to speak to him like I'd promised, and tell him everything I'd bottled up about my past, I decided it could wait one more night after seeing him stumble into his room and collapse face first on to his bed, falling asleep in seconds.

The constant schedule we had all been upholding over the last couple of weeks was finally taking a toll on our bodies, but even though I felt like I could sleep for a year, my mind wouldn't shut off because of Erin. I kept thinking about what I was going to tell her about Tara, about my past, about everything, and it worked me into a nervous wreck. I found myself at the hospital at six in the morning, standing in the doorway of Tommy's room, staring at him.

I'd sent Keller a text letting him know where I was, and he replied instantly saying he'd check in with me in an hour, and every hour after that, like he always did when he wasn't next to me. I pocketed my phone, and with a deep breath I stepped into the room I had been observing for fifteen days. I slowly walked to the side of Tommy's bed, and sat down in the chair closest to him.

"Hey, Tommy," I said, clearing my throat. "It's me . . . Ward."

The steady rise and fall of my friend's chest was the only response I received.

"I know I'm probably the last person you'd want to see," I continued, "but I'm here for you, and your family, and I'm goin' to make things right between all of us . . . if I can."

Silence.

I rubbed my hand over my jaw.

"So much has happened since I last saw you, man," I said. "Some good, and some bad. Mostly good though, the empire we founded is thrivin' . . . but I guess you already know that, huh?"

Darkness fell over me.

"I'm sorry I lied," I said, looking down at Tommy's unmoving hand. "I'm sorry I pretended Friendzone was my idea when it was our baby . . . It belongs to the both of us. I'm so bloody sorry, man. I was bitter that you cut me out of your life, and I guess I did it as a way of gettin' back at you, but once the lie was told, I couldn't take it back."

I swallowed down bile.

"I guess I could have taken it back, but I was too much of a coward to face the repercussions of the lie I'd spun. I had to keep that perfect image; I couldnae let any cracks form because it was so fuckin' important to me . . . but after spendin' time here with my brother, with your sister . . . I cannae think of one good reason why it was in the first place."

I leaned forward, resting my elbows on my knees.

"Your sister" – I swallowed – "I care about her a hell of a lot, Thomas. I've messed things up with her, but I'm going to do everythin' I can to make it right, and pray she considers givin' me a chance, because I *want* to be with her. I've never wanted to just be with someone before, but in the short time I've spent with her and gotten to know her, I want her. I've never met anyone like her. She takes no bullshit, she doesnae give a shite that I've got money, she isnae interested in materialistic things, she only cares about her friends and family. She makes me feel those stupid butterflies in the pit of my stomach when she smiles . . . and when she laughs? I know a true glimpse of heaven. She's fuckin' perfect, man."

I could practically hear Tommy's "No shit, Sherlock".

"If you'd wake up and vouch for me," I joked, "I'd really appreciate it."

I looked at Tommy, and jumped with fright when I found his eyes open and locked on mine.

"Naw way," I stammered. "Naw fuckin' way!"

Tommy blinked a bunch of times, and almost instantly I burst into tears. I quickly got up, ran to the door and shouted, "Someone, help me!" Then I rushed back to Tommy's side. He made a grumbling noise, like he was try to speak, but even though his lips were now parted, words didn't come easy for him. I couldn't make a single one of them out.

"It's okay," I assured him, hitting the button for the nurse over and over. "Dinnae try and talk yet. Give yourself a moment to gather your bearings."

He tried to relax, but his eyes reflected how terrified he was.

"D'you know who I am?" I asked, my heart in my throat. "Blink twice if you do."

A few seconds went by, and when my friend blinked twice in rapid succession, my heart just about burst with relief.

"Fuck, Tommy," I rasped. "You have no idea how happy I am."

He stared up at me with wild, panicked eyes.

"You were in a car accident," I quickly explained. "A man ran a red light, and hit you when you were on your way to get Erin from work."

The confusion that replaced the panic in his eyes was like a sucker punch to the gut.

"It's okay if you dinnae remember," I said with a smile to reassure him. "Everythin' will come back to you in time, there's no rush. Resting will aid that."

He still stared at me, and I saw the unspoken question burn in his gaze.

What are you doin' here?

"I'm not goin' anywhere, man," I said to him, wiping my cheek free of tears. "We've a lot of shite to hash out, but I'm not goin' anywhere. I promise. Don't worry about anythin'. I'm here, and I'll take care of everyone until you're back on your feet."

A nurse hurried into the room, followed by a doctor I'd never seen before.

"Holy God," the doctor said as he came to Tommy's side. "He's awake."

Hell fuckin' yeah he's awake.

I gnawed on my fingernails as the doctors performed a bunch of random tests that involved a small light flicking back and forth in his eyes, and questions that Tommy could only reply to through blinking. I fumbled for my phone, but the only number I could remember was my brother's. I could have gone into my phonebook and found Erin, Jennifer or Emma's number, but I dialled Jesse's number without thinking.

"Hello," he answered groggily.

"Get everyone, and get your arse to the hospital. Now."

"Is he okay?"

"Better than okay," I practically squealed. "Tommy is *awake!*"

"Oh my fuckin' God."

"Get Erin, his mum, Aiden, his aunties. Ring Keller . . . and just get here."

"We'll be there."

Jesse hung up on me, just as Dr Liddle – the head doctor from Tommy's team – entered the room.

"I was just about to end my shift when I got a hell of an excitin' call," he announced with a smile.

I placed my hand on his shoulder. "I cannae believe he's awake."

"Me either, kid," he replied. "It's not unusual though, I've seen people awaken hours after we lift the drugs keeping them in a coma, and I've seen others not wake up for weeks. It depends on the person and their brain, really."

"He isnae talkin'," I said as the doctor moved to the other side of Tommy.

"Not talkin' right away is no cause for worry," he replied. "His brain has been through an awful lot, and it's still healin'. Talkin' may take a while to come back to him."

"How does he look?" I asked, noticing Tommy's eyelids seemed to be getting heavy, like he was going back to sleep.

"A lot better than I expected for someone who had as much swellin' as he initially did," the doctor admitted. "He's alert and aware of his surroundings, even though talking is difficult for him right now. That's incredible considerin' the injuries he sustained, Mr Buckley. He's fifteen days post-op, and to be already awake and alert is incredible."

"You have no idea how happy I am to hear you say that."

Tommy closed his eyes, and I tensed.

"Dinnae worry," the doctor said to me. "He'll stay awake for longer and longer periods each time. He still needs an abundance of rest, so sleepin' as much as he can is a good thing. I know it's hard for your family when you've watched him do nothin' but sleep these past couple of weeks, but rest is Mr Saunders's best friend right now."

Then, just as quickly as the staff appeared, they left the room, and once again I was alone with a sleeping Tommy. I checked my phone and noted the time, and checked my call log to Jesse. I had called him twenty minutes ago, and with everyone rushing, they should have gotten here by—

"Ward!"

I jolted with surprise, then quickly exited Tommy's room and looked to my right. I started walking towards Erin . . . who was sprinting down the hallway directly for me.

"He's fallen back asleep right now," I called, "but the doctor said he'll wake up again soon, and hopefully he'll stay awake a little bit longer."

I was surprised when Erin didn't slow down; she continued to barrel towards me, and I opened my arms just in time to catch her as she jumped into them and wrapped her limbs around me. She cried with delight, and hugged me so tightly she almost cut off my oxygen supply, but did I mind? Not one fucking bit.

"He woke up," she sobbed into my neck.

Over her shoulder, the rest of the tribe came running around the corner, all smiles and tears.

I kissed the side of Erin's head and said, "He woke up, Whisky."

I had never been happier to say any words to another person in my entire life.

CHAPTER TWENTY-THREE

ERIN

"He's not goin' to open his eyes if you keep starin' at him, Erin."

I looked at my auntie and felt myself blush. "I dinnae want to miss it. I want to see his eyes open so I know this isn't all just a crazy dream."

"I know, love," Auntie Emma said as she reached over and squeezed my hand. "But you heard what Ward said, and what the doctors said — he was awake, even if it was only for a few minutes. He seemed to know who Ward was, and understood what had happened to him. That's all simply incredible, hon."

"He's a miracle," I answered, and looked at my brother. "A real-life miracle."

There was no other explanation for it. The odds had been completely stacked against Tommy from the moment his car was struck, and he had somehow survived the accident and surgery when I knew the doctors thought his chances were slim. And not only that, he'd woken up, and not long after they'd stopped the drugs that kept him in his coma, too. I couldn't believe it, it felt like everything had happened so fast but so slow at the same time.

I wasn't taking any moment for granted, because I knew just how quickly a situation could change.

"Where's Auntie Jennifer?"

"She took Aiden and your mum to breakfast."

I nodded, then glanced around the room. "And Ward and Jesse?"

"In the viewin' room."

I glanced at the windowpane, and saw the two brothers sitting inside the viewing room, talking and laughing.

"That's a pretty sight," I said, out loud.

Auntie Emma chuckled. "Aye, it is."

I looked back to my brother. "I wonder what he'll think of Ward being back."

"What do *you* think of Ward being back?"

I sighed. "I cannae answer. I'm so confused about him right now."

"Women are usually in a permanent state of confusion over men."

"Be happy you're gay then."

My auntie laughed, and it brought a smile to my face. At the same moment, Tommy groaned. Instantly I was hovering over him, all up in his face when I knew I should be giving him space. I heard footsteps and movement indicating Ward and Jesse hustling into the room. It was hard to step back, but after a few seconds, when I felt hands grip my waist and gently pull me away, I didn't fight them.

"He groaned," I said. "I heard him."

"Let him breathe," Ward chuckled from behind me, tugging me against him. "He'll probably scream if he opens his eyes and sees you nose to nose with him."

I laughed and cried at the same time.

Ward turned me towards him and wrapped his arms around me. Since I got to the hospital I had been a mess of emotions: I was smiling and laughing once second, then crying the next. I was happy, I knew that much. I was still scared for my brother, and worried out of my mind for his future, but we finally had some good news regarding him, and it felt good. Another thing that felt good was being wrapped in Ward's embrace.

"Sorry," I sniffled, pushing away from him gently. "I dinnae mean to cry all over you."

"D'you see me complainin'?"

"Naw."

"Then dinnae apologise."

"Okay."

I was aware of my auntie's eyes – and Jesse's – on me, so I turned back to Tommy just in time to see his eyes flutter. I held my breath, and so did everyone else. Then, the thing I had been praying for every single day came true. Tommy slowly opened his eyes.

It wasn't like anything from a film where a person awakes from their coma and it's all sunshine and rainbows. It took ten minutes for Tommy to be able to keep his eyelids lifted, and when he managed to focus, he was confused just like he had been with Ward.

Louise, Jesse's nurse, came in and checked his vitals, and everything was looking good. Once she had Tommy's attention, she asked him to wiggle his toes and fingers. He did both. She pressed all over his body asking "Can you feel this?" and he grunted in response. The grunting was a step up from the blinking, and it was such amazing progress so early on after waking up that I could do nothing but cry as I witnessed it.

He tried talking, but it hadn't come back to him yet, and this frustrated him. I could see it in his eyes. Louise was recording all her findings on the clipboard that was at the bottom of Tommy's bed. We were all so focused on her, and Tommy, that we missed the moment Aiden entered the room.

"Dad!" he gasped.

Tommy jerked a little, his eyes darting to Aiden as his son came rushing at him. Tommy grunted when Aiden leaned over him and hugged him tightly. My nephew sobbed, and before I could move to his side to soothe him, my mum stepped in to comfort him. When Aiden relaxed, Mum leaned over and kissed Tommy's face, tears on her cheeks, too. Tommy grunted again and tried to speak, but our mum touched his cheek.

"It'll come back," she told him, her thumb brushing the skin under his eye. "Dinnae worry."

He seemed to relax, and the sight touched my heart. It had been a long time since I'd seen my mum able to relax Tommy as only a mother could, and it gave me true hope that she would find her way back to us again. And like I'd promised, I'd be there to help her every step of the way.

"What's wrong with him?" Aiden worriedly asked the room as Tommy's eyes slowly drifted shut.

My brother fought the sleep that was wrapping itself around him, but evidently he lost.

"He needs plenty of rest," Auntie Emma answered. "When he's awake, he won't be for very long because his brain is tired. He'll get stronger with each passin' day, but your dad needs his rest, okay?"

Aiden nodded, then leaned down, kissed his dad's cheek and whispered something in his ear. Auntie Jennifer moved to Auntie Emma's side and kissed and hugged her when she saw her tears. Everyone, apart from the Buckley brothers, was crying, but no one seemed to mind a single bit.

"Your eyes are goin' to be killin' you all later," Jesse commented, making us laugh.

I turned back into Ward and hugged him. I knew we had to talk, and I probably wouldn't like hearing what he had to say, but for the moment there was nowhere else I'd rather be than wrapped up in his arms.

And that was exactly what the next four days consisted of. When I wasn't rushing through my shifts now that I'd had to return to work, I was sitting in Tommy's hospital room with Ward's arms around me.

It seemed that while we knew we had to talk, we'd silently agreed that it would happen when it felt right. I hadn't talked to Ward all that much since Tommy had woken up, even though I spent an incredible amount of time sitting on his lap and in his embrace. I had heard from chatter between him and his brother that he had been hanging out with his dad. I was happy that he was mending that relationship, because I knew that was one fence Ward would forever regret not mending if he left things unspoken.

On the nineteenth day after Tommy's accident, and four days after he'd initially woke up, my brother did something that surprised everyone, even himself. He found his voice. It was seven in the evening, and the only people in Tommy's room were Ward, Jesse and me. We all stared at Tommy when he opened his eyes, just like we had every day since he'd woken up, and when he focused on us and a small grin curved the corner of his mouth, my heart pounded against my chest.

"It's . . . creepy," he rasped. "When I open . . . my eyes . . . and you're starin' . . . at me."

The brothers laughed, while I cried, of course. I got Tommy some water, and watched as he carefully took sips, cherishing the cool liquid as it slid down his throat. He cleared half of the plastic cup before he nudged for me to move it away.

"Dinnae cry, kid," he said to me.

His voice didn't sound like his own, it sounded like he had been screaming for hours and lost it, and what remained was a raspy reflection. That was to be expected though, after him not speaking for close to three weeks.

"I've never been so scared in my life, Tommy," I said, putting the water to the side. "I've been terrified."

He didn't have full mobility of his body yet, but when I gripped his hand, he squeezed my fingers.

"It's . . . okay."

"I'm so happy you're awake," I gushed. "We've been starin' at you for ages."

Tommy smiled slightly, then winced in pain.

"My . . . legs," he rasped.

"They were both broken," I said, explaining everything to him. "They repaired them with surgery; the bones were fixed with metal screws. You had a punctured lung they fixed, so if it hurts to breathe, that's why."

My brother stared at me. "And what . . . about my . . . head?"

"Your head?"

"I can feel . . . the bandage, Erin. It . . . hurts."

My heart broke for him. "Your brain was badly swollen, so they performed a surgery to take away a piece of your skull to let your brain have room to breathe, so to speak. The swellin' decreased, and it's now back in place. That was two weeks ago. They reduced the drugs keeping you in your coma, and you woke up the next day. You've been out of it since then, but you're awake."

I still couldn't believe it. I knew that the doctors said every person's body reacted differently, but I'd fully suspected Tommy would be in a coma for a long time. I hadn't thought he'd wake up so soon, but I really shouldn't have been surprised, because he was a fighter. He always had been.

"That's a lot . . . to take in."

"Dinnae stress," I urged. "Just relax and let it be."

Tommy grunted, then looked to the Buckley brothers.

"I'm surprised you're . . . here," Tommy said to Ward.

Ward nodded. "I'm sure you are, man."

My brother flicked his gaze to me. "I want . . . to talk to . . . you alone."

"Of course," I said, and looked to the brothers. "Can you excuse us for a few minutes?"

Jesse got up right away and left the room. Ward lingered.

"Ward . . ." I frowned. "Please leave."

He didn't move.

"Ward," I growled. "Get out before I shove my foot up your arse!"

He sighed, but dragged himself to his feet, walked out of the room and closed the door behind him.

"Sorry about that," I said to my brother, turning back to him. "I dinnae ken what his problem is."

Tommy stared at me.

"What?"

"You spoke to . . . Ward," he said slowly, "and you . . . didnae kill him."

I gave him some more water and grinned. "You should have seen me the night of your accident when he showed up. I just about ripped him a new arsehole. I've laid into him a good few times since then."

Tommy smiled slightly. "I can . . . imagine."

"We're on neutral ground now, though," I said with a shrug. "I didnae want to waste my energy fightin' with him when you were in here fightin' for your life."

"Good," Tommy said.

"Is it good?" I questioned. "Is it good that we're neutral? Because I fought hard against him for the first few days. I defended you and what he did to you."

"Listen to me," Tommy said sternly.

I clamped my mouth shut.

"I love how you . . . stuck up for me with Ward . . . about what happened, but Erin . . . I never needed Friendzone."

My mouth fell open.

"You're lyin'," I accused. "It was your dream."

"*Was* my . . . dream," he said softly. "It was, once . . . upon a time, but I've had years . . . to think about it."

"And what conclusion did you come to?"

"That being a father . . . to Aiden in every . . . capacity was more important . . . and became my new dream."

"But Tommy—"

"Naw buts, kid," he said, breathing heavily. "That's how it is . . . I never needed Friendzone . . . Not like Ward did."

"You needed the money aspect of it! That money would have—"

"It would have . . . what?" Tommy interrupted, his voice gruff. "It wouldn't have helped Mum . . . with her alcohol addiction . . . It would have only fuelled it. It wouldn't have given me . . . custody of Aiden . . . It would only mean I had to give Lucy more money to spend on herself."

Out of breath, Tommy took a whole minute of inhaling and exhaling before he spoke again.

"It wouldnae have done . . . anythin' worth a shite to what . . . is worth somethin' in my life. Sure, we would . . . have been livin' like kings and queens . . . but we'd still be miserable with the hardship . . . we'd have to endure like we are now, and our lives wouldn't be . . . private. Everyone would know what . . . we've tried every day to hide for years . . . about Mum."

I didn't know what to say in response, so I kept quiet as I processed Tommy's words. He was breathless, and it took him a few more minutes before he could speak again.

"I dinnae need to reap . . . the rewards of Friendzone to be . . . successful, Erin. I helped Ward . . . write the program for it . . . I helped create it, and it's . . . successful, so that makes me successful. I dinnae give . . . a shite who knows about it . . . Once I know it, that's all that matters."

I wiped away the surprised tears that fell on to my cheeks.

"I understand that, and trust me when I say that's hard to admit."

"Ward beats himself up . . . enough about it, Erin. I dinnae need to . . . do anythin' to make him feel horrible . . . I can see it in his eyes when he looks at me. A guilty . . . conscience needs no accuser."

"How do you know he feels guilty?" I demanded.

"That's why he keeps . . . sendin' me cheques," Tommy replied. "He knows how I helped . . . him with the foundation of his empire . . . and sendin' me money . . . is his way of acknowledgin' my hand in it."

I looked down to my fingers as they knotted around one another.

"You think I'm so forgivin' . . . but I wasnae always so welco-min' . . . with the thought of Ward, let alone his presence," Tommy mused. "For a while I was bitter . . . and I hated Ward for his failure to credit me. I felt like . . . I was part of somethin' that became so huge . . . and I gained nothin' from it. Then I realised just . . . because no one knows about it . . . doesnae mean Ward and I don't know."

"Or me," I added quietly.

Tommy's lips quirked. "Or you."

I leaned my head against the back of the chair.

"He probably won't come back," I murmured. "You heard me, I threatened to put my foot up his arse. He probably won't show his face again, he's probably scared of me now and run off back to London."

Tommy's sudden pained groan grabbed my attention, and in seconds I was by his side.

"Oh God," I panicked. "I'll get the nurse."

I made a move to turn, but his hand gripped mine.

"Wait," he rasped. "Give me . . . a second."

I gave him sixty.

When he relaxed enough to open his eyes and not scrunch his face up in pain, he focused on me.

"I laughed," he rasped. "It hurt more than . . . I thought it would."

I stared down at him.

"What the hell were you laughin' at?"

Tommy smiled, and laughed a little more, only to then quickly wince in pain. I'd had enough of him being in pain when he didn't need to be, so I reached over and pressed the morphine button, and watched as it automatically pushed the medicine through the IV and into Tommy's vein. Seconds passed by, and his relaxed hum relaxed me.

"Feel better?" I asked, my eyes roaming over his face.

He nodded, lazily.

"I was laughin' . . . at you," he said, blinking his eyes slowly. "Just about you . . . runnin' Ward off, and him being scared of you."

I frowned. "Why is that funny?"

"He's a foot taller than you . . . about four stone heavier, and deals with men . . . a mite meaner than you could ever be on a daily basis. I dinnae think . . . you could scare him very much."

"You're wrong, brother," a voice spoke from behind me. "I feared for my balls for at *least* ten seconds."

Tommy laughed and closed his eyes. The morphine became too much for him, and he fell asleep with a smile on his face. With a small smile on my own face, I leaned in and kissed his cheek.

Get better soon for me, big brother.

"I thought I told you to get lost," I said to Ward without turning around.

"You did," Ward agreed. "I just didnae listen."

I sighed, and didn't respond to him.

"Are you angry that he doesnae hate me?"

He was listening to my and Tommy's conversation, and I wasn't surprised in the slightest.

"Aye," I answered instantly, then my shoulders slumped. "Naw. I mean, maybe. I dinnae ken, Ward. A lot is buzzin' round inside my head right now."

"Want to talk about it?" he asked.

"We have to, but I'm too tired, and too scared to do it right now."

"Why scared?"

"Because what if what you have to say pushes me away from you? Or what if . . ."

"What if what?"

"What if it pulls me closer to you?"

Ward hunkered down in front of me. "Would that be such a bad thing?"

"I dinnae ken," I answered. "It falls into the 'scared shitless' category."

Ward smiled at me, and the urge to kiss him was strong.

"Dinnae smile at me," I warned.

He raised an eyebrow. "Why?"

"'Cause I wanna kiss you when you do."

Any playfulness vanished from Ward's demeanour, and he leaned his head closer to mine and smiled wide, clearly trying to entice a kiss from me. I laughed, and pushed his face away with my hand.

"You're daft."

"Maybe," he mused. "But I'll be daft every day if it'll make you laugh."

I looked into his eyes, and found that my body relaxed the longer I gazed into them.

"Okay." I nodded.

"Okay what?"

"Let's talk." I answered. "I'm never goin' to be ready for it, not really, so there's no point in makin' excuses. Let's talk."

Ward stood and took my hand. "Let's go into the viewin' room. Jesse will come in here and sit with Tommy."

As we walked into the viewing room, Jesse passed us and headed into Tommy's room without a word, and I wondered if he knew Ward and I were about to have a serious conversation.

"Where do we start?" Ward asked.

"Tara," I answered, swallowing down bile. "I dinnae want to talk about my brother, or anythin' else. Just Tara, and what you were gettin' at in the corridor when you came back from London over the weekend."

Ward nodded his head slowly. "I'm not engaged to her anymore."

My heart stopped.

"Did you tell her what we did?"

"Naw," he answered. "I didnae see her, not in person."

My mouth dropped open.

"Please." Ward held up a finger, silencing me. "Dinnae judge me, just let me talk."

I closed my mouth, and gestured with my hand for him to get back to talking.

"Tara was blackmailin' me to marry her," Ward continued. "I had an agreement with her that if she kept quiet, then I'd marry her, and when we eventually divorced she'd get a large sum of money. That wasnae enough for her. She wanted to have a baby to receive monthly payments from me. She wanted to ensure that the money never dried up, and she knew if she had a baby by me that I'd never abandon my child, and she'd get what she wanted."

My gut twisted in knots.

"I agreed to it all because I was a coward, and didnae want the world to know of a lie I'd created out of anger."

"What was the lie?" I asked. "The one Tara knew?"

"Tommy," he answered. "It was all about Tommy. I was really drunk one night and told her about Tommy and she used it against me."

"You would let a woman blackmail you into a sham marriage . . . just to avoid tellin' the world that Tommy is the co-founder of Friendzone?" I asked, my body beginning to shake. "Are you fuckin' *jokin'* me?"

"Dinnae get mad," Ward pleaded. "I *was* goin' to let her blackmail me, but that was before I came back here. Before I got to know everyone again – got to know *you* again."

"What does that even mean?"

"It means," Ward stressed, "that you've made me a better person, a braver person, someone who doesnae need to hide behind a fictitious image."

I didn't speak.

"I'm done keepin' shite to myself, Erin," Ward continued. "Tara cannae blackmail me anymore, because as of today, the world knows that Friendzone isnae just mine to claim. She's lost her only piece of leverage and cannae expose me anymore . . . I did that to myself."

My breath caught. "What?"

"Since I returned from London, I've been writin' an announcement, tryin' to get the wordin' just right," Ward said as he took out his phone and handed it to me. "Just read it for yourself."

With shaking hands, I took Ward's phone and looked at the words on the screen.

To whom it may concern,

I am the biggest fraud that I know. For eleven years, the last seven or so in the spotlight, I have lived a lie, a lie I have spun to the public, and added to over the years. No, I'm not gay, I haven't made a sex tape that's been leaked, and I definitely don't have a secret love child. What I do have is an ex-fiancée who was blackmailing me into a marriage I didn't want, for money. A lot of money. What did she have on me, you may ask? She had a coward by the throat, to be blunt.

You see, in an act of bitterness, I told the world that I created Friendzone all by myself, when that is not true. My childhood best friend, my brother-in-arms, dreamed up Friendzone with me. Thomas Saunders is just as responsible for Friendzone being a reality as I am. It's taken nearly losing Tommy for me to re-evaluate everything in my life, and to come out with the truth.

To be frank, I'm tired of lying, I'm tired of keeping this piece of poison to myself.

I know this story will be spun a thousand different ways within the press, but if you're going to take away anything from this announcement it should be that Friendzone has two founders: Thomas Saunders and Ward Buckley. And also, that just because someone appears to have it all does not mean they do. I have all the money in the world, I have all the success I could ever have dreamed of, and I'm hollow inside.

Thanks for reading,
Ward

I looked up from Ward's phone and stared into his eyes. He had done the very thing I had always wished he would do, and my heart adored him for it. I swallowed as I looked at him, noting that my feelings for him were growing by the minute.

"You arenae hollow inside," I told him. "You're sweet, carin' and compassionate. Dinnae sell yourself short ever again, d'you hear me?"

Ward's Adam's apple bobbed as he swallowed.

"Thank you," I said to him. "Thank you for being honest."

His hands gripped my thighs. "It was long overdue, love."

"Be that as it may," I sniffled. "Thank you."

Ward tucked his phone back into his trousers when I handed it back to him, his eyes never once leaving mine. "The press are havin' a field day with the announcement. I'm being dragged by some people as being a liar and a cheat, and praised by others for being brave and honest. Stocks have risen in the company because of the worldwide media attention, and my name has received more Google hits in the past six hours that ever before . . . or so Hope tells me."

I shook my head. "So you and Tara are really done?"

"We're really done."

"What made you break it off from her?"

"Apart from her blackmailin' me to marry her and father her child?"

I snorted. "Aye."

Ward reached out and brushed his thumb over my cheek.

"When I thought of Tara, I knew that she wasn't the woman I wanted to spend the rest of my life with."

I swallowed. "Oh really?"

"Really."

I licked my lips. "Are you interested in datin' again, or is it way too soon to broach the subject?"

Ward's lips twitched as he leaned his head closer to mine. "I'll only date again on one condition."

"What is it?" I asked breathlessly.

"That *you* be the last woman I date."

I pressed my lips against Ward's and kissed him. He pulled me from my seat and on to his lap and deepened it. My fingers were tangled in his hair, and my lips throbbed with the force of his.

"Is this," he said against my mouth, "your answer?"

"What d'you think?" I asked, swiping my tongue along his lower lip.

"I think," Ward groaned, "that you should answer my question with words so there are no misunderstandings between us."

I smiled against his lips.

"Aye, sweetheart," I hummed, "I accept your condition."

"You do?"

I brushed the tip of my nose against Ward's, my heart pounding erratically.

"Aye," I hummed. "I do."

CHAPTER TWENTY-FOUR
WARD

"Stop smilin'."

I shoved my brother as we walked up the stairs of his apartment complex.

"I cannae help it," I answered. "Fuck, I'm just really happy."

"I'm happy *for* you, man." Jesse beamed. "You and Erin? I never would have seen it comin', but you're both good together."

"We're takin' things really slow."

"What does that mean?"

"That we take our time gettin' to know one another more," I answered. "That we do a whole lot of talkin' and make sure we dinnae keep secrets from one another. I dinnae want to mess this up."

"Aye," Jesse snorted. "Naw secrets is a good place to start."

"She's my girlfriend," I said with a shit-eating grin. "My *girlfriend*. This was not how I was expectin' my day to end."

Jesse snickered, then did a little dance on the spot that made me laugh.

"What are you doin'?" I said.

"*Fuck*," he groaned. "I left my phone in Tommy's hospital room."

"I'll call Keller and ask him—"

"Nae chance. I'm not havin' him go back to the hospital and get it for me. It's fifteen minutes away, about seven if I jog there."

"Offski," I snorted, shooing him away. "There's no way in hell I'm runnin' anywhere, I need a year's worth of sleep."

"Lazy bastard," Jesse said, jabbing me in the ribs as he tossed me his keys and headed back down the stairs.

I shook my head, smiling, and continued up toward the apartment.

"Dad is stoppin' by, he wants to look at the blueprints for the hotel once more," Jesse shouted, his voice echoing up the stairwell. "He has an idea he thinks I can benefit from."

I sighed, rested my arm on the stair rail and looked down.

"Does that mean I've to put the kettle on?"

"There's bottles of beer in the fridge, pussy."

I chuckled and continued up the stairs, opening Jesse's door when I was close enough to do so. The second I entered the apartment and closed the door behind me, I knew something wasn't quite right. The lights were on, and so was the television in the sitting room.

"Hello?" I shouted. "Who's here?"

"Who's here?" a voice that plagued my dreams called from the kitchen. "Who d'you think, son?"

My legs felt like chains were attached to them, and each step I took towards the kitchen felt like climbing up a ninety-degree hill. I swallowed down bile as I reached the kitchen doorway and stared into the room. The hairs on the nape of my neck stood up, and my heart pounded against me as I looked at her.

My stepmother.

My abuser.

"What are *you* doin' here?"

Debbie Buckley stopped dead in her tracks when she saw me in the doorway. I could see the shock on her face, and I knew she'd thought I was Jesse.

"What are *you* doin' here?" she snapped back.

I swallowed. "I'm stayin' with Jesse, and I have done for the last three weeks."

"Why?" Debbie demanded. "Why are you back here at all?"

"Be-because," I stammered. "Tommy was in a car accident."

Debbie gasped like it was the worst thing she'd ever heard.

"Is he okay?"

"Naw," I answered. "He's alive, but he's very injured."

Debbie made the sign of the cross, clasped her hands together, bowed her head and began to pray. I stared at her, fear and disgust all rolling through me at the same time. My heart thumped against my chest, and my fingers flexed back and forth. The longer I stared at Debbie, the angrier I got.

"You need to leave," I told her.

Her brown eyes opened. "Excuse me?"

"I said" – I cleared my throat – "that you need to leave. Right now."

"How dare you," she snarled. "This is my son's home."

"He hasnae spoken to you in months, not since you hurt our dad and he kicked you out," I said, my eyes narrowed. "How did you get in here?"

"I've a key."

"Leave it on the table and get out."

"Naw," she bit out. "I'm not goin' anywhere."

"I'm tellin' Jesse everythin' when he gets home, so trust me, you *need* to leave. He's furious about you hittin' our dad, and once he finds out what you did to me . . . Just leave."

Debbie stared at me, and the rage I felt radiate from her would have once terrified me, but not anymore.

"You're selfish," she spat. "You always have been, and you always will be."

"Selfish?" I repeated. "*I'm* selfish?"

"Yeah, you are."

"That is fuckin' bullshit," I bellowed.

"You call cuttin' your family out of your life to live large anythin' but selfish?"

I almost fell over with shock.

"I wasnae cuttin' my family out, I was cuttin' *you* out!" I shouted. "I wasnae leavin' my family, I was runnin' as far away from *you* as I could get!"

"Bullshit," she snapped. "You ran away to live your rags-to-riches lifestyle."

"A lifestyle I'm sure you hated that you couldnae be a part of."

Debbie glared at me.

"You hate it," I growled. "You hate that I'm successful, and have made somethin' of myself. Just like you hated when I hit my teens and you couldnae physically abuse me anymore, but you upped your game with the mental and emotional abuse though, right?"

"I dinnae ken what you're talkin' about."

"Dinnae lie!" I screamed. "Dinnae pretend you didnae hurt me!"

Debbie refused to look me in the eye, or in my direction at all.

"You're delusional," she continued. "You always make up silly stories."

"Did I make them up before or after you sexually abused me?"

Silence.

"Did I make up the blood on my bed sheets that you made sure to wash before my dad saw the evidence? Did I make up the teeth marks on my penis? Did I make up the bruises on my neck and shoulders because you forced me to put my mouth on you? Did I make up all of that, Debbie?"

She spun, her eyes on mine, and pure rage filled them.

"I never touched you!"

"You touched me in ways that haunted me for years. But no more," I said, my eyes narrowing. "I'm not givin' you any more power, not even in my head. You're beneath me. You're nothin'. You always have been, and you always will be. You're a paedophile, an abuser, a low-life monster. That's *it*."

"You better apologise for those accusations right now or—"

"I make *no* apologies," I said angrily. "Not a single one. I did nothin' wrong, and no matter what you say or do to me, it will never change that. I did nothin' wrong. *You* did."

"Get out," Debbie spat. "Get out of this house, you're causin' nothin' but trouble."

"I'm being brave," I swallowed, lifting my chin. "I'm confrontin' my demon."

"Your demon?" Debbie scoffed, swatting her hand in the air. "I'm not a demon."

"You're one of many on this earth."

Debbie looked me up and down, her lip curled up in a snarl.

"You may be grown, but you'll always be the snot-nosed little shite who wouldnae get out of my life!"

"Naw," I said, coolly, "I'm a reflection of all the strength I had to use to survive you!"

Debbie stiffened. "I always hated you. You were never mine. Jesse is my flesh and blood, but you . . . I did what I did because you were *always* there!"

Hearing her admit that she'd hurt me caused a lump to get stuck in my throat.

"You knew my dad had a son when you agreed to marry him . . . You *knew*!"

"I did," she said. "I just didnae realise how much of a disease you would be."

My stomach rolled.

"I'm a nightmare for people like you," I said, my hands trembling. "I'm usin' what you did to me and lettin' it fuel me. I'm goin' to use my newfound courage and I'm goin' be the monster that abusers fear. I willnae let you break me anymore, I willnae let those memories cut me down. I swear to God, I'll haunt you before you'll *ever* haunt me again."

Debbie didn't say a word in response, and it took me a moment to realise that she wasn't looking at me. Instead, she was staring over my shoulder. I turned around, and the moment I saw grey eyes and white hair, my world stopped spinning.

"Erin," I said, my breath fleeing me a second later.

When I realised she had heard what I'd said, and what Debbie had said, about . . . about everything, a weight fell on to my chest and I found it hard to breathe. I fought to hold on to my courage, but fear worked hard to take hold of me. I balled my hands into fists and fought back. All the years I had spent hiding my past, the image I had worked so hard to protect, was shattered. The one person I never wanted to know my darkest secret had heard about it in explicit detail.

And I didn't care.

If Erin wanted me in her life then it was going to be with all of me . . . or not at all.

CHAPTER TWENTY-FIVE
ERIN

Rage flowed through my veins like wildfire. My heart pounded against my chest, and there was a sickness in the pit of my stomach that I knew would never fully go away. After Keller had dropped Jesse and Ward off at Jesse's apartment building, I'd thought of Ward constantly on the drive home. I'd asked my aunties to get Mum settled because I wanted to speak to Ward. I didn't really have to speak to him about anything, I just wanted to see him. After everything we'd talked about at the hospital, after agreeing to start a relationship, I really wanted to be around him.

We were in such a good place right now, and I wanted to experience him in the new light I saw him in.

After Keller drove back to Jesse's apartment building, and dropped me off, I gave myself a pep talk as I walked up the stairwell. I reminded myself that I didn't need an excuse to see Ward, and that I knew he would be happy to see me. I repeated that, over and over in my mind, until I came to a stop outside Jesse's apartment, and found the door wide open and heard shouting inside.

I stood rooted to the spot outside and listened as Ward and Debbie Buckley argued, and what was revealed made me feel like I'd been kicked in the stomach a million times. I gripped on to the door panel to keep myself upright. Everything they spoke of ran through my mind, and like clockwork, all the times Ward said he couldn't stay in Scotland because of *her*, and that he was running away from something, made perfect sense.

He was running away from the woman who'd abused him.

Ward, I thought. *He was abused.*

I never thought it was possible to feel such anguish, but I did. I hurt for Ward, God knows that the pain I felt for him was real . . . but so was the rage that settled in the centre of my chest like a gigantic weight. I put one foot in front of the other and entered the apartment. I walked towards the kitchen, and stepped up behind Ward, who was only a few feet inside the room. I saw the moment Debbie locked her gaze on me, and when pure shock settled in her haunting eyes, I wanted to rip them from her body.

Her silence drew Ward's notice, and when he looked around and clapped his eyes on me, fear instantly filled them. I wanted to go to him, to assure him he had nothing to fear, not anymore, but I couldn't. I returned my attention to Debbie, and with a sudden sensation of numbness filling me, I walked towards her, brushing by Ward who was breathing heavily.

"Erin, love, what you heard wasnae—"

My fist cut Debbie off.

I reeled my arm back, balled my hand into a tight fist and swung. My hand connected with her cheek, but the power I put behind it forced my hand to slide over her cheek and slam into her nose. A sickening crack sounded, and Debbie screamed as she fell to the floor.

"You . . . you . . . you broke my nose!"

I was shaking, and before I realised that I was reaching for Debbie again, arms came around me, preventing me from getting my hands on her. I needed to hurt her, I needed to make her suffer for what she had done. Nothing short of reducing her to a pile of bloody limbs on the floor would satisfy me.

"Let me go," I told Ward, my voice shockingly calm. "I'm goin' to kill her."

I was . . . I was going to kill her, if only Ward gave me the chance.

His arms tightened. "She's not worth it, love."

I struggled in his hold. "It is to me."

Ward hugged me against his body, and he didn't let me go. When the rage subsided, a raw pain struck and I burst into sobs. I turned in his arms and wrapped myself around him so tightly I knew he found it hard to breathe. Then I pulled his face down to mine and I kissed him all over.

"You're perfect," I told him. "You're the strongest person I've ever met, and I wish I could take back every hurtful thing I've ever said or done to you."

Ward rested his head against mine. "Dinnae disregard what I did just because you now know my reason, sweetheart. You didnae know when I up and left, and dinnae feel an ounce of guilt because of that, okay? The only person who should feel guilt of any kind is the monster on the floor behind you."

At the reminder of her, I turned to face her, but Ward kept hold of me. He tugged me into him until my back rested against his chest and his arms were wrapped tight around me.

"You're evil!" I all but snarled at Debbie. "*You* are the monster that parents try desperately to protect their children from. You!"

"Erin, I—"

I cut her off. "You're lucky he's here. Because I swear I would kill you for what you did to him. You're evil! You're fuckin' sick, and you *won't* get away with what you've done to him. D'you hear me?"

Debbie continued to cry, and I felt nothing but anger at the sight.

"Ward?" Jesse's voice hollered. "Why'd you leave the bloody door open? Keller spotted me jogging towards the hospital and gave me a lift back. I've got Dad . . . but he's taking ages walking up the stairs. Is

Erin here? Keller said he dropped her off. *Please* don't be havin' sex in my— *Mum?*"

Things got eerily silent for about five seconds until Jesse took in the scene before him.

"What the hell?" Jesse moved to his weeping mum's side, brushing by Ward and me as he rushed into the room. "What happened?"

"I decked her," I replied. "That's what happened."

Jesse blanched as he helped his mum to her feet. "*Why?*"

I narrowed my eyes at Debbie.

"Go ahead," I snarled. "*Tell* him why I hit you."

She only whimpered, her hands pressed against her face, blood covering them.

"Erin," Jesse snapped. "What the fuck is goin' on?"

I turned and looked up at Ward. "Tell him."

Ward swallowed and nodded his head, his hold on me tightening.

"I've been tryin' to find the right moment to talk to you about this," Ward said, clearing his throat. Twice. "D'you remember, in the hospital corridor, I said I wanted to talk to you about something?"

Jesse jerked a nod.

"It was about your mum."

Jesse glanced at her, then back to his brother.

"What about her?"

"I'm so sorry, man," Ward said, his voice filled with emotion. "But she hurt me when I was a kid . . . She abused me for a long time."

Silence.

Jesse stared at his brother and his eye twitched.

"Dinnae you fuckin' *dare*!" I screamed at Jesse. "Dinnae you even *think* to accuse him of lyin'. Not about this. I heard every word that piece of shite said. She justified hurtin' Ward because he wasn't her flesh and blood, Jesse. I heard her say those exact words!"

Jesse looked at me, then Ward, then down to his mum.

"Please, please tell me they're lyin'. *Please*."

I lifted my hand to my mouth upon hearing the desperation in Jesse's tone.

"Of co-course," Debbie stammered.

"Liar!" I bellowed. "She's a fuckin' liar. I heard everythin'!"

Jesse's hand slowly lowered from his mum and he took a step back. "Mum?"

Debbie looked at Jesse, then at Ward, then back to Jesse. "I hit him a couple of times, that's it."

I tried to attack Debbie, but Ward somehow managed to keep a firm hold on me.

"The sexual abuse," I almost sobbed. "Admit to *that*!"

"*Sexual?*" Jesse repeated, stumbling back. His wide eyes shot to his brother's, and he repeated, "*Sexual?* Ward?"

I looked up at Ward in time to see his nod. His expression was grim, and I knew he took no pleasure in revealing this to his younger brother. None whatsoever.

Jesse stared at Debbie.

"Did . . . did you touch him?"

When Debbie continued to cry, Jesse gripped her arm and said, "Did. You. Touch. Him?"

We all knew in what way he was implying.

Debbie managed a soft "aye".

Jesse dropped her arm like she was on fire, and Ward made a choking sound at her admission. I wrapped myself around him, holding him tight just so he'd know he wasn't alone. How he'd never be alone again if I could help it.

"Dinnae touch me," Jesse said, his hands shaking, when Debbie reached for him. "Stay the hell away from me, and never contact me again."

"Jesse," Debbie whimpered.

"And never," he continued as if his mum had never spoken, "put a finger on my brother ever again. Never talk to him again, never fuckin' look at him again. I willnae be responsible for what *I'll* do if you do."

Debbie sucked in a breath at the blistering threat and stumbled back a few steps.

"You're dead to me," Jesse said, his face a mask of pain.

"Ward?"

I jumped with fright in Ward's arms, and we all turned our attention to the kitchen doorway . . . where Mr Buckley now stood.

"It's true?" he asked, tears staining his cheeks. "That woman hurt you?"

Ward's breath hitched as he nodded.

"I failed you," Mr Buckley whispered, his hand going to his chest. "My job is to protect you from harm, and I failed you."

Ward shook his head. "Dad, you didnae do this."

"I didnae prevent it either," he countered. "I brought that woman into your life. I may not have been the one to hurt you, but I made it happen. I practically gift-wrapped you for her."

A lump formed in my throat when Mr Buckley broke down, sobs erupting from him.

"I'm sorry, son," he choked out. "For the rest of my days, I'll be sorry."

"Naw, naw," Ward said, his voice cracking as he released me and stepped closer to his father, placing his hands on his shoulders. "You did *nothin'* wrong. I dinnae care if you were the one to marry her. She did those things to me. Her, *not* you."

Mr Buckley wrapped his arms around his son, and Ward wasted no time in returning the embrace. I sprang into action when out of the corner of my eye I noticed that Debbie was trying to leave the room. I pushed her with both of my hands until she fell back to the floor with a cry.

"You arenae leaving here unless it's in handcuffs, you dirty cunt!"

267

"Erin," Ward said from behind me.

I spun to face him.

"You need to press charges," I stated. "You cannae let her get away with it."

"I know."

"I'm already diallin' the polis," Jesse answered, devastation in his tone but determination in his eyes.

I stepped closer to Ward as he glanced between me, his father and his brother.

"I was worried about people findin' out. I didnae think anyone would believe me."

"I believe you," I said.

"I believe you, son," Mr Buckley managed to say.

"Aye," Jesse said, his voice tight. "I believe you, Ward."

Ward closed his eyes. "I cannae believe I kept her secret for my image."

"Your image is nothin', Ward!" I implored as I stepped closer to him. "Fuck what other people think. I know you, and more importantly, *you* know you. That's *all* that matters. Why do you care so much about what strangers will think about you?"

I expected Ward to shout, to scream, to do something other than fucking smile.

"I dinnae anymore. I agree with you."

I blinked. "You do?"

He nodded. "Wholeheartedly. My image was all I had for a long time; how people perceived me was the only thing I thought I could control. It's not all I have anymore . . . I have you, my friends and my family. I still have my business and my charity. Nothing has changed, I'm just not keepin' her secret anymore."

My heart broke for him.

"Honey, you're grown now. You know you cannae control every aspect of your life, but that just makes you human. Nothin' needs to be hidden anymore, you're free from that restriction. She has no power over you once you realise that."

Ward reached for me and pulled me against his chest, his eyes burning as he stared at me. He spoke to his father and brother, who nodded, before he led me down the hallway and into a bedroom without casting a glance Debbie's way.

"I know she has no power over me." He closed the door behind him. "I know. Fear was a whole other monster to me for a long time."

I wrapped my arms around him. "I'll fight your fear with you."

"You will?"

I squeezed him. "Try to stop me."

Ward leaned down, brushing his lips over mine. "I want you, and only you."

"You're the only person I want too," I whispered. "You've been back in my life for just three weeks, and I cannae imagine it without you, and I dinnae want to. You make everythin' better."

"You willnae have to," Ward answered. "I'm movin' back here."

"What about Friendzone?"

"It'll continue as normal," he said, brushing his thumb over my cheek. "I can run my company from anywhere in the world. I was in my office on days I didnae even need to be near a computer. When I need to be at a meetin', or in the office, I'll fly to London. It's not far away."

"Where will you live?"

Ward eyes locked on mine. "In a house with you, I hope."

My breath caught.

"Of course," he said softly, "that can be a few years down the road. Right now I'll settle for stayin' at your mum's house with you a few nights a week."

Butterflies filled my stomach.

"I'm sure I could fit you into my little bed," I said. "I may have to lie on top of you, though . . . Is that okay?"

"Is it okay?" he asked, pressing his forehead against mine. "I would-nae have it any other way, Whisky."

"I wouldnae have *you* any other way," I said, nuzzling my nose against his. "You're a treasure, Ward Buckley, and I wouldnae trade you for the world."

"Not for the whole world?" he teased, though I knew he felt the depth of my words in his heart.

"Not for the whole wide world," I answered. "You're my perfect."

CHAPTER TWENTY-SIX
ERIN

As I sat in my brother's hospital room and reflected on the previous day's events, I couldn't wrap my head around it being less than twenty-four hours since Debbie Buckley was arrested and placed in the back of a police car, facing charges that would earn her a very long stint in prison. I'd stood by Ward and held his hand as he gave a very long, and very detailed, statement to the police about the abuse he'd suffered at the hands of that monster.

Mr Buckley and Jesse had flanked Ward too, and I knew their presence and support meant the world to Ward, because even though he was done keeping secrets, he was still scared of revealing the one he'd kept for so long. I wasn't sure how, but news broke about Debbie's arrest, and it made its way to the press, and then Ward's personal life was all over the Internet. Everyone knew that his stepmum had been arrested for sexually abusing a child and that child had been him.

I felt sick every time I thought of the piece of dirt who'd hurt someone who I was now incredibly close to, then I felt even worse when I thought of how I used to think about Ward, how I'd treated him when he came back home to help in whatever way he could for Tommy. All the while I was nasty, petty and couldn't let go of a grudge. I felt a lot of self-hate because of that.

I ran my fingers over the charms of my bracelet and sighed.

"You're thinkin' . . . hard."

I looked up at my brother when he spoke, and smiled tiredly.

"Hey," I said. "How long have you been awake?"

"Not long," he answered. "How long have you . . . been here?"

Hours.

"Not long."

My brother grinned. "Liar."

My lips twitched.

"How are you feelin'?"

Tommy winced. "I've been . . . better."

I got up and got him some water to drink. As usual, he drank a lot of it, which pleased me. After I sat back down, Tommy returned his gaze to me.

"What?" he asked.

I looked down to my fingers, before returning my eyes to his.

"Did you know what Debbie had done to Ward?" I swallowed. "The abuse?"

Tommy was silent for a long moment, which gave me my answer.

"You knew," I concluded.

"Aye," Tommy said with a sigh. "I knew."

"Why didnae you tell me?" I asked, trying hard not to be angry with him. "Why did you let me hate him when he left to escape that piece of dirt?"

"Because he made me . . . swear never to tell anyone," Tommy answered. "I couldnae break his trust, Erin. He's my . . . best friend, I had to let him . . . make a decision for himself since . . . Debbie made so many for him over the years."

I understood that, but it still made it difficult for me. I felt sick with myself. I had hated on Ward, on Friendzone, on everything related to him for years because I thought he'd left us during the hardest time of our lives. I hadn't realised he was escaping the person who'd hurt him in ways I couldn't even imagine.

"I'll never forgive myself for treatin' him so horribly."

"You didnae know," Tommy said. "You could only . . . feel what you felt because . . . of what you knew at the time. You thought Ward left us . . . for somethin' you thought wasnae . . . worth it at the time."

I saw his worth now, and I adored him.

"I know," I said, looking down. "I still feel like shite though."

"It'll pass," Tommy assured me. "Talk to Ward . . . about it, tell him how you feel and he'll assure you . . . that you did nothin' wrong. I know . . . he will."

I glanced up at my brother. "We're together, ye'ken?"

"You and Ward?" Tommy grinned. "Aye . . . I know."

"How?"

"Because I'm not blind," he said with a slight shake of his head. "I know I'm not awake for . . . very long at a time, but I saw you on his lap. And I can hear you even . . . when my eyes aren't open."

I felt my entire face burn and it made Tommy's lips twitch.

"He's pretty incredible," I said.

"Aye," Tommy said. "I know."

When my brother closed his eyes and winced, I frowned.

"What's wrong?"

"I feel weird."

"Weird?" I questioned. "How so?"

"My head feels . . . weird," he finished. "I dinnae ken."

Without waiting for Tommy's permission, I reached over and pressed the buzzer for the nurse. Ten seconds passed by before Louise entered with a smile.

"Is everythin' okay, Erin?"

"He said his head feels weird. I'm not sure what to do."

Louise moved to Tommy's side.

"How are you, Tommy?"

"Sore," he answered. "Sore head."

I sat back while she asked him a bunch of questions and jotted them down on his clipboard. She was going to give him a painkiller less powerful than morphine since it knocked him out so much, but she needed a doctor to sign off on it.

When she left the room, I said to Tommy, "Try sleepin'."

"All I do . . . is sleep."

"Sleep is good," I said. "It gets your brain stronger."

Tommy grunted but kept his eyes closed.

"Sing to me," he suddenly said.

I chuckled. "What will I sing?"

"The same thing . . . I sang to you . . . when you were hurt . . . or sad."

You are my sunshine.

I dramatically cleared my throat, and it caused Tommy's lips to twitch.

"You are my sunshine," I sang softly. "My only sunshine. You make me happy, when skies are grey. You'll never know, dear, how much I love you. Please don't take my sunshine away."

Tears blurred my vision as I realised how our roles had reversed. I'd always wanted to protect my brother, but this was the first time he'd showed some weakness and asked me to do something to make him feel better. It was another reminder of how different our lives were now.

I slipped my hand into Tommy's and gave it a light squeeze, which he returned. I continued to sing, and I saw Tommy was drifting off to sleep with a small smile on his face. I used the back of my hand to wipe away my tears, and focused on taking deep breaths so I wouldn't burst into a sob. I didn't want to cry – crying solved nothing, but it seemed to be all I could do of late. I looked around the room for a tissue but couldn't find any, so I stood up and left the room, stopping off in the bathroom to grab some. I splashed my face with water, and just as the droplets touched my skin a horrible sensation of dread washed over me.

Something told me I had to get back to Tommy's room immediately to check on him. I quickly dried my face off and jogged back, pausing at the door as I looked into the room. Just then, a machine starting beeping like crazy.

"Tommy?" I called, over the sound of the machine, and rushed to his side.

He didn't answer me.

"Tommy!" I screamed.

He didn't move, but my shaking him caused his head to shift, and that was when I noticed his jaw was slack and his mouth was slightly open. His skin was pale, and his lips were turning a shade of blue. His chest wasn't rising or falling anymore. The image of what my dad may have looked like when he died flashed across my mind, and in my heart I knew that Tommy was gone, but my mind refused to accept that.

"Somebody, help me!" I cried as I scrambled around the bed and pressed the nurse's call button.

It turned out that I didn't have to press the button, because a second after I pressed it, two nurses rushed into the room – most likely after hearing my screams and the machine's insanely loud alert tone.

"He isnae breathin'," I sobbed to them.

I moved to the side of the room and watched the nurses zip around the room, pressing on machines and calling out orders to whoever was in the hallway. One second things were silent in Tommy's room, and the next there were people everywhere. A doctor, multiple nurses . . . and Ward.

"Ward," I cried the second he stepped foot into the room, breathing heavily.

His face was panicked as he rushed to my side and enveloped me in a hug.

"What happened?" he asked, his voice thick with emotion. "I heard screamin' from inside the lift and ran to the room."

"I dinnae ken," I cried. "He was talkin' a few minutes ago, then I went to the bathroom and came back and he was just . . . like this."

I placed my hands on either side of my head and stared unblinking as the doctor began doing CPR on my big brother. I cried out when they used a defibrillator on him and delivered shocks of electricity to his wounded body. When he jolted, so did I. Time seemed endless in those few minutes, but everything came to an end quicker than I could have ever anticipated. One by one the nurses backed away from the doctor who was performing CPR, and I watched in horror as his compressions slowed down to a deathly stop.

"Call it," a nurse to my left said to the doctor.

"Naw!" I screamed before he could say a word. "Dinnae fuckin' call anythin'. Keep doin' CPR. I'm beggin' you, *please*."

No one looked at me, and Ward pulled me back against his chest.

"Time of death, 8:31 p.m."

"Naw!" I screamed in desperation. "It's his *birthday* next week, he cannae die so close to his birthday! Keep fuckin' doin' compressions!"

When no one moved, or made any attempt to move, I burst forward out of Ward's arms, pushed two nurses aside – one of them being Louise – and placed my hands on Tommy's still-warm chest and began compressions myself. I only paused to squeeze the bag the nurses connected to his mouth to push air into his lungs.

"Breathe, Tommy!" I demanded of him. "Breathe!"

He didn't breathe, and in my head, and my heart, I knew he would never breathe again.

"Erin," Ward choked as he moved to my side and put his hands on mine, stopping my movements.

"Naw," I shouted as tears burst forth like water from a dam, spilling down my cheeks. "Dinnae leave me." I smacked Tommy's chest. "Thomas, dinnae leave me."

Every ounce of strength I had ever built up to keep me going collapsed within me the instant I realised my brother was gone. In that moment, I became nothing. I died right along with him. I wanted to close my eyes and cease to exist like he had, but the harrowing pain in my chest thrummed harder, faster, louder, and refused me that solace.

My true sentence in hell had only just begun.

I felt arms tighten around me, and I heard hushed words of encouragement being whispered in my ear, but the pain I felt shone over all else until I couldn't focus on anything but the sensation of dread, loss and utter devastation that formed like a layer of blistering-cold ice around my broken heart. I knew I was crying, I felt sobs rack my body, but it was like I wasn't really experiencing it. I was there but I wasn't, at the same time.

The pain came in waves: for minutes I'd sob, then a lapse of recovery breaths broke through for a time before I was hurled right back into the open arms of grief and despair.

"He was talkin' to me," I cried to Ward, who was crying himself. "He was just talkin', then he asked me to sing and he fell asleep. He cannae be dead!"

But he was, he was dead.

"I'm so sorry, baby," Ward said, his words choked. "God, I'm so sorry."

I held on to him for dear life as I broke. I was aware of everything around me. I watched the nurses through blurred vision as they removed wires from Tommy's body and put a folded-up cloth under his chin to keep his jaw from hanging slack. Louise fixed his blanket around him, then quietly left the room, closing the door behind her. I looked at the viewing room, where the curtains were drawn so if anyone went inside they wouldn't be able to see my brother's dead body.

Ward talked to me, but I couldn't recall a single thing he'd said. I heard him on the phone, but I didn't know who he was talking to, and I didn't ask. Nothing could replace the fact that Tommy was dead. I stared at his face, his skin, his lips . . . Everything was a sickly grey colour now, and I was terrified to touch him in case he was getting cold.

I could still feel his warm hold on my hand when he'd squeezed it as I sang to him.

"What if he knew?" I suddenly asked Ward, my throat raw. "What if he opened his eyes, and saw I wasnae there anymore? What if he realised he was all alone? What if he was scared and knew he was about to die? What if he tried to call for me?"

The thought alone made me wail.

"Please," Ward begged. "Dinnae do that to yourself, Erin. You couldnae do anythin', and you know that. Baby, you *know*."

I knew nothing, and that was why everything hurt so bad.

Ward and I were alone with Tommy for a long time, and during that time we were completely wrapped around the other, using one another as something to lean on. We both looked towards the doorway when it burst open, and in rushed Jesse, his chest rising and falling rapidly.

"Naw!" Jesse hollered, his hands flying to either side of his head when his eyes landed on Tommy. "God, please."

Ward and I could only sob as Jesse moved to Tommy's side and touched his face, his chest, then his hands. We both got up and moved to be next to him, hugging him with every ounce of our strength. I hadn't ever seen Jesse cry until that moment, and it added to my pain.

Then I looked at the doorway as a cry sounded.

"Mum!" I whimpered, and rushed to her, grabbing her just as her knees gave way.

Ward and Jesse quickly helped me with her, and we got her into the chair next to Tommy. She didn't sit down; she practically threw herself over Tommy.

"Not my baby," she wailed. "*Please* not my baby."

She placed her hands on Tommy's face and sobbed; she cried worse than when my dad died.

"Wake up, Thomas," she pleaded. "Wake up for Mummy."

I covered my face with my hands, not being able to witness my mum cry for her firstborn baby. I couldn't imagine the pain she felt, looking at her child dead before her, knowing she could do nothing to help him or bring him back. I couldn't even look at my aunties when I heard their cries as they entered the room.

I moved to the corner, back to the chair Ward and I had shared. I drew my knees up to my chest, wrapped my arms around them, and cried as I rocked myself back and forth.

How can this be happening?

I didn't jump when hands came around me and a head rested against mine. I knew it was Ward, and I knew even if I told him to get away from me that he wouldn't listen. He wasn't going to leave me, he had made that clear, and I was glad because I didn't want him anywhere else but next to me. I couldn't cope without him, and I think he knew that.

"Ward," I said, lowering my legs and parting them when Ward moved between them as he knelt before me. His hands were on my cheeks and he pushed hair from my face. I looked into his red, swollen eyes, and I blinked. "I feel broken."

"I know you do," he said, leaning in and planting kisses on my face. "It's okay to feel broken. We have all the time in the world to piece you back together."

We didn't, though; we didn't have all the time in the world. Looking at my brother's lifeless body showed me that.

"Dinnae leave me," I told him. "Please. I cannae . . . I just—"

"I'm goin' *nowhere*," Ward said firmly, pressing his face against mine. "I'm never leavin' you, Whisky."

A sob erupted from me, and Ward pulled me against him, swaying me from side to side and rubbing his hand up and down my back. Time became meaningless then. I wasn't sure how long Ward held me, but one thing I was certain of was that the sound of crying was constant.

"Dad!"

I jumped to my feet from Ward's embrace the second I heard Aiden's voice, and without a word I rushed out of the room to meet him. He was barrelling up the corridor, and he came to a skidding stop before me. Tears stained his cheeks, his face was red and blotchy, and he was shaking.

"Aiden," I whispered.

"It's not true," he said, breathlessly. "Tell me it's not true, Auntie Erin."

Tears blurred my vision.

"I'm so sorry," I choked. "I'm so sorry, baby."

Aiden sucked in a sharp breath.

"Naw," he said, placing his hands on either side of his head. "Naw, he's not dead. *No!*"

He rushed by me then and entered the room, and the scream that left him would stay with me for the rest of my life. I stumbled back into the room, my hand covering my mouth as I watched the scene unfolding before me.

"Dad!" Aiden shouted before he fell to his knees next to Tommy's bed. "Please, Dad! Wake up!"

Ward was next to me within seconds. I watched as my heartbroken aunties and mum comforted my nephew as he stood up and reached for his dad, crying when his hand pressed against Tommy's motionless chest.

"Why?" Aiden sobbed. "Why him?"

I wanted to know the answer to that question too, but I knew no one would ever have the answer. Ward moved with me over to Aiden, and when I touched his shoulder and he looked at me, he wrapped his arms around me and held on to me tightly. He trembled as he cried, and I wished to God that I could take his pain from him and bear it as my own, but I knew I couldn't. I could only be there for him, and try to make things as comforting as I could because I knew exactly what he was going through.

I knew the pain of losing a father.

Aiden had been in Tommy's hospital room for ten minutes when his mum came bursting into the room, breathless.

"I couldnae find parkin'," she said. Lucy covered her mouth with a shaking hand as she stared at Tommy, and for the first time in all the years I'd known her, I saw true emotion. There was shock and pain, but mostly guilt. She looked to Aiden when he called her.

"I want you to leave," he said, refusing to look away from his father.

"But, honey—"

"I. Want. You. To. Leave," he growled. "Get out."

"Aiden," she rasped, her voice threatening to crack. "I'm so sorry."

I didn't know if she was apologising for Aiden's loss or for all the years she'd robbed her son of a relationship with his father.

"I've never had any time with him," Aiden said, and his body was so tense I worried his veins would burst. "You used me as a weapon against him. You stole my dad from me."

Lucy burst into tears, her body trembling.

"All he wanted was me," Aiden continued, his eyes – identical to his dad's – glazed over with tears. "He jumped through all your hoops just to see me, to spend time with me, but you made it impossible for us to have the relationship we deserved. We'll never have the chance to do everythin' we wanted to do together. He'll . . . he'll never get to meet the man I'll become, or the family I'll have."

"Aiden," Lucy cried. "Please—"

"I'll never forgive you for it. Never."

Lucy fled the room, sobbing as she went. Aiden didn't spare her a glance; he kept his hand on his dad's and his eyes on Tommy's face. It was almost like he was willing Tommy's eyes to open, and it ripped me in two because I knew they wouldn't ever open again.

"I'm the last person to defend your mum, Aiden," I sniffled. "I'll *never* forgive her for what she did to your dad, but you dinnae have to hold that grudge. She's your mum, and I know you love her. It doesnae mean you can't be hurt and angry for what she's done, but if you cut her out of your life, you'll be doin' something you *know* your dad would have kicked your arse for."

Through his tears, Aiden laughed.

"He would smack my arse red raw for shoutin' at her like I just did."

"He would," Mum said, smiling through the tears that slid down her cheeks. "And just because he's forever sleepin' doesn't mean his word isn't law anymore, d'you understand?"

"Aye," Aiden said. "I understand."

Mum nodded her head, then looked back at Tommy. I couldn't look at her face anymore, it was killing me to see how much this ripped her apart inside. I focused on my nephew as he turned to me.

"He's gone," he whispered. "My dad is gone."

"I know, baby," I said, my throat killing me from crying. "I know."

Aiden hugged me, and for the moment I put my pain aside and focused on being his auntie, and comforting him, just like Tommy had done for me when our dad died. There would be time later for me to break completely, but right now I had to hold it together for Aiden.

I had to.

CHAPTER TWENTY-SEVEN
WARD

Tommy was dead.

It felt surreal to think that, but to know it was a reality was almost too much to bear. My heart broke for Erin, for Amelia, for Aiden, for Tommy himself, and it broke a little for me, too. I hadn't got to apologise to him properly. The few short times Tommy was awake and I was in his presence, we'd hadn't spoken much. He'd looked at me a lot, and I'd looked right back at him. I knew he didn't hate me, and forgave me for what I did, I could see it in his eyes.

He'd flicked his eyes from me to Erin then back to me the last day I saw him alive, and it was like he was silently telling me to take care of her and protect her, and I'd given him a nod, letting him know that I would. I hoped he knew that I would take care of his sister, his son and his entire family, because I would. They were my family now, and I would do right by them for Tommy.

I swore to God that I would.

It had been four days since he died. Four whole days of darkness, emptiness and gut-wrenching pain. According to doctors, it was a brain aneurysm that killed Tommy. His brain had been through too much trauma and couldn't keep going. We kept busy through all the funeral arrangements and planning during the day, but that meant I held my girlfriend that bit tighter at night when she cried herself to sleep in my arms. Each day that passed meant it was one day closer to saying goodbye to Tommy forever . . . or to his body at least.

We'd be saying that farewell in one day's time, and everyone wanted more time.

Everyone.

I looked at Tommy, all decked out in a fancy suit, as he lay in his coffin in the centre of his mum's sitting room. Neither Erin nor her mum had wanted him at a funeral home; they both wanted him at their home. His home. He'd arrived home yesterday, and since then there had been a steady crowd of people coming in to say goodbye to Tommy and pay their respects to his family. I looked to my right, staring at Erin as she stared at her brother. I pushed away from the wall I was leaning against and moved behind her, sliding my arms around her waist and tugging her back against me. I felt her relax a little as she rested against me.

"Will you come and eat some food with me?"

She tipped her head back and looked at me. "I'm not hungry."

She hadn't eaten in four days, only drank water here and there.

"Please?"

She sighed, and I knew she had given into me without her saying a word.

"Okay," she begrudgingly agreed.

I kissed her cheek. "That's my lass."

She smiled ever so slightly as I led her into the kitchen and put a few sandwiches that her auntie had made that afternoon on a plate. There were people all over the house, some I knew and some I didn't, but I only focused on Erin in that moment. She didn't seem to care that my eyes were on her as she ate the sandwiches. She took little nibbles at first, then those nibbles turned to large bites. Her body must have realised it was hungry in that moment, because Erin gobbled down three sandwiches and a can of Coke before she pushed the plate away.

"Good," I said. "Any more and you'll probably be sick."

She nodded, placing her hand on her flat stomach.

"D'you want to come and lie down for a little while with me?"

She looked torn as she glanced out into the hallway.

"We'll still have time with Tommy, sweetheart," I said, taking her hand in mine. "But he'd beat me bloody if I didn't make you take a nap."

Erin's lips twitched as she allowed me to lead her from the kitchen. I glanced over her head towards her Auntie Emma, who gave me a thumbs-up when she saw I had Erin functioning like a human. I nodded to her then left the room, following Erin up the stairs. When we entered her room, she closed the door behind her and climbed on to her bed, not removing any clothing. Silently, I took off her shoes and rubbed her feet, drawing a deep moan from her as I pressed my thumbs into the tissue, massaging it.

I moved my hands from her feet up to the band of her leggings, and I tugged them down until they were off her body completely. I lay them at the end of the bed and moved to sit beside Erin, finding her staring up at the ceiling. I knew she was looking at the glow-in-the-dark stickers on the ceiling; she had told me her dad put them up for her when she was little. They didn't work now that the light was on, but when it was off they shone brightly for stickers that had been on the ceiling for over a decade.

I helped Erin remove her jumper, and when she was in just a T-shirt and underwear I pulled her blanket over her and tucked her in. I turned off the light in the room, moved around to the other side of the bed, kicked off my shoes and climbed in next to her. Instantly, Erin reached for me, her arm wrapping around me and one of her legs tucking itself between my thighs.

In the past four nights of sharing her small bed with her, I had learned that she needed to touch me in some sort of way when we slept. I didn't care – in fact, I preferred her hands on me – but right now, I knew her need to feel me was purely out of fear of not wanting to be on her own.

"Go to sleep, love," I told her, wrapping my arm around her. "I'll be here when you wake up."

The tears started a minute later, and like the other times when she'd cried herself to sleep, I rocked her from side to side and murmured sweet things until I felt her body relax and she fell into a slumber. I was too wound up to attempt to sleep, so I lay in the dark, looking up at the stickers on the ceiling as Erin slept in my arms. My T-shirt was soon wet from her tears, and would be wrinkled from her hold on me, but I didn't care.

This was helping her – *I* was helping her, just by being there.

It was horrible timing, with her brother's death having just occurred, but we were falling in love with one another, and I found comfort in the fact that Tommy was the person who had brought us together, and his passing was what cemented us together as a couple. I couldn't explain how I knew, but deep down I knew Erin and I were going to be together long-term. I knew we would get married and have babies.

I could see it all play out in my head, and I wanted it.

I had never once considered marriage or babies before Tara attempted to blackmail me into both, but with Erin in my arms, and working her way into my heart, I wanted it all. I was finally in the same mind frame as my younger brother. I was ready to settle down, and Erin was the woman I wanted to settle down with. I didn't care that I'd only known her for a month, I didn't care that we still had a lot to learn about one another, and I didn't care that she knew my secrets, because when she looked at me, she didn't see what I had suffered in my past – she saw the man I was now, and she wanted to be with me.

Everything else would figure itself out.

I wasn't sure how much time had passed, an hour or two maybe, but when Erin woke up, I prepared for tears when she realised that Tommy was dead. It seemed to hit her the hardest when she woke up because, just for a moment, everything was okay and all was right in the world, then reality struck and the walls came tumbling down.

"Did you have a nice sleep?"

Erin's lips brushed over my cheek. "I do when you're next to me."

I squeezed her body to mine.

"Did you dream?"

"Naw," she answered. "I just slept."

"Good," I said softly. "You needed that nap."

Erin didn't reply; instead she placed her hand on my chest, and messed with the neckline of my T-shirt.

"When do you think it'll stop hurtin'?"

I closed my eyes, wishing I had the answer to that question that wouldn't cut her in two.

"Whisky, you know this is a pain we'll carry around forever. It's always gonna hurt, but in time, it'll get less painful. We'll be able to think and talk about Tommy without feeling a lump in our throats. We'll get there, together."

"Together," Erin repeated, her voice cracking.

I held her as she broke down. I worried over her, and found myself thinking that she was soon going to be dehydrated. I had never seen one person cry so much and so often, but I knew she couldn't help it. Her heart was hurting, and she'd cry until it stopped.

"I cannae imagine sleepin' without you now," I commented when her cries turned to sniffles. "Would you think I'm crazy if I want to share your bed every night?"

"Naw," Erin replied softly. "But I think we should get a bigger one. You're too big for this one."

My legs dangling off the end of the bed made me nod in agreement.

"You're hobbit height, love."

I chuckled when Erin poked my side.

"My Whisky," I purred. "You're precious to me."

Erin pressed her lips against the side of my mouth and I smiled, knowing the darkened room had made her miss her mark. She adjusted her head, and when her lips touched me the second time, she got her aim right. I hummed against her mouth, taking a step back and letting her control it. There was no way in hell I was going to push her into something she wasn't emotionally stable for, so I let her take the reins and followed her lead.

The moment she deepened the kiss there was a knock on the door, and I almost growled in annoyance.

"What is it?" I called. "We're sleepin'."

"You need to come downstairs," Jesse replied, his voice gruff. "There's a problem."

Both Erin and I shot upright. I quickly turned the light on, while Erin moved like a buzzing bee, pulling her clothes on. I opened the door to Jesse and asked, "What's wrong?"

"Come with me," he said. "Now."

The urgency in his tone made me walk out of Erin's room without her. I jogged down the stairs after Jesse, and when he opened the front door and blinding flashes went off, followed by dozens of voices shouting my name, I growled, "Fuck."

Jesse closed the door, and as I glanced around I realised the house was empty of all the guests. I peeked into the sitting room, and Amelia, Jennifer, Emma, Aiden, and Lucy were all talking and looking at Tommy in his coffin. Keller was standing at the window, looking through the blinds at the press out front. I closed the door and turned to my brother.

"They know?"

Jesse nodded. "They showed up an hour ago."

"Fuck," I said, shaking my head. "The fuckin' wasters, do they know there's a person being laid out here?"

"I told them but they're still here, so they obviously don't care . . . and that's not the only problem."

I blinked. "Jesus, what else?"

"Tara."

My heart just about stopped.

"What'd she do?"

"Accordin' to Hope, she went on a rampage once news broke that you credited Tommy as co-creator of Friendzone. She's spent the past few days runnin' your name into the ground to anyone who will listen. She's now screamin' to the world that's she pregnant and has proof."

"It's *not* my kid."

"I know," Jesse said. "Someone who used to work for you came forward and said he had an affair with Tara and the kid was his. Whatever she thought she was goin' to get out of this mess has blown up in her face. Keller said Hope had her removed from your property and cut off her access to everythin'."

I scrubbed my face with my hands. "She's evil. Pure fuckin' evil to try this knowin' what's goin' on here."

"What'll be done about the leeches outside?" my brother asked.

"Call the polis, this is private property and they're trespassin'."

Jesse nodded, then went back into the sitting room. I leaned against the wall, but stood upright when Erin spoke.

"Are you okay?"

I turned. "I'm fine. Just Tara tryin' a last attempt to get money from me."

"Is she gone now?"

"Yeah, love. She's gone now, she willnae be a problem ever again. I promise."

She walked towards me and pressed her head against my chest. "I couldnae imagine doing all this if you werenae here with me."

"Dinnae imagine it," I said. "Because I'm here, and you know I'm not leavin'."

Erin looked up at me. "I know you aren't."

I placed my hands on either side of her face. "God, what I'm startin' to feel for you scares the shite outta me."

"Me too." Erin smiled, her tired eyes showing a little ray of the life that had been drained out of her the past few days. "I cannae believe how much you mean to me already."

"Well, get ready to feel a whole lot more for me, Whisky, because you're stuck with me."

"There isn't anyone else I'd rather be with, Ward."

The fact I knew she meant that warmed my heart.

"You're it for me, Whisky," I said, leaning down and brushing my nose over hers. "I'm goin' to take care of you."

"I know," Erin said. "And I'm goin' to take care of you, too."

"Together?"

"Together."

CHAPTER TWENTY-EIGHT

ERIN

I always thought burying my dad was the hardest thing I would ever have to do, but I was wrong. Burying my big brother on top of him was worse. Four hours ago, my family, friends and a huge chunk of the community had laid Tommy to rest. Every minute of the church service felt like an hour, but every minute in the graveyard felt like a second, and before I knew it he was lowered into the ground, and it struck home that I would never see him again.

Not in person . . . Not in this life.

While many people went to the local pub to celebrate Tommy's life, my family and I returned to my mum's house, and we simply existed in one another's presence. There were no more funeral arrangements, there was no more walking into the sitting room and seeing Tommy and being able to touch him, there was nothing – and that was when the pain really set in. With nothing to do to distract us, all we could do was sit and think of Tommy, and the fact that he was dead.

The thought ran through my mind until my head pounded.

I hurt, everyone hurt, but when my mum cracked after the funeral and grabbed a bottle, things really began to crumble. I didn't try to fight her, none of us did. As I watched her escape from reality, I knew it would be the last time I'd let her drink a drop of alcohol. She got one pass, and she was using it. Tomorrow, she was going to the rehabilitation centre.

I'd mentioned it to Ward, and he was glad that I'd spoken to him about my mum's addiction. He admitted Jesse had told him about it, and I wasn't angry over it, more relieved that he knew and I didn't have to drop another bombshell on him. He informed me of a better rehabilitation clinic, one where Mum couldn't sign herself out, because she would be a full-time patient until the doctors decided she could leave.

Ward had told me that he would arrange everything, and all we had to do was talk to my mum about it. Watching her gulp back some more Jack Daniel's made me think that conversation wasn't going to go down so well.

"Mum," I called. "Are you okay?"

"Naw," she replied groggily. "Tommy is dead."

"I know . . . I know."

"God wanted him, Erin," Mum said, her eyes lifeless. "God wanted him."

"I wanted him more, Mum."

She looked at me for a moment before looking back to the bottle in her hand.

"It's your fault," she said, her voice so low I barely heard her.

My heart stopped, and my stomach lurched. It wasn't the first time she'd blamed Tommy's accident on me but it still hurt hearing her say it, especially now that he was dead as a result of it.

"Amelia!" Ward and my aunties snapped, but she paid them no mind.

"If you walked home from work that night, he wouldnae have gone to pick you up."

I'd never felt the emotion that was surging through my veins. It came close to the feeling I'd experienced when I saw Tommy had died, but nothing could ever top that pain. It still hurt, though. It was a mixture of sadness, shock and utter heartbreak.

"Dinnae say that, Mum," I said, my voice breaking.

"Why not?" she replied. "It's true. If you'd walked home, he'd still be alive."

"I would have never phoned him if I knew this would be the outcome," I said, trembling. "I never would have."

"Doesnae matter," she replied. "Nothin' matters because my baby is dead, and he's never comin' back to me."

She downed more of the drink, and I couldn't take it; I reached over to take it from her, and she reacted by swiping at me. I instinctively covered my head. She'd missed me when she swung and didn't try to get me again, but the damage was already done.

"Oh Jesus," Ward said. "*She's* the reason you flinch."

I turned my wide eyes on him, and I couldn't form a coherent sentence.

"She hits you?" he pressed.

"What?" my aunties asked in unison, standing up across the room.

"Ward," I pleaded. "You dinnae understand, she only did it once because she was so drunk—"

"Dinnae defend her."

"I'm not," I stressed. "But it's not her, it's the drink."

Ward turned to my mum.

"You're a disgrace of a mother," he bellowed, his words slapping her harder than any physical touch. "Since this girl was eleven years old *she* has been looking after *you*. When Tommy wasnae pickin' you up from puddles of your own vomit, Erin was. When Tommy wasnae out workin' to earn money to keep your bills paid, Erin was. When Tommy wasnae takin' care of you, Erin was. Where there was Tommy, there was Erin. You seem to forget they lost their father *and* their mother the day Kenny died, and that is *your* fault. You could have held it together for your kids, but you didnae. You fell into a sickness and dragged your children down to the pits of hell with you. You should be ashamed of yourself, because I know I am."

Mum seemed to choke on Ward's words, and my instinct was to comfort her, but Ward grabbed my arm and pulled me from the room and into the kitchen. I couldn't believe what had just happened, and began to tremble.

"You're shakin'," Ward commented.

"I'm not cold," I said. "But I can't stop."

"It's adrenaline," he assured me. "It'll pass when you've had a second to calm down."

"Nothin' will pass, because everythin' is so fucked up."

Ward didn't argue with me.

"He's dead, Ward," I said, my heart wincing as I said the words aloud. "I'm never goin' to see my brother again, and it kills me . . . so I can't be mad at my mum for tryin' to escape the hurt."

Ward's hold on me tightened. "She doesnae have to hurt you because of it, Erin."

"It's the alcohol," I said. "It only happened once."

"That doesnae make it better. Once is too much."

"I hate all of this."

"I know, Whisky."

"I keep prayin' to God, but then I want to scream and curse at Him. I cannae have faith," I said with a shake of my head. "I cannae trust that this is all part of God's plan, and that everythin' happens for a reason. No reason is good enough for my brother to be dead."

"Erin—"

"Please. I just want to be on my own."

"You've been on your own for long enough."

I blinked up at him. "What does that mean?"

"It means I'm puttin' an end to it," Ward answered. "I'm not leavin'."

I knew that; I knew he wasn't going anywhere.

"You dinnae need to keep tellin' me that," I said. "I know."

Ward nodded once before pulling me into a bone-crushing hug. When he led me upstairs, I didn't fight him. When I heard my aunties and Jesse go off on my mum in the sitting room, I didn't tell them to lay off and leave her alone. I moved my feet, putting one in front of the other. Once I was in bed with Ward, I pretended to relax, to go to sleep, and I knew the second he fell asleep because his hold loosened on me and his arm fell away.

For days, I had needed Ward by my side constantly, but right now, not even he could soothe me. No one could. I slipped out of bed, put my clothes back on and ventured back downstairs. I glanced into the sitting room and saw my mum was asleep on the sofa, and so were my aunties. Jesse was gone. I glanced at the clock and saw it was only 6 p.m. I couldn't blame everyone for knocking out, the last few weeks had drained us.

Today's events especially.

I closed the sitting-room door quietly and wandered into the kitchen. I put the kettle on then sat at the kitchen table, my thoughts turning to my nephew. He'd gone home with his mum after the funeral, and I wondered if he was asleep, or awake and thinking of his dad. I hoped he was asleep.

I got up when the kettle boiled, and when I opened the cabinet to get a cup, I froze when my eyes landed on an unopened bottle of Jack Daniel's.

My mum had them scattered around different areas of the house. I usually binned them whenever I came across a bottle, but for some reason I stopped and stared. This was the drink that had taken my mum from me . . . but it must have served some sort of purpose for her after all these years. Did she escape the pain she felt? Did it make coping with death easier?

I wanted to find out.

I gripped the bottle, opened it, and for the first time in my twenty-two years, I tasted alcohol, and it *burned*. I tensed as the liquid scalded its way down my chest. Once I swallowed my first gulp, I had to take deep breaths to avoid being sick. Once I was sure my stomach was steady, I took another gulp. I squeezed my eyes shut as the pain thrummed in my chest. I pushed through it, and after five minutes, and three more gulps later, the burning didn't burn anymore. It felt sort of like a tingling sensation. When I blinked, my head felt a little dizzy and I grinned.

It was working.

I looked around the room, and like the click of my fingers, I felt like I was trapped. I closed my eyes, and my mind switched to all the people who had come to see Tommy when he was laid out. I thought especially of Jensen, my manager at Tesco. I opened my eyes, and without really thinking about it, I kept my grip on the bottle in my hand, walked out of the kitchen and out of my house completely.

"I'm so sorry for your loss, sweetheart," Jensen had said to me. "You take your time, and don't worry about work, okay? Your job will always be here when you're ready to come back to us."

I hadn't replied to him – I couldn't out of fear I'd either cry or snap at him. Instead I'd given him a small smile and a quick hug before I moved my attention to the next person offering their condolences, and that was how the afternoon went.

As I walked away from my house, I repeated what Jensen had said in my head. He'd said he was sorry for my loss, and the wording of it had really bothered me. It just didn't make sense to me. I didn't lose Tommy; he was taken away from me. You lose your purse, you lose your phone or your keys. The word "lost" implies there's a possibility of something being found, but there was no chance Tommy would suddenly turn up in my life again, no chance I'd stumble upon him when I least expected it. Thinking of him as just being lost softened the blow a little, but then the harsh reality came crashing back as a painful reminder that he wasn't just lost, he was gone forever. My only brother was dead. And it hurt like hell.

"I hate this," I whispered to myself as I walked.

I hated everything about it. I hated the pain, the loneliness, the hurt, the anger, the misery, the emptiness. I hated the emptiness the most, because it felt like I had nothing to live for, no reason to go on. I took another drink, and the more of the liquid I downed, the more hopeless my life seemed to become. My mum was a lost cause, and it would only be a matter of time before I buried her on top of my father and Tommy; and even though I was at odds with her, I couldn't survive burying her.

I'd have no one once she was gone.

The more I drank, the more doubt flooded me and my mind began to conjure up the worst-possible scenarios when it came to the people I loved most. I'd probably only see Aiden when his mum decided to let me. I couldn't see Lucy just letting her son see me more often because his dad was dead. And Jesse? I wouldn't be surprised if he never spoke to me again when he realised how rubbish a friend I'd been to him by making him censor himself when it came to his brother – I wouldn't blame him if he blocked me out and focused on Louise. Ward was likely to go back to London, getting back to his old life, forgetting everything that was shared between us.

When all that happened, I would be truly on my own, and in that moment, I had never felt more insignificant.

I was empty.

I was nothing.

I wanted to be with my dad and Tommy.

CHAPTER TWENTY-NINE
WARD

When I awoke, and found the space next to me empty and the bed sheets cold, I pulled my shoes on and zoomed downstairs to find Erin's aunties and mum asleep in the sitting room. I checked the empty kitchen before running back upstairs, checking all the rooms for her, only to find them empty.

"Erin!" I shouted.

Nothing. Silence.

I went back downstairs. Jennifer and Emma were now awake, mostly likely due to the noise I was making, so I focused on them.

"Where's Erin?"

"What do you mean?" Emma asked. "She went upstairs with you."

"I woke up and she was gone. I cannae find her."

"Calm down," Jennifer said, getting to her feet. "Maybe she went to see Aiden."

I quickly got my phone from my pocket and dialled Aiden's number.

"Hey, Uncle Ward," he answered.

His voice . . . Jesus. He sounded miserable.

"Hey, buddy," I said. "How are you doin'?"

"Fine," he answered, and I knew he was anything but fine.

"Is your auntie over there with you?"

"Naw," Aiden said, and I could picture the frown on his face. "I'm with my mum . . . Why?"

"Naw reason," I answered. "I'll see you tomorrow, okay?"

I hung up before he could reply.

"She's not with Aiden," I said to Jennifer.

"What about—"

The front door opened, cutting Jennifer off, and I about deflated with relief until Jesse walked into the sitting room and froze when he saw all eyes were on him.

"What?"

"Is Erin with you?" Emma asked.

"Naw." Jesse blinked and turned his attention to me. "I thought she was upstairs with you."

"She was," I said. "But when I woke up she was gone. She's not with Aiden, and she's not with you. Where the *fuck* is she?"

Before anyone could answer me, I dialled Keller's number.

"Sir?" he answered on the second ring.

"I cannae find Erin, and no one knows where she is. Check the surroundin' hospitals," I told Keller. "Give her name, description and what you last saw her wearin'."

"On it."

The line went dead.

"Everyone calm down," Jennifer said. "Let's think a minute. Where would she go?"

"Where *would* she go?" I repeated to myself, and just like that the answer came to me. There was no person she'd rather be with when she was hurting than her brother.

"The cemetery," I mumbled, then turned to Jesse. "I know where she is."

I phoned Keller to stop what he was doing and to come and collect me. He made it to the house in ten minutes flat, and when Jesse and I jumped into the car and told him where to go, he took off like a bat out of hell. Jennifer and Emma chose to stay at the house to look after Amelia, and in case Erin came back. My leg bobbed the entire journey, and when we eventually reached the graveyard, the sun was setting.

I jumped out of the car without waiting for it to come to a complete stop. I ran up the gravel pathway, passing row and row of graves, and when I neared Mr Saunders and Tommy's final resting place, relief left me in the form of a sob. Lying next to the overturned muck of her father and brother's grave lay Erin. She was on her side with her knees tucked up against her chest, her arm bent and acting as a pillow for her head.

"Erin!" I shouted.

She didn't move, and a fear I hadn't felt since childhood consumed me.

I sprinted to her, dropped to my knees behind her and grabbed hold of her with both hands, shaking her as hard as I could. In that moment, I didn't care if I hurt her, I just wanted her to be alive. I almost collapsed with relief when she jolted with fright and darted upright, almost colliding with me. She snapped to attention, and when her bloodshot eyes landed on mine, she seemed to stare right through me. I checked her over, twice, and it was only in that moment that I realised she was shaking like a leaf.

"Sweetheart," I said, softly. "Let's get you home."

"Naw," she slurred, her voice sounding strained. "I cannae leave them."

It was only then that I saw she had a bottle of Jack Daniel's in her hand. I couldn't see how much of it she had drunk, but from the state of her, it was enough.

I placed my hands on her arms, and rubbed up and down as fast as I could to try to generate some heat for her. I didn't ask for permission as I pulled Erin to her feet. She tried to bat my hands away, but she was drained of energy and could barely manage to swat at me. I shrugged out of my thick jumper and tugged it over her trembling frame, then pulled her against me. The night was cool, but lying on the cold ground wasn't good for Erin. I continued to rub my hand over her arms and back to help her get warm.

She leaned against me and cried.

"I wa-wanted to be with Tommy," she said, sniffling. "I di-dinnae want him to be on his own."

I kissed the crown of her head.

"He isnae alone," I assured her. "Your dad is with him, and has been from the moment Tommy left us. He's lookin' after him like dads are supposed to. I promise you, sweetheart."

"I hurt," she hiccupped. "I hu-hurt so bad, Ward."

"I know, baby," I said, hugging her to me. "I know you do."

"Please," she begged. "Take it away."

"I'd give anythin' to take your pain away," I said. "Anythin'."

The bottle in her hand fell to the ground and she yelped, then laughed like a madwoman.

"I realised somethin' today."

"And what's that?"

"I'm a reflection of my mum," Erin curled her lip in disgust as she tried to pick the bottle up from the ground. "I'm not strong en-enough to face the re-reality that Tommy's dead, so I'm es-escapin' into a bottle. I'm her exact do-double."

"That's bullshit," I stated.

I wasn't sure why, but Erin laughed again.

"You're a reflection of your *deeds* to her," I continued, then grabbed the bottle of Jack from her hands when she managed to pick it up. I threw it on to an empty section of grass, far away and where Erin couldn't get it without me releasing her.

"Hey!" she screamed. "I need that!"

"Naw!" I shouted, and grabbed hold of her hands that desperately tried to shake me off. "What you need is *me*, and I'm here, Erin."

She stared up at me. "You have an ex-expiration date . . . ev-every-one in my life does."

"We all have an expiration date," I stressed. "It's why we have to live every day to the fullest."

Erin closed her eyes. "I'm not like you. I cannae be br-brave and stand tall when I feel so br-broken. I'm not strong enough."

"That's why you have me," I said softly, fingers brushing over her cheek. "You have me to lean on when things get tough."

She didn't reply.

"We're all goin' to be a family," I assured her. "You, me, Aiden, Lucy, your mum, your aunties, my brother, my dad. The whole lot of us. We have a lot to figure out between us, but we're a family, and if there is anythin' that your dad and Tommy have taught us it's that we should never take family for granted."

"I'm so scared," she whispered, her body swaying. "I'm so scared to love an-anyone in case they le-leave me."

"I think it'd be scarier to live a lonely life instead of taking the chance to love someone."

Erin's grey eyes stared up at me. "Are *you* takin' a chance?"

"With you? Definitely."

Her lower lip wobbled. "You mean that?"

"With all of my heart."

Erin's shoulders sagged, and in my arms she turned and looked down at her father and brother's grave.

"We'll have to live for them, since they ca-cannae anymore."

I squeezed her body tightly. "We willnae waste a single second."

Erin leaned her head back against my chest, and let my words sink in.

"There's nothin' we can't do."

"Together?" she whispered.

"Aye, Whisky," I replied, holding her close. "Together."

EPILOGUE
ERIN

Six years later . . .

It had been six years to the day since Tommy died, and it felt like it passed in the blink of an eye.

I traced my finger over the engraved name on his headstone, then I did the same with my dad's. It was still hard to wrap my head around Tommy's passing away, but trying to comprehend my dad being gone *seventeen years* was almost too much for my brain to handle at times. He had been gone nearly two decades, and yet it felt like a single day since I'd last seen him, if even. Every time I sat before my brother and father's shared grave, I understood that time was truly no man's friend, because it just kept on ticking, whether we wanted it to or not.

"I miss you both," I sighed, folding my hands in my lap. "Seein' your stupid faces would make my life that bit more perfect."

I smiled, practically hearing them both argue that their faces weren't stupid.

"Aiden and Jesse are wrappin' up a project they've been working on," I said. "I know you both know what they've been up to, but I like tellin' you either way."

I thought of my nephew, and smiled fondly. At twenty years old, Aiden was an intern at Friendzone's Edinburgh branch, which Buckley Construction just happened to have designed and built two years ago. Aiden also worked at Jesse's construction company, as he liked to get his hands dirty when he wasn't working with Ward. I liked Aiden's drive to try more than one thing. He already had a life beyond any twenty-year-old's wildest dreams, but he didn't just accept the money when Ward offered him his dad's cut from the business. Aiden wanted to earn it.

My nephew was hard-working, he loved his jobs, and most importantly, he loved his life and was happy.

Jesse was happy too; he was soon to be celebrating his third year of marriage to Louise Buckley, formerly Chambers. Together they had a one-year-old son, named Fintan, and Louise was six months pregnant with their second child, a daughter. They hadn't settled on a name for the darling just yet. She would be the fourth grandchild in the Buckley family. Ward and I had a son, and our second child was due very soon.

Thomas Kenneth Buckley, or Tommy for short, was four years old and the light of my and Ward's lives.

I settled my hand on my swollen stomach when my second child kicked as if to say, "Dinnae forget about me, Mum."

"This wee one should be here any day now," I said to my father and brother. "I think it'll be another boy, but Ward is convinced it's a girl. He says I didnae cry or lash out at him nearly as much when I was pregnant with Tommy, so it must mean I'm carryin' a girl." I playfully rolled my eyes. "That's male logic for you."

I thought of my husband of five years, and couldn't help the giddy sensation of delight that filled me. He was my other half in every way possible, and I loved him more than I could describe in words. He was precious to me. His worth was not lessened by what he had been through in life; if anything, his worth was tripled. He was one of the bravest, strongest and most selfless men I had ever met.

His ex-stepmother stopped haunting him a long time ago, and she never would again having died by suicide in prison a few short months ago. She was one less monster on the earth, so rot in hell was all I had to say to her.

I thought of Ward's smile once again, and delight filled me.

"God," I sighed. "I love that man."

Once, where Ward was concerned, I would have never considered the word "love" in a million years, but love him I did. That man owned my heart, body and soul, and he knew it. He had been there for me during one of the hardest chapters of my life, and I had been there during one of the hardest times of his. We had held the other's hand and got through both together, and six years later, we still held the other's hand and tackled life side by side.

Braving the unknown with a smile on our faces.

"Tommy starts preschool in September," I said with a shake of my head. "He was just born yesterday, and now he's startin' school. I'll never get over how quick it's all goin' by."

My son was officially enrolled at the school I worked at, the school that I adored. I lived and breathed my job. Guiding young children at such a developmental age in their lives, and seeing them grow and learn, filled me with such pride and happiness. I loved my job, and there weren't many people who could say that.

I rubbed my swollen tummy. "I love the baby stage, and I told Ward we'd have to just keep on havin' kids to satisfy me. He said he was gettin' a vasectomy when we reach number four, but I'll talk him out of it. I have a way with words that always seems to sway him."

I chuckled at the memory of that conversation.

"I wish you could both meet the kids," I sighed as I rubbed the tip of my fingers fondly over my beloved charm bracelet. A bracelet that had two new charms added to it. A silver ring to represent my and Ward's marriage, and a silver dummy that my husband had gifted me after I gave birth to our son. "I know you're watchin' over them, though."

I knew they watched over all of us.

"How's the conversation today?"

I looked up when my mum sat down next to me, and snorted.

"Lively as ever," I joked.

Mum leaned in and kissed the headstone. "Hello, my loves."

I looked at her, and like every other time, I found myself staring in amazement. I'd lost my mum when my dad died, and it took my brother dying to bring her back to me. Of course, I would have given anything for my dad and brother to still be alive, but if I could only have my mum . . . then I'd take her with open arms.

Ward still had reserved feelings about Mum, but he was slowly, very slowly, starting to warm to her. I doubted he would ever let his guard down completely – I doubted I would either – but he was starting to see what I saw. She was trying. She would always be an alcoholic, but the word "recovered" would now be placed before it. Every day for the rest of her life would be a struggle, but she was ready to face that struggle head-on, and that was why she had my support. It's why she was in my life. If I hadn't seen the determination in her eyes to break free of the darkness that had held her for too many years, I would have turned my back on her without hesitation.

I admit that I hadn't thought her willpower would be strong enough to hold her true to her word, but it had been nearly six years since she'd made the decision to part ways with alcohol for good. She wasn't a shell of a woman, or a shadow of her former self anymore. She wasn't her old self either, not fully, but she was my mum again. I knew she would never be the woman who I'd adored at eleven years old, but no one stayed the same forever, and I found myself looking forward to getting to know the woman she was now. I was excited to form a new bond with her. I had hope for her, and that was something I thought had died long ago.

"I missed you today," Mum said to me as she reached over and rubbed my stomach. "How are you feelin'?"

"I missed you too," I answered. "And I'm feelin' thirty-nine weeks pregnant, so to sum up, I feel bloody awful."

Mum smiled, and I was jolted back to being a child, when her smile had wrapped around me like a warm blanket. In her recovery, I was noticing more and more familiar things about her, but her smile was something that defined her, and seeing it on her face felt right.

"What do you say we walk around and try to get that kid movin'?"

"It's worth a shot."

Mum helped me to my feet, and together we kissed the headstone of my father and brother, said goodbye, and walked towards the car park, where my husband was playing with our son, with our close friend John Keller not too far away keeping a watchful eye. My mum took my hand in hers as we walked and talked, and contentment filled me. I had never thought that feeling would be possible without my dad or Tommy being alive, but I was happy.

Dad and Tommy would both remain two of the loves of my life until the day I took my last breath, but just because they couldn't live their lives to the fullest didn't mean I couldn't live mine to the fullest for them, and that was *exactly* what I intended to do.

I wouldn't waste a second.

I wouldn't go to bed angry.

I wouldn't let fear hold me back.

I was going to live happily with my family, and cause ripples in the pond that was my life. My reflection would always be changing, and I was perfectly okay with that.

ACKNOWLEDGMENTS

There are books authors write because of an idea they couldn't get out of their head, then there are books authors write because of an idea they couldn't get out of their heart. *Her Lifeline* was the latter for me. From the second I thought of this story of love, loss, heartache and healing, my heart beat every single word I typed. My love for these characters bled on to the pages, and they'll forever have a place in my heart.

They say it takes a village of people to publish a book, and in my case it's the truth.

Sending an abundance of love to my family, daughter and friends, whose support, trust and encouragement always have me reaching for the stars. I love you all to the moon and back.

I want to thank Sammia – and everyone at Montlake Romance – immensely, for believing in me and *Her Lifeline*. You're a fantastic crew of people to work with. There is no other team I would trust my stories with more.

A billion virtual hugs to Melody Guy. You're so talented, and somehow make the brutal process of editing very educational. Working with you is as rewarding as it was the first time we worked together. I'm very grateful for you and your ability to read in between the lines when it comes to my stories. Thank you.

A thousand thank yous to Gemma Wain. You scanned through every word in this book to make it as polished as it could be. You're very thorough, and it makes me feel better knowing you worked on *Her Lifeline*, because I know that means it was in good hands.

A solid high five to Monica Hope for your thorough proofread of *Her Lifeline*; thank you so much for reading my story word by word so it could be reader-ready.

As always, a massive thank you to Mark Gottlieb. You're a fantastic agent, and without you, I would have never crossed paths with Montlake Romance and discovered a wonderful group of people.

To you, my readers. Thank you for taking a chance on *Her Lifeline*. I hope you enjoy reading it as much as I did writing it. You all make my world spin.

ABOUT THE AUTHOR

L.A. Casey is a *New York Times* and *USA Today* bestselling author who juggles her time between her mini-me and writing. She was born, raised and currently resides in Dublin, Ireland. She enjoys chatting with her readers, who love her humour and Irish accent as much as her books. You can visit her website at www.lacaseyauthor.com, find her on Facebook at www.facebook.com/LACaseyAuthor and on Twitter at @authorlacasey.

$1/19$